The

Renun

Pragya Agrawal is a dual qual … and an architect from CEPT University, … BIT Mesra, Ranchi. After several years in t … gn and construction industry, she now also builds with words as her second craft.

Born and raised in India, she was deeply shaped by the ancient stories and rich cultural heritage of her homeland. *The Renunciation* is her debut novel, illumining the quiet strength of Sita—the guiding force behind the Ramayana's turns of fate—as seen through the eyes of a believer and a daydreamer.

Pragya lives in London with her husband, their two children, and a head full of stories.

https://authorpragya.com
facebook.com/pragyaagrawal.author
instagram.com/pragyaagrawal.author
x.com/authorpragya

Praise for The Renunciation

'Like a kaleidoscope, where a slight twist of the hand can totally change the picture, Agrawal's Ramayana changes our perception in seemingly tiny ways. The impact is as dramatically different as the best kaleidoscope.'

—Mallika Sarabhai,
recipient of the Padma Bhushan, legendary classical dancer, actor, and social activist

'This tenderly retold story of the earth goddess Sita and her twin sons Luv and Kush addresses the strength and vulnerability of her legacy. The foundational epic text of the Ramayana presents the complex moral dilemmas of the compulsions of kingship and the personal and domestic. Pragya Agrawal's narrative evokes Sita's resolute path through love and marriage, exile and abandonment.'

—Namita Gokhale,
Sahitya Akademi Award-winning author, acclaimed writer, and co-founder of the Jaipur Literature Festival

The Renunciation

Pragya Agrawal

RUPA

Published by
Rupa Publications India Pvt. Ltd 2025
161-B/4, Gulmohar House,
Yusuf Sarai Community Centre,
New Delhi 110049

Sales centres:
Bengaluru Chennai
Hyderabad Kolkata Mumbai

This is a work of fiction. Names, characters, places and incidents are either the product of the author's imagination or are used fictitiously and any resemblance to any actual person, living or dead, events or locales is entirely coincidental.

P-ISBN: 978-93-7003-288-0
E-ISBN: 978-93-7003-480-8

First impression 2025

10 9 8 7 6 5 4 3 2 1

Printed in India

To my Guru, Shrii Shrii Anandamurtiji

Tava drawam' jagadguroh, tubhyam- eva sam'rpaye
Your wealth Guru of the universe, unto you only I surrender

Contents

Author's Note

The *Ramayana* is one of the oldest foundational epics of the Indian subcontinent, echoing through generations. For me, it first echoed in my grandmother's resonant voice, where Sita appeared as a figure of grace and quiet strength. In my mother's telling, her story arrived with questions—how a woman so resilient and deliberate came to be remembered as submissive? Years later, their voices found their way through me in *The Renunciation*.

Somewhere, the injustice to Sita haunts all our collective memory. From *Valmiki's Ramayana* to countless later retellings, writers have sought to fill the silences left by the great sage. In the mesmerising brilliance of Valmiki's verses, Ram shines with celebrated qualities—god, king and ideal—and it is difficult not to be helplessly drawn to him. Yet when that god subjects his wife to one of the most controversial trials in the history of literature, the conversation unfortunately collapses into one of unquestioning reverence or discomfiting silence. It is reduced to a matter of devotion over dialogue, a dulling of inquiry, a slow slide into acceptance.

Painfully, Sita occupies no more than ten percent of Valmiki's text. Though glimpses of her reasoning, defiance and presence of mind are shown, she remains largely relegated to the margins—her absence as telling as her presence. Perhaps if it weren't so, posterity wouldn't have cast her as mainly dutiful but rarely decisive.

Her appearances largely serve the glorification of Ram—his duties, his trials, his suffering. Even the credit for their monogamous marriage is attributed to Ram alone, though Sita's extraordinary brilliance must have also contributed; inspiring devotion from Ram to make a striking departure from the norms of polygamy. We have shaped her as a pious figure, a devoted wife and mother, but rarely as a woman of beauty—though it must have been phenomenally striking, for a war of such magnitude to be waged for her.

Though my retelling is mainly based on *Valmiki's Ramayana*, I approached my research beyond the limits of an 'authentic' version to truly understand the sentiments around Sita. Across centuries, she has appeared in many lights: as the slayer of Sahasra Raavan in *Adbhuta Ramayana*, or as Mandodari's daughter in *Uttarapurana*, *Javanese Serat Kandha* and *Adbhuta Ramayana*. *Ramayana* too differs, where in some retellings Luv and Kush capture the horse and defeat Ram himself. The fact that the text has been captured differently in songs, ballads, sculpture, dance and other mediums, proves that *Ramayana* has never been a single, rigid story; rather a living one, shaped by time and imagination, each reframing the tale according to its own perspective.

Even Valmiki's text is not free from debate. Scholars question whether the *Uttara Kanda*, which narrates Sita's renunciation, was a later interpolation. If so, then how striking that the epic which ends in the *Yuddha Kanda* with a vision of Ram and Sita ruling happily for ten thousand years, begins in the *Bala Kanda* with their sons, Luv and Kush, reciting the epic to an estranged Ram, who listens intently, mourning the wife no longer by his side. Some suggest that parts of the *Bala Kanda* too were later additions. Yet it is only when we set aside such scholarly dissection that the true essence of the *Ramayana* emerges as a treasury of moral learning, revealing human virtues as clearly as our failings.

The Renunciation is my attempt to illuminate Sita without ever diminishing Ram. He is a god—but so was she. They were both heroes, navigating their destinies with grace and conviction. Some may say theirs was a different era, governed by a different set of values. But for them it was a shared world—where they made different choices—each guided by their own personal sense of duty.

Here, it becomes important to reiterate that their love towards each other was absolute; but when we look at their separation, we inadvertently end up pitting them against each other, when contrarily, they both stood united in their vision of honouring the greater good.

That spirit of nuanced understanding is what I seek to bring; an appeal to approach our epics with reverence but remain open to questioning, and to finding answers offered by the very characters we worship as gods.

Sita's final act should not be reduced to one of private despair or even personal redemption, but an empowered visionary choice, establishing her blazing legacy as no less enduring than Ram's. Let us not remember her as someone who was renounced—for the truth of the final renunciation was altogether different.

It is time to pause and look back at Sita—not simply as a consort, but as a woman who dared to think beyond her times. Writing this book allowed me to see her, know her and love her—entirely, in her own light.

Map of Key Sites

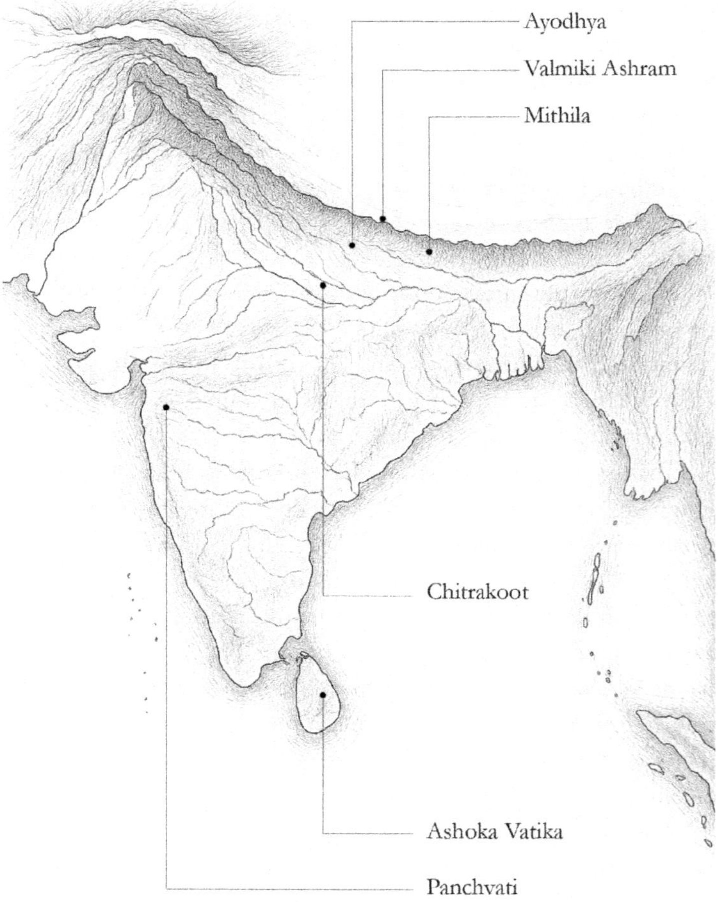

Major characters

Sita: Divine princess of Mithila; wife of Ram.

Ram: Divine prince of Ayodhya; revered for his righteousness and sense of duty.

Luv and Kush: Ten-year-old twin sons of Sita and Ram; raised in Valmiki's hermitage.

Sage Valmiki: The composer of the Ramayana; guardian of Sita in his hermitage.

Raavan: Mighty demon king of Lanka; revered for his knowledge, feared for his pride.

Laxman: Ram's devoted younger brother; companion through the years of exile.

Shiva: Ascetic god, venerated by all, especially Raavan; bearer of the mighty bow Pinaka.

Maharaja Janak: Philosopher king of Mithila; Sita's father.

Maharani Sunaina: Queen of Mithila; Sita's mother.

Maharaja Dasharath: Powerful king of Ayodhya; father of Ram.

Maharani Kaushalya: Eldest queen of Dasharath; mother of Ram.

Maharani Sumitra: Middle queen of Dasharath; mother of Laxman and Shatrughan.

Maharani Kaikeyi: Youngest and favoured queen of Dasharath; mother of Bharat.

Manthara: Kaikeyi's shrewd maid.

Bharat: Son of Kaikeyi; younger brother of Ram.

Shatrughan: Twin brother of Laxman; devoted to Bharat.

Urmila: Younger daughter of Janak; sister of Sita, wife of Laxman.

Mandavi: Cousin of Sita; wife of Bharat.

Shrutakirti: Cousin of Sita; younger sister of Mandavi, wife of Shatrughan.

Sage Naarad: Celestial wanderer; messenger between heaven and earth.

Sage Vishwamitra: Revered sage, fierce of temper; guide to Ram and Laxman in the Tataka forest.

Sage Sarbhanga: Hermit of Dandakaranya; revealed to Ram the deeper purpose of exile.

Sage Suteekshna: Forest hermit; guide to Ram, Sita, and Laxman on their southern journey.

Sage Agastya: Revered sage; gifts Ram and Laxman celestial weapons.

Anasuya Devi: Revered ascetic woman; offers Sita counsel, gifts and blessings.

Sage Atri: Revered sage; husband of Anasuya Devi.

Surpanakha: Raavan's fiery sister.

Khara: Raavan's brother.

Vibhishan: Outcast brother of Raavan; unlike him in spirit.

Trijata: Chief demoness in Ashoka Vatika.

Hanuman: Forest warrior, devoted to Ram; blessed with the boon of giant leaps.

Jatayu: Aged vulture-king; heroic friend of Dasharath.

Guruma: Aged matriarchal figure in Valmiki's hermitage.

Vasuki: Spirited eight-year-old girl in Valmiki's hermitage.

Part One

I

An Enduring Labour

'Ma, tell us the story of the princess who wasn't born from her mother's womb,' urged the ten-year-old Luv.

'Oh yes, the princess born from no womb at all,' chimed in Kush, his excited twin.

Sita shook her head, and her eyes creased with warm crinkles.

'What, Ma! Isn't this how you always begin?' Kush's ears tinged with sudden heat.

Listening to stories had become a part of the nightly ritual. To settle down after a long day of lessons, the boys spread out an old reed mat, which, worsened by holes, was hardly much respite from the cold mud floor. Although winter was in its final stretch, the forest still lugged a significant chill. Outside on the verandah of their humble cottage, a fire burnt and the children crouched to splay their hands in its warmth.

'Move aside a bit, I need to warm the oil.' Sita placed an earthen bowl by the firelight. The boys smiled, their eyes glinting under its amber glow. But what caught her attention was the flicker over their high cheek bones and full lips. *How uncanny their resemblance to their father. A father they knew nothing about.*

'I am not repeating that story!' retorted Sita, as she picked up a log from the pile of woods by the wall and plonked it into the fire. Seeing that it too had seared with red heat, she headed indoors to fetch the cotton blankets from the alcove. 'You heard it yesterday only. Why don't I tell you the story of the god who created rain or the one who created the world, including himself?'

'Ah no!' protested Luv following his mother inside. 'Those aren't half as exciting. Please, Ma, we want to listen to this one only.'

Sita hesitated, trailing her fingers over the blankets. Not because it wasn't a good story, but unbeknownst to them, it was her own story. Now known by a new name, Vandevi, her once wondrous past had been reduced to nothing more than a fable over which she had no claim. No claim either to her name, Sita. Suppressing a wistful smile, she dropped the blankets over the mat and settled down.

On the branches outside, a *myna* called for attention, its hoot distinct in the sticky silence. Tucked in the dense solitude of Chitwan forest, life was sparing here. It was here, in Sage Valmiki's hermitage, that she had given birth, and to her surprise, it had been to twins. *If only her husband knew.* But Ram, the infallible king of Ayodhya never came looking. For her—or his heirs.

'Here Ma, the oil has warmed enough.' Kush carried the bowl inside. 'Is it okay if Ma oils my hair first?'

'I don't mind,' replied Luv, pulling her by the arm, 'as long as she lets me rest my head on her lap until then.'

Sita patted Luv's cheeks and unfurled Kush's top bun. The

soot-black hair tumbled down his round shoulders. The fire crackled in the quietude like it too waited in keen eagerness for her to begin the story. And this time when she did, it wasn't with the princess that she began, instead with the childless man to whom she was proffered as a blessing.

On the eastern frontier of the great big Jambudweep was the small kingdom of Mithila, ruled by the virtuous Maharaja Janak and Maharani Sunaina. Never were the rulers seen without a smile on their face, for their lands were rich and their people happy. There was no threat from enemies, no woes in court or malice in their subjects' hearts. With everything so perfect, it seemed the king and the queen had everything that their hearts desired. Everything but a child.

Irrespective of the couple's ardent efforts and numerous prayers, blessings from pious saints, or performance of great *yajnas*, Maharani Sunaina's womb never swelled with promise. It was only when most of her hair turned grey that her tears finally dried. They must accept the ordinance of fate, the king coaxed her. Was not the prosperity of their kingdom a blessing any less?

But fate, in its scorn found no joy in their inviolable contentment. It made the very object of the king and queen's solace, their kingdom, its next prey. That monsoon, when the fields were sown with crops and flower-strung swings hung down the branches in quiet anticipation, the clouds gathered, swelled, bloated and coagulated, and then, capriciously drifted away without a single drop touching the earth. Mithila managed, for the ground was pliable from prior dampness. It offered them produce, however stunted or half-sweet. The subjects thought it only a matter of time for abundance to delude their lives again but the following monsoon brought no luck either. The sky remained dazzling. In fact, it spewed angry lines of orange. No wonder that the stunted crops then perished too.

Distraught at the vulnerability, the king decreed for the royal granaries to be opened to his starving subjects. They gathered by the heavy gate with pots in their hands and hopes in their hearts, waiting for the ornate wooden doors to creak open. When it did, they saw not the gold of wheat, or the white of rice, or even the multi-coloured promises of different pulses, but an assurance of their very life for the next few years. Gratitude rolled down their faces as the grains tumbled down their hands in a long-forgotten feeling. But they were the righteous king's subjects—weak in body yet strong in spirit—and took only what was absolutely essential.

That frugality proved to be a good thing, for it didn't rain the following year, or the year after, or, for that matter, the one after. Seven monsoons later, Mithila was afflicted with acute dryness. Hot days turned hotter, unusual for the pleasantly cool kingdom in the foothills of the great mountains. Warm air bellowed to the skies, thudding, and beseeching it to break down and pour, but no clamour could shake the sky's deaf obstinacy.

As for the earth, left ignored for too long, it started swallowing its own bounty. There started a series of disappearances: first the delicate fields and the resilient orchards, then the redolence of the air, followed by the cooling ponds, lakes and rivers. With these, happiness disappeared, and so did honour when the earth was left bereft of even a humble cover of dry leaves. Its surface broke out in reprehensible lines. The lines cracked, and the cracks deepened, and a jagged maze of ugly webs took over. The wind blew unfettered, scraping across any oddly surviving stumps of the once majestic trees. It whistled through sorrowful carcasses, adding to the dissonant cries of jackals and vultures. The happy, thriving public squares, marketplaces, courtyards, all became deserted in fear of its wild madness, as it blew down long alleyways, thumping down closed doors and windows. Stepping out was a punishment, no less when the earth enticingly swayed and danced under the light of the vacillating sun, deceiving everyone with hollow promises of water.

Despite it, the ghostly skeletons of the subjects never complained. Their trust in Maharaja Janak remained unscathed, even with the rapid dwindling of the royal granaries. They tied their bellies to shrink their hunger, and in croaky, parched voices consoled one another that their benevolent ruler would somehow deliver them from this plight.

Their unwavering faith was precisely what haunted Maharaja Janak more than any tragic afflictions of famine. It kept him awake at night, as he lay in uncomfortable pools of sweat, well past when the lamps would have burnt low and suffused his nostrils with the pungency of charred wick. If ever he managed to fall asleep, nightmares would rouse him up with a shiver, a scream or the deplorable lament of his crushing incapability. That pattern continued for years, until there broke one such morning when the king rose instead with a vision.

As usual, the air in his chamber sweltered even though the sun had barely broken through.

'The earth still has bounty!' he said, turning to his wife.

'Huh! Maharaja?' Maharani Sunaina mumbled as she wiped sleep off her eyes.

'The earth still has bounty and is willing to offer. In fact, it is more than eager—' he looked her in the eye, 'I heard the voice right in my ears. So clear.'

'What voice?'

'The voice. Clear as crystal. Beseeching me to come and claim it.'

'I don't follow—what kind of bounty?'

'Exactly what I am wondering! What could the earth's bounty possibly mean? Might that be…its yield? Its crops? Wait—is it hinting me to…plough?'

Maharani Sunaina looked on, dumbfounded.

'Yes! Oh yes! It's quite likely prodding me to struggle—plough the barren fields. Yes, that's one thing I haven't done. Yes, I am a warrior, but isn't the fight against nature this time? That can't be won with weapons. No, no. A plough. Most definitely a plough!' The early light of the day glimmered on his face, and the king appeared strangely broad despite his frail self.

'The famine may be a design of nature. But so am I. It's time to test whose will is more tenacious.'

Maharani Sunaina gulped. This sounded like the unfurling of a million imagined manifestations. 'Then hesitate no further! Let's make it happen!' Taking the drape of her saree, she wiped the sweat off the king's forehead and clapped thrice. A few attendants shuffled in.

'Maharaja is going to plough the fields. Let's begin this endeavour with a sacrificial *yajna*. Inform all ministers and priests to start preparations. And open these windows. The stuffiness is unbearable.'

That command only had to be passed for everything to change. The attendants stared back at their king; a breach of courtesy, but today everything was pardoned. Soon, the jingle of anklets and excitement filled the air, as one by one, heavy curtains were pulled back and tied. Hungry sunlight, kept at ward for long, leapt in at the first opportune moment. It drenched the black granite floor in intermittent patches of gold and stirred the dust, which glittered and glimmered ethereally; and finally, after a long time, the rigidly frozen palace began to thaw.

By mid-day, a sacrificial pit was readied out in the open fields and chants of a hundred and eight priests rose in the air. They fed the sacred fire in turn with *ghee*, *karpour*, *naivedyam* and scented *ahootis*. Throngs of people assembled on either side; little children perched atop their father's shoulders, ladies, young and old, with the border of sarees drawn as humble shades across their heads.

The prayers lasted a *prahar*, and Maharaja Janak took a vow not to take an ounce of water until he had managed to prove his mettle—such fast not to weaken his body, rather bolster his resolve.

A tinkling of bells was heard, and all heads turned towards the pair of spotless white bulls, the king's accomplices in the task. Their horns shimmered with golden sheath—a testament that any hindrance to their path would be met head on. When the plough was mounted over their backs, and heavy that it was, it made the bulls lose their balance and buckle. But that was only for a moment, before they shot their defiant knees back up, ready despite the harsh day, and despite the sweat quivering down their flaring noses. Today, every plopping sweat was going to be a humble contribution towards their dry state.

Maharani Sunaina stepped forward and venerated the bulls. She applied them with a vermillion *tilak* and offered a sweet drink of roasted gram and jaggery which they greedily slurped. After petting them in gratitude, she made her way to the Shiva temple across the field.

Finally, Maharaja Janak stepped behind the bulls and pulled their strings in readiness. A little distance behind him, stood other farmers, an army replete with vision and plough; and with determination fuelled by the incessant chanting of priests.

'Come, let's do this together.' The king patted the bulls, and they bucked and willed their burly bodies forward. But try as they might, the buried plough did not even budge. The earth had parched into a fury of solid rocks. The bulls heaved and hmphed, but every effort resulted in vain.

Maharaja Janak looked up at the heavens for mercy. Sweat prickled in the folds of his arms. It ran down his forehead and blurred his vision. With crushing pain, he realized that bringing forth the change would take a measure of his own. So, he stepped in front and sat between the bulls, ready to surrender his all. With one knee bent and the solid brace of plough balanced over his shoulders, he started to rise. The relentless earth held on to its intractable grasp. The king strained. A deep guttural sound escaped his clenched teeth. His veins throbbed, his eyes turned bloodshot and his shoulders bulged painfully. The crowd shrieked and cheered, but every sound was dulled to his being, which remained in a deep state of worship.

With tremendous might, he raised one foot in the air and landed it forward. And finally—with a clamour much anticipated—there appeared the first rip.

A collective sigh rose from the sides. Followed by a deferential silence. In only a matter of time the shock was picked up by loud cheering, thumping, cries, and the sound of conch shells. Even the sound of prayers notched higher, and everyone's focus started to feed that one common purpose.

'Huh! Did you see?'—'Our king made it possible'—'Our saviour made it possible!' Tears rolled down everyone's disbelieving eyes.

The king went on to drag another foot. Then another.

Slowly and steadily, markings of a furrow began to appear. Crust started to break loose, dust started to rise and along with that, what started to rise was indefatigable hope. Inspired by his infectious determination, more and more farmers followed suit. And just like that, the face of the lustreless earth began to be embroidered, with a sight so beautiful—that pattern with furrows—a long-desired reminder of prosperity.

What had lain dormant inside was at last brought back to splendorous glory. As the earth tumbled, so did the sky; it rumbled ever so vaguely, without distracting anyone's attention just yet.

Thwack!

That extraneous sound made the bulls freeze mid-air. They turned towards their benefactor; eyes marked with caution.

'Are you tired?' the king stroked them. 'You are doing so well, so well. Not long to go, I promise.'

But the unusual glint by their hooves caught his attention too. He placed down the plough and squinted. There was a bright glare. He started to dig with bare hands. First cautiously, then frantically, and eagerly, and ever so captivatingly.

The shape revealed further.

A pot!

A golden pot! Out in the field?

His heart thudded, hurrying him with unexplainable urgency. He lifted the pot; scraped off the mud. It filled his nails, scratched his palms, but he didn't care. Carefully, he untied the red cloth covering the mouth.

A child!

His eyes widened with shock, and he peeped closer. Therein, lay an infant girl, squirming, squinting to the light falling over her beautiful face. How was it even possible? Were his eyes deceiving him? How was he to discern any sense out of this.

But never have miracles and blessings gone hand in hand with reasoning. They are simply rewards to be graced without questioning. So, with trembling hands, the king gently drew the child out into the world of light, into the world of emotional bondages, and into the world of joy and suffering.

'Why has the king stopped?'—'What has he found?'—'Do you think it is some kind of treasure?—'Is it indeed a child in his arms?' The denizens peered from the distance. They had witnessed the most bizarre happening of their lives; as well as the most blessed.

The child's fists were shut tight, her skin was soft and pearlescent, and with her feet all curled up in a fetal position, it seemed to suggest she might have been lying inside for quite a long time. Could the voice in the dream have belonged to her? Was it she who urged the king to come and claim her? Soft tufts of deep black hair framed her head. Her eyes seemed black too but it was difficult to tell as she kept blinking, still adjusting to the newfound brightness. She wanted to be secure; she needed warmth, and let out a wail that snapped the king from a grim past to a promising future.

The fact that she demanded loosened a smile over his face. He brought her close; and she snuggled, brushing her soft little head on his beating heart. The king himself let out a great gasping cry—one of gratitude for his blessed fate, and one of disbelief for his blessed fate. She looked up at him, tiny eyebrows arched in a puzzled frown, then closed her eyes and snuggled back unaffected.

By then, the crowd had turned delirious with happiness. Finally, Maharaja Janak saw his kingdom rejoicing; at long last he saw them dancing, frenzy with excitement, that made him aware of his own slow self. It felt like the contentment of a lifetime spooling out of that single moment.

Meanwhile, the sky too, started to darken, not in gloom but with jubilation. Cottony shapes, out of nowhere started to stretch over the clear Mithilan sky. They were the long-awaited clouds that reverberated and rippled. Streaks of celebratory silver light rushed across in jagged lines in a wondrous display of ecstatic beauty. And finally, after seven long years of immense patience and prayers, unbridled joy burst through. It ran down the heavens, as well as everyone's eyes.

The earth drank hurriedly. It drank greedily; drank all the water the sky could offer to quench its long impossible thirst. With it, the air cooled, and mingled with an intoxicating smell of wet mud to please the senses.

The king suddenly became aware of the delicate child in his arms. How could she not complain getting wet like that! Wasn't her tolerance extraordinary! He stretched his silken drape over the infant, nodded something to her, and rushed to the temple to meet his wife.

The steps leading up the temple had turned slippery. Despite the loud pour, the queen sat with her eyes closed and rolled the *rudraksh* prayer beads feverishly, like it was on the very grace of her prayers, the rains depended. Their drought thirsty Mithila needed all that water, and more, and nothing would make her stop, not even the gentle tap on her shoulder.

Only when the king placed the child on her lap that she opened her eyes. It was with a flash. She could not utter a single word, yet a thousand questions spilled out at once.

And to all those thousand questions, her husband answered with a single vehement nod, and said, 'Sita.' He took her by the arms, 'Look, our Sita. Mother Earth has relented. She has blessed us with this child.'

The queen sat agape. Slowly she gathered the squirming child to her cheeks, feeling her soft, warm head. The child reached out with her little fingers and touched the queen's lips. Everything stopped, apart from Maharani Sunaina's swelling heart which pounded loudly in her chest, filling her entire being with unbounding maternal love. Her bosom ached, and in an inadvertent act of miracle, the golden elixir started to flow freely.

It was true that Sita wasn't born from her mother's womb—instead from a deep-seated desire, answered in the most sublime manner. While nature gives at least nine months for most mothers to sink into the realization, it was impossible to understand the state of Maharani Sunaina, who transitioned through this exultation in a fraction of a moment. As for Maharaja Janak, Sita was more than just a daughter. If it wasn't for her, he would never have realized the limitless potential of his own self.

And so, like any gruelling labour which preludes sacred sanctifications of birth, Sita's happened to be much longer, more arduous, more testing. For her blessed arrival, evidently not her mother, certainly not her father, but the entire kingdom of Mithila heaved, and heaved for seven long years, eventually to see her arrive and miraculously reverse their fates.

The pleasing winds which until now had been bringing in fine sprays of rain stopped; and the night sky, suitably clear, bejewelled itself with the twinkling of stars. However, no changes could break the stupor of Maharaja Janak and Maharani Sunaina. For them, time remained in limbo, as together they lay in an eternal state of deep embrace, with their daughter, their blessing, their bounty—their Sita.

2

Crushing Conundrum

In Sita's hand was a bowl of paste, made from grinding soaked rice. She dipped a finger into the slurry, and with assured strokes painted a fresh *alpana* onto the mud floor. This time, she drew a creeper hugging the three steps of her frontal verandah. Clustered over were dainty white flowers—the scented *raatrani.* For Sita, there were no flowers quite as cherished as the raatrani. After putting the finishing touches, she placed the bowl aside and leaned back; not quite expecting the commotion that followed.

'Uh-oh! Watch out, you two!'

But her warning came too late. The bowl was already toppled, and the verandah was blotched with white feet marks.

'So sorry! We are ever so sorry, Ma,' said Kush, visibly flustered.

'Here, let us clean it for you.' Luv seized the wet cloth off her hands and started to wipe. It only made matters worse.

'You know it wasn't our intention,' Kush lifted her chin and added in a placating manner, 'You will pardon us Ma, won't you? If nothing else, they will at least make up for a comforting reminder in our absence.'

'What absence! When you are off for lessons? Nah! Your mother is far too busy herself,' replied Sita, suppressing her smile.

'Who's talking of lessons! We are going to Ayodhya!' he said, springing open his arms.

Her eyes shot up. But Kush, too chuffed to notice, continued, 'That is true Ma. We are finally going to the fabled land.' He grabbed her by the shoulders, searching for a startled reaction. But Sita only stared back in incredulity. Then she turned towards Luv.

'Which is why the reckless rush, Ma,' said Luv, still regarding the blotch marks apologetically, 'We had come to relay Guruji's message. He wants us to fetch our veenas to begin practicing the Ramayana.'

'The Ramayana?' Sita winced, 'Do you mean...Guruji has finished it already?'

'Only this morning,' replied Kush. 'He read us the entire script and...Oh Ma, it is wonderful. I doubt if another tale could surpass it in rhythm and sublimity.'

'Twenty-four thousand!' chimed in Luv, 'That's how many verses are in the tale. And each one of those with the same number of syllables. Honestly—nothing short of a miracle!'

Sita had long been aware of Guru Valmiki's epic endeavour—the composition of a tale exalting King Ram's life, virtues and infallibility; something Guruji had been on working well before she took refuge in his ashram. If that alone wasn't irony enough, never in her wildest dreams had she envisaged her own sons reading it. Discomfiting. Especially to realize they were oblivious to many important truths. The past had already stripped her of everything. It now came for her children.

'You are not going anywhere. Ayodhya is a long way off and you are much too young.'

'We are not young! We are ten!' Kush pounded his foot.

'Please Ma, don't stop us,' Luv implored, 'Guruji said if luck favours, we might even get to meet Maharaja Ram. Tell us now, what challenges, forget walking a few simple miles, could dissuade us of such opportunity. Maharaja Ram is the perfect example of an ideal being. Wait till you read the epic, and you will find out for yourself.'

'True, it isn't every day that a man like him takes birth. Guruji even says that he might be an incarnation of Lord Vishnu!' added Kush.

Such lofty praises, such distant adulation—for a man who was their own father. Sita bit her lip and rose to put away the rice paste; but ended up bumping her foot on the threshold.

'Ma, are you okay?' Kush leapt forward and took hold of her feet to massage them. But there was enough excitement bubbling in him to quieten for long, 'Did you know, Maharaja Ram was born through divine supplication.'

'That's right,' joined in Luv, 'When his father, Maharaja Dasharath could no longer beget an heir, despite having three wives; he decided to organise a big sacrificial prayer. The grandiosity was unheard of. Fed with copious amounts of ghee and *ahootis* and powerful chants, it is said, the sacred fire had churned for days before it finally reached a state from which was obtained a celestial *kheer*. It was the sharing of that pudding made of milk and rice between his three wives that changed the king's life. So much so, that he ended up being blessed with an abundance of four sons. Ram was his eldest, and his dearest.'

'And the most supreme,' smiled Kush.

'And the most supreme,' agreed Luv, 'Afterall, he was conferred with the blessings of a million saints and million more gods.'

'But wait till we tell you who his wife was,' Kush winked, '...a princess who was a divinity no less!'

Hot flame seared up Sita's back. 'Here, let me keep this away,' she motioned to her bowl of rice paste.

'None other than princess Sita! Imagine, the great king Ram married our princess, Sita! Now wouldn't you call that a stroke of serendipity!' shrieked Kush.

Sita's head swam with the apprehension of how much her children knew.

'At least now you wouldn't find us pestering you for her story,' Kush let out a chuckle. 'Why, now we could regale you with our learnings instead. You don't know her story much beyond her birth anyway?'

'These divine births, aren't they wondrous?' continued Luv. 'What with all the yearning and prayers that lead to their arrival. No wonder the ones born from them are special and achieve exemplary deeds.'

'You, my children, are no less special.' Sita drew the boys into an embrace. 'Remember, every soul, divine or otherwise is equally capable of achieving greatness.'

'Hmm, Guruji says the same. It is exactly the reason why Maharaja Ram was born as a mortal being.'

'All that is fine.' Sita's lips tightened, 'But must you really go?'

'Ma, we need to support Guruji,' Luv reasoned. 'Hearing the Ramayana will inspire people to imbibe the great king's qualities. Why, we ourselves feel so motivated!'

'And equally by Maharani Sita,' added Kush.

'True, they are both astounding. It is why destiny brought them together. A true marriage of equals,' said Luv.

A lump went down Sita's throat.

'Now here's another fact—it was Lord Shiva who was instrumental in bringing them together.' Kush said, with a twinkle.

'Oh yes, if it wasn't for his Pinaka.' replied Luv, 'Pinaka was the Lord's sacred bow, that was only ever—'

'Err...don't you think we are getting late,' Kush interjected.

'Oh yes, so we are. Ma, we'll tell you the rest tonight. For now, we really must hurry back with our veenas. Guruji won't take us along if we don't learn the epic. That too in ten days! We better leave.'

And away they ran, gone as quickly as they had come, only this time careful around the alpana.

Sita sighed. It was a relief that Guru Valmiki hadn't revealed more than was needed. At times, it startled her, the fact that her children never enquired about their father. Either they didn't feel the curiosity or were simply content with her. Whatever the reason, it spared her an uneasy predicament. A soft smile curled her lips at the thought that they considered her marriage to Ram as that of equals. It was something only ever said by one other person—her father.

In the initial years of her arrival, Maharaja Janaka had openly embraced Sita's divinity. He saw how her arrival proved to be a balm that healed Mithila and turned it into a pretty picture of bounty. He saw his grounds swell and sprout with the softest grass. Sparkling water once again tumbled down the framing hills. And once again, his heart was gladdened by the sweet swish of golden harvest, and the grateful songs of those who toiled in his name.

Most miraculous of all, he saw his wife's belly bloom at a bewildering age and witnessed the birth of another daughter—Urmila. The sisters loved each other deeply, as did the parents, who loved them both equally. If accusation could ever be made of favouring a child more, then that slightest inclination would be for Sita, the daughter they had adopted—a fact that they preferred not to be reminded of.

Growing up, Sita continued to astonish her father with surpassing beauty and wit, but he would not address her as a divinity. Not in the least because he didn't value her uniqueness but because the disconcerting realization widened the gap between his mortal being and hers. She was too dear; admittedly a blessing proffered a different way, but his own, nonetheless. Years passed under deliberate pretence. Then the day she turned sixteen, an incident jolted the king right back to reality.

The momentous day began as usual Sita had bathed early and was headed to the temple with a basket in hand. This was her daily ritual; readying the temple for her father's morning prayers, though there was still time for that. For now, the horizon lay stretched in pink light, slowly plucking the night away. Upon seeing her, the sparrows waiting over the gulmohar tree glided across—making Sita smile, at which the birds twittered louder, darting back and forth towards the temple.

It was difficult not to be charmed by Sita's smile. Or her beauty. Ethereally carved to perfection; she had a slender waist, shapely arms and a suitably small chin. Her lips were a beautiful pink and accentuated the gentle curves of her cheeks, perfectly framed beneath her large, expressive eyes. She usually tied her hair into a thick bun, a neat parting running down the middle of her face. Although not very tall, she walked with her shoulders arched back; the manner not proud, just self-assured.

Sita stepped into the puja chamber where a black *Shivalinga*, the sacred oval stone, lay in perfect harmony with the dim interiors. Keeping the lord company were a few brass lamps, whose light had turned fuzzy in the early hours. Sita began to clear the previous day's lamps, utensils and withered flowers, replacing them with fresh ones.

She took the sandalwood mark off the Shivalinga, and it came off smoothly. As she put down the wet cloth, her eyes landed on an unusual amount of dust at its base. It was a presence quite odd, as if the dust was purposely sprinkled there. Not believing anyone to commit such blasphemy, Sita cleared it, only to notice more leading off in a curious trail. It stretched to the chamber's corner, all the way to the heavy coffer laid atop eight large wheels.

Sita gulped. It was no ordinary coffer. She was aware of its sacred content, but equally was she aware of its inviolability. It was only ever to be opened on the day of its annual veneration.

Making the moment more opportune, a shaft of light seeped in and illumined the heavily carved chest. Surprisingly, it too was filmed with dust. A puzzled frown caught Sita's face, and she began to wipe the coffer—its top, the sides, the front, the edges; the dust was everywhere in the carvings and in between the grooves, and she pressed harder, trying her best to take it all off, when her hand scraped the latch. It was only ever a gentle scrape, but everything fell heavily silent. Sita's shoulders slumped and there took over her a powerful urge to open the lid. For a while, she regarded it. Then, in a trance, did the unthinkable.

The lid came off, and Pinaka, Shiva's grand bow was revealed. A formidable force emanated outwards and sucked her in. Despite the dull wood, the bow shone mystically. So colossal was its thickness, that it could only ever be grasped by the lord's large hands, and so overbearing was its weight, that it could only ever be lifted by the one able to bear the weight of the world.

Sita reached over and wrapped her delicate fingers around the ancient bow. Only a touch was needed for her soul to realize that she was no different from the primal lord. Under such inextricable connectivity, she began lifting the bow, and with unbelievable smoothness it came off, like it was nothing more than child's play. Its immense weight melted away as she stretched it to the ceiling, showing the heavens what belonged to the heavens. A deep meditative solitude descended and wrapped the place.

'Shiva's bow!'

The gasp broke her stupor. Her father stood at the door. Whether his mouth was agape in wonder or condemnation was not clear. Sita swivelled her own gaze at her hand, baffled by how the bow even got there.

'I am…I'm so sorry, Father.' She carefully placed back the Pinaka, closed the coffer, and rushed out with choking embarrassment and the mortifying jingle of her anklets, leaving the basket and wet cloth behind.

That day Maharaja Janak had not witnessed Sita's disrespect for the bow. It was instead a truth he was irrationally overlooking. Later when he returned to the royal chambers and recounted to his wife, with stupefaction in his eyes and incomprehensibility in his voice, the disbelief he had witnessed, a heaviness slumped upon them both. They both realized the gravity of their endowed responsibility. Sita was unique. If they were ever to find a groom equal to Sita, he had to be one equal to Shiva. And who other than Shiva could ever be equal to Shiva.

A long time had passed since the famine, and their nights turned sleepless once again as restlessness clawed into their consciousness. But this time the king didn't sit idle. Instead, he made the very source of his worry, his stipulation. Any ruler, powerful enough to lift the Lord's bow and brace it with a string would be offered his daughter's hand. The message was sent out to all valiant kings, near and far. As expected, having heard of Sita's alluring beauty, rulers from far and wide came in great numbers; some with torsos wide as tree trunks, others with fists heavy as iron, with moustaches thick and black, and with backs marred with honourable war scars.

These were all burly, powerful kings. However, despite their appearance and all the heaving and struggling to pick the bow, none amongst them could as much as shift it even. The great Pinaka lay mockingly rooted on its deep red velvet casing, waiting for the right man to come and lift it.

That man, however, took close to two years to finally come and claim Sita.

3

Equal Forces

Despite her usual occupied self, Sita sat on her cottage's verandah, enjoying the odd luxury of a winter afternoon. The overhead sun prised in jagged lines through her thatched roof. It fell over her face, her ochre yellow saree, the colour a soothing blend to her simplicity. At places, the caked mud on the floor still showed the sweeping brush pattern, otherwise it shone over with constant treading. And then there were the feet marks; white, little, messy marks. A smile lit up her face before her eyes returned to the view outside.

Not only the sun, but the shadows raced down too. On the little clearing outside, they cast stark shapes of bare branches. It was nice how the forest stood proud in bareness; dressed for the final breath of winter, with barely a few leaves on the mango, *jamun*, banyan and jackfruit. As the wind tried to pluck them, they flittered and flickered in futile desperation before falling. A sluggish moment later, the dry pods of *amaltas* went *khan, khan, khan*, their music delightful to the ears, especially when the lazy warmth had dulled every other senses. Sita rested her chin atop her knees and stretched her palms to the creamy light.

It glimmered over the lines on her palm, those telling of love and fate. With a jolt, Sita curled them back in a fist.

Even though she never believed in their foretelling, her younger sister, Urmila thought otherwise. Growing up, she would often cajole Sita to accompany her to the soothsayers and dissuading her proved to be a difficult battle, especially when Urmila would drag her by the arm, pucker her face, talk sweetly and become teary-eyed—basically try every gambit possible to have her will. Once there, she would compel Sita to show her own hands, and every time when Sita would hold it out in the light of the dimly lit lamp, the old lady's face would crease up with a thousand and more wrinkles. Cackling, she would relay the same prediction from the previous week. A man unrivalled in charm to Indra, in power to Shiva and in wisdom to Brahma was soon to enter Sita's life. When the giggling Urmila would question as to how soon that was destined, the soothsayer would burst out, crying, 'Next day, why, the very next day!'

But no such man came. Not the next day, not the next month, not even in the next two years. And the impossibly heavy Pinaka lay rooted, with no more kings willing to sacrifice their ego only to face humiliation. However, not every word of the soothsayer was false.

That evening Sita was spending time in the garden with her younger sister Urmila. Mandavi and Shrutakirti, their uncle's daughters were over too. Mattresses and bright cushions were sprawled on the stone terrace under the overladen branches of *basantrani*, which profuse with the fluffiest white flowers, drooped down. Every passing breeze relieved the tree of some of its treasure and aroused a delighted giggle from beneath.

'Sita, would you please sing for us?' requested Urmila.

'But I sang just a while ago,' protested Sita.

'You did. But when did I say I have had enough of your melodious voice?' Urmila thrust the veena forward, knowing fully well her sister would oblige.

True to her praise, when Sita did start singing, it wasn't just plain melody that rose from her throat, but honey that was sweet and warm, and had the power to pierce all senses. One only had to look at Sita's delicate fingers plucking the veena, the soft clenching of her beautiful eyes, the quiver of her throat, the gentle swaying of her pretty round face pooling and stretching those honey drenched notes, to realize there wasn't a beauty more alluring than hers. The afternoon's receding light shimmered on her face and illumined her round, pink lips that culminated in captivating grooves.

A few swans, which had been swooping and looping in the air, now huddled alongside the other entranced spectators. But the song ended all too soon, once again leaving everyone with a sense of longing. When Sita opened her eyes, it felt like any melody left hanging around would instantly be absorbed into her deep black pools of wonder.

By now, her parents, who had been taking a walk in the garden, also reached.

'Father! Did you hear her singing?' beamed Urmila.

'Most entrancing!' replied Maharaja Janak. He wrapped his arms around Urmila and took a seat by the platform. Sita smiled and passed him a cushion. Her father's affectionate praises meant the world to her.

'Hail our Maharaja!' An attendant followed up from behind.

'Yes?' The king turned around, surprised at this sudden interruption.

'Maharaja, we have just received news that the honoured Sage Vishwamitra would be visiting our kingdom with the Ayodhyan princes, Ram and Laxman. He has thereby requested an audience with the Lord's bow.'

Maharaja Janak's eyebrows shot up, soon followed by a relieved smile. It didn't go entirely unnoticed by Sita, but Urmila, not as moderate with restraint, openly nudged her.

'Make sure appropriate arrangements are made for their stay. And inform me when they are close to the gates, I will greet them myself,' said the king.

'As you wish, Maharaja.' Saying this, the attendant left.

'The Ayodhyan princes! Maharaja Dasharath's sons? Did you invite them?' Maharani Sunaina asked her husband.

'Oh no! It is most definitely the Lord's doing, surprising us when we least anticipate.'

Those words weren't exactly explicit, still it was not difficult to understand what her parents had on their minds. Sita tried her best to feign sobriety.

'What brings them here then?' Maharani Sunaina continued.

'Last I heard, Sage Vishwamitra had sought Maharaja Dasharath's help in sending his valorous sons to kill the demons at the Tataka forest. Those menacing demons had been wreaking havoc, interrupting the performance of vedic rituals, even killing the hermits. I believe the princes have relieved the hermits and are en route to Ayodhya. Anyway, I should get going. It wouldn't be long before they are here,' said the king.

'Yes, it also is getting dark. About time we head indoors,' agreed the queen.

A faint sound of bells followed from the palace. 'Looks like the priest is getting things ready for *Gauri poojan*,' said Maharani Sunaina. 'Why don't you girls get changed and assemble for the evening prayers. Meanwhile, I will go and see to the arrangements for their stay and dinner.'

The evening had indeed spilled quickly, and in dimness, the scattered flowers of basantrani stood out in exquisite beauty. As they rose to leave, one last flower tumbled down Sita's shoulders, and she caught it just in time. She blushed, thinking how the flower would make for a nice offering to Gauri, the goddess of marital boons, the wife of Lord Shiva, the one who begot her own husband with stubborn will.

Sita never met Ram that evening. At night, she lay in bed, looking at the sky outside her window, knowing that she wasn't really looking at the teeming stars but was consumed with the thoughts of the Ayodhyan prince. Odd to feel such strong inclination for someone she hadn't even met, and it vexed her all the same. Her father had hinted that Ram was valorous. But was he strong enough for the Pinaka? An answer only tomorrow would unfold. *Ram—Ram—Ram*. There couldn't be a name with a sweeter ring. She didn't realize how much time had passed before she finally fell asleep.

The next morning broke with his presence in the cool air, and in the teasing chants of her friends.

'*Ram—Ram—Ram*!'

'Stop it!' called Sita, half laughing, half flustered.

'*Ram—Ram—Ram*!' they chimed again, more emboldened than before.

'Enough! Someone will hear you!'

'Good!' one of them chortled, 'Maybe he will! The one with the sweet name?'

Sita huffed and snatched the flower basket. 'I'm going to the Pushpa Vatika, and please don't follow me,' she said and walked away but the impish ones hovered after.

'Look at her anklet! Where was this hiding!' remarked a friend.

'It's the same I always wear,' retorted Sita.

'Liar!' they sang. 'Even your mirror knows better.'

Not that they were completely wrong. She had, after all, spent longer in front of the mirror, tucking her bun just right, adjusting her drapes with care. While the bangle, the earrings, and the necklace were the usual, the waistband and the anklet were more exquisite than other days. But they weren't for anyone in particular, of course.

Once at the garden, they thankfully dispersed in different directions, embossing the dew laden grass with dainty footprints. It was the early magical hours, and the beauty of the garden was more pronounced. A few bees, the other early morning risers, were already at work, drawing sweet nectar from flowers. Seeing the girls get closer, they buzzed off to the next bush. Sita reached for the *champa* flower, when her eyes caught sight of a large dew sparkling on its waxy white surface. As if aware of her watchful eyes, the iridescent pearl slithered shyly to the edge, quivering, gathering all its water, before going down with a plop. Sita smiled and proceeded to collect *belpatra*, *tulsi* and *harsingaar*; whose white petals with orange stalk made an excellent choice for Shiva. As she plucked the large *udhul* flower from the upper branches, it came off with a playful lurch. It sprinkled heavily over her face and hands. Where the drops landed on her saree, deepened its colour from pink to magenta. She shrugged it in haste, but it was too late; the attire chosen after much contemplation ruined in a matter of moments.

She was still wiping her face when an intriguing silhouette of a man walking against the rising sun caught her attention. It felt as if the rising sun was nothing but the man's own distinctive aura. She parted the *udhul* branches and peered closer while he walked over with firm stride. Before she could come to her senses, he had already stepped out of the blurring silhouette into reality, standing right across her. Not someone she had seen before, he had wheatish skin, broad shoulders, and long arms, which somehow accentuated his masculinity. There was an endearing charm of a young man over his face, yet the effulgence over his forehead suggested a degree of wisdom, that would take a lifetime for most men to impossibly gain. Despite his strong build, he had kind eyes, framed beautifully by sweeping lashes. It was with those twinkling eyes that he regarded Sita with as much a lost expression as she regarded him.

Sita loosened her grip on the hibiscus branch, realizing it was awkwardly late to avert her gaze. He greeted her with a barely perceptible nod, and she responded with a gentle lowering of her own lashes.

'Brother Ram!' followed a voice from the other side of the bush.

Her heart skipped a beat. She looked at him again, then at the other man who might not have taken note of her presence. Possibly his younger brother, Laxman. He too was clad in a white pleated *dhoti* and *angavastram*, with hair tied in a top knot. 'Guru Vishwamitra should be expecting us back soon. Do you think this makes enough flowers for the prayers?' He pointed towards the basket in his hands.

Ram nodded to Laxman, then turned back towards Sita. Fortunately, in this time, Urmila had also walked up from behind and without exchanging any words, Sita abruptly swivelled and left. To make matters worse, Urmila turned around with the worst quizzical look at the men.

It troubled Sita to know that her emotions had laid transparent like a sheet of water, that her heart had beaten loudly, and that every dire attempt at calming breaths had only resulted in shivers. She was acutely aware of Ram's gaze on her and did not know what to do with her idle hand. When Urmila shook her to pry, Sita squeezed her and continued walking away with her best attempt at utmost grace.

Soon, the sound of trinkets from their anklets and waistband dulled, along with any incessant laughter from her prying friends. Once again, the buzzing of bees on the champa flowers picked up in the air. And now brighter than before, sunlight sparkled on the remaining dews, as the men too, left from there. They themselves needed to return for the prayers before heading off to see the holy bow.

The atmosphere in the court was intense later that afternoon as everyone had assembled to see Ram lift the Pinaka. Sita sat beside her parents who sat with their backs stiff, as did every other minister in the courtroom. A thumping was heard. In walked, fifty attendants straining a thick rope across their burly shoulders and wheeled in the Pinaka. The creaking continued, grating the granite floor and the air, and finally stopped when the chest reached the centre. All eyes turned towards Ram, seated alongside the assembled ministers. He took Guru Vishwamitra's approval and proceeded forward. There was not a single falter in his steps or hesitation in his expressions. He was unbothered. But when he reached the bow, he turned towards Sita with an expectant gaze. A shiver ran down her spine and she became aware of the prayers already on her lips.

Ram folded his hands at the mighty bow smeared with sandalwood paste and flowers. He reached over and clasped it in his palms. Not only did he pluck it easily, but within a fraction of a moment, mounted it on the floor. An immediate smile broke across Sita's lips, and it was difficult to keep them from quivering.

As for the rest of the ministers, they sat agape, and understandably so. For their limited mortal minds, such a reality was impossible to accept. But not for Maharaja Janak who had witnessed its precedence before. His vision altered between the past and the present, between Sita and Ram, and he knew that they were no different, only equal parts of the same force that needed to be brought together. His shoulders slumped in relief, and there escaped a relieved sigh, as he squeezed his wife's hands.

With one hand still holding the Pinaka, Ram started to brace its ends. He checked the tautness by pulling the bowstring all the way to his ears and released it.

But the bow creaked!

A sudden deafening roar followed: one that stunned both the heavens and the earth. Everything lay in suspension; shock, heartbeats, panic. The great Pinaka had been snapped in two, and a part lay by Ram's feet. Sita's heart stopped beating. It was a calamity. What would her father make of it?

But Maharaja Janak understood. He understood the breaking of the Pinaka was not a travesty, instead a realization of its intended purpose. He rose from his throne and began to applaud with unbridled ecstasy, and it was only then that Sita was able to breathe.

A furtive smile escaped Ram's lips. He turned to check Sita's reaction, knowing he had claimed her. But Sita's eyes were downcast, knowing her parents were watching her. So was Urmila, her cousins and everyone else in the court. Amidst all that clapping, thumping and crying, it was declared that Sita would be wedded to Ram.

That joyous message was sent out to Ram's father, Maharaja Dasharath. Overly delighted, the old king rushed to Mithila, bearing gratitude and gifts, as well as his other two sons—Bharat and Shatrughan. While Maharaja Janak had only planned to wed his elder daughter to Ram, Maharaja Dasharath was looking for more. He had four sons, and Mithila, four princesses. In ten days, rushing on the fastest steeds, he arrived at Mithila, to a city decorated like a bride, garlanded with the finest flowers, its streets sprinkled with perfumed waters, and was received with great fanfare and showered with utmost hospitality.

The day of the wedding was special. It was a new chapter in Sita's life and was suffused with a plethora of emotions—from the nascent joy of a new relationship to the pain of parting from her parents' unconditional love. Sita squeezed her mother's cold hands as Maharani Sunaina decked her with her own jewellery. A chapter was about to close from which she would only carry forth tenderness.

The whole palace was bedecked heavily in flowers, with intricate *bandanvaar* that stood guarding the threshold. Long streams of plump champa and *palash* wrapped every pillar and ledge, and hung from balconies and windows in a striking display of celebration. The *vivaah mandap* was suffused in their intoxicating aroma, as well as that of ghee, holy fire, incense sticks and perfumes of different kinds. The glow of countless lamps on the black granite wall reflected a magical aura that diffused and spread in a supple manner, drenching the entire atmosphere in their golden haze.

Seated next to Ram, Sita smiled blissfully. Her wedding saree, red and orange, was embroidered intricately in gold, and with her eyes downcast, she could make out the delicate quiver of her nose ring. She hadn't yet looked directly at Ram but could tell he looked serene and assured. Maharaja Janak took hold of her hands; her fingertips coloured beautifully in red *alakata* and placed it over Ram's. Her bangles chinked as it rested over the man she could lean on her entire life. She felt herself softening under his warm touch; the moment soon made more special with the pouring of sacred water to sanctify the hymns. Thereafter, with their hands clasped together and amidst the chants of *mantras* and ringing of bells, they went around the holy fire. It cast mesmerising glow over their beautiful young faces as they each took sacred oath of togetherness.

With this, Sita was married to Ram. As was Urmila to Laxman, Mandavi to Bharat and Shrutakirti to Shatrughan. All the treasure of Mithila graciously offered to Maharaja Dasharath of Ayodhya. The latter was moved by the display of this greatest order of generosity and assured the Mithilan king that he would take utmost care towards ensuring his daughters' happiness.

Yet Maharaja Janak's eyes were supple like that of an overcast cloud. Afterall, he was parting with a child who was an unexpected gift, taught him an important life lesson, and enveloped his life with unbounding happiness. Tenderness emanated from his eyes as he regarded the young couple with welling satisfaction. As he presented Sita with the acclaimed *choodamani*, the bejewelled hairpin from his royal treasure, he said, 'From now on, you will also be known as Ramaa of Ram,' remembering how he often referred to her as Janaki, her name of endearment from his own addressal as Janak, or as Maithali, the princess of Mithila. But he probably saw a surprised unease on Sita's face and added, 'My dear daughter, you may have many names, derived from your father or your husband, but they will all be inconsequential towards how you will be eventually known. It is my blessing that may you always be remembered for your exalted qualities alone.'

With withered hands, he cusped his dear daughter's cheeks and took a moment regarding her glittering eyes with his rheumy ones. Something told him it was the last he was seeing of her. Then he closed the raatrani flowered curtain over her palanquin.

Those were the parting words of wisdom from Maharaja Janak to his daughter. The sound of flute and *turhi* picked up the sharp strain of separation, as well as the conflicting joy of union. With it, the bearers picked up her palanquin and Sita's round face wavered behind the fragrant strings of delicate flowers, as she made her way to a different world—to Ayodhya—a world of splendour and budding happiness.

4

Jeopardizing Jealousy

Outside, the forest lay steeped in the smell of wet grass. Every strand was bejewelled with dew that would soon be collected by the day's first light. There was still time for its cracking, but Luv and Kush stood ready, with their veena and a bundle of clothes strapped across their backs.

The only light came from the cooking fire, where Sita was roasting rotis over hot stone. Her sons favoured the flatbreads rolled from *bajra* dough. The stone was hot and smoke watered her eyes, offering a good excuse to conceal her true emotions.

Luv tapped Kush's shoulder. They knew her displeasure all too well but what was the point of breaching the topic if their hearts were set. So, they sat beside her and chatted about the most banal things—the sound of crickets that didn't let them sleep so well, the change in weather, the bubbles on her rotis and whether she would roast them crisp or soft. However, Sita replied in mere mumbles. In reality, her throat ached from the strain of suppressed words.

It was only after she spread out the rotis to cool that she glanced up. The boys had neatly tied their top buns themselves. When had they grown so independent, so self-assured? From the start she knew that they could memorize the epic. Five hundred chapters, or twenty-four thousand verses, there was not a barrier dissuading enough. Just like there were none for their father.

Behind their eager faces, the nascent light finally broke through, ushering in the tenth day. The awaited day, the dreaded day. The day her sons would leave for Ayodhya.

'Ma, promise to take good care of yourself,' said Luv.

'And skipping no meals, please,' said Kush.

She wanted to fill them in her arms, press their little faces against her aching bosom and smother their cheeks with kisses. But she gulped her unease and got on with packing the food in a muslin cloth: ten rotis each, generously smeared with ghee and a lump of jaggery. It would be days before she would see them again. They had hardly been around in recent days, spending most of their time in Guru Valmiki's cottage and returning only for quick meals or a few hours of sleep. With such possessed intensity had they recited the Ramayana, that by the end of it, the verses were inexplicably spilling out of their mouths even in deep sleep. Those mumblings, those inaudible snippets of her previous life, had troubled her all the same.

'Is that him?' The sound of approaching footsteps caught Kush's attention, and they leapt to the door.

'Wait, put on your *khadau* at least.' Sita followed after with their wooden slippers.

The air outside was chilly and their threadbare clothes too light. But she bit her tongue, thinking it best not to offend Guruji. She couldn't refrain from slipping the small bundle of food though.

Guru Valmiki brushed it back, 'Now, now, daughter. Don't forget these boys are ascetics. Let them beg, and I am sure some kindly soul will take mercy.'

'At least take these fruits,' Sita insisted, 'They are very fond of *ber*.'

'Trust me, they will be fine.' Guru Valmiki's tone was a bit firm this time.

'Ma, we will be back before you even realize,' assured Luv.

'In the blink of an eye,' smiled Kush.

What did their innocent hearts ever know about separation and its knotting pangs. But Sita nodded and gave them her blessings. Skipping and chattering, they walked away, in the direction of the creeping sun, soon lost to her watery sight.

It wasn't like she faulted their eagerness. Twenty-eight years had passed since her first Ayodhya visit, yet the memory was clear as the morning sky. She was only a young bride of eighteen then.

Twenty days and as many nights had passed since the convoy had left Mithila. The lurch of the palanquin on its bearers had turned laggard. The monotonous motion made Sita's stomach churn. She ached to step out, allow her limbs a little stretch and breathe in the fresh air. But the sight of Maharaja Dasharath, riding austerely up-front crushed her desire in its fledgling. She peeled the netted curtain for her sisters, but none were in sight. Throngs of guests and ministers trailed after, and trailing after them were the gracious gifts offered by her father—a never ending cavalcade of chariots, servants and female attendants. The generosity of Maharaja Janak was unmatched, what with countless cows, and enough numbers of elephants and camels, all beautifully decorated in golden harnesses, goads and necklaces, and bearing precious carpets, silk clothes, caskets of gold coins, diamonds, pearls, topazes and emeralds. Now even the animals moved wearily, kicking up clouds of dust that settled on the ones behind.

'Are you looking for something, my dear?' Ram drew her curtains. Mounted on a regal white horse, wearing a yellow dhoti with a crimson *angavastram*, he looked resplendent.

'Uh-no…I was just…Do you know how much further before we reach home?'

A teasing smile flickered across Ram's face. Was it too soon that she had called Ayodhya home? Sita twirled away. He was making her feel so vulnerable.

'Almost home,' he replied gently.

As if on cue, there rose a call from attendants at front. 'We can see Saryu!' An instant cheer went up.

'They are talking of Saryu, the river!' Ram explained. 'It is much loved by all for the prosperity it brings to the kingdom. In fact, the way it loops around Ayodhya is almost as if it is garlanding the kingdom…well, that's what people say.'

Once again, Sita's heart skipped a beat. Was he too thinking about their own wedding, her standing across him at the *mandap*, with thickly knotted raatrani garland in hands?

Feigning unaffected composure, Sita peered to catch the river's first glimpse. Saryu sparkled gloriously and lapped forth with assured playfulness. Fertile fields, result of its generous benefactions, lay on either side. Every now and then, the abutting land stretched inwards in a wily attempt to embrace the river, but the spirited one, tantalizingly gushed out.

Sita's heart pounded with trepidation. In no time, she would be before Ram's family; his mother, his sister, other cousins and everyone else who couldn't make it to Mithila. She smiled at Ram and leaned back, hoping he would get the cue. After all, she needed time to smoothen out her crinkled saree and retie her bun.

In only a matter of a prahar, the convoy halted. Large imposing gateways, the portal to Ayodhya's magnificent kingdom stood in front, and huddled behind was a congregation of people, who had lovingly laid a welcome carpet of flowers. It was a striking display of colour and intricate patterns, of dancing peacocks, and flowers in bloom, that heart-melting, devoted effort. Soon the sound of drums reverberated through, alongside exuberant chanting.

'Ram-Sita! Ram-Sita! Ram-Sita!'

It was the first time she had heard their names called out loud, wrapped together. It sounded sweet, as if honey bound. Her cheeks flushed red, and her hands were no use in cooling them down. Ram trotted up front to acknowledge the outpouring. He raised his hand, beaming, for all to see how delighted he was about their union.

The chants and flowers trailed them through the great palace gates. At last, her palanquin swayed to a halt and was lowered, the curtains lifting to the blaze of colour and sound. Incense drifted in the air, mingling with the neigh of horses and the clamour of drums. A flutter of nerves rose in her chest, but as her feet touched the stone courtyard and she glimpsed her sisters stepping down beside her, her unease began to melt in their familiar company.

An opulent palace stood ahead, shimmering under the sun like a jewel of stone and story. The new brides climbed up a staggering flight of steps, leading to a podium behind which stood royal buildings. Columns, tall as the sky and heavily embellished with motifs of vines and flowers, of dancing *apsaras* and fighting warriors held up the roof. Waiting there were the three wives of Maharaja Dasharath, each carrying a welcome *thaal,* replete with *diyas,* flowers and vermillion powder.

Ram touched their feet, and Sita followed suit, the flutter of nerves and wonder picking up again. She watched quietly as Ram greeted each queen, but did not speak their names. Sensing her confusion, the one with completely grey hair smiled, 'I am Kaushalya, the eldest and mother of Ram. And here is Sumitra, mother to the younger princes, Laxman and Shatrughan.'

'So you must have guessed that I am Kaikeyi, mother to Bharat,' Sita's eyes flicked to the youngest queen, the most radiant. She had blue eyes, framed with thick lashes, a beauty that carried quiet power.

Each queen blessed the brides, tilting their chin, talking of beauty, blessings, and long-awaited happiness.

Then Kaushalya took hold of Sita's palms and dipped them into the vermillion slurry, 'It's for the welcome ritual. Go ahead and press your palms on the wall.' As Sita lifted back her palms, a vivid red imprint glowed back.

'Urmila, Madavi and Shrutakirti, do we need to tell you to do the same?' Sumitra added with a playful smile.

'Your first mark in Ayodhya!' Kaikeyi's voice was warm with pride, 'And now your destiny is sealed to it.'

The mothers handed them each a cloth to wipe their hands and led them inside. Outside, the handprints glowed like a promise of belonging.

Over time, life settled into a state of interminable bliss and joyful discoveries. Sita learnt many truths not only about Ram but also herself. She became aware of how crimson her cheeks blazed under Ram's gaze, how involuntarily her lips quivered at his close embrace, how her dainty waist fit snugly in his strong arms, and how, every time he came close, her knees went weak from his musky smell.

She came to know what his favourite food was—that he liked sweet more than sour. His mannerism was always calm, in joyful times or otherwise, always awe-inspiring. As for Ram, he learnt that she preferred wildflowers over neatly manicured gardens, and loved animals dearly. To please her, he would often take her on nearby forest sojourns and spend a few loving nights undisturbed by the bustle of palace life. Those nights he was free to admire her beauty. But more than her beauty, it was her intense and independent mind he admired most; the way she challenged rituals in need of reform. To Ram—a descendant from the illustrious Ikshavku dynasty—a dynasty with predecessors like Sagar, Bhagirath and Raghu—rituals were sacred. Yet he found himself listening with interest.

One day as they were strolling in the palace gardens, Sita whispered, 'Why are the ministers of the court all men, Ram?'

Ram paused, searching for words, 'It is tradition. Maybe men are deemed more decisive.'

'Shouldn't traditions change? Justice needs all voices.'

'You may be right. Why don't you start with setting up a women's chamber. I will speak to Father on your behalf.'

Some nights, out on their terrace, she would entertain him playing veena and he would shower her with incessant praise; all the while acutely aware of the sprig of *raatrani* in her dark hair. Later, drunk on the heavenly sweetness of her voice, and the irresistible allure of fresh marriage, he would sweep her off to the bedchamber. There she would nestle up close, often caressing the mole beneath his left ear. He would smoothen out her silky tresses and gently lift her chin to make her look him in the eye.

Most mesmerizing would be the moonlit nights when

milkiness would drench her ivory skin with ethereal glimmer. Ram would trace his fingers, and the hushed silence would fill with the clear jingling of her bangles. In time, that jingling replaced by sweet whispers, and finally the soothing rhythm of sleep. Sita always slept with her head propped against his chest, and Ram with his hands strapped across her—that deep entwine separated only by the morning's unforgiving light.

And with that cracking of the first light, Sita would head out to the women's chamber to hear appeals, and Ram to the court. Only a few months had passed since their marriage, but Ram's responsibilities kept increasing swiftly. Maharaja Dasharath had been urging him to take over military and state affairs, then administration and finally cultural matters.

One fine morning in the royal hall, as Ram stood before his father, recounting to him the proceeds from each ministry, he caught his father watching him with a curious smile.

'Father, is something the matter?'

Maharaja Dasharath remained silent, his gaze steady but unreadable.

'Please, tell me.'

'It is time, Ram. Time, you took up the throne.'

A thunderbolt struck Ram. 'Father! Ayodhya still needs you.'

'It is the tradition, Ram. As inevitable as the rising of sun.'

'But your wisdom guides us all. The ministers, they trust you.'

'Ah! They already trust you. Last evening, I asked them if you would make a worthy ruler and every voice rose in fierce, unwavering support.' He added with a smile, 'It has been many years ruling, and I now desire to go for *vanaprastha*.'

'If the kingdom falls without you?'

'Then it is your burden. But I know you will not let it happen.'

That decree was borne out on streets; the news received with frenzied dancing and jubilation. At the palace, however, much preparation was in order. After all, Ayodhya was unmatched in esteem, and Maharaja Dasharath left no stone unturned to showcase its burgeoning prosperity. Overnight, invitation scrolls were weaved in threads of gold and adorned with intricate calligraphy for every ruler near or far, priests, advisers, commanders as well as the foremost citizens. By morning, the fastest horses carried them. After all, the coronation was only a fortnight away.

Marquees, huge as palaces and rich in opulence, were propped for accommodating guests throughout the royal grounds. On one corner, stables were readied, and tents and ancillary accommodation set up for the entourage on the other. Jewels and precious stones were accounted as gifts, and gold coins for brahmins. The best artists and warriors were summoned for singing, dancing, wrestling, archery and sword fighting. For discussions on *shastra*s, scholars were invited. The ghats of Saryu were scrubbed, incense of *agaru* was lit in the streets, and the marketplace bustled with excitement never seen before. Thankfully, it being the month of *Chaitra,* the gardens and groves were full of blossoms and needed no special tending.

At the palace, the floor was polished to gleam like water. The same treatment was given to every ledge and corner. As the day neared, aroma of various delicacies started to fill the air. *Payasam, halwa, modak, rabri,* along with *shashkuli, khāṇḍavana* and *gauḍa* were being prepared. It was a delightful smell, that of flour and lentils being roasted with ghee, sugar and nuts.

For the ceremony, golden pots of water from the four sacred

rivers were brought. More pots were filled with honey, curd, ghee, milk, parched grain, along with *darbha* grass and flowers. A whisk of yak was brought to fan Ram, and his chariot was yoked with supreme horses as tall as elephants. Tall camels, white horses and handsome elephants lined the yards. Music filled the courtyards, with bards and minstrels singing the heir's praise, matching the sound of trumpets, tambourines and drums, to which danced the happy denizens.

The palatial ladies became occupied with their own grooming. Their maids bathed them in *champaka* filled basins and scented oils, washed their hair with honey and curd, scrubbed their skin, and smothered them in thick sandalwood paste, in assurance that by the day of the celebration, the lustre of their skin would rival that of the sun.

What was ironic then was that amongst all this frenzy, invitation was missed out for Bharat, Ram's younger brother, son to Maharani Kaikeyi. At the time, he was away at his maternal uncle's kingdom, but the kingdom itself wasn't unreachable. Equally ironic, that Maharaja Dasharath hadn't taken note of that gross oversight. Neither had Ram. Nor Kaikeyi. But Manthara, the queen's long-serving maid, wasn't so naïve.

The day before the coronation, she stood oiling the queen's hair. There was a kind of hypnotic magic in Manthara's hands. As she pressed her fingers in gentle spirals, Kaikeyi's earrings chimed in time with the drowsy, pleasured tilt of her head. How could Kaikeyi's closed eyes then see the reflection in the ornate mirror as was visible to Manthara. To Manthara, the mirror was a relentless judge, harsh and punitive. Without pretence, it captured the stark contrast of the queen's silky saree against her own plain brown, her patron's lean and beautiful frame against her disfigured hunchback. It was true that fate had been unsparingly cruel to Manthara. Not only was she crippled by birth but was then painfully subjected to life surrounded by the beautiful palace women. The hankering reminder of her own insufficiency turned out to be too much for her jealous mind. The feel of Queen Kaikeyi's shiny tresses in her calloused hands started an involuntary twitch of her nose.

'Big day tomorrow. Our Ram will be crowned king.' Kaikeyi struck up a conversation.

But the maid simply carried swivelling a spouted brass lamp under her hair. The scent was jasmine, Kaikeyi's favourite. Despite her earlier restraint, Manthara ended up blurting, 'Ram will be crowned...*aaa-aachooo!*'

'Careful! Don't you know it's inauspicious to sneeze. Besides, you are standing right behind me.'

'So sorry, my princess. It is the perfume.'

Manthara was special. Having once been Kaikeyi's wet nurse, she still held onto calling the queen by her maiden title. And despite her lower ranking, she was the only one who could get away by speaking her mind.

'You are quite right,' Manthara continued. 'It indeed is inauspicious—Ram's crowning.'

'Manthara!' snapped Kaikeyi. 'You are again deriding Ram!'

'Pardon me, princess. I can't help but feel wronged.' She placed the lamp on the table, which felt more like thumping, and picked the comb.

'Why so?'

'Why so! Well princess, you may have forgotten Maharaja Dasharath's promise—that of only ever crowning your son as the king. But I certainly haven't. If it wasn't for that assurance, your father, the great Maharaja Ashwapati, would have never consented to you marrying an old king—a king who had already been married twice!'

'Yes. But that was a long time ago. Much has changed since.'

'Exactly. Much has changed since. But not you! You never bothered to look after your interests then, and are gullible to overlook it now. My princess, with your beauty and wit, you deserved to rule as a prime consort. Unfortunately, that didn't turn out to be the case. The least you can do now is to secure Bharat's future.'

'Things changed when neither of us queens could beget him an heir. We couldn't do it for years. Why, you know everything. You also know how these four princes were born out of the same divine blessing, that *kheer* we shared. Isn't it one source, after all? True, we mothered different children, but does that make any difference?'

'Ha! Conveniently not for Kaushalya and her son. They are hogging the empire. They will chant that all brothers are equal. Are they though?' She hissed in her ears, 'Okay tell me, does it not strike you as odd, the sudden urgency behind the ceremony?'

Kaikeyi's eyes shot up. Those blue eyes, wide and beautiful.

'Why else, but to protect the kingdom from Bharat!' continued Manthara with her conspiratorial hissing. 'It's detestable how everything is planned in his absence. Sly of Maharaja to draw on this opportunity. And even if he were to break his promise, the least he could have done was to check with you. See if you were okay with the changes. So much for harping about you being his dearest!'

Those words. Dipped in venom, they pierced right through Kaikeyi's heart. It was true that Dasharath considered her his dearest wife, coming to her most nights. She turned heavily silent.

'Do you remember princess, those two boons the king granted you when you saved his life?'

'Huh?'

'At Sampasura! I am talking about that fated battle, where you fought alongside him. How the enemy's arrows had knocked him unconscious, and how you had charioteered him off to safety, tending until he was strong again? That time, my princess, he promised you two favours in return. Any...two... favours, that he could not refuse.' Manthara placed the comb down and whispered, 'I don't think you ever claimed them.'

It was true. There were so many promises Maharaja Dasharath hadn't fulfilled. Kaikeyi's thoughts rattled in her stiff mind. Too many questions, too many missing answers. She rose off the padded velvet stool, but Manthara shoved her down.

'Wait, princess! Let me finish putting this *choodamani* on your bun, this very symbol of marital bliss. There, there, just how nice you look now.'

Kaikeyi's gaze returned to the mirror. The large ruby on her *choodamani* caught the sunlight and splintered as bloodied daggers across the room. Behind her, Manthara was cackling. Her laughter started slow and raspy, and then, turned chilling.

5

The First Decree

Sita untied the bundle of ber, those plump green fruits, and tipped them into the wicker basket for air.

Guru Valmiki could have at least taken the fruits; after all she had risen before dawn in hope to pack some for the children. They were still wet from fresh plucking, and even one rotten ber was enough to spoil the rest. Just like the rotten Manthara, the nemesis of Ayodhya's grand collapse. A figure entirely insignificant, but dangerous, nevertheless. Murmurs had later reached Sita on how she had oozed her bitterness to Kaikeyi and rocked the bearing of a kingdom otherwise wrought in harmony.

That morning, the wily Manthara had only pretended to get Kaikeyi ready, while weaving schemes with every stroke of the comb. Now all Kaikeyi could hear was the hollow promise of her husband. *My dear, the one born from your womb would rule Ayodhya one day. Yes, the one born from your womb...Ayodhya... one day. Rule, womb, Ayodhya.* It rattled with unstoppable chaos.

She shut all her windows and doors, allowing no escape for her trapped hurting. With every attacking thought, she toppled the lamps, hurled her clothes, tore off her jewels—including the *choodamani* on her head—and flung the pillows off her bed. In the confusion of such tramplings she paced non-stop, until her legs turned weary with resentment, her eyes angry with questions, and eventually, the chamber dark with night. The man who claimed that she was the absolute love of his life, was clearly more concerned about the welfare of others. Of course there was every reason to hate Ram.

Oblivious to what was brewing in the other end of the palace, the envied heir retired to his bedchamber. Sita stood by the window, regarding the storm brewing outside. The white and gold flaps of the marquees fluttered loudly, which the panicked attendants tried to pin down.

'Not the most favourable of weather, is it? What with so many guests arriving by daybreak,' Ram said to Sita, caution etching his brow.

'Don't worry, it will turn around by tomorrow,'

'Tomorrow is all about turning. A rather momentous turning.'

Sita looked up, her eyes sparkling at Ram's wit.

He continued, 'It will bring a big change into our lives.'

'More so, it will offer us the ability to bring changes. Maybe I should already start calling you Maharaja.' She placed her hands over his chest, proudly looking him in the eyes.

He smiled and drew her close. On the walls, their distorted shadows wavered like mad spirits.

'All that is good, but looking after a kingdom is no trifling responsibility. I hope I do justice, live up to the reputation of my forebears.' His expressions turned sombre, more focused.

Sita wasn't sure if being overcautious was a good thing. Before she could reply, the heavy snarl of the wind distracted their attention. Outside, huge *sal* trees bent down to unseen force.

'Ram, all you need to do is follow your heart. No shadow of any predecessors can be a better guide than your own conscience. Just shine with your own light, and that will be enough. Come, let's try and get some sleep. There will hardly be any respite after the crowning.'

'Crowning might be mine, but the ruling will be ours. I hope you will keep offering your brilliant advice, Maharani Sita.'

Her face lit up. The world could wait for their turn. Tonight, Ram was only hers. As per the ritual before coronation, they settled onto their separate *darbha* mats over the floor, and looking into each other's eyes for a while fell into deep sleep, undisturbed by the howling and the whooshing, and the fluttering and the wavering; for they weren't living in the present, but the turnings of tomorrow.

Only the turnings had no patience for tomorrow.

Hardly had they slept a proper wink before a rattling shook their door. Ram, still groggy with sleep, went to answer it.

An attendant stood outside, half trembling, half panicking. 'Maharaja Dasharath...he...he has taken severely ill. Maharani Kaushalya...she has asked for your immediate presence.'

Those broken words were cold daggers that pierced through Ram's bones. But he didn't flinch, didn't scream. His eyes remained wide but unseeing. Sita came up from behind and shook him by the elbow, and they left, slowly at first, before Ram's stride turned urgent, and his hands clammier in hers.

Out in the gardens, the attendants carried forth holding down the tent and putting away broken boughs. The fated night had clearly been wrecked by more than one portentous storm.

Even though Maharaja Dasharath's mahogany doors were shut, it couldn't stop the palpable unease from spreading outside. Sita saw Ram taking a moment before pushing the door open. Over the large bed lay the king, pale as a piece of dry log, huddled against pensive wives—the middle and the eldest. The dearest oddly missing.

A stream of tears ran down Maharani Kaushalya's bleary eyes. In a voice that had turned hoarse beyond recognition, she kept calling her husband's name, as if the pointless pleading would bring him back to consciousness. On the other hand, Maharani Sumitra sat in stoic silence, her eyes open, yet unresponsive, like she had already accepted the inevitable fate. The king whimpered in a hum of distant bees. *Ram. Ram. Ram.* It was his dearest son's name he hummed over his lips.

'Right here, Father.' Ram took his hands But unfortunately, the king's heart had already ferried to another world, hanging here only for the compelling fondness for a son he no longer recognized.

'She claimed her boons. Ram…exile…' Maharaja Dasharath started to howl, his delirium rippling like a rain struck pond. He banged his head on the pillow, an unsuited behaviour for his regal state. As Maharani Kaushalya leapt to steady his head, she broke into a fresh wail of anguish. Sita rubbed her back. All this was so sudden, puzzling.

'I never knew she could be so heartless,' Kaushalya cried.

'What do you mean, Ma? Heartless? Who?' Ram's impatience was mounting.

'Kaikeyi! Who else!' barked the queen, 'She has asked you to be banished to the forests. Not just that...but for Bharat to be crowned king.'

Colour drained from Ram's face, quick as water out of sand. He grabbed the bed post tighter. If only this was a nightmare. Outside, the sky rumbled with threat, the dark clouds cracking, splitting the sky with light. Everything confirming the moment's reality.

'After all these years she is claiming the boons your father had supposedly promised. And look at what the wench has chosen.' The hurt had turned Kaushalya coarse.

'Fourteen years...my Ram...' the king slurred. Kaushalya bent down to wipe his dribbles.

'He is talking about the duration for your banishment. It's fourteen years. Fourteen...years.' Kaushalya continued between sobs, 'And your father, adamant as ever for the sanctimony of his words, relented. Why?' She looked around for empathy, 'Why the pointless nobility?' Time heaved forward cruelly. The first drops speared on the windowsill and with the gust, fine sprays got in. Sita drew the curtains, but they still bellowed in the wind, and returned to Kaushalya. She could understand her mother-in-law's rage, her sorrow. *Kaikeyi might have seemed inclement, but was Dasharath any less? If she had held on to her stubborn will, the king had equally clung to his own pious image—the one who would uphold his promise at all costs. It felt more like he couldn't risk being maligned, despite the heavy price. Was he soothing his own ego then—his righteous ego?* There was so much Sita could have said but knew this wasn't her place.

'Father did the right thing.' Ram finally spoke, 'A promise is a promise after all. It has always been the way of the Ikshvakus, and we cannot sullen it. Not least in the name of self-interest.' He looked his father in the eye.

Self-interest? Sita's eyes shot up. *It was one thing to be selfless but agreeing to chicanery risked overlooking the collective welfare of all. Who would benefit from keeping this twisted promise? Not the king. Not Ram. May be Kaikeyi. But definitely not Ayodhya.* She didn't agree with this new facet of Ram's personality.

'I will do as she wants. Besides, isn't Bharat equally your son, Ma?'

His voice wavered and it was all he could say. He then clutched Sita's hands, and they left, leaving his mother more distraught than before.

The corridor stretched endlessly. Ram was trying hard to feign indifference, but Sita saw how his hands glided onto the wall, how his legs crossed each other, how he stood for a while, unsure how to carry on. It was the closest she had seen of his vulnerable side, especially knowing what self-respect meant for him. Thankfully, the patter of rain provided a welcome distraction. It sucked in the soundless sobs. Sita wanted to stop him, hold him, wipe the pearls of rain off his face and hair and tell him that she understood—the situation was cruel and unfair, and that she understood. But she did none of that. Instead, she squeezed Ram's hands and walked together in hurting silence.

Time carried forth. It limped, but carried forth. Ram announced the annulment of the coronation on behalf of Dasharath. Afterward, he spent the day with Sita distributing their belongings to the brahmans and returned to the court to attend to the usual affairs. By nightfall, when he finally returned to his chambers, he found Sita standing on the terrace, her hands resting over the parapet. The storm had calmed, and the weather turned surprisingly peaceful. A gloriously round and profuse moon outflowed with silent light, and splashed it on the terrace, over Sita's silver saree, and trickled down the dense raatrani creeper by the bedchamber. The wet leaves gleamed, amidst the dotting of fuzzy white flowers. A breeze stirred from somewhere, carrying the smell to Ram. He walked to his wife, her face as beautiful as the moon, admiring the one in the sky.

'Ram! When did you come? And how is father now?'

'Still the same. In deep remorse, conflicted between oath and emotions. Doesn't want me to leave, but I know either option will crush him. I would much rather he keeps his promise.'

'Hmm. And you? Are you okay?'

'Oh yes.'

Sita knew her husband was good at soaking everything, especially the predicaments. His tranquillity an uncomfortable contradiction to the surge of emotions tossing within. He had trusted his youngest mother like his own and it was no small blow that she wanted him exiled.

'Mother Kaikeyi refuses to let Father bathe or eat anything until I leave. Best I depart at dawn.'

A wave of shock swept across Sita's face, both at Kaikeyi's cruelty and Ram's hurried decision.

'Whenever you say,' she said, matching along to his unaffected composure.

'No, not again! The decree is mine alone. You must stay—for Mother's peace.'

'And what of mine? My wishes? My happiness?'

'I understand—Yet, I forbid you.'

'You cannot.'

Her sharpness stunned him, but only briefly. Soon, his face loosened with a bemused smile. Sita's expressions, however, remained taut and beguilingly beautiful.

Before she could speak again, Ram interrupted her, 'Try to understand. Mother is beside herself. It pains me to see her this way. Were it not for my duty towards Father—'

'And what of your duty towards your mother?' she asked, in a low but resolute voice.

'It's not like I don't know. My heart weeps equally. But the past revers sons who bore bigger burden when heeding their father's behest; Kandu Rishi killed the sacred cow, Parshuram his own mother, Sagara's son dug up the earth, all to follow their father's command. I am simply following the path already set—better I bear the sin, than Father. Besides, so much has changed in a single night—can that be mere chance? I was to be king, Sita, yet all has fallen away in a night. Surely, it is destiny's call, and I must honour it.'

Sita met his gaze.

'Talking of destiny, mine is no different,' she said. 'A great brahman, and another mendicant had predicted to my parents that I would be living in forests. Never believed it then.'

'But Sita, the forest is full of dangers. How will you live—'

'Exactly, how will I live—without you?'

'I am not alone. Laxman will be accompanying me.'

What! A flash of anger coloured Sita's face. It wasn't jealousy against Laxman, only concern for her younger sister. Would Urmila be separated from her husband? All in the prime of her youth?

'Well, I tried to dissuade him...but you know how stubborn he can be.'

Sita held her gaze, unthinking and unwavering.

'I see that you will not listen?' he asked, lifting his eyebrows.

'No, I will not.' she reciprocated with similar such lifting.

Parting from her wasn't easy for him either. He sighed and took hold of her hands.

'Look at them, so delicate.'

'They will toughen up.'

'My dear, the decree is not binding to you. I am going because I have a duty to fulfil.'

'Then don't stop me from fulfilling mine.'

'Forest life isn't easy. It's a world of danger.'

'And opportunities.'

'Oh! There would only be frightening challenges.'

'Which would offer the best learnings. Ram, you will see, how they will prepare you towards becoming the best ruler the world would ever have.'

'My love, how innocent you are! Does it not strike you, why Mother Kaikeyi has asked for fourteen years? I will be forgotten by the time I return. Irony is, I would have never asked it back anyway.' His voice shook a little as he tried to drive out the swarming syllables. 'She could have just asked me to step away. Did she not trust me even that much?'

Sita squeezed his hands, 'For me, it honestly doesn't matter whether you get to rule Ayodhya or not. I wasn't even alluding to that. All I know is that you will rule for undefined period and undefined territories. You will rule the hearts of people. Don't you see how the subjects are already showering support for you?'

Ram drew her closer, and she rested her head over his shoulder. He did not feel like talking anymore. A soft smile lapped about her face. It was remarkable how she could pull him out of any misery. Her hands were stretched out, saying something about the Rohini star always following the moon. But he was scarcely listening, only happy for her beautiful voice, full of life, full of vigour. Despite what he said, he was secretly happy that she was coming.

Outside, the water fountain sparkled with light. A soft fuzzy glitter rose off its base and was instantly swallowed by the hungry night. After all, what was the moon without its wondrous light. Similarly, what was he without his wonderful wife.

Ram rested his head atop hers and they peered ahead, two separate sets of dreamy eyes, wrapped in the same intoxicating dream of the future. The raatrani bush stirred once again, filling the air with its sweet smell.

Part Two

6

Voice of Honey

Fuelled with unbridled excitement, the stride and the pace of the boys on the first day of the journey was remarkable. Their enthusiasm more or less sustained over the next two days before it started to wane. They had walked for eight days, covering over a hundred miles across dense forests and interspersed settlements. Despite their vigorous walking, Ayodhya kept slipping away. Their limbs turned weary, clothes dusty, voices faint and eyes red. But never once did the young ones complain.

'Look! The city walls! Do you see it?' Guru Valmiki said.

'City walls? Where?' Luv craned his neck. It was quite hazy.

'I can just about see something faint...oh, look, there it is!' squealed Kush.

They bounded forth, fatigue magically forgotten. The faint apparition of the city walls turned steadily distinct, like someone had wiped the air clean. They rose tall, in height and manner, and in caution against silenced enemies. Luv and Kush stood holding each other's hands, their mouths agape, eyes darting bemusedly from each other to the ramparts. They could no longer wait to enter this oasis of peace and prosperity.

From the watchtowers, a reverberating sound of *dundhubi*, the exceptionally large drums, announced the start of the second prahar. The morning sun splintered through from behind.

'It is like a dream!' wondered Kush, his little chest heaving.

'It is better! Much better!' whispered Luv.

'Thank you Guruji. Thank you ever so much for bringing us. Shall we go in?' asked Kush.

'Wait! Who will offer obeisance to the sun lord? You are forgetting everything!' smiled Guru Valmiki.

The boys did as told. Saryu's water was cold and the surface glossed with the touch of the golden sun. After making their offerings to the holy deity—the giver of life—they prayed in gratitude and submission. They then drank from the river, and true to their Guru's descriptions, found the water sweet as sugarcane.

The crisp and chilly air made the children shiver as they walked out of the water. After putting on fresh clothes and bolting down whatever food they had begged the day before—two rotis and a chunk of jaggery—they patiently waited for their Guru's approval. Slender-necked white birds scraped over the water, carving temporary indentations, before flying across the city walls.

'Guruji, now? Please, can we go in?' asked Kush.

'Just look at you! Alright, go. But after you are done exploring, come right here. You will find me resting by this tree.'

'Wait, aren't you coming? Are you suggesting we go all by ourselves?' asked Luv.

'Wouldn't you at least like to see Ayodhya?' Kush was equally incredulous.

'My old body demands rest. Besides, one doesn't need only a set of apparent eyes to see everything,' he said with a twinkle.

'You can tell me later if Ayodhya was any different from my descriptions.'

The boys smiled, they knew that Guru Valmiki was bestowed with the gift of clairvoyance, the ability to see things beyond reach. In fact, this was how he had written the Ramayana.

'Besides, you are big boys now. Come on—off you go! And let me rest in peace.'

The boys broke into pearls of giggles. Then Luv asked, 'Do you think we might get to see Maharaja Ram?'

'Why not! If you wish it deep enough, you will.'

'We do! We most certainly do!' they replied, eyes clenched with a hundred hopeful wrinkles. And away they tottered, crossing the long moat with ornate carvings, transitioning at last from anticipation to reality.

The scene that unfolded staggered them. Wide boulevards stretched straight to the horizon. Lining either side were flowering trees, some red as flames, some white as the calming moon, some with the sprinklings of yellow, orange or purple, and some plain green. They were all full of sweet shade, where birds picked on ripe fruits and sang melodiously.

The grandiosity of the houses was unlike anything the brothers had seen before. Huge storeys clambered atop each other. Stuccoed walls with intricate patterns made of rubies, emeralds, topazes and aquamarines, glinted more ferociously than the stars in the sky. In between some of the houses were large flower gardens.

Luv and Kush ambled stupefied. Just like the ordered streets, these houses too had well-laid front yards, where robust horses were tethered. Women sat with heaped plates of powdered colours and decorated their yards with beautiful patterns, much akin to their mother's simple rice paste alpana.

'I miss Ma. Wish she was here,' Luv sighed.

'I know. Let's soak it all in so we can tell her later,' said Kush.

A faint hustle and bustle could be heard from the other end. Luv and Kush followed the sound, and sure enough, a market was waking up to copper being beaten into vessels, the chatter of friendly shopkeepers decorating and readying their shops and the squeaking loom of weavers who transformed spools of coloured threads into exquisite clothes. A potter sat across, skilfully balancing his creation on the wheel, and as the wheel swivelled, the pot grew with a wondrously odd shape.

The place was busy. While sellers called, enticed, and coaxed, buyers haggled, bargained and bickered. A bunch of women stood in one corner pinning garlands in their hair or slipping shiny gold bangles down their wrists, as praising shopkeepers tried to influence their fickle minds. They finally gave in, offering him grains in return, and the shopkeeper thanked them, gleeful for the first exchange of the day. Some vendors yelled louder than their neighbours, trying to cajole their own first customers, beckoning them with cries of 'have a look at the best silk', 'don't miss the best mangoes of the season', 'no exchange for trying this fennel', and so on.

The boys wound their way through the busy market, gawking at and admiring things they had never seen before—wonderful jewels, rugs, lamps. A cool draft of wind pushed them from behind and made its way down the alley. It fluttered displays on awnings—clothes and glinting metal, and lifted off rich aroma of cardamom, cloves, and cinnamon from big piled up heaps.

'Just look at their turbans. Some are even beaded in gold and pearls,' remarked Kush.

'The Ayodhyans must like to groom themselves. They seem so prosperous. Did you see the jewelleries on the ladies? Ma will be astonished; she must have never seen anything of this kind,' said Luv.

The sound of *mridangams*, cymbals and veenas came through, and reminded them of the mention of *gaayanshala* in Guruji's description. But before they could head in that direction, they were stopped short at the artistry of a stout man with a bushy moustache, who shuffled flavoured milk from one tall glass to the other, a hint of saffron and cardamom perceptible. It was only then that they realized how much time had passed since they had been wandering about.

'Are you feeling hungry too?' asked Luv.

'More like starving!' said Kush.

'Shall we do something about it then?' Luv asked, raising his eyebrows, the manner fictitiously grown-up.

'About time!' beamed Kush.

They settled down on a podium by a large banyan tree and swivelled forth their veena. The long-necked, pear-shaped lute was smaller than usual and suited to their age.

Their little fingers plucked the copper strings, and an inviting melody swarmed through. People started to gather, and the market fell rapidly quiet, to hear not just the singing, but equally the song.

They began with recounting tales of the illustrious Ikshvaku dynasty, its descendant Maharaja Dasharath, who was comparable in valour to the famed King Indra in heaven, and his Ayodhya more splendorous than that of Indra's Amravati. The kingdom had known nothing of sickness, poverty or misery, which wasn't simply a fortuitous blessing, but more the result of the king's remarkable ruling.

They sang of Dasharath's painful yearning for an heir, at which point, a collective sigh rose. But the mood turned again as they sang of the great yajna and the blessing in abundance of not only one, but four sons. The whole of Ayodhya was drawn in to that banyan tree. Ladies, shopkeepers, little children, old men; all came forth with offers of food, grains, clothes or a piece of whatever little they had. Everything stood still, except the sun, which carried on rising, urging the stupefied to get on with their day.

A lot of time, probably a prahar, passed before the enchantment was finally broken by the metallic tapping of spears.

'Greetings children,' said a royal attendant, 'Our king has requested your attendance. He would like you to sing for him.'

They looked up, stunned. It was as if the ground had fallen off from under their feet.

'Maharaja Ram...do you mean he has called for us?' asked Luv.

'Yes please! Please take us to him!' pleaded Kush.

They threw their arms about and jumped with elation, gathered all their gifts, thanked the people, and rushed to meet the very man for whom they had undertaken the arduous journey.

The attendant walked rather fast, unaware of the knots in the boys' stomachs, caused by both hunger and nervousness. Whichever direction they looked they saw glinting lanterns and grand furnishings. They gaped at the high ceiling and the numerous columns that held it up. The walls with intricate carvings of flowers, dancers, chariots and wars glowed with light reflecting off fire lanterns. The floor was cold and slippery smooth wherever it wasn't covered by thick embroidered carpets.

It was a world beyond imagination. As they crossed over rooms, smartly dressed attendants announced their arrival, the whole act making them feel distinguished. Finally, they were ushered into Maharaja Ram's court.

He was seated on a golden throne, clad in a yellow dhoti with pink *angavastram*, hands resting on his knees, a soft smile on his face. Beautiful necklaces, earrings and thick bracelets adorned him. They knew that his eyes were shaped like lotus petals, and so were his lips; that his arms were exceptionally long and his persona resplendent like the sun. Yet, all their million imagined fabrications failed against the beauty they stood witnessing.

'Salutations, Maharaja. Please accept our warmest and sincerest greetings.' Both fell to their knees.

'Welcome, children. I am told your singing is divine—so much that you have held my entire kingdom in your rapture since morning. I hear that the traders haven't yet left the city, the shopkeepers hardly sold anything, and that the fields are still waiting to be threshed.' Ram made a mock expression of solemnity, yet his voice dripped with affection as he regarded the ten-year olds.

'So, is it true then? Are you guilty of keeping them off duty?'

'Apologies Maharaja,' replied Luv, 'We were hungry, and being *gurubalaks*, it is only through the favour of *bhiksha*, that we can feed ourselves. Our Guruji insists we offer something in return so as not to accrue worldly favours. And we possess nothing more than our voices and veenas.'

'That is right, Maharaja. We were simply doing our duty. We humbly beg your pardon if your denizens forgot to perform theirs,' said Kush.

'I see! Not only are you talented but also quick-witted. So, what is it that you sing about? I am told it's about Ayodhya?'

'About you, Maharaja. And your impeccable qualities.' Luv said, hands joined in devotion.

'Yes, Maharaja. We hope to enlighten people of what they must do in order to move towards perfection, a state akin only to you. We sing the Ramayana, composed by our Guru.' said Kush.

'And who is your Guru?' asked Ram.

'Sage Valmiki.' They cried out in unison, their small chests puffed, pearly teeth peeking from behind their rosy lips.

'Sage Valmiki! The revered saint! You are indeed very lucky. What else has he taught you?'

'Oh, he has taught us the shastras, the vedas. He has given us lessons on economics, warfare, administration. But most importantly, he has taught us to love you. Aspire to become like you,' said Luv.

Ram smiled solicitously. *These boys, so confident in a foreign court, so assured in the way they talk. If his own child was with him today, he probably would have been nearly as old.* Their unabashed praises made him think of Sita. How she had once professed he was meant to rule not just the limits of a kingdom, but the undefined boundaries of people's hearts.

'Would you oblige me with your singing then?' Ram asked.

'It would be our utmost honour, Maharaja,' they curtsied and began, but only after holding their idol in gaze. Their fingers plucked the veena, and once again, sweet melody started to surge and swarm. The court plunged under a hypnotic spell as the boys nodded and swayed their heads, acknowledging each other as they hit the right notes. And under such spellbinding synchronization, they started to sing, their pitch rising, falling, pausing, cruising, cascading. Ram closed his eyes, ready to be carried back to kinder times.

Luv and Kush sang of the great king Dasharath and his undying love for Ram. They sang of Ram's prowess at archery, at vedas, his love for nature and acuity at shastras. Of his unparalleled valour, strength, wisdom and persona. Of his wedding to Sita. At that, a soft smile swept across Ram's face, as he thought of the Pinaka, and the demure Sita with the wedding garland in hands. He saw the shy quiver of her nose ring and the string of scented raatrani wrapped over her lusturous bun.

Verse by verse, his life was unraveled by the little magicians, whose chest swelled up and down to deliver him that past. They sang of Ram's exile with Sita at Panchvati and Dandakaranaya, where they spent many invaluable years together. It felt wonderful to return to Sita, even if vicariously. Nothing was more valuable than her kind face, her comforting smiles, her encouraging praises.

Soon, the verses turned painful. He saw her far away, calling out for him. He saw the flames, thrashing, lapping, and with a shudder, his eyes opened.

But the boys were singing of no such flame. In fact, they were singing no longer of Sita. Only of Ayodhya under his glorious rule. They were singing of *Ram Rajya*, the fairest of all kingdoms, and how happy the people were under his rule. Finally, the song reached its end, to the emphatic lauding by the court. But something had soured in Ram's mouth.

'Your singing was most beautiful!' He finally said, 'And your praise equally generous! Please offer my deepest regards to your Guru for helping me relive lost time. And your command over the veena was effortless!'

'Thank you, Maharaja. Our mother taught us the veena,' beamed Luv.

'Yes, there is no one who can play quite like her,' added Kush.

'In that case, you are indeed lucky to have such a talented mother. Please thank her too.'

Ram peeled two necklaces off his chest and gestured for the boys to come close. 'Thank you for coming. May you prosper to great heights. Here is a little token of gratitude.' He placed a necklace each around their little necks.

An unexplainable surge of deep love inundated Ram, as he marvelled at their round cheeks, the loose tufts of hair over their shoulders and their eyes shining with pride. He wanted to reach out and enfold them in his arms but the weight of the crown and the decorum at court stopped him. He simply smiled as they bowed down and retreated.

As destiny would have it, it was in this strange way they connected, as mere formality and in complete oblivion. Maharaja Ram with Luv and Kush. A father with his two sons.

7

The Tinkering Bells

When Luv and Kush flitted out, they were surprised to hear the dundhubi sound four times, wrapping down the last prahar of the day. The sun might have dimmed by now, but not their excitement. Ayodhya was splendorous, and it's allure irresistible. There was so much left to see. When would they ever get another chance to visit? But conscience nudged them otherwise.

Torn between the sense of responsibility and burgeoning curiosity, Kush asked, 'Do you think we could wander just a little longer? Would that upset Guruji?'

'Not sure. We did promise to be back before evening. Although I really wanted to see the *akhaada*, the gaayanshala, and the *kalakendra*.' sighed Luv.

'And the *ghats* by the Saryu. We have hardly seen anything!' said Kush.

'We saw Maharaja Ram!'

'So we did!' A smile lit up Kush's face.

Luv gathered his brother's hand and said, 'Let's head back, shall we? It's quite a walk to the city gates.'

With heavy footsteps, and still heavier hearts, the responsible young boys retreated. Hardly had they walked a little distance when they stumbled upon an open field. Built at its centre was a huge marquee, with various attendants milling about. A few ministers inspected the work, while talking of some kind of sacrificial offering. Some attendants carried humungous vessels, presumably to cook the feast. Others carried heavy sacks of grains that they stowed to a corner. There were priests smearing a sacrificial pit with coloured pastes—white from rice, yellow from turmeric and red from vermillion.

Tethered to one corner was a magnificent horse, spotless white, with rich mane that fell across its face. Adorning its back was a red cushioned saddle, with silk tassels, brocade embroidery, and gold beaded strings. A priest venerated it with vermillion tilak on his forehead. As if cognizant of its aristocratic charm, the horse stood tall and robust, swishing its neatly trimmed tail. With equal grace, it flicked its slender limbs by the knees and landed it down, making its anklets go *chan, chan, chan*.

'A horse wearing golden anklets? Incredible…' A low hum escaped Luv's mouth.

The boys came closer and squatted by the horse. Aware of its young admirers the horse started to prance about and the ringing notched higher.

'You are right,' replied Kush, 'up until now, I had only ever known of ladies wearing anklets. It is true—anything is possible in Ayodhya.'

The sculptor sitting nearby smiled at their gullibility and said, 'Oh, this is no ordinary horse. It is the *Ashwamedh* horse—which is why it is worshipped and adorned regally.'

The horse swivelled towards the boys, agreeing about its privileged status.

'The *Ashwamedh* horse? Now what is that?' they asked in unison.

'Really? Haven't you heard of the horse sacrifice ritual? Well, it is an old ritual where an eminent king lets loose the horse to travel in any direction of its choosing. And any kingdoms it crosses en route must submit to the emperor's allegiance.'

'Submit allegiance? What! On the whim of a horse which happens to cross their lands? That's bewildering!' said Kush.

'Well, if they don't, they would have to challenge Ayodhya. And no ruler of any sound mind would want that. But you see, the aim is not driven by conflict, only to foster law, order, and friendship across regions. The acceding kingdoms still gets to retain their autonomy, along with a share from the collective wealth of Ayodhya.'

'Does the yajna begin today?' asked Luv.

'Oh no, not today—thankfully. There is still a bit of work left on our queen's statue.' Saying this, he proceeded to chisel the toes. Luv and Kush peered curiously but everything apart from the toes was draped in red cloth.

'Is that a statue of Maharani Sita?' asked Kush.

'Who else! One queen is all we've ever had. Maharaja Ram is so unlike other rulers,' nodded the sculptor with a thoughtful expression.

'Please may we see?' pleaded Luv.

'Oh no! It's inauspicious to unveil the statue before the yajna! This cloth will only come off when we place her beside our king.'

'But why would you place her statue! Wouldn't the Maharani like to participate in the yajna?' asked Luv.

'Is she not allowed to come in public?' Kush interjected, a little too soon.

'Does Maharaja Ram refrain her from doing so?' Luv followed soon after.

'Stop! Don't you know our Maharaja is the most supportive of all kings. He respects women a lot.'

'Then why her statue?' asked Kush.

'Come on boys, enough questions.' The sculptor appeared flustered, 'It has been a pleasure meeting you, but really, I have a lot to finish before sundown. Now if you will please excuse me!'

'You're pushing us away', Kush protested.

'We only asked because it sounds strange.' said Luv, his mouth puckered up.

'I am sorry children. It just brought back difficult memories. To tell you the truth, our beloved queen doesn't live here anymore.'

'What! Why?' asked Luv.

'Did something happen between her and the king?' asked Kush.

'There you go again! Our queen loved our king deeply. And before you ask again, so does our king. In fact, he has never loved any other, never remarried. This important yajna couldn't be complete without the participation of a spouse, which is why placing her golden statue seemed like the next best recourse.'

'So, if—' Kush was still unsatiated.

'No! No more questions now. It is quite late. Shouldn't you both be heading home? Your mother must be waiting.' Saying this he picked up his tool and started chiseling.

'Not our mother so much, but definitely our Guruji,' Luv mumbled. 'Come one Kush, we must hurry.'

And the boys tottered off. The streets had quietened down,

the awnings of the market rolled back, their displays stowed away, and by now all houses were aglow with lamps.

The streets looked different and confusing, but they somehow managed to reach the city gates. Early darkness had already settled over the fog, and only a faint silhouette of Sage Valmiki was visible. He rushed towards them, and in haste, forgot to put on the other *khadau*. Turned out he didn't quite believe they were that big after all.

The boys recounted everything, squealing that they had the opportunity to not only meet, but sing for Maharaja Ram. Contended and happy, they walked back, hoping the excitement and memories wouldn't fizzle by the time they reached their mother.

They couldn't wait to tell her how kind Maharaja Ram was, how charming. They would tell her that he agreed—that too in front of the whole court—that there was no one quite like her. But what they wouldn't tell her was that he was only talking of her skill at playing veena. As they looked at each other, hands clutching the gifted necklace, which mysteriously carried a deep scent of lotus, they smiled. They pictured the puzzled expression on their mother's face at this inaccurately presented fact. *It would be fun.*

8

Lurking Shadows

Back in the palace, the hours that had stalled now rushed to be reclaimed, leaving much to resolve after the boys' departure. Cases dragged on for a while, accounts were sorted until at last the court was adjourned and the weary returned to the warmth of their families. Ram, however, was an exception. He had only remorse and loneliness waiting in his bedchamber. As he passed through the warmly lit corridors of the palace, he heard his brothers' children in their courtyards, the ringing of bells for the evening *aarti*, the smell of camphor, the chanting of hymns in a ritual to bind the family together in the evenings. And it was difficult not to think of a life—with his wife and child, possibly even children over time.

After Sita's departure, the courtroom had turned into his safe haven. He listened to the court with seasoned maturity but recognised what a fallacious judgement he had borne against his own wife.

Ram reached his bedchamber and bid away the waiting attendants. The room was hollow despite rich furnishings. They were useless anyway, for he always spread out a reed mat over the cold floor. After all, this is how Sita—wherever she was—

must be sleeping. The sky outside his window lay blotched with grey clouds. His words to Laxman hovered in the air and gradually took a life of their own. *'Take Sita away. The rule is the same for everyone.'*

Deep down, Ram knew that Sita was as pure as morning dew. It was his own judgement that was clouded with personal attachment. *Was he harsher than required? Did he overbid under the worry of appearing unfair? But if he let Sita stay, would that have been fair either?*

The cruel night carried on with sporadic bouts of ephemeral longing. Ram's own decree punished him in the worst possible way. In banishing her, he had inflicted the pain of separation not only on her, but equally on himself. And Sita, who was once his strength, turned into his biggest weakness.

Like every night, he tried in vain to return to her, desperately sketching her delicate face from memory, but the impressions faded away like markings in the sand. He only saw her with an obscure smile, and shuddered to find that it was bruised. He thought of the many bangles on her wrist, but their clinking was distant. He imagined the flowers in her hair, but the smell was faint. The more vividly he sketched her, the more quickly she dissipated. Miserable was his state—remorseful when he saw her, and distraught when he didn't, and he wondered which was better.

That was the state of the reigning king of Ayodhya, with only mocking regret lurking in his bedchamber. It never quietened, musingly passing the room with the flutter of a curtain, or the wavering light of the night lamp. Outside, the night birds twittered in deep lamentation. It quietened the wounded silence, but only until the raatrani on his terrace stirred, and brought back pain and longing.

The moon slunk lower in the horizon with a cold light. The night darkened, the shadows lengthened, and leapt into his room for their own turn of mischief. Sita might have left forever, but these shadows visited him every night. With persistence. With loyalty. With reproach.

Part Three

9

Pink Lotuses

Sita returned to her cottage after teaching the ladies in the ashram. She had been doing this for many years now; teaching them how to weave mats, collect honey, make earthenware and read vedas. The women listened, with utmost attention, for they were awed that she had once resided in the prosperous kingdom of Ayodhya. If only they knew she had in fact ruled the place. Her identity may have shifted—from Sita to Vandevi—but not her proclivity. For her, life mattered more than the limited bounds of personal concerns.

A gentle breeze coursed through. It was no longer chilly, and carried a subtle scent of change. Winter was finally losing grip. Under the shining warmth of the sun, long-knotted braids of moss on the pathways had started shrinking. *Malti, nirgundi, aparajita* and other winter flowers burst forth with departing glory. Bobbing over their heads were bright red flowers of *eranda*.

Sita's eyes fell on a mother sparrow by her steps. It preened its young ones' feathers, and they, in due obedience, tucked and twitched their heads from side to side. The sight brought a wistful smile to Sita's face as she creaked open the bamboo door of her lonely cottage.

A ray of uninvited afternoon light leapt in. As if familiar with the surroundings, it raced to the edge of the opposite wall. There it stopped, climbed up the alcove, and rested snugly, lighting up the pebbles, shells, seeds of wood apple and other such artefacts gathered by her sons. Sita reached for the necklace of rounded pebbles and turned over its cool beads. It was something her children had gifted her.

'Missing the boys, are you?'

Sita turned around, surprised.

'Sorry, didn't mean to startle you.' Guruma stood at the door. She was a lady with a big bosom, rounded arms and a voice steeped in warmth. Her hair, with a generous sprinkling of silver, was always tied high in a thick bun. Guruma had looked after Sita like a mother when she first arrived, and it was she who had guided Sita's first steps into motherhood.

'They should be back by tomorrow. If not in the morning, then surely by sunset.'

'Ah! I was only looking at this necklace,' Sita said, her face flushed with embarrassment. 'See how perfectly round they have ground the stones. Children! And their little gestures of love!'

'It is beautiful,' remarked Guruma.

'I have never been without them. Not this long.' There was an unmistakable quiver to Sita's voice.

The old lady held Sita's hands in hers and patted them. 'I tell you what. Let's gather tonight for a *ratjaga*. We ladies are forever occupied with life, chores, husbands, children. Never a restful moment for ourselves. Why don't I prepare a nice meal and we can all eat together and talk ours hearts out? Sounds alright?'

'Are you serious?' squealed the eight-year-old Vasuki, who had crept up from nowhere.

'Vasuki! When did you come?' Guruma's eyes flashed open.

'I saw you walking over to Vandevi's cottage and thought I must check in on her too. Now, Vandevi,' she said, shaking Sita's hands, 'Say yes quickly or Guruma will change her mind. You know how she can be.'

'But Vasuki, did I ever say you were invited?' reproached Guruma. 'This night is only for ladies.'

'How rude!' The little girl stomped her foot and puckered her lips. 'I'll tell you what; the gathering won't be half as much fun without us.'

Her stubborn pretense faded away when she saw Guruma unrelenting, 'No one bothers whether we children need some change too. Please now, Guruma! I will only ask Sumriti, Damyanti, Kalyani...and Brinali...and Sunehria...and—mmm, if you don't want so many, we can leave the boys out. Okay?'

Both ladies burst out laughing, and Sita drew Vasuki close. 'Alright, Guruma. I am sure this will be a nice change. Let me know if you need any help.'

'None at all. Just show up. But you Vasuki, come with me now. Let us check whether or not the ritual woods have been chopped for the evening prayers. See you later Vandevi!'

Guruma and Vasuki left, once again leaving Sita with her necklace of round pebbles. She returned it to the sill. By now, the sunlight had crept sideways to the thick bundle wrapped in red cloth. It was the stack of bark leaves beholding her buried truth.

Up until now, she had only heard fleeting snippets from her boys, that too from afar. Intentionally, she had willed her ears to obscure any sounds. Now, with unsure hands, she reached for it. The cloth slipped away and the Ramayana in Guru Valmiki's graceful handwriting shone in black ink. Sita's heart thudded in the emptiness. Her fingertips tingled. She eyed the scratchy bundle for a while and then leafed through the pages.

vaidehi ramase kaccic citra kūṭe mayā saha |
paśyantī vividhān bhāvān mano vāk kāya samyatān ||
darśanam citra kūṭasya mandākinyāḥ ca śobhane |
adhikam pura vāsāc ca manye ca tava darśanāt ||

They sucked the life out of Sita. Those were indeed Ram's words, something he had said to her in Chitrakoot. The echo of his voice from more than two decades ago rung with unsettling clarity. At that time, their exile was in its early days—barely two months since they had left Ayodhya.

Ram was wonderstruck by the beauty of River Madakini. Since they had left Ayodhya, they had seen quite many rivers—Tamsa, Gomati, Syandika, Ganga and Yamuna—but none amongst them quite as beautiful as what lay in front.

Profusely bejeweled with dark pink lotuses resting atop wide leaves, Mandakini's water flowed placidly. The morning was memorably cool. Having arrived in Chitrakoot only the evening before, Ram and Sita stepped out for a bath. For miles, no life was visible or any sounds heard. Some sleeping deer and the sporadic hoot of cuckoos were the only exceptions.

Sita dipped her toes, but the water was shockingly cold.

'I am not going in.' Sita drew back.

'It will not be so bad once you step in. Come, take my hand.'

'I am certainly not coming.'

'Look! That white bird soaring above!'

It was only a ruse, a playful ploy to splash her over.

'Ah!' A gasp escaped Sita's lips. 'You will not be spared, not after this!'

Losing her inhibition, she stepped in. Before he could wet her further, she started splashing water on his face, his hair, his eyes...all the while, her laughter rippling like that of a mischievous child, pausing, then springing again. Ram threw his arms in the air, 'Wait Sita, stop!'

'Oh, is it! No, not until you show me that white bird!'

Her defiance only made Ram laugh harder, proving that he was not taking her seriously. Sita splashed harder.

Ram covered his eyes with one arm and glided across. Before she could react, he pulled her by the waist and drew her close. For a while the splashing and giggling continued. Then Ram pressed her closer and everything fell silent. Not a sound apart from a few odd plops. A moment of complete silence, with just the river drinking its own water back. Ever so slightly, Sita twisted in an attempt to break free, but his grip was firm.

She saw him dip his hands inside, and the river burbled. Her doe eyes regarded the ripples yieldingly. Slowly, he cusped his palms and dripped the water over her head. It trickled down her face, her chin, her shoulders, her warm bosom. She stood still, letting herself get wet, letting him regard the honey-like sparkle of cascading water. She lay wrapped against his heaving chest, as he swept back the strand of hair from her face. A white swan swam close, almost too close. Then went away to nibble on lotus petals.

'The white bird,' he whispered and she smiled weakly.

Then he took her by the hands and led her deeper until they were completely immersed. Water swirled around her saree and his dhoti as they paddled to stay afloat. He took hold of her bare shoulders and glided closer, until only her face was visible amidst the dark pink lotuses, her lips more succulent than any of them. For a moment time stood still, then Sita giggled. It was a nervous giggle—more of an effort to break his trance. Finally, Ram sighed and loosened his hold. Together, they swam to the shore and sat down on its soft bank, their clothes sticking to their limbs.

It was then that he had said those words. His face was beautiful and chiselled, and his eyes marvelled at the surrounding emerald green mountains and the lotus-filled Mandakini. A soft breeze stirred the grass. He had asked her if she too found everything equally pretty and if she too was as happy. She smiled, dipped her toes back into the water, and splashed it all the way to the lotuses. The drops fell with the sound of ringing anklets. Then she replied with a soft mumble—so he had to come close—that she had never been happier. Such was the magical beauty of the place, which healed them of all the hurt they carried from Ayodhya.

Or so they thought.

Later that evening, they sat under the stars outside their cottage. Ram and Laxman had roasted an antelope over an open pit. The venison, having rested a while, was sufficiently cool for Sita to slice into pieces. Thick juices ran down her dainty fingers, sending a repelling shiver down her spine, but to survive, they had to make do with whatever was on offer. Judging there was enough for the evening, Sita decided to put some away for the next day. As she got up, a sudden chaos caught her attention. A flock of birds took off in a sudden flight. Next followed the trumpet of elephants, and the sound of thrashing amongst the bushes.

'Who could that be?' Sita spun to Ram, alarmed.

'Sounds like a large group. I doubt they are hermits.'

'Here, let me check!' Laxman, always alert, climbed over the nearest sal tree. 'Looks like an army of sorts. The light is too dim to tell whose that might be. Quick! Put out the fire.'

Before Laxman had time to climb down, the army was already outside their grassy clearing. Thankfully, they had nothing to worry about. Bharat had come to meet them. He had brought along an entourage of around twenty soldiers bearing the Ikshvaku standard.

The blaze from the fire fell over Bharat's face and illumined his straining tears. His clothes were dusty from the long journey, and surprisingly he wasn't adorned in regal clothes. Instead, was wearing a rough bark dhoti, much like Ram and Laxman.

'Bharat! How...how come you are here? And how did you locate us?' Ram rushed to embrace him.

Instead, Bharat fell to his knees, ashamed of enveloping Ram in his hands, of even touching him. 'I...I want nothing with the throne, nothing with Ayodhya...nothing with my mother. Hope you know this.'

Ram lifted him off the ground, but Bharat was beside himself, the sobs and hiccups kept swallowing his words. He flung himself into Ram's embrace, wetting his shoulders completely with his tears.

'Please don't say that Bharat. Aren't we all Father's sons? What difference does it make who rules Ayodhya?'

'It does. It certainly does. Ayodhya needs your guidance, especially now...especially now that Father has passed away.'

Bharat had spoken so casually that it took a moment for Ram to comprehend what he meant. Ram still had the placating smile on his face when he peeled Bharat off and locked him in the eye.

'Father…he passed away,' Bharat sighed. This time his voice was smaller even than that of the popping wood by the firepit. 'He left lamenting for you, cursing mother, cursing himself… this cruel play of fate. I wasn't present either, but I hear he was in a deplorable state. With Shatrughan also away, his body was placed in an oil jar until I returned and performed the last… his last—'

Ram collapsed. Like a tree hacked with sudden impact, he flopped down right where he was standing.

'Ram!' Sita rushed forward to hold him up but he was too heavy for her. She too went down.

'Quick! Laxman! Get some water,' she shouted, propping Ram's head on her lap. With a few sprinkles, Ram was back, but his face was ashen. He looked around at everyone, and then at Sita who was rubbing his palms. He pulled away and propped himself up.

'Father stood for his duty,' he finally spoke. 'The price he paid in this life was heavy, but the rewards in afterlife will be sweeter. The least we can do is to follow his example. Stand by our duty, whatever the repercussion. Let us not sullen the great man's oath, not for the sake of a mere kingdom.'

'Don't say this brother,' Bharat howled, 'Please return with me. Don't burden me…not with any more sin. We need you more than ever. Brother, please! Do you not care for Ayodhya?'

'Of course I do, Bharat. Of course I do. But no, I won't return. Not for fourteen years, anyway. Then I will willingly take over the kingdom. For now, you must take care of Ayodhya. And don't come looking for us again.' Ram got up and lumbered inside, turning his back on all the wailing supplicants, summoning the restraint he needed for doing right by his father.

Next day, Sita walked up with Ram to the Mandakini to

perform the great king's last rituals. Cusping his hands into the river, Ram offered it to appease his father's soul. The water sparkled in the sunlight and fell in a sad stream. Sita sat by the banks, patiently waiting for him. It had been hours that he had been standing knee deep in the cold water, motionless, well after the sun had set. The colour of the lotuses, which were so bright only a day ago, seemed to have faded overnight.

In time, autumn came, and the emerald leaves on the trees faded too. They turned light green, then yellow, then russet and finally brown. Like every worldly thing must reach its end, they too were shed. Ram saw the branches, bare, knobbly and bereft of all that was once dear. Sita instead saw a new beauty, sunshine now uninhibitedly painting the once-hidden branches with a glorious gold. They were sitting out in the open. A mist fell from above, and with the sun still in sight, it splintered the sky into a faint band of seven colours.

'I wonder where the ends of the rainbow meet the ground,' Sita mused, sliding her arms into Ram's. In front, peacocks fanned and swayed their iridescent feathers, and she motioned their play to Ram. But he was far too occupied following the path of a soaring black hawk.

'Ram, I understand your pain. You can talk to me about it.'

Ram picked up the yellowed sal leaf and turned it over.

'Ram?'

'I can't help this restlessness.' He looked her in the eye, 'You are right, it hasn't been easy to learn of Father's passing. I know one can't escape destiny, but to know a ruler—one so powerful—went away pining for a simple wish. One last sight of his son…'

Sita had mindfully refrained from sharing any thoughts. But

the unspoken words were no good either. 'Pardon my saying,' she said, 'Father was a righteous man, but was tied down by his own rigid oath. Hope you understand that you are not required to do the same. You could still return to Ayodhya, the kingdom he spent his lifetime nurturing. In my honest opinion, nothing would be a better tribute than serving his kingdom, looking after his subjects.'

Once again, her forthrightness stumped Ram. He cleared his throat. 'You think it does not crush me? To send Bharat away…and all my subjects? Every night, I am haunted by their faces. I see their tears pooling into a lake, drowning me under. Their lamentations throb in my ears. The pain is ready to burst. It's not easy, but I ask myself, what good is a ruler who can't even suffer for the sake of what's right? What teachings will I impart? There is nothing greater than duty. Not father. Not me. Not you.'

Sita flinched. Thankfully, Ram was looking ahead. By now the peacocks too had stopped dancing and had moved away.

'Besides Bharat is equally capable. I am sure he will serve Ayodhya well.' Ram said.

'Then don't go back to Ayodhya.' She squeezed his hands, 'But at least be willing to look at this exile in a different light. Maybe it is not simply to spend time away from the kingdom. Fourteen years is a long time for doing just that. Maybe you are meant to serve a greater purpose here. You will only know if you start searching for it!'

Ram considered this for a while and then said, 'Do you think we should move from here?'

'If that is what feels right. As for me, I will happily follow you anywhere.'

'Would it be alright if I followed you instead, my love?'

And just like that, the twinkle was back in Ram's eyes. Sita smiled. It felt enough, enormously enough, after the gruelling gap of the past few days.

True to their conversation, Chitrakoot, though lovely, was not the place for them. Destiny wanted them to demand for more, and once they did, it thrust them forward with its own two hands.

Ram and Sita returned to their cottage to find an unexpected crowd of ascetics assembled outside. Seeing Ram, they fell to their knees, pleading, 'Save us Ram, save us!'

'The demons are wreaking havoc in the Dandakaranya forest down south.'

'So many hermits have fled, and many more killed. We managed to escape from there.'

'How will we practice our austerities? Only you can do something about this.'

The warrior prince looked at his wife, his face shining with renewed purpose. Sita nodded back.

Ram and Sita decided to spend the final hours of that night by the moonlit river. The lotuses had all curled back to sleep. However, they themselves were not at all sleepy. They lay on the soft grass and waited for the sun to rise and partition the sky with directions. When it did, Sita helped Ram and Laxman load the quiver of arrows behind their backs and they started their journey southward.

10

The Rousing Raatrani

Sita kept flicking the pages of the Ramayana, but her eyes remained fixed on the wall. She needed no script to find what happened next. It was her life after all. The long journey from Chitrakoot to Dandakaranya wavered in front of her eyes with vivid clarity.

Ram, Sita and Laxman had walked for miles and for days—through forests full of wild beasts and other kinds of danger. They had walked over hills which rose steeply and made them tired, and across valleys which slowed them with mesmerising beauty. The scenes shifted from rocky outcrops to lush valleys, from river plains to dense jungles. Regardless, they kept moving with hunger to witness all of nature's ecstatic beauty. In a way, walking had become meditative and taught them so much about perseverance and resolution.

The exile offered Ram and Sita an opportunity to know each other better. Ram discovered that the delicate appearance of Sita's limbs was only an illusion that hid her tenacity. The way she matched Ram and Laxman in every quick stride as they wedged through dense forests, be it in wide leaps or ardent climbs, was awe-inspiring. He also saw her playful side, splashing puddles, kicking wet grass, jumping across stepping-stones, her laughter rising over and pounding his heart.

The journey allowed the couple plenty of tender moments. It warmed Sita's heart to see Ram pull thorns from under her dainty feet, his eyes squinting with effort. In those moments, she could admire him without restraint, look at his thick, curly lashes, the glimmer of sunlight over his bare shoulders, the pinching of his nose feeling her inflicted pain and—most precious of all—his innocent smile as he showed her the pulled thorn, completely unaware of her thoughts.

Sita walked between Ram and Laxman when they crossed streams. Some of these were calm, while others gurgled with current. There were also some that deceived to be shallow but ran deep, or ones with abundance of wildlife around and those slimy with mud.

They foraged for food and learnt to rely on their instincts and strength. Some days they got by merely on the pulp of inguda and *badar* and at times indulged in feast when the men killed an antelope, a boar or a tiger. They learnt to cook over fire, to charr and soften food. They ate their meals over large leaves and made drinking vessels out of fruit shells and sculpted branches. At times when they couldn't find a source of water close enough, they learnt to hack the trunk of *saaj* which held just enough water to quench their thirst.

After the clothes from Ayodhya tattered, they made ones from the bark of *shahtoot*, *peepal* or *kathal*. They peeled the inner bark and pounded it with stones, until it was soft like sheet. They wetted and dried the garments under the light of the sun to turn them soft. To make her saree look beautiful,

Sita patterned it with dyes from flowers and plants, and her eyes would twinkle with joy when showing it to Ram. She drew flowers, creepers, deer and peacock feathers, or anything that took her fancy. Each time Ram washed his hair, Sita would mat it afresh with the pulp of inguda and bind it into a half top knot.

Their feet blistered, for they walked tirelessly and endlessly, but over time even that toughened. Nature was gracious, providing them plenty of herbs to heal their sores. When needed, just the right herbs, or leaves, or flowers, would glimmer from the thicket, almost asking to be gathered and brewed into a potion, and with their strengths revived, they learnt the lesson of gratitude.

Every day was different. Sometimes thorns from acacia would stretch to scratch them, and on other instances, soft grasses would caress their ankles. Bees and butterflies would join their trail, expecting to be led to a better place, and for a brief while, monkeys and rabbits would become their faithful companions. Birds would scream from high branches, pointing towards a more opportune spot, or warn them of the impending danger. When it battered down with heavy rains, a sheltering cave would never be too far, and with time, they learnt how different the forest smelled between the summer and winter rains.

After walking this way for four months, they finally reached Dandakaranya—the land of their new purpose. The sages at Chitrakoot were right. The forest here grew dense with thorny bushes, and sal, palmyra, date and peepal trees loomed large under the blocked-out sky.

'Ah!' Sita squeezed Ram's hands and staggered back, as the group suddenly came upon the corpse of an ascetic hanging by his feet from the branches, eyes open in shock. The light was dim and the sight too morbid. His rope-like coiled hair dropped all the way to the ground.

'Laxman, watch out! There are even more over there,' said Ram, and the buzzing of flies got louder. Indeed, there were a dozen more ascetics hanging down the branches.

'Such awful stench!' Sita clamped her hands across her face.

'The stench is coming from that direction. I can hear the river.' Laxman edged warily.

Their stomachs clenched as they saw more horrifically mutilated bodies by the blood-soaked banks of the Pampa.

'Unbelievable! We really must do something about this,' said Ram as he held Sita's hands and moved away.

The trio, more alarmed than before, visited many hermitages that had had their *havankunds* smashed and cottages wrecked. The sages were too horrified to resume their ceremonies but Ram and Laxman spoke to them with calm resolve, urging that fear would only embolden the enemy. They promised to guard the rites with their bows, that no harm would reach the hermits under their watch. At last, the sages yielded to their words, and chants rose with the crackle of fire, with Ram and Laxman circling the hermitage in turns, arrows notched, listening for every rustle in the dark. As the the scented smoke of sacrificial fires returned to the air, it once again drew the demons, which was all Ram and Laxman ever wanted.

Killing the demons was a slow, relentless process, and they moved between different hermitages, staying for months, years or as long as it took to drive out evil. Life felt a little more settled living amongst the hermits. They studied the vedas under the guidance of the sages and learned how they subsisted on leaves, water, air and sunlight. The knowledge they gathered from the hermits provided a good stimulus to their curious minds. The sages didn't just share their knowledge, but a select few shared their visions of clairvoyance and bolstered their beliefs about the real purpose behind their exile.

Sage Sarabhanga was the first to share his insight. They had arrived at his hermitage that morning, but he had not said anything. Later at night, he knocked softly on Ram's door, He had with him a pot of water and clean clothes which he said he had forgotten to offer in the morning. Sita invited him in but the sage refused for the visit was hardly about comfort.

'You weren't born of fire without reason,' the sage said to Ram. 'You are here to end a darkness equal to your own strength. It will come. Be ready.' And he left, leaving Ram and Sita in perplexed silence.

At dawn, as the trio prepared to leave, Sarabhanga offered one final instruction. 'Seek Sage Suteekshna. He will guide you further.'

The forest grew denser as they moved, the light dimmer and the paths narrower. By twilight, they reached Sage Suteekshna's hermitage. He sat outside a lotus pond, dressed in rags and matted hair. His voice shifted between tears and trembling ecstasy as he kept referring to Ram as Lord Vishnu.

'Welcome, welcome, Vishnu. At last, you are here. Your path is long, Vishnu. Go south. Go south.'

So they continued southward, the terrain gradually shifting—flatter now. The air clearer, even tinged with the scent of sacred smoke. They had reached Sage Agastya's hermitage, and he welcomed them with warmth, his eyes lingering on Sita.

'You carry strength few can see,' he smiled at her. Then, turning to the brothers, he bestowed them with divine gifts;

a bow and a sword from Lord Vishnu, and a quiver with inexhaustible arrows from Lord Brahma.

'These will serve you well,' Agastya said, and smiled again as he saw Sita bowing to the weapons. 'She knows how power is to be wielded. Take her to Panchvati. It is full of beautiful groves, she will like it there.'

Sita looked at Ram and they both knew what the other was thinking. Ten years had passed wandering, and finding a place they could call their own wouldn't be so bad.

That is how they came to Panchvati, a land nestled amongst hills, with forests bathed in cooling green, and enclosed by sparkling hills and many waterfalls.

Sauntering down its valleys, they came upon a spot where the lazy Godavari River widened into a basin. The scene took their breath away. Clear as crystal and blue as the loveliest blue could be, its lake was laced with drooping hyacinths, dotting lily pads and lotuses, which were all pink in health and beauty. Grasshoppers called from time to time, and in response, frogs croaked. Grasses swished with every movement of scampering rabbits.

Ram and Sita edged closer. Its water was a still sheet where cumulous clouds, amused by their own reflection, playfully melted away. All around the flowering trees—palash, *amaltas, mahua, kodivara, kachnaar* and *kanak champa*—either gracefully drooped down or proudly bore the weight of the creepers in embrace. Aware of this hidden gem, spotted deer and rabbits came here to quench their thirst.

Sita lifted the border of her saree and dipped her toe to break the surface. It warmed Ram to an earlier memory. He waited for her to splash but she was distracted by the glimmering shoal of small blue fish. They wriggled up in beautiful patterns that shimmered as they caught a touch of sunlight, before going back down. Sita turned to Ram, her eyes prancing with delight.

'Beautiful, isn't it?' He offered his hand for her to climb back.

'Perfect! Look at the swans, waterfowl, cranes and ducks,' she said, soaking in the lovely smell.

'Laxman, what do you think?' Ram looked back, 'Do you also agree it's a good place to settle?'

'Not for me to decide. But yes, I would say it's the loveliest we have come across. I can see *ashoka,* sal, *aam, ketaka, kathal, khajur, lakuch,* champa—all with ample fruits. There would hardly be any need to venture far.' Laxman's tone was serious as ever.

'Sita will also be able to fetch her prayer flowers right here. How about we build our lady a cottage? With a little garden in front?' He smiled at her.

Sita blushed and nodded back. Living here would be like living in a dream.

'The kitchen could overlook the lake, and could have another window facing the hills at the back.' Ram motioned with his hands, carving her dreams. 'Sprawled to this side would be the resting rooms, one for me and Sita, and the other for you.'

'Not for me. I am only here to look after you. As always, I will stand guard outside,' Laxman replied respectfully.

Ram silently appreciated Laxman's selflessness. This is what his younger brother had been doing since the start of the exile, and wouldn't heed otherwise.

The men set about the task at hand. A mud wall was soon raised, and as it dried and hardened, they hacked wood to lay the roof. They made its frame from *shahtoot* branches, which Sita helped interweave with leaves of *khejri, kaash* and other grasses. The men then secured it with sturdy vines. They carved small doors and windows, and Sita lovingly smeared the floor with mud. The verandah would be where she would wait for Ram to return with food and stacks of firewood. In time, she would train flowering creepers over the roof and let them hang by her windows. At night they would light a fire, sit outside, count stars and tell stories. Such simple joys of life, yet unparalleled.

There were also many waterfalls that rolled down the steep hills of Panchvati that Ram and Sita loved climbing. From there they could catch glimpses of their newly built cottage.

A few nights after settling down, they sat atop a boulder overlooking the valley. It had rained a while back and an inviting coolness had settled over. The flowers and leaves were all plump with vivacity, although a few delicate ones had drooped. The black boulder they sat on was wet too, as was the mossy grass under their feet.

It was a full moon night and the lake by the cottage sparkled under the touch of the amorous light. The distant trees, puddles, hills and the wet grass beneath their feet, all shone beautifully. In that solitary vastness, the two of them sat undisturbed. Sita in front of Ram.

Kept on the black boulder were a few raatrani flowers, Sita's favourite. Her hair cascaded down her slender waist and made Ram think of the night sky. He carefully tucked the white flowers in her tresses, adorning them just like the clusters of stars above. A few strands blew in the breeze and brushed his face. He marvelled at her delicate shoulders, her saree wrapped across one, leaving the other bare to sight. From time to time, some flowers slipped down her silky locks, which he duly tucked back in.

The breeze didn't help. It was satin-like, gliding and caressing, and made them even more conscious of their desire. All Sita wanted was for Ram to enfold her, but she could not bring herself to say so.

'Are you done?' She asked. She hadn't spoken in a while and her voice quivered, just like the delicate wings of a butterfly.

He replied with a mumble, equally soft. She felt his warm breath over her neck, and unable to pretend any longer, swivelled around. But Ram grabbed her mid-way.

'Steady there,' he cautioned. But a few more flowers tumbled down.

Sita squeezed her eyes. Such unflinching concentration, despite the obvious tenor of the night. Probably his most endearing trait. After fixing the last of the flowers, he came around and sat beside her. In the creamy light, their silhouettes glowed. A fine mist picked up and the air turned cooler. She missed his touch. His musky smell was strong.

Ram looked Sita in the eye, and noticed that they were sparkling. It made her conscious—the fact that he knew.

Without saying anything, Ram put his arms around Sita's waist, and gently drew her in. He enfolded her, resting his arms over her soft hair. Her hair brushed his warm cheeks. Their hearts started to beat. Beat loudly. The flowers began to tumble. It tickled down his wrist, her waist. But neither of them cared. Not any longer.

Then the drizzle stopped. Much too soon it stopped. It was alright, for Sita was already in Ram's embrace.

II

The Shrilling Cry

The Ramayana was laid open on Sita's lap, but the words had started to swarm and turn blurry. She placed it back on the shelf and wiped her cheeks.

It was not like their love was any less perfect. On the contrary, it was the kind that people would only dream about. So absolute was its depth that despite everything that ensued between them, they continued to love each other in a completely helpless and broken sort of way.

Sita stepped onto her verandah and stood by the doorway. Her frame was narrow as ever, and with golden light illumining her face, she looked youthful. Time had spared her from leaving any marks of its passing except for the few strands of hair that had recently begun to turn grey.

Across from her, a few sleepy rabbits rested under the amaltas tree. Their soft fur glistened as it gently rose up and down. But Sita was hardly paying attention. Her mind was consumed by the mangled web of interconnected fates, where one commits sin, and calamity befalls the other. Dasharath's sin bore its mark on Ram's fate, and in turn Sita had to bear the doing of not only Ram, but also Laxman.

A parrot called from high above the branches, its squawking deep and clear. But Sita had already been sucked into another world. Their cottage back in Panchavati, one that was built and nurtured with love.

The creeper Sita grew over her thatched roof crept more than just her window. Its delicate tendrils caught and curled over the roof's wooden rafters, palm fronds, twigs, thatch, and any in-between spaces it could crawl into—its scent and colour bursting forth. The sight of those bright flowers appeased Ram and Sita, especially when they lay wrapped in each other's arms after a night of contended togetherness.

The house that was born out of their dreams, took shape exactly that way. It had beautiful views on all sides. Deer and rabbits often sauntered around, hoping to find food, get thorns picked or simply a caress. Dandakaranya may not have been Ayodhya but proved to be a kingdom no less. The exile was now in the twelfth year, and soon all this would be over. The realization that they would no longer be all alone brought on an odd sense of yearning over Sita.

Only it was a folly to think they were truly alone.

Someone other than the deer, rabbits, monkeys, swans and reptiles also lurked in these forest. She was enigmatic and cunning; bereft of love and pining for it. She lurked in the dense trunks and thick undergrowth, keeping an eye on the trio. Never should she have needed such stealth, for this beguiling forest was in fact her rightful territory.

That evening Ram and Laxman were hacking wood for the night fire. The sound of falling axes pounded through the still air. Sita was indoors, tending to the *Shivalinga* she had crafted from mud. She wrapped raatrani flowers in a belpatra and offered it to the idol. Praying at dusk had become a ritual. Not only did it offer a sense of routine but also helped ward off malevolent forces most prevalent during such times.

Despite the prayers, evil appeared.

With a jingle of anklets, the genesis of their misery walked up. The unexpected sound made the brothers drop their axes and look up. There she was—a damsel dressed in a flowing pink saree with green blouse. Her small lips were painted a deep red and she was wearing a nose ring, bangles, necklaces and earrings. It had been a while since they had seen anyone adorned with so much jewellery. With every languid step, her hips swayed delicately and her ornaments chimed with bewitching allure. Her blouse was short, exposing her milky waist, on which sparkled a *kamardhani*. She walked with her bosom thrust forward, which made her dainty waist appear even more attractive.

'Greetings, young men! I was passing by when I heard the sound of chopping.' She fluttered her lashes, drawing attention to her dark eyes. 'Pardon me, but I have never seen you before.'

'Greetings. I am Ram, the eldest son of Maharaja Dasharath from Ayodhya. And this is my brother, Laxman.'

'No wonder your ascetic garb had me confused. They can hardly disguise your princely features.' Her eyes widened with a bewitching look.

Through her small window, Sita could see and hear everything. She heard attempts at seduction drip like honey from the enchantress's every word and noticed that her eyes had not moved from Ram's chest—pumped from the effort of hacking wood—even once.

'So, princes of Ayodhya, what brings you to these dark forests?'

'A penance,' Ram replied. 'We have been ordained to spend a few years away. But I wonder why you called these forests dark. We love it here so much that we have even built ourselves a small cottage.' Ram pointed to their humble house.

'Hmm, not bad. Still, these forests come with their dangers. There are demons and wild animals, arduous terrains and belligerent nature. You could lose your life any moment.' She lowered her voice, making it difficult for Sita to hear what she said next. 'What you need is someone...someone who knows this place like the back of their hands.' She floated closer, not saying anything in words, yet making her proposal evident.

'Thank you for your kind offer.' Ram stepped back. 'But my brother and I are prepared to avert such dangers.' Sita noticed that Ram kept his gaze turned away.

'Oh, the way you talk! Isn't that impressive!' The enchantress followed Ram in circles, a bit too close. She pursed her red lips smugly. 'Of course, you are fearless. Look at your long, strong arms. That puffed...broad...chest.' Her exceptionally long fingers sliced dreamily through the air.

Sita came out to the verandah. It was difficult to tell in the dying light, but perhaps the hint of a blush was visible on Ram's cheeks.

'And may I ask who exactly are you?' asked Ram.

She laughed tantalizingly.

'Who am I?' Her laugh turned into a playful giggle. 'Ha! I am Surpanakha. These are my forests you are in.'

At that, Ram looked her in the eye, and she giggled yet again, throwing her head back, elated to finally have his attention.

'It is true!' She swivelled delicately. 'These mountains, this lake, this river, this patch of sky—all mine.' She leaned back against a low slanting branch to allow them a more inviting sight. But when she continued, it felt like she was talking more to herself, 'Unfortunately what also belongs to me is a tormenting loneliness—one that has not been filled since my husband's death. He…he was killed by my own brother.' Surpanakha spaced out, but not for long. She sprung forward, and her bewitching voice turned enthusiastic, 'Tell me, would you like to fill that emptiness? My deep and dark emptiness. In return, I can show you sights more exquisite…' she paused for effect, '…more exquisite, than anything your eyes would have otherwise seen.'

Ram was stunned. She was so uncouth. A disturbing contradiction to her beguiling beauty. Surpanakha, oblivious of his thoughts, suggestively rubbed the sides of her neck and continued, 'These forests are full of hidden caves, underground rivers, secret vantage peaks and crystal waterfalls. Come, let me reveal it all to you. Let me snatch your breath away.' She hissed as she spoke.

'Thank you for your offer, but I already have a wife.'

Laxman chuckled at Ram's unease that made the latter say something out of character. 'My brother here might like some company.' There was a discernible hint of sarcasm in Ram's remark and Laxman was amused by such playfulness.

Surpanakha grew annoyed but she continued. 'Is that so? Well, your brother is equally strong and handsome. Then tell me young man—' She turned towards Laxman and continued with cloying sweetness, '—would you rather like to come along with me?'

'Thank you for the kind offer. But I am only a humble

servant to my elder brother, while you are so beautiful—and clearly, so powerful. Betrothing me would hardly befit you.' Laxman was trying hard not to laugh.

Surpanakha's amber eyes glowered. She wasn't taking the rejection too well.

Laxman continued, 'If only you could convince my brother. But you see, there's his wife. Not only is she beautiful but is mannerly too. Honestly, his refusal doesn't surprise me.' A soft chuckle escaped his mouth, but unfortuntely, it was loud enough for Surpanakha's ears.

She shot a glance at Sita. Indeed, she was young, delicate, beautiful. Surpanakha scoffed, 'Who—that crone? Just look at her plain clothes, her unadorned self. Her…her matted hair. Ha! That hag is hardly a match.'

'Surpanakha! Mind your words!' Laxman pointed an accusatory finger.

'My words! Really! Didn't you just say she is the obstacle between Ram and me? What if I kill her? Surely your brother wouldn't mind then!'

She hissed and charged in a terrifyingly ferocious manner. Her form disturbingly massive, despite her fragile frame. Everything happened too quickly for things to make any sense.

'Laxman!' Ram screamed out.

Laxman promptly shot an arrow. It hit Surpanakha's nose and blood gushed down her face in ghastly spurts. Her shrill cry rent the air.

Surpanakha touched her face to find it dripping with blood. Her saree and hair had also been smeared. With a twisted mouth, she panted and cried, 'You will pay! You will definitely pay! My brothers, they will not spare you!' Then she snarled at Sita, pointing out her long blood soaked nails and screamed,

'You will pay! I will make sure of that!' She fled, dissolving into the very darkness she had come from. The echo of her warning, however, lingered in the air.

Ram, Laxman and Sita stood rooted for a while. Laxman's shoulders still taut, still holding out the bow. Ram stunned with anger. Sita in disbelief, as she regarded Ram and Laxman and the trail of blood around. *Why did Ram entice Surpanakha in the first place? Had he forgotten about Urmila, Laxman's wife who, back in Ayodhya, was carrying no less than a gratuitous penance of her own?*

Evening spilled quickly, engulfing the forest with a nervous darkness.

12

Red Rain

The sun had begun its recede into the horizon—turning the shadows faint and skewed—but there was still light in the verandah. The rabbits sleeping in its warmth had long moved away and the glint on fluttering leaves too had dimmed. Yet, Sita remained standing, oblivious to such changes.

The thing with bitter memories is that one always follows the other. The loose thread, which may seem short when pulled, turns out to be an unending spool. *Could the past have been managed with greater wisdom?* But past always comes with closed doors, which can never be revisited; only repented.

Surpanakha had fled but the darkness she had brought never fully dissipated. The sun rose, the sky brightened and the time rolled, yet the gloom stuck to Sita's skin like a leech. It was difficult to shake off her shrill cry. Everything from the crunching of dry leaves to the thud of falling fruits and the howling of the wind sounded like her scream. Sita looked at every tree with suspicion, perpetually anxious that Surpanakha was hiding among them and could swing down crying any time. She remembered the trail of blood—dripping, sullying her garden of prayer flowers.

Until now, Sita had only seen her union with Ram being celebrated. Now she also got a taste of the raging jealousy it could inspire. A welling premonition much like Surphanakha's long nails dug into her sense of tranquillity. She knew that it was only a matter of time before the enchantress would try to prise her off Ram.

Sita's restlessness started to bother Ram, so she started to feign normalcy. She smiled more than usual, but it looked hollow. She strained to converse but the silence no longer felt comforting. It irked them, reminded them of exactly what they were trying to push away. Ironically, it was only when Ram left to forage did she feel free in the company of her weighing thoughts, and then whether time would pass—quickly or slowly, she could no longer tell.

One evening, she was so preoccupied that she did not hear Ram walk in with a stack of woods. The room had turned gloomy in the absence of any firelight. Hunched to one corner, Sita sat with hands resting on her knees, regarding something in the distance. Ram dropped the stack and lit up a small fire. Almost instantly, the warmth seeped through, yet Sita didn't look up. She didn't move. Probably done with her pretences.

'It's been unusually windy the last two days.' Ram struck up a conversation, 'You should have seen the trees outside. They are swaying madly. I wouldn't be surprised if there are uprootings tonight.' He wiped water off his forehead and sat beside her.

'Why didn't you just send her away?' Sita asked abruptly, her gaze still fixed ahead.

'I tried. But she would not leave.'

'But was that jibe necessary?' She looked him in the eye.

He had no words. In the silence the wood crackled. Their eyes stayed upon each other, but not a single word was uttered. It was clear that Ram had acknowledged his fault, and it felt enough.

'You do realize that she will be back?' Sita said.

'She most likely will be. But we are not afraid, are we?'

'No.'

'Good. Tell me, wasn't that our whole purpose—to relinquish evil?' Ram asked, his expressions sombre in the glinting light. Small pearls of raindrops were scattered on his hair. *Maybe he was right; maybe the welcoming peace over the last year was only transitionary.* Sita wiped his hair with her saree.

'I could not let her attack you,' Ram continued.

'All I am saying is there will be a price to pay.'

'There will be none,' he said, taking her hand.

Sita leaned over his shoulder and the wetness from his clothes seeped through.

'You haven't brought them to use.' Her eyes returned to what she was gazing at earlier.

'Not brought what to use?'

'Sage Agastya's bow. The one we received before coming to Dandakaranya. He said it had once belonged to Lord Vishnu and you will need it to fulfil your purpose,' she said in a whisper.

Ram looked at the celestial weapons kept in the corner. They were adorned with fresh garlands which Sita wove daily. She didn't just pray to the *Shivalinga,* but also to their weapons—imploring that they always guide Ram towards their righteous use.

'Maybe it is time,' she said. The cold winter air filtered through the roof, shaking the flowerless creeper above.

'Sita, are you worried?'

'About your abilities? Never!'

She lied down and rested her head on his outstretched legs. Ram stroked her gently. Maybe she was right, maybe things were serious this time. They looked at the glinting bow, its golden surface sparkling with rubies, emeralds, and topazes. Next to it was the quiver of arrows that had once belonged to Lord Brahma. For the first time, they saw the bow blaze with potent power. The more they looked at it, the brighter it blazed, like it was the only thing worth seeing. Next to it was a sword from Lord Vishnu. If the worst came, they were prepared.

In the corner, the firelight flickered. Threatened by a spray of rain, it faltered momentarily before steadying back. It stayed resolute—towards its sole purpose of warding away the darkness.

By morning, the wind gathered ferocious speed. True to Ram's prediction, some trees had been uprooted. Not only fragile palms, but also the sturdy sal, palash, *mahua* and *semal*. It was baffling that their cottage stood intact. Sita tried shutting the windows in a hurry, but they clattered against the frame, letting in the red dust that the wind had brought from mysterious lands. Every now and then, flashes of lightning ripped through the sky's belly and stunned their hearts.

Soon it started to pour in frightful sheets of water mixed with red dust. The whole landscape was washed out with the colour of blood—the colour of retribution. Oddly, the sun cowered down, plunging the forest into inexplicable darkness. Surpanakha's warning had indeed come true.

Sita's heart shuddered to see Ram by the doorway, ready with Sage Agastya's bow. *How her words had tempted fate.* She rushed to grab his shoulder, but his eyes were fixed ahead, gaze intent, eyebrows knotted with caution. Sliding off her hold, Ram stepped into the deluge and peered around. He shouted something to Laxman but the sound was muffled by the howling wind. All that could be seen in the murky darkness were his white teeth and eyes.

'Laxman! I said, take Sita away!' he hollered louder.

'No! I am not leaving you!' Sita stepped back.

'Didn't you say you trusted me?' He screamed and stepped inside, picked up the scabbard and secured it around his waist.

'Brother, even I can't leave you alone. Please, let me help you—' Laxman cried.

'Try to understand. Sita's safety is paramount. Up there in the mountains is a cave. Follow the rivulet. By the lake. Leave! Now!'

Sita's throat tightened. She did not want to leave. Instead, she wanted Laxman to assist Ram, but there was no use arguing. She embraced Ram, but he hastily prised her off and motioned for Laxman to depart.

The storm was implacable. With great difficulty, Laxman and Sita forged ahead, holding onto tree trunks, clinging onto boulders, braving their way against the battering wind. It kept whipping Sita's hair and her saree. They only paused to catch their breath or steady their constantly slipping feet, until at last they reached the cave.

It was a safe shelter, but everything below was shrouded by foliage. The wind's howl was made worse with the screeching of jackals and vultures. The darkness itself was agitating. Weeping, Sita fell to the ground. It was crushing not knowing how Ram was.

She heard cries, almost human-like, yet abhorring, filled with a deep sense of resentment. The wind continued to howl and the downpour just would not stop. *Had Surpanakha come with her brothers? How many were they?* Laxman paced outside, equally helpless, and time passed with cruel, aching clarity. Then slowly, those cries fell silent, and the sky eventually brightened.

When Sita and Laxman hastened down, they found the ground strewn with flowers. They were not the usual *kaner, kumkum* and *kachnnar* but varieties she had never seen before. Her eyes searched for signs of destruction. Oddly, there were none. In fact, the forest was resurrected—more beautiful than before. Ram was standing near their cottage, proud, with flowers tumbling down his shoulders. A large group of ascetics from the surrounding hermitages stood in mute submission. Ram lovingly raised them by the shoulders.

'No one will disturb you now. You can practice your austerities freely,' he said.

By now the ascetics had seen Sita and Laxman and one of them proclaimed, 'Ram killed fourteen thousand demons. He has brought an end to evil.'

'Khara and Dooshan—Surpanakha's brothers were here with an army. But Ram freed us all,' said another, 'At long last, we can live in peace. The gods in heavens are rejoicing too. Glory be to Ram!'

'Glory be to him!' joined in the rest.

Fourteen thousand! Sita's head reeled in confusion. She felt the ground—one which was strewn with otherworldly flowers—slip from under her feet. Amongst the euphoric chants and the relief of seeing her husband, she could not make complete sense of what was and was not conceivable. She rushed towards him.

'Ram, are you okay?' She threw her arms around him. In the presence of Laxman and the gathered ascetics. She couldn't be bothered. Her husband was so valourous, so kind—a true king. Tears rolled down her eyes as she looked at him. He had wielded Vishnu's bow the way he had Shiva's Pinaka. Her father had been so right about insisting to choose such a man. She ran her hands over his shoulders and peered over his back.

'Not a scratch!' Ram smiled.

A smile broke on Sita's lips too, and she embraced him again. Ram beamed. In that moment, nobody else mattered. Not the blessings from the heavens, not the gratitude of ascetics, or the shower of flowers, or even Laxman's approval. Sita knew that it was her approval that mattered to Ram. It was she was who mattered. Ram looked at her and gently wiped her tears.

But she was smiling.

13

Pools of Wonder

Sita stood at her cottage's verandah looking at the late afternoon sky, which stripped of colours, had started to dull just like her past. Her memories were fading, the textures, the smells and the sounds were no longer as vivid. There was this desire to guard them—despite their assaulting nature—and keep them safe in her heart like a sacred wound. She gazed into the endless sky, and would have remained in that stupor, if it weren't for that tug.

A deer stood beside her, pulling the drape of her saree. Its innocent eyes trembled with fear.

'Are you okay?' Sita bent over. A faint mewl slipped from the deer's throat. 'Oh, look at your belly! Are you with child? And why are you alone? Where's your herd?'

The deer peered at the thicket and Sita tried to follow the cue. But everything was shrouded in dense greenery. No sound, apart from the distant hymns. It sat down close and placed its head on her feet. Tears clung to its lashes.

'Don't you worry. I am sure your herd is looking for you… just like you are looking for them.'

The swell of its belly suggested the deer was close to its time. Sita stroked it gently. Who better than her could understand the pain of abandonment at such a time? Hopefully, this one was just lost. She brought a bunch of sedges, but the creature looked too upset for anything.

'Not hungry, are you? Alright, come, let us have another look.' The deer sprang up, and once again caught hold of her saree. Just what Luv and Kush used to do when they were little.

'Don't worry. I am not leaving you. Not until you are reunited.'

They walked behind the cottage and stared into the thicket beyond the ditch, straining for any signs of movement. The deer let out a few groans. Still nothing. All that filled the air was the smell of grass and a feeling of heavy dejection.

All of a sudden, they heard a long grunt followed by frantic movement. A herd came rushing—an adult and three fawns. Looked like a father and his children. Once at the ditch, the father stomped its feet and grunted.

'See, I told you. They are—'

Before Sita could finish, the deer had already taken off. Then, remembering something, it halted and swivelled. It gazed at Sita, eyes glimmering with unspoken appreciation.

'Go now! They are waiting,'

The deer pranced around in circles for a bit and then leapt off. All too soon it was over. Sita's throat tightened to see their reunion—the mother licking its young ones, the father rubbing its face over her, his nose black and shiny, its mate reciprocating with equal enthusiasm. Then entire family then slipped away, once again leaving Sita with her cold and empty afternoon.

It was marvellous how the deer spoke with nothing but its eyes. Eyes are the mirror to the soul and few could match the allure of a deer's. If Sita could be accosted for a mistake, it was her unrelenting pull towards exactly those enchanting eyes. At the time, they were living in Panchavati.

Sita was in the kitchen, preparing the last meal for the day. The air inside the cottage was thick with the smell of the earth, and the roof's damp palm fronds. It was also full of the rough-skinned *aluka*, the starchy tuber that she was roasting in a pit. It was the smell of the home; the thought made Sita smile. Plumped under heat, the tubers sputtered and hissed with sprays. She wiped her face and carefully turned them over, their white smoke filling the cottage. After they would cool down, she would peel their skin, mindful of taking out any burnt bits, and mash them with wild herbs. Seeds of carom lent a lingering sharp taste, perfect with alukas' nutty warmth. She took them out on palash leaves and placed the other lot in the fire.

The patch of sky outside her window was a playful mix of deep and light yellow that tumbled one over the other. It was autumn and the forest lay in joyful harmony with the surrounding haze. Evening would be upon them soon, and Ram and Laxman would be back home. Just like that, another day in exile would be over, with only a year left to bide.

Judging the tubers would take a while, Sita stepped onto the verandah. The berries she had spread to bask under the sun needed to be stocked away before the scampering squirrels stole them away. The forest was no palace, yet she had flavours to balance—sweet, sour, bitter and salty. She loved it when Ram remarked on her quiet magic, and for not making them miss the palace food so much.

Strangely the sky was not the clear yellow she had seen a moment ago from her window. A dense fog had descended, filling the air with an unsettling allure. Sita squinted. It was only afternoon, but the sun seemed to have reeled back its light. Some forgotten bits lay suspended in the air, lending it a surreal glow. The trees in the distance were engulfed in fading clarity.

From the thistle bush came the chirrup of sparrows, and Sita reached for a bowl of grain by the verandah. Clearly, they too weren't prepared for the evening's abrupt onset. It was then that she saw a faint glimmer. A skittering amongst dry leaves. She looked up but nothing was visible. Probably just her imagination. The flash advanced forth and blazed. It swooped in circles and halted revealing itself in full glory.

It was a golden deer.

A surreal being from another world. It was the only thing that stood out in the dense mist. Sita blinked, and the deer blinked back.

Its almond eyes were mesmerising. Its head bobbed and swayed, as did its neck. It called on to her, pulling her with a deep, hypnotic tug. Its every movement was graceful: from the lurching of its head to the dropping of its feet, from the digging of its hooves to the swivel of its back. It edged closer towards Sita.

There was a golden shine to its fur, and the spots on its back dazzled, or more like swimmed. Sita stretched her arm, and the deer twitched its ears. She tilted her face, and it followed, the act broadening a smile over Sita's lips.

Holding onto her gaze, the deer started to retreat with elegant footsteps. It turned and began walking away, but not without stopping every three to four steps to look behind. Sita felt a faint discomfort taking over. Finally, the deer jerked up its ears and leapt into the bushes. Gone. Swallowed. The sparrows she was feeding followed after, with a mad tug of their own.

She slumped over the verandah, her frame bent with deep helplessness.

When Ram and Laxman returned with a bunch of large *kavat* fruits and a few hares, they sensed a strong charred smell. Laxman dropped the crossbar and dashed in. It was the forgotten tubers.

'Sita? Are you alright?' Ram asked, taking her hands.

'Huh! When did you come?'

'Just now. But what happened? You look lost?'

'Lost? No, not me. It was the deer…it went that way.'

'What deer?'

Sita pointed towards the thicket where the object of her fascination had eloped.

'Was it just a deer?'

'Not any deer. A golden deer!'

'Golden deer? That doesn't make any sense.'

'Oh, it had golden horns and shimmering fur with these… these bright white spots.'

The wonderment in her voice bothered Ram. His eyes flew towards Laxman, who looked equally bewildered.

'It leapt over the bush and vanished. Did you not see it? On your way back? Please, can you go look for it?'

'Oh, Sita! This all sounds very strange. I have never heard of a deer being golden!'

'Believe me, it was. Why, it mustn't have gone far. Please go look for it,' she pleaded.

Ram, being pragmatic, reasoned with her not to believe in it, but Sita continued imploring. 'Ram! Go! Please!' Her pleading got louder.

'Even if it were true, don't you think it might likely be a trap?'

'A trap?' Sita shrugged off his hands.

'Likely! You know how these forests are full of enchanted beings.'

Sita fell silent. Then replied in a vexed voice, 'All the more reason to seek it then. Maybe our troubles aren't over yet. If you really believe it was evil, then why don't you go and kill it? You never hesitated before incensing Surpanakha. Why spare the deer?'

Ram knew he could not deny Sita—not after the reasoning she had presented him. *Hadn't he been just as impetuous once? Maybe it really was yet another summon.*

'Laxman, Sita is right. We must seek the trap before it seeks us. I shall be back soon. Guard her.'

He grabbed his bow and bolted off, hoping it would not be too difficult to spot the golden deer. After all, evil forces blaze brighter in darkness.

'Laxmannnnn!'

It had not been very long before they heard a cry knotted in pain. Sita looked at Laxman.

'Laxmannnnnnnnn!'

Was it Ram's holler? The wind and the distance had added a layer of deception. Sita rushed forward.

'Is Ram in some kind of danger? Laxman, go! He is calling for you!'

'But he has asked me to guard you. What if the holler isn't his?'

'We cannot risk it! Quickly, go!'

'This might be a ruse. It all sounded suspicious from the

start. Besides, I cannot refute him.'

'Refute him! What do you mean? I am safe here. It is Ram who needs help.'

'Believe me, he will be fine.'

'And why should I? My husband screams for you, and you stand here without as much as a hint of concern. Do you know what is suspicious here—you, and your family. They didn't spare Ram anything, and now you refuse to respond to his call for help!' She bore her eyes at him, 'Why? So that only you and me would be left behind? Was that your plan all along? To win me?'

'How could you say that!' Laxman yelled. 'This is abhorrent! Simply abhorrent! I only had respect for you. You've broken that trust. I no longer want to stay here with you. Only I am not sure that you will still be here upon our return. It is your doing, sending my brother away and then making me disobey him.'

'Laxmannnnn!'

Another ringing call pierced through. Sita and Laxman both looked on with alarm. Without saying another word, Laxman darted in its direction.

Sita slumped over her verandah. She did not doubt Laxman but what other recourse was there? He was stubbornly senseless, bound to a baseless promise, when all that truly mattered was Ram's safety. Her heart didn't just ache, it twisted, caught between the concern for Ram's safety and the hurt of Laxman's rebuke.

The shrill of the cicadas picked up, masking every other sound. She strained for Ram's cries but there were none. They had at least provided an odd sense of reassurance. With time, darkness deepened, as did the eerie shrill of the cicadas.

14

Abduction

Dusk sifted down the heavens, cloaking the dramatic orange sky. Lingering over the horizon was the fatigued sun, waiting for the sages to return with alms from surrounding villages. Sita made her way to the evening hymns, a quiet ritual that wound down her day. Some young *gurubalaks* pattered by, carrying their bhiksha of small sacks over their backs. They weren't simply sacks of rice, wheat or barley, but learnings on humility and gratitude. It made her think of Luv and Kush—their big round eyes, delicate arms and curly long hair. They too must be subsisting on similar generosity.

The *ashramwasis* were already gathered under the ancient banyan tree, and even though it wasn't yet dark, long torches were ablaze. Sita brushed away the dry leaves from under a *parijat* tree and rested against its smooth stalk. Today's sermon was going to be from the Rigveda, on the Sun God—the gracious giver of life. He alone was the omniscient god, privy to all happenings, knowing equally the virtues and sins, the good and ill, of every being.

A rueful smile touched Sita's lips. If it was so, then surely the all-seeing Sun God must have known her truth despite the world's misgivings. He must have seen what had transpired when Ram and Laxman departed in the pursuit of the deer. And yet, the sting returned when she thought of how even the sun had turned its face away that evening.

Sita had been pacing non-stop, rubbing her palms, clicking her fingers. Her ears strained for any crunching of leaves amongst the thicket, any news from the birds on the high branches. None. The evening only darkened with a grainy appeal. She thumped her head on the pillar, caring not for the tears that streamed down her ruddy cheeks.

'Alakh Niranjan. Jai Shiv Shambho! O Bholenath!'

Sita faltered. Dressed in a crimson *angavastram* and dhoti, a hermit forged towards her. He had an exceptionally formidable build: broad shoulders, carved-out arms, and a pinched waist. A shock of black hair was partly tied up in a knot with the help of *rudraksh* beads, while the rest cascaded down his back. Smeared across his forehead were three lines of red sandalwood paste.

A flicker of hope leapt Sita's heart. *Sages are omniscient. Perhaps he comes bearing a message, or better still, a solution.*

Still, she couldn't overlook the air of imperiousness about him. A deep scar ran just below his chest, like a relic from some brutal combat. Draped from his shoulder across his chest, was a white *janeu*, the sacred thread reserved for Brahmins. He swung his staff and pitcher as he strode. Oddly for a sage, he wore a ruby necklace that rose up and down his heaving chest.

Now all too soon, he stood across her, looking directly into her eyes. His own deep-set yellow eyes stood against his dark skin and inspired a sense of caution. Suddenly, remembering the rightful etiquette, Sita bowed down.

'Greetings lady! I was passing through when I noticed your cottage. What are you doing outside? And why is there no fire lit? Surely you know how the wild beasts prowl at night?' There was an ocean-like depth in his voice.

'I am grateful for your concern, kind sage. But I live here with my husband Ram, and his brother Laxman.'

The sage's eyes bore down on her. She worried if her answer had somehow displeased him.

'I…I'm sorry they are not here to receive you. In fact, I am very worried. It's been a while that they haven't yet returned.' Her eyes tracked the woods.

A smile peeked beneath the sage's moustache. Sita felt unnerved but tried to dismiss the suspicion. It might have been her anxiety and the dusk playing tricks. She wiped her tears and the wet lashes accentuated the beauty of her daunted doe-eyes. Her hand caught in her bun which came loose, and tumbled down her waist, but she chose not to move. Something told her he was following her every movement.

'You have such long hair!' The sage smoothed his hands over his beard.

Sita eyebrows pinched with a sudden frown, but she kept her head bowed low.

'You don't look to be one from the forests…no, you belong elsewhere.'

'I…I am the daughter-in-law of Maharaja Dasharath, from the Ikshvaku dynasty. Misfortune has driven my husband into an exile.' Sita looked up, surprised at his lack of response, 'Which is why we live here.'

'Outrageous!' He banged his staff, startling Sita. 'What kind of a husband forces his wife on an exile? To bear his shame of punishment! Lady, you have been wronged.'

'Oh, no. It's not that.' Her eyes darted in confusion as she rummaged for the right words, 'My husband was in fact against it. His whole family was. It was...it was I who insisted.' she broke off, reminded of a similar such insistence only hours ago. 'He is a very compassionate man. Wait till you meet him. He has gone looking for a golden deer.' Her shoulders flinched at the strangeness of her own words, 'Well...there had been one just earlier today.'

The sage reserved his odd silence. Not a word of sympathy, not even mockery. His face turned into stone, hard and harrowing. An owl hooted from the banyan tree.

'Ram will be back soon.' It felt as though Sita was reassuring herself, but her words rung like mockery, and she noticed a malicious curl on the sage's lips.

His eyes were over her threadbare saree, and she pulled the drape over her exposed waist. But his eyes tracked over to her bosom. A looming premonition welled inside her. *Would it be rude if she asked him to leave and visit later?* A snake slithered under the cover of dry leaves right where she was standing, but she made no effort to move.

'I haven't eaten anything in a long time,' he said.

'I am deeply sorry. Unfortunately, I have no food to offer. Also, I...I need to go in to light the evening lamp. If you don't mind waiting here,' Sita said, motioning to the *bakula* tree, 'my husband will soon return with something.'

'You say I should wait outside?' He looked around at the growing darkness. 'Is this how you treat a hermit?'

'Oh, pardon me. You are right, I'll wait here too. Of course, the lamp can be lit when he returns.'

She curled in her toes, hoping to shrink and disappear. The sage stepped closer. Her heart, distressed as it already was, now started to beat outside of her. Her fingertips too started to tingle.

'What about you?' Sita endeavoured to converse. 'I mean... Do you come from far?'

At that the hermit let out a bellowing laughter.

'Did I say something wrong...I...I haven't seen many hermitages close by.'

'Do you remember Surpanakha?' He crouched over.

Sita's eyes flew open. She stared at the man in crimson clothes, the same colour as that mad gush of blood from Surpanakha's nose. Her face turned pale.

'Do you remember Khara?'

'Who...who are you?' Sita staggered back, and a sharp mango twig snapped under her bare feet. But the sage only laughed in returned.

'Who are you?' Sita screamed.

'I am Raavan!' His voice thrashed like gigantic waves. 'I am the lord of suffering, the harbinger of misery. I bring despair to those foolish enough to cross my path. Every tear, every anguished cry...my doing. I make the world tremble in fear... Foolish woman! To ask who I am! Well, I am none other than the emperor of Lanka. The devotee of Shiva. The one blessed with ten heads and twenty arms.'

As if on cue, nine more enormous heads jutted through, and started to bob and swarm ignobly, with dangling gold hoops on every ear. Sita's hands shot to her head. Raavan hurled the water pitcher and staff, and roaring, thrust his arms, which went from two to twenty, revealing his boon in all its arrogant glory. A number of golden armlets encrusted with lapis lazuli blinded her eyes.

Raavan jerked forward, and in a trice all his abnormalities

vanished. Ten heads and twenty hands swallowed back. Sita's head reeled with wild confusion. His voice took an unusually soft tone as he addressed her, 'I have a thousand wives, but none as beautiful as you. Your skin…' He took a deep whiff. '…sandalwood. And your hair…' He twirled his finger in the air, '…a silken cascade. It is aching for the weight of a crown. Pity, such beauty is being wasted in the forests, when it in fact needs to be celebrated in a palace, alongside a man like me. Come to Lanka, radiant one…surrender to me, and reign in my arms as my queen!'

'Enough!' Sita trembled at his crass adulation. She had intended to lash out more fiercely, but was choked. It made Raavan's eyes glow.

'You have no shame? Wait till you meet my husband.'

'What wrong did I say? It's a fine thing, that taste of power. You can have the best palace in my kingdom, surrounded by the prettiest gardens. My Ashoka Vatika, the most exotic of all. I could have a thousand maids wait on you. They will dress you in the finest silk and the best ornaments. If your heart still aches for more, why, I will even have all my queens tend to you. With a husband like me, the great Raavan, mightiest of all…you will never miss a thing in the world. Can that Ram ever offer anything close in comparison?'

'You compare yourself to Ram! Disgraceful! You are no match…not for him, and neither for me. Leave! Now!'

Sita stomped her foot and turned to go inside but her feet slipped. There was a painful tug at her hair. Raavan's big burly hands were clamped over it. He began dragging her. Dry twigs and stones scratched her waist, and she heard the mortifying tear of her saree. She screamed, but not a soul was around. The birds screeched and flapped and flew for their own safety. Even the serpent underneath the cover of leaves stared in stunned silence. Raavan's ugly heaving suffused the air. He clamped her wrist, grasped her thighs and swung her delicate body over his shoulder. Sita thrashed out, but to no avail. He tossed her inside his chariot. It was baffling to see that there had even been a chariot all along. It gleamed gold and silver, and was heavily studded with rubies, topazes, and emeralds. There were several storeys to that chariot. Strange wings sprouted at its either ends.

Sita's head pulsated. Her body was scratched. Her limbs ached. There was mud in her mouth which she spat out. She yanked, thrashed, twisted her arms to break free, banged her head. Her hair flew about in a mad rage of its own, and once again, Raavan pulled it back, making her yelp. The more she struggled, the tighter his grip became, so tight, that his nails dug into her skin. After a long struggle, she gave up.

Without warning, the chariot started moving, and the whole world swayed in revolting jerks. The wings unfurled completely, and the thing took flight. Bewildered, Sita rushed to the edge, but Raavan's clasp was strong. He pulled her towards him, pressing his arms on her waist. 'Raaaam, Raaaaam! Help!'

But her howl was absorbed by Raavan's deep laughter. His ten heads had sprung out again; their emotions multifarious, all speaking concurrently, all demanding to be heard at once, playing acute havoc on her senses. Meanwhile, the chariot kept rising.

'You are mine,' claimed one head.

'You are so beautiful,' chimed in another.

'I will teach your husband a lesson,' jibed another.

'Ha ha ha,' celebrated yet another.

'You want a golden deer? I will get you one,' ridiculed still another.

In her mind, Sita saw the deer again. Only this time, she saw it for what it really was—the spots on its back glinting in deceit, its sickly horns, the sharp twist of its neck as it beckoned her with its unnatural grace and its menacing leap into darkness. Clearly, the creature had compelled her life in a direction that had already been framed.

Laxmannnn. Ram's cry rung in her ears, and she understood that the call had never belonged to her husband, but the deer, which truly never was a deer. Hot tears streamed down her cheeks. She kept struggling to free her arms, but they had turned weak from all that fighting. She bit Raavan, and he shoved her to the floor. It was no use, for the chariot was now significantly high in the air.

'Sitaaaaaaaaa.'

She heard the holler from down below. It sounded like Ram.

'Sitaaaaaaaa. Where are you?'

It indeed was Ram. Sita edged to the railing and saw the forest from above as no person would have ever seen. She saw the emerald green treetops; the turquoise lace of the Godavari flickering and disappearing. The lake beside her cottage kept turning smaller as she rose higher. Somewhere beneath that green veil must be Ram, wailing and seething in anguish. Back at the cottage, unable to understand her strange disappearance, unable to bear the pain of separation or find out what happened. Dejected, she slumped down.

'Hurts you, does it?' Raavan feigned compassion. Then, he leaned and glared, 'Did Ram really think he could get away by dishonouring my sister, killing my brothers? Never!' Vengeance marred his dark face. His amber eyes burned. He bent closer and hissed, 'Now you will become my queen—like it or not.'

His maniacal laughter reverberated through the clouds, hitting her with an almost physical force.

Her hands crept to her trembling heart. It was flailing. Raavan had turned delirious with screams and laughter. Her hands squeezed around her chest, and her fingers wrapped around her necklace. She prayed to Shiva, pleading him to show her a way.

And in a way Shiva did.

When Sita pulled down her hand, her necklace came away. The solution gleamed back at her. She considered it for a while and dropped it down the cloudy skies, hoping it would carry her message to Ram. Thankfully, Raavan was far too occupied to notice, holding the reins of the chariot. Next, she took out her bangles, her earrings, her anklets, and her ring—every piece of jewellery that could be a tell-tale for her wise Ram to put together, and fed them down the grey clouds one after another. With all the fervent desire that her quivering heart could hold, Sita hoped the benevolent clouds would rain. When the time was opportune, they would rain down on Ram carrying the message from his helpless, abducted wife. They would help him track her down.

In time, the clouds parted, and the sky turned dark and clear. Sita remained slumped over. The scenery had shifted. Tall dense trees gave way to rocky outcrops, which in turn gave way to coastal plains and then to the sea. The chariot must have been gliding at a great speed. She must be a long way afar. By now, Raavan had turned quiet, and all that could be heard was the odd whimpering of the wind. And all that was visible was just miles and miles of indiscernible grey light. She felt lonely up there, with Raavan and just the chariot gliding across.

Just when she had lost all hope, something gnawed at her

ears with fervent desperation. A giant bird beat its enormous brown wings to block Raavan's way. In a hawking voice, it demanded that Sita be released. It called itself Jatayu, a friend of Maharaja Dasharath.

Raavan staggered. He hadn't expected any obstacle, not this high up in the sky. He pulled out his sword. The bird flew away and attacked from behind. A part of the chariot broke and fell down. Then it dug its large pointy beak in Raavan's back, and swung the chariot with both claws. The chariot was deflected from its path and Sita's heart leapt with hope. The bird tore Raavan's hair, and then came straight for his eyes. But unfortunately, Raavan dipped and slashed its wings. Sita cried, she attacked Raavan but he threw her back. The wounded bird still forged on, and Raavan brought his sword down on the other wing.

With that, Jatayu fell.

Right in front of Sita's eyes, with a pitiful look on its face, its eyes pinned on her, mouth open in remorse, it kept receding in a helpless fall with half-spoken words that melted in the sky until it became smaller and smaller—its giant bulk gradually turning into the size of a grain—and then disappeared altogether. With that, Sita too faded into unconsciousness.

15

Paradoxical Paradise

'Vandevi, what are you doing here all alone?'

Sita opened her eyes, slowly reeling back to reality to the buzz of night insects. Vasuki, the eight-year-old spirited child stood before her. She was clad in a short white saree with matching champa flowers in her hair—large white petals with yellow centres. Over her head swarmed a glittering crown of fireflies.

'Oh, I must have fallen asleep!' Sita sat up from the tree trunk.

Vasuki rolled her eyes, in a facetiously grown-up manner. In the distance, the banyan leaves dappled gold and orange under the blazing torchlight. Those who had been sitting in its inviting warmth must have returned to their cottages.

'What are you doing out so late?' asked Sita. 'Isn't it time for your evening recitals?'

'Exactly why I am hiding.'

Before Vasuki could catch the reproach in Sita's squint, she had already crouched down beside her. Now she pulled the drape of Sita's saree over her thin, bare arms.

'Ugh! Mother doesn't let me off until I have chanted my hymns a hundred and eight times! A hundred and eight times! And if I ever refuse to practice, she wastes no time reminding me of how focused Luv and Kush are. Honestly, by learning the Ramayana so quickly, they have made life difficult for the rest of us!'

Sita embraced the little one and gave her a gentle squeeze. 'Your mother's insistence doesn't come without a good reason. Chanting *mantras* is the only way to unfurl the power of their blessings.'

'Pfft! But why?'

'The repetition helps to draw you in.'

'And why do we even need to reach inwards?'

'Because it's the only place that truly matters. It's where lies your immense potential.'

'Hmm?' Vauski's eyebrows remained pinched.

'These are very powerful words, you see. As you chant, it's almost as if you start rubbing and releasing their powerful vibrations. More or less, they all have the same essence—that you are a part of Shiva. That there is no distance, or for that matter difference between you and him.'

'Hmm, would that mean I could do anything Lord Shiva can?'

'Of course! Just don't reason; surrender to him in complete faith.'

'Alright, if you say so. I shall try to be more focused.'

'I expect no less from you. Come now, your mother must be worried.'

When they reached Vasuki's cottage, her mother was already at the door, a diya in hand, prepared to go and look for her. The little girl flashed her mother an impish grin, and slipped in as if nothing had happened. Returning to the threshold, she called out, 'I will see you later, Vandevi. Don't forget the ratjaga tonight.'

'How can I? Not after your dozen reminders through the day!' Sita left the chuckling child with her worried mother, who was wringing her daughters arms in questioning, and walked back to her own *kutiya*.

It was indeed the power of staunch belief that got Sita through her gruelling captivity. Realizing that Raavan's chariot had flown across an ocean would have made anyone give up. But not Sita. She was born with the same tenacious will as her mother earth. Even as the chariot glided through the sky, a dim hope still throbbed within her exceptionally drained self.

A sudden turbulence threw the chariot about and made Sita look up. Raavan yanked the reins, and the chariot started descending. Shimmering like a mirage—Lanka—Raavan's famed kingdom, built entirely in gold and white stone started to materialize. It carried a similar boastful impression as its ruler—powerful, vulgar, ostentatious. The kingdom was shielded from the thrashing waves by a radiant rampart. On its top, large flags snapped in the sea wind. A huge palace rose at its centre, its walls sparkling with coloured gems and draped in flowers. Illuminated paths and courts with fountains separated the palace from other smaller palaces. There were platforms encrusted with sapphires and emeralds that gleamed under the blazing lamps, and where people milled about to the sound of trumpets and drums. But this wasn't where the chariot landed. Instead, it landed in Raavan's famed pleasure garden—Ashoka Vatika.

Night had already fallen and the garden was covered in a

blanket of darkness but for pockets of light where torches shone over the luscious emerald foliage. A net of bells was visible in a corner, tinkling to the whisper of the sea wind. In between, the plaintive cry of curlews drifted through. Raavan clambered out and wrenched Sita's arms, almost knocking her over.

'*Raakshasis*!' he bellowed.

In an instant, several of them materialized from everywhere—behind the trees and bushes, clambering down the branches and the smooth rocks, or rising out of the tall grasses. They gathered around their master, heads bowed in submission. On the trees behind, a low murmur of roosting peacocks could be heard, their long tails spilling like shadows from the high branches.

They were big burly women, with skin the colour of black sand and jute-like braided hair. Their red and yellow patterned saree was draped oddly high, baring their dense calves. Ivory bangles of many different sizes adorned their ankles and wrists. With lips painted the deepest red and eyes richly rimmed with kohl, they huddled together, staring at Raavan's unflinching clasp on Sita's hand. A flicker of resentment stirred across their faces as they whispered about her torn clothes and the absence of her jewels.

'Trijata!' Raavan yelled. 'Keep a close watch on her. Let this rebellious woman stay under your guard until she begs to be taken to the palace.'

Sita glared at him. Unaccustomed to such defiance, he was momentarily stupefied. The demonesses too glared, but with eyes dark with unease, stiffening at the exchange between their master and his captive.

The silence was broken by a jingle as Trijata stepped forward. She was a tall woman, with the frizziest, greyest hair.

The sharp light of one of the torches caught the deep pockmarks on her face.

'Take her!' commanded Raavan.

He thrust his captive forward. Sita winced, not so much from pain but panic. Where Raavan had clasped her for so long, a black ring-shaped mark had formed. It felt like a disconcerting reminder that he still clung on to her. In a vain attempt, Sita started rubbing her wrist vigorously. A sigh escaped Trijata as she put her fists over her big waist and bore her eyes upon her.

'Does Maharani Mandodari know about her?' Trijata asked Raavan in a low rasping voice.

'Not yet,' he replied, his tone more sombre than before.

Once again, the demoness assessed Sita from top to bottom with a curious disdain. By now, Sita understood Trijata was special. She could not only dare to look straight at Raavan but brazenly question him. She also guessed that Mandodari was Raavan's prime consort and was not one to be dismissed easily.

'Would you like to tell me who she is?' Trijata continued.

'Sita.'

Trijata let out another rigid sigh, which almost suggested she had known Sita previously. But she said nothing; only stepped forward and grabbed her, clamping not just one but both wrists. It made Sita's palms thrust forward in supplication.

'Don't you worry, master; I won't take my eyes off her for a single moment.'

'Good!' said Raavan before glowering back at Sita. 'Let us see, how long your stubbornness lasts.' With that, he turned and left with a huff, denying Sita the opportunity to hit back. He left her with a deep burning scorn—and the company of her new companions.

The silent looks on the demonesses' face was enough to

tell Sita how the sight of seeing her so close to Raavan had inspired a raging kind of jealousy in them. Their hearts were restless with a teasing torment, for it implied that their master no longer found his own woman worthy of admiration. She saw them staring at her waist, limbs and hair. Trijata turned Sita's wrist to see the mark closely under the firelight, as others huddled close. The crushing force of their gaze made it evident how irresistible they found Raavan.

That night, they didn't say a word to her, not even in disdain. They pretended disinterest by abandoning her under the *shimshapa* tree. Sita brushed off the fallen flowers from the stone platform and sat down. With time, shade darkened beneath its swooping branches and the air turned pricklier. Her throat burnt with shame and tears welled up her eyes. She looked up, hoping to soak back that vulnerability. The large, silver moon shone in the unfamiliar patch of sky. Looking at it, a wistful smile flickered on her face and the lingering drop of tear finally fell.

With its inspiring light, the moon showed her the power of love. It still bound Ram and her together under one light. With a prayer on her lips, Sita sent herself out. Perhaps Ram was touching the moon with his sight too, and they could reunite, even if vicariously. With that thought she rested her head on the rough trunk and finally closed her eyes to the terrors of the day.

16

Blade of Grass

As Sita returned to her cottage, she happened to step on an acacia twig.

'Ow!' She jerked back.

A spear-like thorn had jabbed through her feet. She lowered herself and squinted at the injury. Then very slowly, biting her lips, she yanked it free. A bead of blood oozed out, and she pressed her foot against the grass, hoping for the cool surface to soothe the sting. Under the pale light, each blade pulsed with quiet energy. She plucked one and turned it over. It was this delicate, green, thing that had been her weapon in captivity.

Sita woke up to the luxuriously beautiful sight of the Ashoka Vatika—so different from the night before. Blooming in pompous glory were flowers of every imaginable kind. There were heliconia, birds of paradise, *agnimatha* and bright eranda. There was *nagkesar* weaving the border with dark green leaves, in front of the tall *munja* grass. There were mahua, palash, jamun, ber, *sugandha, agaru,* as well as *karpur,* champak, *kodivara* and *ingudi* filling the garden in an array of shades. All around, bees buzzed and birds chirped, as dreamy sunlight filtered through The peacocks, now awake, fanned their feathers, which looked nothing less than shimmering jewels.

Despite that immaculate beauty, something was amiss. Sita looked around. There wasn't a single leaf that strayed from the rigidly trained borders, or a single flower that withered amongst the profuse bushes. There was no place for imperfection. All around, the demonesses seemed busy, sweeping the pathways that shone without a speck of dust, or scrubbing the basins of the fountains which sparkled with their own light. Some of them trained shrubs into whimsical shapes. Amidst such extensive pruning and plucking, it seemed they had plucked death itself from nature, lending the garden a very tense, fearful expression. They continued to ignore Sita—lending her neither greeting nor rebuke. Diligent and unyielding, these meticulous guardians of Ashoka Vatika made sure that everything adhered to their tyrant master's command.

A putrid smell penetrated Sita's nostrils and made her look up. Hanging from sunlit branches on the tree opposite, were hundreds of guavas, oddly large, more yellow than green, their flesh nauseatingly ripe. With the day waking up, their aroma woke up too. Sita felt queasy to the bones. The smell here was also trained with overwhelming opulence.

A sound of heavy footsteps drummed through the earth, and everything fell silent. Raavan was coming. No longer dressed as a trickster he was clad in bright silks and shining gold ornaments. An immaculately bejewelled crown lay on his head. The only similarity to last night were the three lines of sandalwood paste across his forehead, his ruby necklace and the thick moustache framing his cavernous mouth. His janeu also hung across his shoulder.

'So, how are you? Has the night made you change your mind?' He lifted a feet and placed it on the stone platform.

Sita let out a sharp sigh. The silence burned as the demonesses huddled around.

'Still adamant? What for? Do you really think your husband will come? He cannot! He doesn't even know where you are.' Raavan slapped his thigh. 'You are across an impossibly wide ocean.'

'He will come! Not only for me. But also for you! And then you will regret it.'

'Regret it! Then you clearly have not heard of my valour. There is no man quite like me—no man!' He thumped his chest with wild agitation, and his face, which had been beaming a while back, hardened.

'Of course, there is no man like you! One who disguises as a hermit! Who abducts another's woman! You took me by force…physical force! You think that makes you valorous? What you really are is a deciever! A coward!'

Raavan flung his hands and reached out.

'Stop!' There was a ferocious blaze in Sita's eyes. The drape of her saree had tattered amidst all that dragging and pulling, and there was nothing to screen her from his ugly view. She snapped out a blade of grass sprouting at the base of *shimshapa* and held it out as an allusive shield. 'Never again! Don't you ever dare touch me again! I am a married woman! An impossible barrier lies between us. If you dare cross it, I promise, you will regret my curse…much worse than you will repent Ram's revenge.'

Raavan stood stunned. That blade of grass was ordinarily frail but held out as a barrier in Sita's hand, it seemed transformed. Caution spilled out in shocking waves. It wasn't like Raavan couldn't have grabbed hold of Sita in her unarmed fragile state and drag her all the way to the palace. Yet he didn't. For some baffling reason, he didn't.

A deep colour of exasperation rose up his face and he edged away. His muscular shoulders remained puffed. His chest, however, heaved sharply.

'Trijata, see to it that this woman knows her place! Spare no mercy until she learns,' he said in a gruff voice, and with an imperceptible murmur left the place.

Silence returned, and everything seemed to be caught in a stun. Sita was afraid to move, she did not want to break the spell. Through the corner of her eyes she saw Raavan retreat. The beads on her forehead turned chilly, and only once he was completely out of sight, did she wipe them. From all sides, accusatory glances bore into her. This was not a place she wished to be.

Up in the sky, the sun had turned into a dim yellow ball, hardly warm enough to be comforting. Sita wrapped her saree tightly across her shoulders, stifling the sobs that threatened to break through. Thankfully, grey clouds tossed in and after a short soft rumble, ripped open.

Chin, chin, chin.

Water dripped down the large ovate leaves of *shimshapa*. It soon turned into a steady downpour, and began scraping and chafing her arms, washing down every raw emotion. The sky paled, and the stone platform turned cold. On the tree opposite, ripe guavas fell, their pulp splattering on the ground. Water flowed in thin streams down her hair and her long lashes. It rolled down her lips, chin, onto her wet saree, which clung to her limbs. For a long time, that melancholic rhythm continued over the treetops.

In time, the sky cleared and darkened to a pitch black. Toads came out of hiding and croaked exuberantly. They sprung across wet puddles gleaming in the moonlight. The air turned cool, suffused with the aroma of wet mud. Every once in a while, a thick drop of water plopped down the *shimshapa* and made Sita shudder. She rubbed her cold hands over her shoulders but to no avail.

A bonfire was lit in the distance. Not close enough to offer any warmth, it was premeditatedly far to only carry the voices. The demonesses sat toasting their hands and drying their hair. They shared some kind of nut, whose tough shell after cracking open with their yellowed teeth they flung into the fire. Every time they did so, the fire hissed and sprayed up with golden glitter, and a sound of a cackle followed. They were exchanging bemusing tales of enigma, cruelty and rumour—perfect antidotes to the weariness of night-long vigils.

'Just hear the disgust in her voice!' said one.

'Who does she think she is?' shouted another.

'I mean, look at her waist, thinner than this piece of burning log.'

'Ha! I don't know about that, but it surely is thinner than your arms!' The mockery turned distasteful.

'Oh, stop it! But her eyes—forever dazed. And her ugly mouth, I haven't heard a single word spill out of it. You would think this poor thing knows not how to speak—but wait till she does and you will be shocked at her insolence.' Their jibes turned crude in dialect and their voices rose to uncover suppressed jealousy.

'Honestly, I don't understand master! What does he even

find in her? Why so smitten? Her petite frame is hardly attractive.'

'Meh! Don't be a fool to believe master is in love with her,' Trijata spoke, her low gruff discernible amongst others, 'His real aim is to kill her.'

'That's what I would have liked to believe. That she is only here paying a price for princess Surpanakha's insult! Now, she was beautiful, but how they mutilated her! Poor princess!'

'Pity, isn't it?' concurred her friend. 'Now she mostly remains locked indoors. Still, master's eyes tell a different story? The way he regards this wench. What was he saying to her this morning—that he is ready to make her the queen consort! I wonder what Maharani Mandodari has to say about that.'

'Uh! How do I explain? It is not just for princess Surpanakha,' replied Trijata with an unsure expression, 'Okay, promise me that you will strictly keep it to yourselves?'

The demonesses huddled their inquisitive faces closer. Their voices had hushed down, but the intrigue was too great for the silent air to mask any revelation. Sita's heart churned. She did not want to hear any of it.

'It is believed she is none other than Maharani Mandodari's daughter!' said Trijata.

'What are you saying! Her daughter? Are you out of your mind Trijata?'

'Well, if there is any truth to the hearsay. Maharani Mandodari, had once given birth to a girl. But when the sages saw the child, they were shocked. They called it the one who would become master's undoing. Imagine the shame, the cause of his death—forget the gods, not even a man…but a mere girl! Master took out his sword and dashed for the child, but the queen came in between. She pleaded, rebuked, even threatened to give up her life. Master had to relent. He put that girl in a golden pot and tossed it across the ocean. It is said that master and queen stood on the shore a long time, making sure the waves carried her away and relieve them of ill luck.'

Sita's heart pounded. It was painful to keep up with its pace. What they were saying was not true. She knew her reality. She was mother earth's daughter and nothing would make her believe otherwise.

'And do you know what is said about her birth?' Trijata said, gesturing at Sita, 'That…she was first found inside a pot before being adopted!'

A collective gasp rose up. The demonesses' eyes gleamed brightly as the bonfire's light caught their slick, oily hands clamped over their mouths. They swivelled, stealing furtive glances at her.

'Why, now that tells us something! Why else do you think a man like master is cautious around her? She is no ordinary woman, not like you and me. She is but an enchantress.

'A curse!'

'An omen!'

'A wench!'

They seemed to be relishing this detail, the animation in their voices steadily sharpening, their hushed tones once again losing inhibition. Joining in their depravity, the wood cackled, the fire splintered and sputtered, and the ghostly shadows danced to the tunes of gusty winds.

'Now, here's one more thing—this is not the first time our master has abducted another woman,' confessed Trijata.

'Oh yes, we all know about the beautiful Rambha.'

'And Tapaswini.'

'Maya too.'

'Not them, I meant more like kidnapping a woman only to put an end to her.' Trijata's eyes gleamed with dark temptation.

'What?'

'Yes—and the woman was none other than Sita's mother-in-law, Kaushalya. Rumours go that a long time ago, Kaushalya was similarly captured in a chest by master and flung across the sea, but a king named Dasharath rescued her and later they married. Their first born son is the wench's husband. Ah, the play of destiny has been unfairly kind to these wenches.'

'If only master were not so kind! Why didn't he just kill them when he had the chance? At least, we wouldn't be sitting here, keeping an eye on this abhorrent one.'

'Abhorrent did you say! Ha! Ha!'

'Isn't she? Okay, evil, if you prefer!'

'Or ugly!'

'No, let's keep to wench.'

Every time their mouths opened in malevolence, the light from the bonfire caught a glint on their crooked teeth. The wind snapped and swivelled the fire, making shadows leap and dance, and the dark mood of the night continued to pass with rattles and mockery.

Sita was deeply hurt, but she didn't blame the demonesses. She knew their souls hadn't known any mercy or their hearts any compassion. Such a waste—a long life spent in ignorance.

Sita looked up at the sky. The moon was right there, dutifully smiling with consoling light. She closed her eyes and tried to fight her way to Ram. He must be angry, worried and utterly distraught. By now, he must have found her clues—the necklace, bangles, rings and anklets. Hopefully, he must have followed the direction and must have reached the coast, plotting a way to forge through.

He had overcome a lot of impossible hurdles before, surely he would do it again. Her lips involuntarily uttered his name—'Ram'. It felt good to say it out loud, to soak the sound back in. She repeated it again. And again. And again. It provided her such solace.

That night she chanted his name silently, and thereafter feverishly, and constantly. She chanted it on nights when the moon, her only known companion in the sky, would appear bright and full, and on nights it only came as a thin slither. At times, it would appear late, fighting its way through the punitive clouds, or at times, too tired to put on a challenge. Focusing her mind helped her transcend her emotions and reach a completely different plane. It stopped to matter whether the demonesses were being cruel or kind. She no longer lived in the world she saw—but the world she willed to see.

17

Unfolding of Miracles

Baaaaa. Baaaaaa. Baaaaaaaa.

Sita was halfway indoors when she heard the restless call.

'Oh, I am so sorry.' She hurried outside to the shed. Before she could even finish untying the calf, it sprinted to its mother and started suckling. The loud smacking noises made it evident how ravenous it was. The equally impatient mother nuzzled and licked her young one, bringing a smile to Sita's face.

'Pardon me! I just didn't realize how time flew by. And you'd expect I'll be less occupied without Luv and Kush.' Then she said in a whisper, 'I miss them.'

The cow's ears shot up.

'Do you understand?' A soft chuckle escaped Sita's lips. She dropped some fodder into its trough and filled the other with water. The cow took a few hasty bites, slurped some water, and looked up again.

'It's okay. You should eat.' Sita stroked it, and it returned to the fodder. Having finished nursing, the satisfied calf ambled over to Sita and began rubbing its little forehead against her, like it too sensed her loneliness. Sita gathered it to her chest and patted it gently, before tying it by its mother.

However, the cow still shifted uneasily. Its udders were swollen.

'Forgive me, let me relieve you of some weight,' Sita said, setting an earthen pot in place. Settling down, she reached out for the gentle, rhythmic ritual, and a steady stream of milk swished and frothed through.

'Waiting is never easy. I know it isn't,' Sita said in a stupor, her words drifting past the cow. She was no longer speaking of the present, but of the arduous wait she had once endured.

By now, the calf had curled up on the floor and its eyes had begun to droop. Sita too fell silent, and once again all became quiet in the hushed night, except for the low buzz of mosquitoes, and the monotonous swishing and frothing of milk.

With great agony, the initial days in Ashoka Vatika crawled into a month, and then nearly into a year. They were not much different. Sometimes Raavan came bearing gifts, sometimes threats, at times, profuse pleas to join him in the palace, and at times, warning to kill her if she did not obey. His colours changed like the turning hues of a whimsical sky, yet Sita sat unswayed. She was a piece of stone under that *shimshapa* tree, hardly flinching, hardly reacting, uttering not a word except for the incessant chant of her husband's name.

Every time, vexed by their master's humiliation, the demonesses pounced upon Sita with worse taunts and jibes, but she never allowed herself the luxury of breaking down. Her victory was hinged on nothing else but her response. So, she willed herself back to the cocooned safety of more forgiving times. On one such occasion, her mind drifted back to Panchvati.

Back at the hilltop, over their favourite boulder overlooking the orange lace of the Godavari looping and swirling through the valley. It was late afternoon, and a clear sheet of golden light glinted over the river's placid waters. The forest shimmered with life, as if someone had breathed colour and spirit back to it. Beside her, Ram rested, his face flushed with the burnished sunlight.

'Ram?'

'Hmm?'

'I still find it hard to believe what happened yesterday—it was a miracle. How did you make that happen?'

'Make what happen?'

'Don't be sly—you know I am talking about you killing Khara, Dooshan and their fourteen thousand men! How is it even humanly possible?'

'Why curtail oneself in the limits of possibility? Limits are nothing but a paradox—forever expanding.'

A smile crossed Sita's lips, 'All that is fine. Still, it was no mean feat.'

'My dear, what you can or cannot achieve is only a play of mind. What truly matters is your belief—your complete conviction. If you set your mind on the goal, and only the goal, limitations fade away.'

'Huh! You will not give me a straight answer then?'

'There is none.'

'Alright. At least tell me, when you sent me away, did you envisage victory at all?'

'I don't know. I just cleared my mind to everything but the goal.'

Sunlight glinted on his long lashes. There was certain charm in his finely drawn lips, which was sculpted with great care. Down in the valley, the river had turned pink and the evening muskier. Ram moved in closer, but Sita rose to her feet, a playful glint evident in her eyes.

'Sita!' he frowned.

'Ram,' she smiled.

'What is she saying?' said a jarring voice, not belonging to Panchvati.

'Isn't that her husband's name?' said another.

'Why does she keep chanting it?'

'Who knows? The woman is strange!'

Those voices wrenched her out of Ram's embrace and brought her back to Ashoka Vatika.

'Hush you all!' roared Trijata, 'Don't you have anything better to do. Leave her alone! Go tend to the gardens!'

Sita woke up, baffled at the hint of compassion in Trijata's eyes.

Later that night, when her throat was parched from constant chanting, Trijata came with a pot of water and Sita didn't refuse. She patted the ground beside her, and the demoness sat down. But Sita didn't stop her chants, so Trijata, not knowing what else to do, echoed after. She too started chanting. Not because she loved Ram, but because somewhere she had recognized the resilience in Sita; the power in her chants, and was looking to unburden her own mind from the trappings of her dark thoughts.

That night, Trijata fell into a blissfully deep sleep. A kind she had never experienced before. With their chief demoness asleep, the other demonesses, also weary from night long vigils, stole a chance for the much-needed respite.

The following morning Sita awoke to witness yet another miracle. Charred smell, thick enough to clog nostrils, filled the air. Enormous plumes of black smoke whipped and billowed up to the sky. It came from the palaces. Ashoka Vatika was safe, but a wild commotion overtook the place with the demonesses howling and frantically running about.

'Someone called Hanuman has set fire to Lanka!' A demoness came running.

'Who is Hanuman?'—'What about master?'—'Speak! Is he alright?'—'And how are the queens?'

'An entire wing of the palace is burnt down,' cried the demoness, 'Thankfully master and his wives managed to escape in time. But the damage has been colossal. Most of the council chambers, the treasury, stables, all minister's houses...have burnt to ash. Our golden city...burnt to ash! Everything except the Shiva temple.' She eyed Sita before continuing, 'And—surprisingly, this Ashoka Vatika.'

'Lord Shiva, have mercy on us!' cried her companion, 'But who exactly is this Hanuman? Why would he do such a thing?'

'That is something we should ask her! Tell us, wench! Wasn't he your husband's emissary? Is it true your husband is planning a war against us! Against our master?' She bent down, and bore her face over Sita, 'That husband of yours has no idea what's coming for him. Especially not after this foolishness!' She spat and walked away.

Trijata looked at Sita with a solemn expression, but Sita only smiled with sadness and relief. The time had come. Unfortunately, it was destined to bring annihilation.

Of course, Sita knew about Hanuman. Under the cover of darkness, when all the demonesses had oddly fallen asleep, Ram's emissary had sneaked into Ashoka Vatika. With the ease of apes, he swung over treetops to reach the *shimshapa* tree. And when time was propitious, he dropped Ram's valedictory ring into her lap.

When Sita looked up in shock at the sight of that deep red ring that had always adorned Ram's fingers, Hanuman clambered down and cautioned her to stay quiet. He told her how some of his friends had found her dropped ornaments and had joined Ram on his search. He told her how distraught Ram had been, not eating, not drinking, hardly sleeping, just walking miles until he came upon the sea—that stretch of impossibility. It was then that Hanuman told her about his unique boon—that he could take giant leaps. So giant, that he could even carry Sita across the ocean, and reunite her with Ram.

That suggestion brought a sudden change upon Sita. Her eyes, which only a moment ago had welled with her husband's memory, now blinked in disbelief. She was not a coward to escape in disgrace, grabbing hold of someone's back.

Her voice boomed as she said, 'My pride has been violated! Ram must come and reclaim it. Only by defeating Ravana will his own honour be restored.'

She pressed on, 'Tell me—how does he plan to cross the ocean? If he has no way, then he must find one. Crossing the sea won't be easy. Insist that he comes up with a strategy.'

It was then that Hanuman saw what Ram had always seen in Sita, a woman with strength and clarity, whose self-worth mattered more than any temptation or torture. He left embarrassed, carrying Sita's *choodamani* in exchange, the only jewel left behind in her hair. The task of crossing the sea would be impossible. Yet he knew Ram would. For a woman like Sita, anyone would.

And Ram did.

It had been a week since the burning. The plumes of smoke had lightened in colour, with the remaining few trailing out from Raavan's atrocious rule. Sita knew her own time would follow soon.

A demoness came running, 'Did you hear, her husband is here in Lanka? He is stationed at Mount Suvela.'

Sita sprang from the tree, her gaze flashing northward. Nothing was visible except an endless stretch of green. Still the proximity was comforting.

'You mean to say he managed to cross the ocean!' asked another. 'How so? Does he own a flying chariot too?'

'Ah, no such thing! I heard he managed to build a bridge of sorts.'

'A bridge! What? Across the entire stretch of the sea?' A collective gasp rose up. Sita's eyes sparkled, for the first time in ages.

'As for you, wench,' the demoness pointed at her, 'before you start to get your hopes up, let me add that he has only come with a bunch of forest dwellers.'

'Ha! You don't say!' laughed her companions.

'Exactly! Can you believe his audacity…here with a bunch of savages to take on our master! The Lord of Lanka! And they bring the most basic of maces and spears.' Her insensitive barbs continued, 'Huh! For all you know, the war will be over before it even begins.'

But no such thing happened. The war waged with utter desperation and determination from either side. Even from Ashoka Vatika, the incessant raining of arrows could be seen. It painted the battlefield with blood. Fallen bodies, devoid of limbs, or heads, or torsos, lay scattered all around, for pickings for eager vultures. The dark air flickered, as maces banged on maces, spears chinked against spears, and the swords cut through each other. Those deprived of any weapons took on the others with their limbs, fists, nails, and even teeth. The passion was terrifying.

Messengers filed in from the battlefield, bearing the demonesses news more grim than comforting. They told them of the growing demise of their prolific warriors—Indrajit, Jambumali, Shatrughan, Virupaksh, Khumbhkarn, and then of their husbands, brothers and sons. Lanka was steadily losing it all. Raavan was steadily losing it all.

The demonesses repented their jibes, and every act of previous malice. They beat their chests and banged their heads, and lay on the ground in delirium for days, turning their matted hair one with the dust. In distress they pulled at it, and out shone their dagger-like teeth. Their bloodshot eyes became bereft of kohl, having washed over their cheeks in a dry stream of caked mud. But everything, including this futile infliction of pain, could not assuage their suffering hearts.

Wishing such agony on her tormentors was not something Sita had desired. She picked them off the ground and smoothed their hair. That tranquilizing measure of magic in her embrace calmed them. Albeit a little too late, they too finally discerned for themselves what Trijata had discovered in Sita a while ago.

Finally arrived the most dreaded news. After a month of intense combat, Ram's arrow had whipped through Raavan's heart. He had looked at the arrow in disbelief, his feet unsteady, still not ready to give up. Then, with a deafening thud, he collapsed. The battlefield blurred, and the last thing he saw was the sun setting over Ram's back.

The sun behind Ram's back was how Sita too had seen Ram for the first time. Only then, it was rising.

Part Four

18

Chariot of Wings

Sita carried the freshly squeezed pot of milk inside. Although Guruma had insisted not to bring anything, she decided to prepare *payasam*. The ladies cherished her cooking, and it would be a nice gesture.

She set the pot on fire. Once the milk came to a boil, she removed a few logs to reduce the heat and added some jaggery. Soon everything took on a brown tint. Sita took a whiff; the sweetness seemed right.

Once the milk reduced by half, Sita added the soaked rice. At once, everything frothed and rose, threatening to fall off the rim. She picked up the wooden spoon and stirred it until it sank back. The sight of the froth stirred a memory—of the surging sea foam she had seen from the Pushpak Viman.

Sita was back in the Pushpak Viman, the flying chariot, only this time returning to Ayodhya. Raavan's righteous brother, Vibhishan, who had joined forces with Ram, had been newly consecrated on the Lankan throne. The grateful successor had offered Ram a lot of treasure, but Ram refused everything apart from the aerial chariot, to help swiftly make their way back. Fourteen years were over, and now every moment away throbbed like a bruise.

Ram stood beside Sita, watching the clouds curl and drift. Laxman, Hanuman and a few others who wanted to go to Ayodhya were on the storey above, leaving Ram and Sita to themselves. There was so much to talk, but somehow an unsettling distance had set between them. Ironically, it had nothing to with their long separation.

'Your presence of mind was remarkable. If you hadn't dropped the ornaments, how else would I have reached you?' Ram looked deep into Sita's eyes.

The colour on her cheeks rose. He never withheld from showering her with praises. Yet today, it sounded forced.

'The forest dwellers had seen it falling from above. They clambered onto treetops and saw you being carried away.'

Sita gripped the chariot's rail so tight that it turned her knuckles white. It was on this very carriage that Raavan had clasped her, had held her close while she screamed for help. Sensing her discomfort, Ram reached out and rubbed her shoulders. Months of captivity had left her frail, reducing her to half her size.

'I am sorry, I couldn't come sooner.' He kissed her forehead and smoothened the floating strands of hair. Sita hadn't uttered a word and it saddened him.

'I searched for you everywhere. By the lake, on the other side of the river, climbed the hilltop, went to our boulder. But you were nowhere. Then back at the cottage I found a pitcher discarded by the bushes. Saw the drag marks run a certain distance, and then, nothing. I knew something was amiss. It took me four months to come across these tribes. They handed me your necklace, told me about the chariot. They even followed you a long way until you disappeared. Very kindly they offered to help, and together we forged ahead, meeting many such tribes who reiterated similar stories, handing me your anklet, your bangles. Then we saw broken bits, of what might have been the hood of this chariot.' Both of them looked up, before Ram continued, 'At last, we came upon Jatayu by the sea. Oh, the poor bird! Had pus and blood all over. He had saved his last breath only to inform me about you.'

Sita shuddered, remembering his helpless fall, then pointed at the miracle below, 'How did you build it, Ram?'

Slashed across the impassable sea was a curious black stretch with waves breaking on either side, and edged with foamy white borders. It was the famed bridge the demonesses had mentioned. Massive boulders were piled one atop the other, rising from the mysterious depths to the ocean's lapping crest. Over it, Ram's returning army leapt and bounded happily.

'Putting together the bridge itself wasn't so difficult, except it took a while.' Ram said, 'Appeasing of the sea proved more trying.'

'Tell me about it. I want to hear everything,' she said, finally turning to face him.

The last rays of the golden sun picked up Ram's sharp nose and chiseled cheeks. Hesitatingly, she rested her head over his shoulders and allowed him to paint her a picture.

And as he narrated his journey, she imagined him scavenge the forests, the deep valleys, walk tirelessly without much food or sleep, until he was upon the edge of the land. She saw his face, wrinkled with worry and exhaustion, scanning with dread the impassable sea. The waves crashing under his feet, each crash mocking his helplessness; every sweep back, a teasing invitation.

The sea, both a barrier and a bond—dividing them in distance yet joining them in touch. She knew that strange intimacy would have turned him even more restless.

'I wanted to swim,' Ram continued, 'To waste no time. But the sea was relentless. You could call it unnatural, as if under a spell. No matter my ardent efforts, it wouldn't let me pass. In fact, the more I strived, the stubborn it became.'

He continued, and she imagined him dive into the foamy sea. She saw waves like waterfall crashing down; the water screeching, roaring, tossing him back on the shore. His knees crumbling into the sand, him lying beaten like a piece of dead wood, panting, coughing up brackish water. She imagined his face covered in gritty sand, water dripping down long lashes, regarding the sun plunge with a despairing sound, and even at night, picking himself again and hurling at the morbidly white waves.

'I fought, I begged, I prayed.' Ram continued, 'I prayed to Shiva. Built a Shivalinga with sand, but the enemy wasn't just the sea. Never could I have imagined the heavens rain with the vehemence as it did then. It washed away my Shivalinga into a stream of brown. I understood that Shiva himself was against me. After all, Raavan was his greatest devotee.'

Sita flinched at the mention of Raavan's name. Ram took a brief pause, then continued, 'So, I prayed with my eyes closed. Summoned him. If Shiva wanted to desert me, then he better take my life. I was ready to give up everything but never my quest for you. Days blurred into each other, they stretched to a month, but the deluge kept worsening. It was only when I understood there would be no answer to my prayers, that I picked the *Brahmastra*.'

Brahmastra! *The weapon of total annihilation!*

Sita's eyes flared with a mixture of confusion and shock. It bewildered her to think that the one who had borne the loss of his kingdom without a flinch, had been driven to such desperate extremes. Suddenly, she felt a pang of deep regret for all that had passed upon their first meeting in Lanka.

He kept talking and she imagined his face hardening, his eyes turning an intimidating shade of red, aiming the gleaming arrow at the sea—that *Brahmastra*—the string stretching, the bow creaking, and with it the world plunging into nervous silence.

'Just as I was about to strike, an unexpected miracle unfolded,' said Ram, 'Lightning struck, splitting the sea and turning it wilder. The water rocked and rose in mad rebellion, and then, very suddenly slumped down. It oozed all the way to me. And retreated. Like it was nothing more than a shallow pool of placid water. The netherworlds seemed to have drunk a part of the sea. The downpour also ceased, and a golden shaft of light peered down the clouds. Finally cleared of all obstructions, we built the bridge.'

Ram looked down, 'I can never thank them enough, these men. Despite only knowning me a few months, they kept going, with not a care of day or night, hunger or sleep.'

Sita also looked down. In their hands were bows, maces, axes and long spears. Some also carried flags bearing Ram's name. She could make out euphoric cries of exultation. How attractive was Ram's persona, to inspire devotion from complete strangers. How powerful his will, that not just men but nature itself succumbed in complete subjugation.

True, their meeting in Lanka was not ideal. But the fact remained that he loved her fiercely. And while the world vied for his love, he only vied for hers. That spoke quite a lot for itself. The strength of a union lies in its acceptance of both virtues and vices, and she was ready to overlook everything.

The Pushpak Viman glided through the cumulus clouds, carrying them back to Ayodhya. Miles and miles of white light filled the vision. After fourteen long years, the days of darkness were finally over.

19

Aloofness

Sita took the payasam off the *chulha* and doused out the cooking fire. The cottage now felt dim, with the light of the single diya on the alcove no longer sufficient, so she picked more and lit them using the one already burning. The damp wicks took a while to catch fire, briefly sizzling before springing up. She took a diya to the cow shed. The mother and the calf were fast asleep, heads snuggled against one another.

She brought the *payasam* to the verandah under the cooling light of the moon and sat down placing a diya beside her. Its flame twinkled and wavered delicately, casting a golden glow across her face. She remembered a similar such glow on the face of Ayodhyawasis. With diyas in hand, that is how they had welcomed her back with Ram. The light of their lives and their rightful heir was back—even if fourteen years too late.

Night had already set in by the time the Pushpak Viman descended on the outskirts of Ayodhya. Ram's younger brothers, Bharat and Shatrughan stood waiting with a vast assembly of ministers and soldiers. The brothers rushed into each other's arms, faces buried on one another's shoulders, their joy indescribable, their words lost in tears and laughter. Ayodhya, too, had waited with equal eagerness, and already a din of euphoria was rising in the air.

Bharat insisted that it would hardly be appropriate for the heir to enter the city on a gifted chariot, and had brought another. The chariot gleamed under the light of torches, and had the proud Ikshvaku flag fluttering atop.

Ram held out his hands for Sita. 'We are finally home!' he said.

'And finally, the world shall have its greatest ruler,' she reiterated to her beaming husband.

The wheels rolled on, and the sound of drums and conch shells grew louder, mirroring the thumping of their own excited hearts. Soon, their cherished Ayodhya was in front of their eyes, dressed in a manner that took their breath away. The chariot came to a slow halt, as did the music on the other side of the gateway. Everything felt silent just like the night. And just like the night, Ayodhya twinkled with a million or more earthen diyas—that framed the parapets, lined the window sills and door openings, and shone over colourful rangolis in the front yards. Sita squeezed Ram's hands as they took in the sight. The light shone as well on the streaming tears of the subjects who each held a diya in their hands. Tonight, every kind of darkness would be warded away—including that of the night.

They were greeted into the palace by Mother Kaushalya and Mother Sumitra who expressed love and relief, and by Mother Kaikeyi who shared her remorse. Thereafter, Kaikeyi shut the doors of her chamber and retreated into oblivion.

Otherwise, they were good days, jubilant days. Ram was

crowned king, and Sita sat beside him at the court, both as his queen and a valued advisor. The cries of *Ram-Sita, Ram-Sita* once again filled the air, and once again, it felt good to hear their names wrapped around, like they would never be separated again.

Or so they thought.

In the quiet streets of Ayodhya lived a washerman. His house lay outside the walled city, surrounded by other houses of cobblers, potters, carpenters, artisans and court-bards. The house had a slanted roof, a small verandah opening onto a front courtyard—quite similar to the other houses in appearance, though not in upkeep. Cobwebs framed its patio, dirt piled up its entrance. The plants in the front yard were stunted in growth, with none that fruited or flowered.

Bitter voices were usually heard from the house. But one fateful morning, the rebuke got so loud that a crowd began to gather outside.

'You spent the night away! And you still have the audacity to bring back your sordid face!'

The washerman shoved his wife out. He carried a copper vase, and a repulsive smell emanated from him, that of sweat and *tadi*, the provincial alcohol of date palms. The woman herself was dressed gaudily.

'Get a grip on yourself! How are you even talking! You're disgraceful!' retorted his wife.

'Get a grip—! You say I should get a grip? Listen, you woman, I am no Maharaja Ram that I will take back a tainted wife. Out of my house, you disgraceful hag!'

He smashed the vase, which clattered noisily, spilling its content all over. The humiliated woman covered her face and left. As did everyone else, shocked not so much at the washerman's treatment of his wife, but more at the deprecating remark against their king.

In no time, that spark kindled a suspicion which spread like a wildfire. It stirred up disparaging thoughts in everyone's minds and turned them restless with curiosity. They wondered if the same doubts pounded the conscience of others.

'Do you think the washerman might be right?'—'Haven't we all heard of Raavan's famed lust; what happened to Rambha and Tapaswini...'—'Twelve months is a long time after all.'

There were a few conscientious subjects, but their rebuttal was feeble against the appeal of dark voices. They gathered by the fire after a day of hard work to debate and repeat their suspicions. This continued for so long that the lines between fact and fiction started to blur. They replaced Ram with themselves and Sita with their own wives, and based on this sense of personal affliction, passed a verdict. Every turn of the prahar, they intended to disperse from around that treasonous bonfire, but temptation held them back. The closing comment kept sliding from 'but who knows the truth' to 'what if this is the truth' to 'if it is so then...'—'our king should set an example'.

By the time the light of the bonfire finally dimmed to that of the rising sun, the entire kingdom was infected. Taints were laid on the character of an innocent woman. Sita was declared guilty.

While the rumours were welling outside, something tender was budding within the palace. Sita's belly swelled with Ram's heir.

It swelled beyond comfort, heavy for her delicate feet. Her already thick hair shimmered with new life, falling in waves more lustrous than before, and the hint of roundness on her cheeks made her look more endearing. The ever-doting Maharani Kaushalya ensured that Sita spent most of her time resting in her chambers.

That evening, Ram returned from the court to find Sita painting. A large canvas lay before her, alive with colours—bold strokes of green, blue, and orange coming together in vibrant harmony.

'Beautiful!' The sudden voice made her swivel. Ram was regarding her work in awe.

'Isn't it!' she replied with a captivating spark.

'Panchavati?'

'Indeed! Our favourite spot. Just how many evenings we spent by the boulder there.' She reached out to put the last touch of white paint over the raatrani bush.

'A loving memory indeed.'

'But it doesn't need to be a memory.' A hint of mischief had crept into her voice.

'What do you mean?'

'That we can still go on a little sojourn. I dearly miss the smell of greenery, the play of animals. Do you think we could go? Just for a few days?'

Ram didn't react, like the question had never been asked. Just kept looking at her with a vacant expression. There was an odd foreboding expression on his face, an inkling that weakly tugged at her. Sita wondered if he hid something. If something had happened at court.

'Will you not take me Ram?' She gazed into his eyes, searching, but he remained unresponsive.

She reached out to touch his face, endeavouring to peel through the mask, but he averted his gaze. Then he took hold of her hands, and placed it on her belly. There was life thrumming inside, the promise of a bright future. Their bond had strengthened. He laid his head atop hers and they stood like that for a moment.

Then Ram closed his eyes, shutting the secret behind. It was discomfiting, his crushing silence—that proverbial habit of not condifing much especially his predicaments. They were the sacred riddles he kept detangling on his own. But Sita put the thoughts away, lest they attract ill fate.

She simply lay wrapped in his arms, thinking of the future, knowing not for a moment that he was thinking of an altogether different one. That, in that moment, only he knew—it was their last embrace ever.

20

The Second Decree

After the growing darkness had engulfed everything in its path, it crept into Sita's mind like a stealthy, uninvited guest. She knew she needed something to occupy herself with. With the *payasam* already prepared, and the dinner at Guruma's, there was hardly much to do. Her eyes scanned the dimness and fell over the mat with the gaping holes. It could certainly do with a bit of repair. Sita fetched a pile of dry reed from the shed and began knitting.

But as she tried to weave, the reed snapped and pierced her thumb, leaving a speck of blood. She tried again, and again it splintered. Disregarding the prickings, she worked furiously, which only left her with a heavily sore thumb, and a still unfilled gap. Sita stopped, knowing fully well the problem wasn't with the reed, as with the splintered memories. Those memories carefully wrapped in the inner recess of her heart now surged through—bitter then tender, intimate then sweet—pinching her all the same. Sita tossed the mat aside and squeezed her eyes, under their almost physical impact.

Sita tried not to make much of Ram's aloofness from the evening before. In fact, they slept particularly deep that night, for the fallacious worries had sapped out too much energy. When she woke up at the crack of dawn, with the sun gently touching her face, she found Ram already awake, regarding her with unusual tenderness. The inkling from last night returned.

'Is something the matter?'

Once again, he chose not to reply. Just gave an unconvincing shake of his head, and left for the court. His reticence was unsettling, but she decided to overlook it, and got ready to embrace another day. Heavy on her feet, she conducted most of her engagements from her reception chamber. There was a proposal for laying new streets on the edge of town, followed by an appeal for different handiwork opportunities for women, and thereafter a meeting with the philosophers. By midday, Sita was exhausted. She had only had a brief respite before the next visitors were ushered in.

They were her sisters.

'Urmila! What a pleasant surprise!' beamed Sita, 'Come in, my dear. Oh look, there's Mandavi and Shrutakirti too.'

'We thought we will check on you,' beamed back Urmila, 'How are you keeping?'

'Just look at that glow on your face!' remarked Mandavi.

'Isn't she the most charming expecting mother?' chimed in Shrutakirti.

The sisters embraced Sita and sat around her; the rich drapes of their sarees elegantly spreading out. It didn't take long for a heartening conversation to strike up and the chamber reverberated with the sound of laughter. A cuckoo on the mango tree outside cooed emphatically, as if in a bid to outweigh their cadence. The innocuous envy made the sisters giggle, and in turn the cuckoo raised its pitch. From the finely carved windows, a sweet-smelling breeze drifted in, and reminded the ladies of their childhood orchard in Mithila.

'Fate has been really kind to us. Otherwise, it's rare for sisters to continue living together,' smiled Sita.

'It has been equally cruel, separating us for years,' said Mandavi. All eyes flicked towards her. Although she had intended that remark only as a separation from Sita, they wondered if she implied it for Bharat.

After Ram's denial to return with Bharat from Chitrakoot, the younger brother didn't accede to the throne either. Instead, he resolved to lead a life of asceticism by the outskirts of Ayodhya, leaving Mandavi alone in the palace, much like Urmila without Laxman. As for Shrutakirti, she only had the fortune of being around an extremely torn and distant Shatrughan—who had to administer the kingdom on everyone's behalf. Those were distressing times. Maharaja Dasharath's assurance to Maharaja Janak, that of looking after his daughters, had indeed fallen short.

'I am so sorry you all had to go through so much,' Sita said in a small voice.

'Oh, please don't. While we may have had our share of woes, none was quite as testing as yours, with your abduction, and everything that followed. Truth be told, your courage is an inspiration, not only to us, but to all the women of the kingdom,' said Urmila. The younger sisters agreed, shuffling a bit closer.

Urmila squeezed Sita's shoulders and continued, 'The worst is over, and here we are finally sitting together.'

'Yes Didi, your motherhood has brought a fresh start to everything!' joined in Mandavi.

The discussion once again turned jovial, from one about the imminent arrival, back to the loving stories of their own childhood. And once again, the ring of laughter seeped out of the chamber.

Unbeknownst to it all, a pair of feet headed towards Sita's chamber. They carried a message. Its burden such, that they moved with dragged effort.

'Maharani, Prince Laxman requests your audience,' interrupted an attendant.

'Laxman? Yes, please send him in.'

Laxman walked in, his eyes pinned to the ground.

'What a surprise! Welcome, Laxman! Today seems like a lucky day. But I wonder if you have only come looking for me or…someone else?' Sita said with a friendly jibe. Urmila recoiled, and a suppressed round of laughter went around.

But Laxman only had to look up for everyone to fall heavily silent. His eyes were bloodshot and his forehead was creased deeply. It was evident, the message was meant only for Sita. Taking a cue, everyone got up. Urmila shot an anxious look towards Laxman before heading out. He waited until the tinkering of their anklets completely dulled down.

Sita felt the weak inkling from last night return.

'I have—' Laxman began, but his throat was jammed.

'What is the matter?'

'I have come with a m-message…from brother.'

'From Ram?' She squinted. Strangely, the tips of her fingers had started to tingle.

'There has been an …unrest in court.'

'And?'

'There was a case of domestic dispute brought in at court… between a washerman and his wife.'

'So?'

'The washerman was forced by his neighbours to…accept his wife but the wife—'

Sita's temples pounded at the sight of sweat on Laxman's forehead. Something told her the affair was related to her, and it was not pleasant. 'And did all this happen yesterday?' Sita cut him urgently. Her voice firm, in an odd contrast to Laxman's.

'Yesterday? Yes, yesterday.'

A welling sickness rose within Sita. Ram had not confessed anything, but it was evident how uncharacteristically disturbed he was. Now she knew Laxman carried the secret behind Ram's aloofness, he carried the words Ram could not bring himself to utter. The question remained—*why Laxman? Why did Ram not tell her himself?* But she reserved her silence, leaving Laxman with no choice but to finish the message.

'The washerman has denied taking his wife back as she had…had spent the night at another man's.' Laxman cringed, the ordeal of conveying the message was too much for his troubled mind. 'There has been an unrest in the masses after he…he accused brother.'

'Accused Ram! What for?'

He nodded, vigorously. Then said no more. A tense silence hung in the air—silence that screeched louder than words. Of words which were loathsome and unsparing. Words of accusation. Of insult and humiliation. Sita had been carried to Lanka. She had been there for many months, many days and many nights. Of course, the world crafted a clearer tale—a helpless woman and a ravenous king. Her face contorted, but she was stronger than that.

'The *dhobi* accused brother of being an unjust king. He said the king should follow the same rules set for the rest of society.

'The rule?' It was a question asked flat, in the manner of a statement.

'Erm...a woman who left her husband's abode shouldn't be accepted.'

Laxman gulped, then continued, 'It has led to an uprising.'

'And?'

'Ayodhya thinks brother has broken the rules he set for others.'

The horror of realization had already gripped Sita before Laxman could confirm everything in utterance. After a long painful silence she said, 'I am listening.'

He gasped for breath, like he was suffocated.

'Brother Ram...he has asked you to leave the kingdom. I am so sorry. I am terribly sorry.'

Sita blinked. Those were strong words. She had already been anticipating them but now that they had been confirmed by Laxman, she found herself fighting. She wondered if Laxman had really said them. *Did he not know how much Ram loved her? Wasn't their trust in each other too strong for such confounded accusations? Besides, Ram was well aware of her truth. Didn't he know she was expecting his child? What did Mother Kaushalya have to say? Surely, she must be broken, pleading him with inconsolable sobs? Ram could never have said this. Wasn't he born from the gods? His judgment could never be clouded. He had loved her ardently. He sought her out from another world.* The thoughts made her dizzy, and her beliefs crumpled like quicksand. Her knees buckled over.

'Watch out for that child,' Laxman leapt forward, but she would not let him. The concern was a mockery. She was not weak. She thrust her hands and commanded herself back on her trembling legs.

Laxman was saying something, but her ears had started to buzz. Was he giving explanations on behalf of Ram, saying how Ram's hands were tied, that it was as much a sacrifice for him? Was he saying that Ram's duty towards the kingdom was more noble than their personal affliction? Or maybe he was simply saying 'I am deeply sorry' but with pursed lips, 'I know this is wrong. I will speak to Brother,' but with weak tears.

It no longer mattered. Quicker than she had expected, everything turned hollow and useless. This should have been a private matter between a husband and a wife, but Laxman had become a chasm between her and Ram. This was not a sin he deliberately committed, nor a punishment he deserved. Still, how could she disregard being belittled so terribly?

'Where can I take you? Is there somewhere you would rather be?'

What a question to ask a person being evicted from their home? Where did she have to go? But being the graceful woman she was, she showed no reaction, but for the faint shake of her head.

'I am really sorry...but in this case I am left with no choice but to escort you to the forests. I will be waiting by the chariot.'

And so he left, leaving Sita with her hands pressed on her belly.

21

A Deep Sleep

Sita sat on the verandah, regarding the fireflies swarming in sinuous laps, their lights blinking every now and then. How inspiring they were, these independent little beings, carrying their own light. She too had once carried the light of the Ikshvakus in her womb—alone, helpless, left to fend for herself. A wry smile escaped her lips, and she reached out to wipe it. If only thoughts could be as easily wiped. It had been more than ten years since the verdict. Still the memory brought fresh pain.

Laxman had left her alone in her chamber of crushing emptiness. Everything fell strangely silent. From somewhere, a soft wind fluttered the raatrani creeper outside her window. A flower tumbled and fell at her feet. Sita tried counting its petals—six or five. Her eyes, heavy with tears, defied her. She tried again, and again she failed. She could only see its withered petals, much like her husband's withered love. Yet her heart wished, wished with a fervent desire, that he would come and say it was all a big mistake; that banishing her was unthinkable, abhorrent. She imagined him breaking down on his knees, taking her hands in his own tear-soaked ones, lamenting and cursing; that he would embrace her, ask her to forget, to forgive. After all, one only hurts their loved ones, not strangers.

But no such thing happened. Ram was a righteous king. And righteousness is a burdensome thing. He must have been sitting at court after having had made up his mind. Now she had to make up hers.

She may have stood like that for an hour or two, and when she finally stepped out of her chamber, she was unmistakably distant. There was no hesitation in her steps or tears in her eyes, no anger, bitterness or pity. No anklet rung on her feet, and no bangles chimed on her wrists, for she had taken them all off. Clad in a simple saree, all she carried from Ayodhya was an unnerving hollowness. When she reached the carriage, there was not a soul waiting for her. That epitome of dignity got into the carriage on her own, flinching not even once when Laxman yanked the horse. Ram saw his wife discreetly from the palace windows, holding her spine erect, looking gracefully ahead.

The wheels began to crunch the gravel as they rolled ahead, and a kindly dust gathered after. Soon she was lost forever. Ram clutched the curtain in his sweaty palms and convinced himself to stay strong. He couldn't commit the same mistake as his father. He wouldn't let his personal life come before his duty towards his kingdom. Ironically, he ended up committing the exact same sin as Maharaja Dasharath. He never afforded his wife the dignity of seeking her counsel. When Ram decided to put forward his duties above his personal life, he inadvertently took a decision on behalf of Sita, about her life. Not only did he command her wishes but also painted her truth. Or much rather a lie, for Sita had never so much as even stepped a foot inside Raavan's palace.

The carriage forged ahead unhindered with the numbing sound of the wheels and the tapping of the horses' hooves. There was no one to stop them. The people had all stayed inside as per their desire—to banish their queen in disgrace. As the wheels rocked and swayed over the uneven path, bile rose into Sita's throat, but she decided to stay quiet. Soon they crossed the imposing gateways and rode past the gurgling Saryu, with sweeping fields and farmers toiling in the late afternoon light. Even there, nobody seemed to notice. Either they were too busy with their lives, or she was simply invisible. The scenery melted into open grasslands, where the portly cows grazed unaware of her passing, stopping only for intermittent breaks to admire the beauty of the ever-so-sparkling Saryu. Then the vegetation started to grow dense, and the trees turned ancient. They stretched to the sky, as a portal into the forests, inviting her into their world of gloom. The *bargad*, sal, peepal and mahogany all stood clustered—their branches long and entwined, whispering and exchanging forbidden secrets. Soon they would discover hers and absorb it too.

In a manner that felt too abrupt, the carriage halted, and made the horses neigh and skitter. Laxman froze. He took a while before slithering down—the courageous, well-built one's face was flushed as if on fire.

Sita realized it was the final halt, and climbed down unaided, her face without a trace of malice. Beyond the clearings, the sun was speedily sucking its light. She gazed confounded, as if it too were dying.

'You had been our companion for fourteen long years during the exile,' Sita said to Laxman, her eyes still pinned on the dipping sun. 'Never slept a wink to watch over us. Now that protector leaves me in the forest. All at a time, when I am due with the future heir!' A sigh escaped her lips. 'The same protector who once insisted I remain indoors when he left in search for Ram, now ushers me outside. This time it's not the bounds of home, but an entire kingdom.' She let out a little laugh, 'But what causes me greater pain is that look of pity on your face—for me.'

There was no wind and the syllables hung in the air. Laxman stared dumbfounded, for it was all very true. What right did he have to pity her, when he himself wasn't a man in harmony with his own thinking? Pointless tears streamed down his face.

Sita turned and started to walk away, caring not for his silent sobs or the sound of the departing carriage. Everything had ceased to matter. She walked away from the setting sun, further into the forest, which turned colder and lonelier.

In time, night fell with an unfamiliar darkness. The sky abandoned by stars showed up with a dismal moon. Without knowing where she was headed, Sita kept going. Soon, the clouds turned against her, sullying whatever remained to vision. In time, the clouds parted, and once again everything took on a ghostly glow. The wind rushed with a kind of madness suggestive of someone chasing it. It scattered dry leaves on its passing, whipped through Sita's saree, and then returned, like it was stuck in a terrible maze, from which it had no escape. Neither was there any for Sita. Everywhere danger lurked—stones and dried branches for her to topple over, hunger or thirst to die of. As if heartbreak alone wasn't simply enough.

The animals began to warn each other of the presence of an uninvited visitor. After all, the forest was theirs. Sita saw their eyes glowing; they were slithering, prowling, leaping; here one moment, gone the next. She quickened her pace, but no matter where she went, the eyes just kept following.

A shrill cry came from the high branches, but it was difficult to tell who it belonged to, for the branches were all snaked in and knotted tightly, trapping her in their distressing world. And then she heard another sound, an all too familiar pattering of rain, and waited with nervous trepidation. But it took an excruciating while as it gathered on the canopy, before trickling down.

Plop!

Plop!

A few angry birds, aroused from sleep, began screeching and blaming her in a deathly chorus. Every mistake was now hers.

Sita shut out the sounds and strode ahead, caring not for the thorny branches. Mud kicked off her feet. She was shivering. The rain had turned the ground slippery, including the moss covered stone she stepped on. She stumbled. Her head hit something hard. There was probably blood. The darkness in front merged with the one behind her eyes. And then her eyes began to close, and very slowly, the hooting of the owl turned distant, and stopped altogether.

Part Five

22

Perplexing Patterns

A certain mystic quality had taken over the cloudy night sky. Sita looked up. A few lazy clouds lay unsurely scattered in the patch over the ashram. They had nowhere to go—homeless and abandoned—just how she had once been. If it wasn't for Sage Valmiki, her life would have been very different.

'Are you alright?'

The cool air was abuzz with the frenzied twittering of birds.

'Are you okay?'

She could hear the singing of birds—it was a mix of melodious tones, high-pitched calls and cacophonous cawing. In between, a brief flapping of some large wings.

'Daughter, can you hear me?'

The call caught her attention. She hadn't opened her bleary eyes but could discern a kind voice. The eager, dissonant chorus of birds took over again. Sounds mixed dubiously with each other, like dream with reality, hope with delusion, rejection with compassion.

'Open your eyes, daughter.'

And Sita did. Slowly and weakly. Rough thick trunks shot all the way to the sky, holding up a blanket of dense green. From between the gaps, white light streamed in, bringing tears to her eyes. She blinked. Then blinked again. Her head was hurting. The twittering was real.

'Your forehead—it's bruised.'

A kindly face peered over and masked the dazzling glare. A compassionate face, one with serene eyes and a faint resting smile. He had dark skin and a very narrow frame. His flowing beard was milky-white, as was his hair, tied in a bun with *rudraksh* beads. The same beads adorned his neck and wrists. His *angavastram* and dhoti were ochre yellow. A sage! Sita sat up, brought the drape of her saree above her head in reverence and bowed down.

'Blessings be upon you! Whatever happened to your head, daughter?'

For a moment Sita was stunned, not knowing what he was talking about, but once the realization dawned, she did not know what to reply. *How to choose between embarrassment and a lie?* Her answer could have entailed everything or nothing at all. She kept her head bowed low.

'Why don't you come with me? My hermitage is only a few steps away.'

Sita peered ahead but the thicket was too dense. She had reached the forest's deepest part, forsaken of all settlements. She turned towards the sage, feeling overwhelmed at his show of concern, and then remembered the last time she had trusted a sage.

'You are very welcome to stay there for as long as you like. It is a small hermitage beside the peaceful Tamsa river.'

Sita remained silent. It felt awkward, uncomfortable.

'Don't worry, daughter, everything will be alright. Just allow me to guide you.'

Something about his calming demeanour felt strangely familiar. Of course, she had never met him before, yet he strongly reminded her of someone. Or something. A sense of comfort? Safety?

'The hermitage has about fifty people, including men and women. Even little children.'

Sita looked down at the swell of her belly. Her saree was covered in deep blotches of mud. But the embarrassment ran much deeper.

'Don't hesitate so much. Trust me, you will be very welcome there. Why don't you just follow me?'

Sita nodded faintly and got up. In the situation she was in, the sage felt like a light out of a trapped world, sent from the heavens to steer her. He walked slowly, mindful of her state; yet with an assuredness that indicated his familiarity with the surroundings. He spoke to keep her company, told her about the various trees, plants, animals and insects. He talked of the meditative calm of the forest, cautioned her of the fallen branches and waited patiently when she took time to climb difficult paths.

'Shall we rest for a while to catch some breath?' Saying this, the sage sat on a large rock and gestured Sita to take another. Out of respect, she chose a lower one. Blue and green winged butterflies swarmed in the air camouflaging in and out of the foliage. A friendly one rested on the sage's shoulder.

'I...I don't know what I would have done if you hadn't found me,' Sita tried to find her voice.

'I would have. I was looking for you.'

'Looking for me!' Sita's eyes shot up, 'D-do you know me?'

'You are Maharani Sita—the queen of Ayodhya,' he smiled gently.

'And you knew you would find me in the forest?'

'Yes, daughter.'

'Ram? Has he sent—'

'No. Not him.'

Sita's face fell.

'I am very sorry to disappoint you,' he apologized. 'Having said that, I am certain he would have made sure that Prince Laxman dropped you close enough to my hermitage, even if not exactly there, so sooner or later you would have found a safe place.'

It didn't make any sense. How did he know so much?

'From what I see, Prince Laxman might have hesitated to drop you at my hermitage. He would have feared my disapproval.'

Sita's eyes began to well up. The indignation was still fresh. 'But how do you know so much? I guess, it relieves me in a way. Still?'

'It's a long story. But one you must know.' He gathered his thoughts before continuing, 'You see, our lives are connected in ways too bewildering to understand.'

'Connected? Our lives?'

'Yes. And Maharaja Ram's.' He nodded in acknowledgement, 'As it happens, I am blessed with a divine gift of clairvoyance by the most revered of sages, Naarad Muni. He blessed me to see what others cannot—visions of events far away as well as those yet to come. This is so I could write the happenings of your lives.'

'The great Naarad Muni? You mean, the divine sage?'

'That's right...the one who carries news and wisdom between gods and men.'

'But why would he ask to write about our lives?'

'It's a lot to take in. Allow me to tell you everything from the beginning.'

And so, the sage, took a deep breath and began.

'It was a long time ago. I was studying the vedas at my cottage when I heard an all too familiar calling of '*Naarayan Naarayan*'. I was honoured to find Naarad Muni at my door. It was a great honour. His visits had always formed the pivotal turning points in my life. After enquiring about the many gods, I asked whether he knew of any mortal on earth whose virtues might compare to those in heaven. You see, I had heard a prophecy, that in time an idol would come to earth, blessed with all sixteen virtues considered unattainable for mortals. You know, the sixteen virtues, right? Courage and wisdom, truth and compassion, strength—'

'Patience, humility...' Sita replied.

'Yes! Basically, every virtue the gods themselves take pride in. Such a being, Naarad Muni said, is already among us.'

Sita continued to listen in respectful silence.

'And that's when he told me about Maharaja Ram. Not only was he righteous and gracious but brilliant at scholastic learnings and war skills. He told me about his rare beauty—his lotus-shaped eyes, his long, powerful arms, and above all, his kind, compassionate, and selfless nature.'

Sita's eyes pooled. It was true. Ram indeed had all those qualities, and much more. Yet she felt slighted. Not by what the sage said, but by her own heart, which, despite everything, still loved Ram.

'Daughter, as much as I am devoted to Lord Ram, I know

that you yourself reflect the same qualities. There is no difference between you and him. You yourself are a gift from mother earth. A result of great conviction and tolerance.'

His words comforted her and a brief flicker of a smile crossed her face. But only brief, as she implored him, 'Why did he leave me then? He, who is so compassionate, and such a well-wisher of humanity? And then you, with your divine blessing, must also know that I was falsely accused!'

'It is not my place to tell whether the verdict was right or wrong. Only to remind what phenomenal forces you both are. I believe your coming together was destined to achieve a much higher purpose.'

'Coming together!' Sita said mirthlessly. 'You know he has abandoned me!'

'Who said you need to be together to accomplish that higher purpose?'

Sita's eyes flicked up. The sage spoke in riddles.

'Forgive me, daughter, but don't you see a pattern? Your first separation brought about the end of Raavan, the greatest evil on earth. With his annihilation, several abominable sins were vanquished from society, but there might still be some unresolved fragments. And now once again, you both have been separated…' The sage paused for a moment. 'I understand it must be painful, for this time it was brought about by his own decree. But I believe this separation too will achieve a higher purpose. It will end some kind of evil. What kind, I don't know.'

But it was already an end, and they were never going to meet again. Sita remained silent; her face marred with intense hurt.

'Daughter, pain is not always a bad thing. That is, if one uses it to allow the blessing of transformation.' He suddenly fell silent. 'I used to be a dacoit once. It was many years ago. Looting, robbing and harming innocent travellers was my life's banal truth. But when I returned with food and valuables, the joy on my wife and son's face was worth more than any treasure. Then one day, I came across Naarad Muni. Being a dacoit, I knew nothing of his excellence. I grabbed him by the arm, held the knife over his neck and peered into his eyes...they were deep blue. But he laughed. I brought the knife closer. And he laughed louder. He asked me the reason for stealing. When I said it was for my family, he laughed again. He asked me to find out whether they would partake in my share of sins. It could have made me slit his throne. Instead, I loosened my hold. And he simply walked away, carrying the laughter, and wrapped within it, a secret. Later when I asked my wife about it, she rebuked me. As did my son. Each of them said that my sins were mine alone. How I cried that night—thinking of the weight of rejection, the burden of insurmountable sins, that unbearable hollow, ignorant life! But what I had mistaken for a heartache, was in effect a mould breaking within. I started my penance and prayed for years, until one day Naarad Muni visited again and blessed me with a new life and a new name—Valmiki. So, you see, my life has seen a great transformation too, and incidentally it has been within these introspecting forests.' He looked around. Leaves dappled with sunlight trembled in the soft wind, as if in acknowledgment.

'Life has brought you to an equal crossroad. Now it is upon how wisely you choose. Allow yourself to grieve, if you must, but only to shed the past's burden.'

Sita listened, enraptured as he continued, 'Allow me to give you a new name too. From now on, you will be known as Vandevi. It will be true to your primal identity since you come from nature. Besides, our souls are above any binding of names. Names, though important, are ultimately inconsequential towards our real identity.'

Names will all be inconsequential towards how you will be eventually known. May you always be remembered by your exalted qualities alone. Those were her father's words! Something he had said as he gifted her the choodamani when she was departing for Ayodhya. Finally, it dawned on Sita who the kind sage reminded her of—her own father. He offered her the same concern and the same open acceptance. No wonder she felt that inexplicable connection. In the manner her father had once adopted her lying abandoned in the fields, the sage too had adopted her when she was abandoned by the world. A pattern was indeed repeating.

'Come now, daughter, let's get going. It is going to be time for sermons soon. Let's better make haste, or the disciples will come looking.'

23

Breaking of Mould

Sita was so engrossed in thoughts that she barely noticed the rumble overhead. The scabby clouds hovering over the ashram had turned thick and grey and begun to batter down fat drops. A cool breeze drifted in, confirming that there was no scent more rousing than that of rain over mud. The drops turned heavier, and as they dug down, they kicked and splattered mud all over Sita's feet, prodding her to head indoors. By now, the *payasam* had also cooled slightly, so Sita wiped her feet with the saree's border and retreated to the safe comfort of her cottage. Not just a safe comfort, but a safe haven—that is what this hermitage had been for Sita.

She began following Sage Valmiki to his ashram, and with every step, the forest grew thinner and lighter. Soon they came upon a clearing with little clusters of mud cottages with thatched roofs. Clumps of champa groves stood in between, surrounded by paths bordered with *kaner*, *chameli* and *harsingar*. Little children played under the shade of a banyan tree, while some climbed its branches, giggling as they did. Everyone was dressed in ochre yellow clothes—the ladies in sarees, and men in dhotis and *angavastra.* Chanting sages fed the sacrificial pit with scented *ahutis*. Everyone was busy; some broomed the paths, while others collected flowers for the prayers.

Sita didn't hear the old lady when she crept up from behind. 'Greeting, Guruvar! I see we have a new guest?'

'Greetings, Guruma. Indeed, we do. This here is Vandevi. And she is your responsibility now. Look after her well, for she is expecting.'

Guruma's eyes fell on the muddy stains over Sita's saree, but she pretended not to notice.

'You are very welcome, my child. Come, let me show you the hermitage. You can change and rest for a while. And whatever happened to your head? Come, I will put some *agaru* and turmeric on it. By tomorrow, the swelling will be gone.'

Thankfully, she didn't ask further questions and led Sita to an empty cottage. It was by an amaltas tree, full of bright yellow flowers. A few children followed after, regarding their new guest with delighted expressions. Some ladies also rushed to meet her. Even before Guruma could make Sita comfortable on her wooden *khaitya*, they had already taken their place on the floor.

'Guruji said you are called Vandevi. What a beautiful name! I am Suhasini.'

'And I am Kumuda.'

'And I—'

'Guruji said you come from Ayodhya? That must be such a vast kingdom! What brought you to the forests then? And... where is the father of your child?'

Sita's fingers tightened around the wooden frame of her *khatiya*, her head bent low. A faint whimper escaped her mouth.

'Suhasini! Don't you know better than to ask until someone

feels ready to tell?' Guruma's eyes flared with alarm, then softened as they lingered on Sita.

'Oh, I am extremely sorry. I really didn't realize I was upsetting you.' Suhasini stammered, panic rising in her voice.

'It's okay, but I feel you all should now leave.' Guruma commanded gently, setting down a pitcher of water and a set of folded sarees in one corner. 'Vandevi is tired—let her rest.'

'Yes, but may I first offer her something? Suhasini asked, turning again to Sita. 'The jamun tree by the cow shed is heavy with fruit. Only, do watch for the large beehive on the old peepal.' She untied the end of her saree and held out a handful of plump, purple jamuns. But Sita politely declined.

'Not long to go now,' remarked another lady, looking at her belly, 'Hope you have been eating *amrud* leaves? It makes the child fair.'

'I thought it was orange. *Amrud* leaves will be so bitter.'

'They can always be mixed with honey,' she quipped. 'And even so, it's not as bitter as the *kadha* from *lodh* fruits that Guruma makes you drink after childbirth. Ugh! Vandevi, you will soon know what we are talking about.'

'Is it!' Guruma, eyed her complainants, 'I gave that *kadha* to bring back colour to your cheeks. Little did I know it would bring forth sharpness to your tongue!'

'Oh Guruma, I was only joking,' she smiled. 'But honestly Vandevi, the most important tip to remember is to always lie on your left side. I did that when I was expecting. Good for the child's heart they say,' and the lady ruffled the hair of a little girl, probably her daughter.

'We are going to collect flowers. Would you like to come along?'

'Not now!' Guruma interjected, 'Didn't I ask you to let her

rest. Come back tomorrow and chatter all you want. Then you can also show her around the hermitage.'

'Good idea! We will take you by the Tamsa. It is beautiful down there.'

'Forever blabbering, you lot!' roared Guruma. 'Just can't stop once you start. Come on, off you go!'

'Vandevi, please don't mind Guruma. She can be bitter as kadha and but also sweet as honey. Alright, alright, we are leaving.'

'See you tomorrow.' they said in a chorus.

That's how they welcomed her. With simplicity, with warmth, with excitement. But Sita did not go for a walk with the ladies. Not the next day. Or the day after. A week passed like that, and then a month. Every day the ladies came to cajole her and left hopeless, for Sita remained lost in her world of fresh heartache, sitting on her khatiya, looking at the amaltas tree outside her window. All that rattled in her ears were Laxman's words. *He has asked you to leave the kingdom.* At times, mustering a little strength, she tried to replace Laxman's voice with Ram's, but even that imagining shuddered her heart so wildly that she recoiled at once. Her days were spent in delusional hope, waiting for Ram to come. At times, self-esteem would tug at her, which she would silently brush away. She could just not stop loving him. Every waking moment she wondered if he too was in similar pain, drowned in deep remorse, once again searching for her. And when many days passed, she grew restless. He had sought her once before; surely this time would be no different. But that depended on whether he really wanted to. Her mind oscillated between different doubts, all of which left her battered. When she knew, Ram was miles away in Ayodhya, tending to his duties, ruling over as the most just king—little knowing that he was also ruling her heart.

Sometimes Guruma would come with hot oil to massage her hair, or the ladies would bring whatever they had cooked, and as grateful as Sita was for their effort, she couldn't help the spark missing from her eyes. When anyone checked if she had eaten her meal she would answer yes, and when they cajoled her to join for a walk she would politely reply no, the conversation never stretching beyond.

At night, disappointment would swell in her dreams like mighty oceans. She would wake up weeping, then console herself back to sleep. All in vain, for the pattern repeated night after night. And then she experienced a nightmare of a different kind.

The night was silent, save for the occasional howls. Her forehead was covered with beads of sweat even though the room was oddly cool. She had a dream that she could carry on without Ram. The thought unsettled her, and she rushed outside to throw up. After splashing water over her face, when she looked up, the ashram was getting ready for the early morning prayers. In fact, a faint sound of chants was already discernible. In the darkness, the yellow flowers of amaltas called out to her. Her belly stiffened. She unsurely walked to the tree and stood gazing at it in confusion, not knowing what to do, how exactly to carry on. It was when she noticed Sage Valmiki walking her way.

'Greetings Guruji.' Sita brought the veil over her head.

'Greetings daughter! How have you been? I haven't checked on you in a very long time. Hope everything is well?'

'Yes Guruji, I cannot complain. Guruma and the ladies have been exceptionally kind.'

'That's good! I was on my way to the *aushadhishala* to prepare medicines. A cow hurt her leg a few days ago and now the poor thing is now running a fever. Would you care to help?'

'Of course. Whatever you need.'

Several large trees framed the narrow path to the aushadhishala. Over the high branches birds were waking up.

'This *vat* tree that you see, is extremely valuable. Its roots are known to soothe swellings. And this here, is jamun. If you rub its leaves on a bee sting, the worst of them will be healed in an instant. Finally, they reached the aushadhishala and he handed her a bunch of *neem* leaves.

'Do you know this is good for—'

'For healing wounds,' quipped Sita, who herself had learnt much about the forests during her time in exile.

Guru Valmiki smiled, 'That's right, it can heal all sorts of wounds, including some stubborn ones.'

Sita smiled and started to grind. A bitter smell rose from the black *silbatti*. Sage Valmiki gave her a small bark of karpur to help bring down the fever.

'You know daughter, it is important to heal the wound before it begins to fester.' Sita looked up, unsure if Sage Valmiki was looking for some sort of acknowledgement.

'You see, change is only born out of pain. Even a child isn't delivered without it.' Sita's hands involuntarily shifted towards her belly, 'Pain is purifying. It is healing. It delivers you to the other end. But you must channelize it towards attaining your purpose. Do you remember the time I told you about my family refusing to partake in my sins?'

'Yes, Guruji.'

'Well, that wasn't the most painful moment of my life. At least not enough to propel me toward my purpose.' He took a moment's pause before continuing, 'The most painful day, ironically, happened to be here, by the banks of Tamsa. I was offering morning salutations, when I spotted a pair of divine cranes. Spotless white, they had long slender necks which swayed as they sang gloriously. I can never forget that sight. The way their beaks rose to the sky, then dipped back down, all with contentment and harmony. It seemed like a song of devotion and praise for each other. Right then, an arrow came whizzing. It hit the male crane. He died. And instantly, the melody from a while ago was swallowed by deathly silence. There was a pounding on dead leaves. A cruel fowler came charging. Before he could reach the spot and claim his prize, the other crane burst with fervent pain. I sometimes still hear her cry—chilling, almost human-like. Exceptionally terse. Then, she too flopped on the banks, lifeless, unfortunately a moment too late. You see, their souls had departed, but not their pain. That remained suspended over the water, and before I knew it, was absorbed into me. It was under the spell of her deep, tearing agony, that I uttered a curse.

Maa Nishaada Pratishthaam Twam Agama: Shaashvatee Samaa: Yat Krauncha Mithunaadekam Avadhee Kaama Mohitam

Only the curse welled out as a rhythm and meter. A beauty that wasn't apparent at first. Later it became the inspiration for the meter for the Ramayana. Remember, the composition on your lives I told you about. It is written in lyrical form. Ironical that those cranes had to die in order to be reborn as the melody.'

Sita looked on absorbed as the sage continued.

'Now as for the epic, it is simply a recital of the happenings, but how well you craft your story is entirely up to you. Become your own storyteller, daughter, and become the fiercest one there is. Shape it, carve it, steer it in the direction of your choosing. You see, stories are important for they become the paragons of tomorrow.'

Sage Valmiki left Sita at that, with a sense of wonderment and responsibility.

'I think the paste looks about right.' he said, scooping it in a small pot, 'The cow should be fine and walking by tomorrow.'

'Greetings, Guruji!'

'Always be happy, daughter,' he said, then added quickly, 'Will I see you over the prayers?'

'You most certainly will.' There was a gentle smile on Sita's face.

Sita didn't follow him out right away, just stood there in silent reflection. Outside, the rising sun had already turned the day brighter, more real. But sparkling brighter was a sense of conviction in her eyes. After a long time, she became more mindful of the life throbbing inside her, the soft grass under her feet, the gulmohar flowers which lay scattered around, and the sound of prayers from the sages sitting under the banyan tree. Her hands crept to the raatrani bush by the doorway, and she plucked a flower, which after a slight hesitation, she tucked into her bun. She was ready to step back. Ready to salvage the once strong, fierce Sita, the one who always had powerful resolution, a mind of her own and the will to live through tough times.

With every passing day, she changed a little. Sage Valmiki was right. Her tears hadn't been entirely useless. They toughened her in a way she hadn't expected. As her obsession with the past ceased, she occupied herself more and more with the gratifying rigours of daily routine.

She never waited for the sun to wake her up. By the time it reached the apex she would have already gone through her prayers, her daily chores, helped Guruma make pottery, the ladies weave the mats. By evening, she would be flushed with tiredness, having tended to the ashram cows, educated the women and taught them vedas, then drawn honey. She would only rest after the day was wrapped under the blanket of darkness. The chores grew miraculously out of themselves, filling all her time and worries. With every passing day as she proved herself capable of more, life started filling her with equal abundance.

So much so that when she finally gave birth, to her surprise it wasn't just to one child, but to twins—two boys. And while her joys should have doubled, they multiplied, as she held the children in her arms, gazed into their dark round eyes, and felt their plump little fingers curl around hers—their grip so tight, as though they would never let go. She was now a mother, and was determined to be the most resilient one. Her boys may not have a father, but she wouldn't let that be a hindrance. She would play every part, even those denied by fate.

Part Six

24

Night of Revelry

It was almost time for rarjaga and Sita quickened her steps to cross the long stretch to Guruma's cottage. Black columnar trunks with crisscrossed branches stood dimming the moon's milky light. The air had come to a still after a brief and windy spell of rain, leaving the winter leaves in restful peace. Occasionally, a drop or two fell down and sent a shiver down Sita's spine. But it was alright. Tonight, was not for complaints, only celebration.

Even though the payasam had cooled, some heat still seeped through the double layers of muslin wrapped around the earthen pot. Sita had covered it with a lid to enhance the earthy aroma. Balanced atop was a small lamp to show her the way. Its light shone over her neatly oiled hair, combed in a bun and adorned with a white champa flower. Such occasions were rare, and Sita had made an effort by changing into a fresh crisp saree—one that had been patterned in lotus motifs by Vasuki's mother. Over time, she had gotten so used to her simplicity that even the slightest change felt like a disturbing aberration. In fact, she had even put on the stone necklace gifted by her sons, remembering their innocent grumbles about not dressing up as much as other ladies. But she couldn't even cross the door before weighing it unsurely in her hands only to take it off.

Sita shrugged the raindrops off her shoulders and climbed Guruma's verandah. The women were already assembled, looking resplendent even in their simple attires. Reed mats dyed yellow, red, and green were spread out. Everyone leaned against the walls, filling the room with an excited sound of laughter and chatter. Little children huddled next to their mothers, some shuffling their bottoms to carve space in the cramped room.

'Here she comes! Vandevi, daughter, come sit beside me.' called out Guruma.

'Not a chance! Vandevi will sit with me.' Vasuki walked up and defiantly grabbed hold of Sita's hands. A string of raatrani flowers adorned her dainty wrists, 'Do you like it, Vandevi? We just finished making one for all. Here, one's for you.' Saying so, she picked up a bracelet from the wicker basket and wrapped it over Sita's wrist.

The room was painfully alive with the smell of raatrani, the heady smell of her past.

'Look at you, coming in with that big pot of food! I told you not to bother!' called Guruma as Sita placed her *payasam* alongside other pots.

'It was hardly any trouble,' said Sita. By now the old lady was peeping inside, and her mock reproach melted into a gratified smile.

As she lifted the lid further, a scent of saffron, nutmeg and cardamom escaped, inspiring a delighted mmm sounds from the gathered ladies. Soon *pattals*, plates of stitched dried sal leaves were passed around. Heaped in the centre was Sita's payasam along with the nut-brown barley gruel, *moong* lentils and roasted lotus roots Guruma had prepared. The women always appreciated Sita's cooking and it warmed her heart to watch them eat. Young Vasuki licked her fingers and her eyes sparkled at Sita.

Following that, there was dancing. The ladies held onto each other's wrists and took to swirling until they felt dizzy. They were openly laughing, giggling. A few, who were better dancers, swung their hips and tapped their feet to the onlooker's clapping rhythm, the expression of their kohl laden eyes complimenting the mischief in their smiles. The same sparkle was visible in their children's eyes, who hardly got to see their mothers' uninhibited side. Thrilled, they rushed forward to become a part of the revelry.

Sita sat with her back against the mud wall, her face soft with kindness and love, as she regarded these women, who over time, had lent a new meaning to her life.

'Why don't you join in, daughter?' called out Guruma.

'I am fine here with you. Afterall, we need some audience too.'

'Won't you sing at least?' requested Guruma.

'Yes please Vandevi, we would love to hear you sing.' cajoled one of the ladies.

'But—'

'No ifs and buts! Everybody come here and take your place,' Guruma called. 'It's very rare that Vandevi obliges us with singing.'

Needing to catch some breath themselves, the ladies obligated.

'What song shall I sing?' hesitated Sita.

'Whatever pleases you. We just want to hear your voice,' said Guruma.

It turned expectantly silent. Sita closed her eyes and beckoned a song from the deepest crevice of her heart—a song about the unfathomable love of the Great Shiva for his first wife, Sati—a song of love, pain, and longing. Not that Sita had chosen the song consciously, but perhaps she was overwhelmed by the air around, heavy with the smell of squashed petals and longing.

She sang with her eyes closed, recounting the tale of the innocent Sati, who despite Shiva's repeated refusals, left for her father's abode to attend a grand yajna. It was an open secret that her father had disliked Shiva from the onset. But never had she expected all the assembled guests to join in the rebuke, laughing at the jibes hurled by her father. Shiva's honour meant everything to her, and when the atrocity got too much, she jumped into the very fire of the sacrificial yajna. When the unfortunate news reached her husband, it made him distraught with impassioned grief. He straight away left for the yajna and gathering hold of his wife's ashes, smeared it all over his bare body, hot tears streaming down his unblinking eyes. Losing all control, he began to dance, like a man possessed, the sight equally mesmerising and threatening. It was how the supreme Shiva came to be known as the Destroyer and that dance form, one of the greatest ever—*Taandav*.

It was a story that ached with raw emotions. Unbeknownst to Sita, tears had started to stream down her face. She opened her eyes to a similar such expression over others.

'What a beautiful song and what a powerful story!' remarked Guruma, folding her hands in obeisance to the great Lord.

'Fascinating that the divine Taandav is an outcome of intense love and wrath. Come to think of it, when they are in fact two opposing emotions,' said one of the ladies.

'True, some of the greatest miracles find genesis in these intense emotions. Take for example, the Nala Setu—the incredible bridge built by Maharaja Ram,' remarked another.

'Ah yes! The one he built to reach Lanka?'

'Yes, that! Now, wasn't that an outcome of love and wrath too?' asked her companion.

'How so?'

'What do you mean? Haven't you heard Luv and Kush reciting Guruji's great epic.'

All eyes darted towards Sita. For a moment, it appeared like they knew she was Maharani Sita—the wife of the man they just spoke of. Her ears turned red.

'Maharaja Ram's state was no less anguished than Lord Shiva's when he found out about his wife's abduction. I heard that he went so delirious with grief, that he even began asking the plants, trees, bees, butterflies, and any passing animals if they knew her whereabouts.'

The women exclaimed in unison and the mood turned somber. In that silence, Sita's own heart thudded sharply.

'When he finally reached the tip of the land, it is said the ocean was unrelenting. But it eventually succumbed under the indestructible will of the great king, and let him build the bridge. I say, to have a will to join two landmasses is nothing short of a miracle!'

'It's quite telling of their love. How deep must it be!' sighed one of the entranced listeners, a yearning visible over her face.

'And how unfortunate!' followed another.

That remark sucked the life out of Sita. It was true. By now her ears had started to burn.

'Unfortunate?'—'How so?'—'Tell us, you're making us uneasy!' cried out a few ladies.

'Well, my husband recently returned from Ayodhya, and tells me that Maharani Sita has now been banished.'

'But Guruji hasn't mentioned any such instance in the Ramayana,' said one of the ladies.

'He says their story is not yet complete.'

'Why was she banished?' Two or more voices asked the same question.

'Apparently, the people in Ayodhya questioned her chastity following her abduction. Maharaja Ram was compelled to pass an equitable verdict, something which he would have imposed on any other woman in the kingdom.'

'What an irony! A loving man, who had once turned the world upside down to reach his wife, finally ends up relinquishing her. Then why ever did he rescue her?'

'Hmm, that is questionable, and I don't completely disagree. The sin of abduction was for Raavan to bear, not Maharani Sita.'

All this while Sita's breath was quickening. The air in the room felt too dense. She rose to open the window.

'Decisions are always imposed on women. Even Maharani Sita's younger sister, Princess Urmila was separated from her husband for fourteen long years. Can that be called fair?'

The women carried on with their deliberations, but Sita wanted no part of it. She stood at the window, praying for the breeze to numb her ears and mind. Living a life of concealed identity was hugely burdensome. Now for the first time, hearing other's opinions, as well as agreement had somehow loosened a torrent of emotions. She held onto the window's frame, inundated under its impact. The silhouettes of stark branches wavered in front of her eyes, and she kept looking at it for as long as it took for the eternal chatter to die down.

'Vandevi, why are you standing there all by yourself. Come, sit with us.' One of the ladies patted the floor beside her.

'Oh yes, I just…I thought a little breeze would be nice,' Sita added abruptly. 'Doesn't the forest look particularly beautiful tonight?' A cuckoo called, even though it was oddly late.

Everyone looked outside. The moonlight had indeed drenched every upturned leaf with a silvery glow.

'It does! But the forest is the only life we know. Why, you had once lived in Ayodhya yourself. Regale us about life there.'

'What is there to tell? It's just a little different.'

'Must be more fascinating?'

'Not really, the forest is far more fascinating.'

Sita's laconic response didn't satisfy them. Everyone was quite enthusiastic, especially the children, who without an ounce of sleep in their eyes hoped for conversations to forge ahead, lest everyone's enthusiasm died down and the night came to an early close.

'My husband says there are tall buildings there,' started the same lady. 'Apparently, there are storage houses so huge, we can hardly imagine them. And people there don't wear clothes like ours. Their garments are shiny and bright.'

'Really?' marvelled the lady beside her.

'Yes! And they eat many kinds of dishes. Similar to the payasam you prepared for us, Vandevi—they eat similar such varieties there. And have attendants to carry out chores,' she said in revelatory manner. The eyes of the other ladies shone in bemusement.

'Then what do they do themselves? How do they bide time? Do they not mop the floor, chop the woods and collect water?'

'Well, they have other things to occupy themselves with. Like dressing up in lavish clothes and exquisite jewellery. Surely, that must take a while. My husband said, they are so fully covered in gold that—'

'My husband said this...my husband said that!' interjected Guruma. 'Next time, why don't you just visit Ayodhya with him?'

A hearty chuckle filled the room. The lady, red as ruby, brought her saree's veil to cover her laughter, but it was only a brief pause, 'Okay, you tell us Vandevi, are their jewelleries really that beautiful? Why, you must be wearing some yourself, even if not as heavy as the women in palaces?'

'Their jewelleries may be beautiful but less so than the ones you all are wearing,' Sita replied warmly.

'What are you saying! We only wear flowers! You think this champa, *parijat* and *karira* is better...oh now, don't lie to comfort us.'

'Honestly!' said Sita. 'They too wear flowers, but moulded out of gold. Their adornments are just a marker of wealth, heavy with dead weight. While yours is...actually alive—with fragrance, with attraction. It can draw anyone with its simplicity.'

'Quite often the bees and butterflies!' remarked a smiling lady. 'At least the women in the palace don't have to bother about that.'

The rest of the ladies broke into pearls of laughter. Sita continued, 'Your jewellery becomes new every day, dressing you with a completely different look. It teaches you to follow the course of nature, the changes, the seasons. Here we respect nature while in kingdoms—'

'In kingdoms?'

'While in kingdoms...you only respect the rules set by the king.' After a brief pause Sita picked up, 'There are no changes to his rules, no seasons, no exceptions. It's rigid. Rules in nature, however, are pliable, and the forest responds differently to every situation. For instance, *kaner* flowers early spring, but if the preceding winter were harsher, it will flower a fortnight later—it would simply adjust. There is respect and consideration for every truth.'

'How beautifully you explain,' said Guruma, rubbing Sita's shoulder. 'You have such a wise outlook on everything.'

The mood had become quite reflective. Amidst all the talking, no one had realized that the children were fast asleep, their little limbs stretched across the mat, the corner of their mouths dribbling. Just then, a small boy happened to cry and his mother picked him up.

'On that note, how about we respect the rule of the night—let's steal a few hours of sleep before daybreak?' suggested Guruma. 'It wouldn't be long before we are needed to fetch water from Tamsa.'

The ladies shuffled out of their host's cottage, hoisting their sleepy little ones over their shoulders. They thanked Guruma for a rare and wonderful night, expressing how full their hearts were. Sita too returned to her cottage, her own heart full, but with loneliness and pain.

And also, a fresh budding anger.

25

Of Unseen Vices

In the stillness of the sleepy forest, the prattle of the ladies rang out clear. Everyone hastened back to their cottages, except Sita. Her feet had grown heavy, like it hauled along a heavy weight. She ambled through the thicket of tall, slender trees, with her empty pot and diya. Those trees, despite their generous bathing in the moonlight, had undeniably dark shadows. They fell on her face, creating random patterns. Light could alter the appearance of most things—but not all.

The night was cool, yet her ears burnt. After what felt like a lifetime, she had heard his name called out loud. Heard his love for her question by some, and his dedication justified by others. It pained her all the same. What did they even know of him? A sigh escaped her lips—for neither did they know much of her.

Over time, she may have turned into Vandevi. But the past remained the same, one she could neither share nor erase. Just like the moonlight—a new identity could alter the appearance of most things—but not all.

She reached her door but instead of pushing it open, gravitated back to her lonesome verandah, the place having recently turned into an ideal spot of reminiscence. All around, the forest lay restfully asleep, without a hoot or a shuffle. The insects lay perfectly still, as did the air, disturbing not a single leaf in the vast expanse. It was silvery dark under the thatched roof, except for the light straining from the small diya. It fell onto her ochre yellow saree and lit it gold. The same glow highlighted her face leaning on the cool mud pillar.

It pinched her to realize that everyone saw irony in their love. As a young, dreamy girl of eighteen, she had never expected such harshness from life, not when she had first seen him in the gardens at Pushpa Vatika; how he had looked at her so reliably. How his eyes had beamed with promise as she had placed the wedding garland over him. The night was turning colder, but she didn't care. The world had no idea how much he had loved her—dearly, fiercely, completely—at times, even possessively.

It was a drowsy afternoon in Panchavati, and they rested on the grassy clearing outside their cottage. Sunshine, sweet over their backs, had turned them vaguely listless. Drifting in the air was a deep scent of new grass and wildflowers. Sita sat with her legs folded, while Ram rested his head on her lap, his eyes closed, palms tucked beneath his face. Sunshine glittered on her toes, peeking from beneath the gathers of her saree. She playfully looped a blade of grass around one toe, curling it in and out. A contended quietude filled the air, broken only by the wavering of grass across their backs, the random droppings of ripe fruits, a rustle in the bushes, the crack of a dry twig or the occasional hoots.

Serenity lapped over Ram's face. His soft eyelids were framed by long lashes that curled all the way back. Very softly, his chest swelled up and down. Creamy light glimmered on his chiselled jaw, his distinctly attractive chin, and the ruffled charm of his hair. Sita didn't want to wake him, but could not resist running her hands through his hair. A sweet flicker of a smile touched Ram's lips. Sita drew her hand back, gathered the seeds kept beside, and scattered them across the moist grass. With a sharp swish, the grains fell, and soon birds fluttered down to peck at her offering. Ram longed for her touch again; its caress had felt so good. But he was too lulled by drowsiness. It was then that he heard it—the sound. At first like a bird's tread, but heavier, almost giant-like. Then came the anguished wail. His eyes flew open. Sita's face was drawn in pain as she looked at the blood on her toes. The crow had swooped to peck at her again.

Blind rage swept over Ram. Without a moment's hesitation, he grabbed hold of a twig lying about, and with a swift motion, stabbed the crow in the eye. The bird stumbled back; its morbid cawing filling the air. Then it scampered, and as soon as it could, fluttered away. Sita looked at Ram. By now he had sat up, his eyes following the bird's flight. It was true the crow had pecked her, yet Ram's action felt mercilessly punitive; and equally unexplainable.

'Are you okay?' It was a question Ram should have asked Sita. Instead, Sita asked him.

His chest hadn't stopped heaving. His nose still flared. Taking a long deep breath, he tore a piece off his dhoti and tied it over her bleeding toe. He still hadn't looked her in the eye. The cloth blotted red in no time. Irritated, he tore another piece.

'It…it was just a crow,' she stammered.

'Was it?' His eyebrows were raised, and he only looked at her sideways, momentarily pausing to tighten the knot.

The oddness in his voice made it evident it wasn't simply a crow. On many previous occasions, enchanted beings had fallen for her beauty—like Viradha the giant—and though Ram had saved her, she often feared her presence had made the exile harder for him. Nothing vexed him more than anyone casting a salacious glance at her.

Her throat tightened. But how was she to know? Especially when the beings came in disguise? Still, it felt as though she had failed him. For the first time, she felt sorry for her beauty. Ram's protectiveness should have made her feel cherished, yet it left her strangely alarmed. Sunlight still glimmered on her toes, which were now blood-stained, and she curled them in, carefully hiding any bareness beneath the gathers of her saree.

Ram lay back, but was light on her lap. A certain stiffness had crept in and neither of them moved or spoke. At least not until Laxman returned from the day's hunt.

The following morning, she made no hurry to return from the river. She filled her pot with water, only to let it topple over, then thumped it aside in frustration. Unfortunately, there was a stone she hadn't noticed, and the pot cracked. She would now have to mould another one, and leave it to harden over fire. Ram would have usually helped her with the baking, but she was not going to ask him. She flung the broken pieces into the river and waited for the ripples to settle. That's when she saw her face; sad, without a smile. On her thick, black tresses, wavered a champa flower, its whiteness almost obscene. For a while she kept squinting at the reflection, until a grimace rose over. She tore the flower and tossed it away. The flower, with its pure white petals, bobbed abandoned. There were no currents to take it away, so Sita furiously splashed it over: and it drowned.

From then on, Sita left her hair unadorned. Two days passed in this manner until one evening she saw Ram return, not with fruits or hunt, instead a dainty bowl modelled of sal leaves. Another leaf covered it as a lid on top. He rested the bowl on log pile. It was late evening and everything had turned a shade of grey. She reluctantly walked out to find him kindle a flame for bonfire. Having rained only a while back, the air was dense with the smell of wet moss and damp wood. She had not greeted him, and neither had he. After rousing the fire, which took a while, he threw in a few sprigs of scented lemongrass. Almost immediately, a relaxing aroma wafted through. Then he walked up to her and held out his hand. Sita didn't take it right away. Unswerving, he left it hanging, something he always did if she ever got upset. Finally, she relented. He gladly took her delicate hand, then reached out for another, and pressed both against his cheeks, not uttering not a word still.

They stood like that awhile, the warmth seeping from her hands onto his cold cheeks, and the silence beginning to fill with the delightful crackle of logs, burning much more steadily now. Gently guiding her towards the log pile, Ram made her sit down. Then he unwrapped the bowl. To Sita's delight, it was full of beautiful red and purple flowers, the kinds she had never seen before. He picked a flower, and it came off as a garland. *So, he had not only simply picked flowers but also strung them with sturdy vines.* An apologetic look lingered in his eyes as he placed it around her neck. Her own eyes mellowed. There was a garland for her neck, and one for her hair, along with the bracelets and anklets. Sita blushed, holding out her hands and feet for her husband to lovingly put them on one by one.

'How pretty you look,' he said.

'How do I know?'

'Look into my eyes and see it for yourself,' he lifted her chin.

Of course, she couldn't see her reflection in his eyes. The light was too dim for any of that. Only a glimmer of burning logs was visible in the earnest depths of his eyes. In time, faint stars pricked through the dull sky. They sat over the logs, admiring the sky as it continued to glimmer with many more stars. Then Ram got up, doused the bonfire, and they headed indoors.

Ram was a good husband. He didn't need words to understand her hurt, and patiently tended to her every whim, big or small. So many times, he had brought her fruits and flowers from the thorniest bushes and the highest branches. Truth was, he loved to see her adorned. Perhaps she had been unnecessarily hurt when he only wanted her to be more careful. To be aware of the evil, for there was nothing more precious than one's honour. Honour was sacrosanct. Once lost, could never be reclaimed. But those were ponderings for another time. For now, love must do. Those flowers—purple and red and sweetly scented—around her neck and her hands, must do.

26

Bliss of Ignorance

Sita slid the raatrani bracelet Vasuki had tied on her wrist, and removed the *champa* from her hair. The back of her head felt heavy, so she loosened her bun. Thick, black hair tumbled down to her waist. She set the bracelet in a playful ring around the diya, admiring the petals glow under the mellow light. It was true that Ram loved to see her adorned—and it was exactly what she had done before their long-awaited reunion in Lanka.

It was a clear day in Ashoka Vatika. Stark pockets of sunlight scattered down the *shimshapa*, the tree which had been her steadfast companion for almost a year of captivity. She usually sat underneath it in silent rebellion, but today she kept pacing non-stop.

Beneath that tree she had manifested her future—and everything was unfolding just so. Ram had been fighting her captor relentlessly for over a month, yet the war was still not over.

That is when she saw a man walk up with an assured gait. Clad in fine silk and gold ornaments, he looked a figure of importance, as was evident when the demonesses rose to receive him.

'What brings him here?'—'Hadn't he fled Lanka to fight the war on Ram's side?'—'Such a treachery!'—Sita heard them mumble, a touch of concern tinging their nasal voice. 'I hope all is well?'

'Greeting, Prince Vibhishan!' They said in a chorus.

Vibhishan!

The name rang familiar. Sita had never seen him before, but she recalled the whispers, how the demonesses huddled around the bonfire, often spoke of him in enraged tones, of how he had defied Raaavan by openly denouncing her abduction, and had been cast out for it. For Sita, is stirred a quiet feeling of solidarity. At least someone in Lanka understood her.

'Greetings, Queen Sita! I am Vibhishan, the successor of Lanka, and I bring the joyous news of your husband's victory. Raavan has been vanquished.' His voice quavered ever so slightly.

A smile broadened over Sita's lips, but the glee was all too soon was distracted by the renewed wailing around. The demonesses had started thumping their chests.

'Please do not cry for him,' Vibhishan consoled them, 'My brother was a great man, a great devotee of Shiva, the most powerful emperor, but he was also afflicted with sins. Think of his death as a liberation. Pray for his soul if you must, but do not cry.'

It took a while for the demonesses' sobs to stifle. Their devotion for Raavan was absolute, but they must now listen to the new successor to the Lankan throne.

'Lord Ram has requested for you,' Vibhishan said to Sita.

'What's the wait then! Let us go!' Sita hurried down the platform.

'Not like this!' he cried, then sensing Sita's surprise, added, 'Nothing will give me greater pleasure. But, he has asked for you to be bathed and changed, brought over with utmost respect. I shall look into the arrangements for a palanquin. Meanwhile, my attendants here will tend to you.' He motioned to Trijata.

'Tend to me? But why? I am only going to meet my husband.'

'I understand. Still, that is his explicit wish.'

'Ram's wish?'

Vibhishan shuffled on his feet, the conversation was uncomfortable, 'Lady Sita, please understand, you are no longer a captive. In fact, you are our most honoured guest—The wife of a man who not only rescued you, but also Lanka—' Once again, his ears turned red.

'Still, I have never known Ram to care about such trivialities. Especially now, when I will see him after so long.'

'Apologies. I am simply repeating his command.'

Although his gaze was fixed to the ground, Sita wondered if he referred to her tattered saree. Sitting under the sun and rain for so long had given it a frayed, threadbare look. Sure it sounded strange, but equally Ram would not do anything without good reasoning. Afterall, he had redeemed her honour by annihilating Raavan and maybe this was yet another gesture. Maybe he wanted her to arrive proud in front of his entire army.

Trijata stepped forward and wrapped her burly hands around Sita. 'Master, please don't worry about the Lady, we shall get her ready without much delay,'

A surge of emotions washed over Sita. She had often imagined this moment filled with relief, but now her stomach fluttered, like she was a bride meeting her husband for the first time. Trijata smiled at her, as did others. Over time, everyone had warmed up to her and hugged her freely.

They led her to the sparkling lotus pool, with its water mildly warm, and made her sit down. With sultry scented petals, they scrubbed her delicate arms and back, remarking on the wonderful glow of her skin. They washed her hair, opening any knots; then dried and oiled it. A beautiful mustard saree and matching gold ornaments was brought from the palace.

'There was no use for all this. I know Ram doesn't care,' Sita said to Trijata who was braiding her hair in small sections.

'It's a little gift from us. Why, you're seeing your husband after so long! Wouldn't you at least make him realize what he has been missing!' She winked and gathered the braids into a lovely knot. The surrounding demonesses broke into desirous giggles.

They kept fussing and teasing as they carried on getting her ready.

'Hold still Sita, these crushed red petals will make your lips irresistible.'—'Only a faint hint of blush on your cheeks, especially since you wouldn't stop naturally blushing,'—'Let's apply some kohl, and give those eyes more fire,'—'And now, with this string of the finest flowers around the bun, you will have your fingers wrapped around him in no time.'

Once finished, they coaxed her to peer into the still pool and indeed colour rose on her cheeks. She hadn't looked like this in a long while. Happier days were finally here.

Soon, an exquisite palanquin was brought forward. Made of fragrant sandalwood and inlaid with ivory in floral pattern, it shone wonderfully under the afternoon sun. Trijata helped Sita into it, then smoothened the drapes of her saree and kissed her beaming forehead.

'I will never forget you. Meeting you has been the biggest blessing of my life.' she said. The sight of big drops rolling down her cheeks moistened Sita's own eyes, but before she could say anything, Trijata swept back the silken drapes. The bearers picked up the palanquin and soon started walking away.

The palanquin swayed gently to their synchronized steps, finally carrying her towards Ram. Inside the small chamber, the smell of unguents and flowers was overpowering, and Sita's lips quivered with unbridled excitement. She bit them, but in vain.

The sun was close to the horizon and filtered through the thin curtains. It was bizarrely similar to the time she was being escorted to Ayodhya as Ram's new wife. Only he was riding beside her then. How he would slyly steal a glance at her! So restrained with the rest of the world, but so different with her.

Left to her solitude, she hugged her knees and laid her head atop it. Would Ram come running, seize her in his arms? And that musky scent of his—how she had missed it. A smile crept up her lips, thinking of all there was to say, but she doubted any words would follow. Anyway, it was the eyes that needed contending first.

Time dragged slowly, as did the bearers. She thought of pulling the curtains, imploring them to gather pace, but every nearing step raised her trepidation, even though the battlefield was still not visible for miles ahead. She sat back hoping to be lulled to sleep. At first, it was an attempt in vain. But soon the trailing thoughts and dreams began to mix—and they were both of an inseparable embrace in Ram's long arms.

27

Fire that Raged

The night had deepened further in the time Sita sat on her verandah. A sudden gust surged out of nowhere, making the cotton wick of her diya shiver. It brought about a dramatic flickering over the mud pillar, pulling Sita out from her reverie. She reached out to shield the flame and noticed the oil had run low. It was time to sleep anyway.

Once inside the comforting warmth of her kutiya, Sita filled the diya with oil, and freshly rejuvenated, the wick sprang up.

'Why do you even worry? Do you have any idea of your strength? You may be small but only until you are challenged. Your power is such that it can bring the whole world down.' Then sensing the sombreness, she added, 'But those in power, must use it for the right reasons!'

As if in response, the wick steadied and brightened. Resting over the wall was a jute khatiya. Sita pulled it down and smoothened a cotton sheet over its rough weavings. Sighing, she curled over and in no time sank into a deep sleep. Outside her window, the silver forest stood silently still, save for some occasional hoots, and inside, that little flame of light kept a watch; shimmering its mellow light on her benevolent face, which at last was empty of thoughts. Despite her age, Sita hadn't lost the sharpness of her chin and nose, or the thickness of her hair which splayed in dense gathers behind her.

What she had said to the diya was indeed true. Out of all the five elements—air, water, fire, earth, and ether—fire was more than warmth and illumination; it was transformation. Sita had witnessed that closely in her life. The day she had finally met Ram was also the day, when under its impact, their whole relationship was melted and forged anew.

The palanquin bearers slowed their pace and jolted Sita out of her slumber. Slanted rays of creamy sunlight trickled in through the silken curtains. Sita shielded her eyes and squinted. There stood a large gathering—mostly tribal men, chatting in little groups, maces and bows flung over their shoulders. Some lounged on the ground.

'You can lower the palanquin!' A distant command was heard, and the bearers froze. *Was it Ram?* Sita's heart pounded.

With a soft thud, she was lowered. Dust rose in the air followed by a peculiar stillness. After a moment's hesitation, Sita peeled the curtain. Laxman stood across, his hand outstretched to receive her. *But where was Ram?*

Her searching eyes found him standing back with the crowd.

It was surreal to see him finally. Though leaner, he looked proud, holding a bow and quiver, covered in battle scars, a deep long gash running down his left shoulder. Still, nothing less than a vision of perfection.

Sita stepped outside and the sudden onslaught of malodorous stench overwhelmed her. The ground was grisly with mutilated bodies, many with missing limbs, heads, some with just the torsos, their eyes open; all confusingly heaped together. Her own attire felt excessive, the delicate fragrance of flowers hardly fitting in with the surrounding morbidity. She felt Ram's eyes on her silk saree, her neatly oiled hair, maybe a bit too many gold bangles glinting in the afternoon light. She squeezed the drape of her saree, and her bangles slid; clinking. Ram smiled, but for some reason it was different from her imagination.

'Greetings, my lady!' he said. And remained rooted.

Perhaps the presence of so many people around. Ram was a restrained man after all. Her throat tightened.

'At last! It is good to see you,' he continued. The right words, but an odd stiffness. Again, perhaps the lapsed time

'I am sorry for all that you've been through. It takes immense courage to withstand an evil like Raavan. But now, he has been vanquished.'

An instant roar went up. 'Victorious Ram!'—'Saviour Ram!'—'Praise be to Ram!'

Sita heard none of it. They were fixed on the hollow look over his face; those unnecessary words of apology—hardly a proper greeting after a lifetime of separation. She knew a silly smile was pasted on her face, about which she could do nothing. Nor could she do anything about the thumping of her heart, the tingling of her fingers or the heat on her cheeks.

'You are finally free,' he said.

Of course, she was. Why state that?

She took a step forward. He recoiled.

'As you may know,' he cleared his throat, then fell silent, considering the gathering around. A slight breeze stirred the air, and Sita felt the prickling on her bare arms. She rubbed herself in irritation.

'As you may know,' he repeated, lifted his eyebrows, pulled

back his bruised shoulders and uttered the jammed words. 'I know you have been forcefully taken against your will. A grave ordeal. But, it also means...that you have lived with another man. With Raavan.' His voice momentarily quietened, 'As you will realize, it changes things.'

Lived with another man! Sita's head reeled in disbelief. *But wasn't he here with an army? Hadn't he just rescued her?* Nothing made sense.

'Unfortunately, your purity has been sullied...after...after he laid his hands on you.'

Sita looked around. Everyone's faces were hung low.

'Changes things? 'What do you mean?'

But silence was all she got.

'Do you not trust me?' she asked.

'It's not you. It's Raavan. A man like him can never be trusted.'

'Ram! You are the only man—'

'Please—say no more! No...more. As much as I believe you, what has happened cannot be changed.'

'I was abducted!' Her voice rose.

'I know. Which is why I came. And I am sorry...sorry I couldn't come sooner. But now, my duty is fulfilled.'

'Your duty?'

'My duty to protect you. Look, I know this is difficult. But—'

'But what?'

He straightened his shoulders, looked past her, and said, 'You are free to leave. You can go anywhere you wish.'

Those words, they quivered straight through her. Was he suggesting that they part ways? With growing dread, she realized it wasn't Raavan he had killed with his last arrow but her very heart.

'You don't mean?' Her voice welled weakly from her throat.

He shifted on his feet. 'It's the rules. They forbid us to get back together. After a lady has left her husband's abode…you know the dictums as well as I do. She can never return.'

'I've heard you! I…have…heard you!' A sudden jolt of energy coursed through her, then left her abruptly silent. Never before had she spoken to him in such a manner and she felt drained. Incipient anger, shame, and confusion, stacked up her chest, ready to rip it apart. She gasped. If only she could howl, but not in front of all those people, especially not with their doubtful eyes upon her.

'How could you ever question my faithfulness?'

'I don't! That's not what I mean.'

His tone was soft, yet the words undeniably hard. She desperately needed the courage to retaliate but this was not something she could have ever imagined.

'Why are you saying this then? Why are you putting me through this?' Tears welled up in her eyes.

'It doesn't matter what you and I believe. It's the rules—'

'And the rules matter?'

He remained silent, and she understood. Sarcasm budded up in her own tone as she said, 'Spoken like a true king! Of course…of course you care for rules, your dictums. It's all about following the footsteps of your dynasty, isn't it? We have been together for so long. Has that not told you anything about my character?'

Ram didn't reply. Once again, she stood feeling foolish. Was he purposefully taking long to answer? The incipient shame started to burn her. Overhead the evening light was waning, making it difficult to see.

'You want me gone. So be it! Laxman!' Sita roared, not

taking her eyes off Ram. Laxman took a while to understand he was being summoned.

'Build a pyre! Your brother wants me gone!'

'Sita! I ask of no such thing!' cried Ram. 'Even you know that. All I said was your honour is restored and are free—'

'Restored? Nobody has the power to restore anything. The truth of my honour lies with me. And with Lord Shiva.' She didn't want to cry, but the words came out in an angry wail. 'But…if the Lord too thinks I have so much as even thought of another man…then let me burn with the pyre.'

'This is insanity!' Ram cried.

'So be it! Besides, I wonder who is being insane here!'

'Sita!'

'No! You just gave up all your rights over me. Now stand back!'

'And Laxman, did you not hear? I said lay the pyre!' She roared, 'Now!' Her bangles chinked. A single lady in the assembly of the so-called chivalrous men, who had all fought bravely to free her.

Everything plunged into an oppressive silence. Even the trees stood motionless against the grey sky. Sita and Ram looked at one another, both stunned by each other's unrelenting will.

Laxman shuffled over his feet. He didn't know what to do. Ram had not said anything. The matter was serious. Before her arrival, wood was already collected to cremate the fallen warriors. Many pyres were built, some even lit.

When Sita saw Laxman not pay heed, she lit a torch from the burning fire and walked to the stack of logs close by. She climbed over a step, and despite the fragility, the logs didn't roll back. She climbed one step over the other, caring not for the knots and knobbles, sharp edges and prickly needles, which bloodied her feet. In no time, she reached the top, and sat down, directly facing all the shameful sorry men, her own gaze fixed on Ram. Hot tears streamed down her unblinking eyes.

'Laxman, light the pyre!' she hollered.

Laxman swivelled towards his righteous brother. Sita's bold visage was intimidating. He desperately hoped for Ram to stop him, but no such thing happened.

Sita looked at Ram, the burning torch still in hands. It was only when she saw Ram unblinking, staring back without a reply, that she let the torch drop. The fire started with a gentle cracking and popping, with splintering and hissing, and with insidious flying of sparks. But sooner than anticipated, it took to its intrinsic nature. Hungry flames leapt up, and started to devour the wood, lending a bitter smell to the air. It raced around and encircled the pyre, turning the air hot. Sita's yellow saree and innocent face began to waver. The whole appearance dramatically surreal, like it wasn't actually happening; like it was just an illusion, a mirage, a shameful trickery to the eyes.

And just as the pernicious fire started to crackle the logs on top, a blaze of lightning stunned the sky. An extraordinary glare ruptured through. A few more followed in quick succession. The sky let out a deafening roar in condemnation of the drama beneath. Everyone looked up, petrified, except for Sita, whose eyes remained fixed upon Ram.

The grey sky furrowed through with glowering silver lines. Sita was not alone. Someone was looking after her. Someone equally aggrieved. Then the sky burst, with a robustness that had only ever happened at her birth. Only this time, its heavy and mad raining was mixed with heartbreak that follows when trust is challenged. The flames cowered. Everything was obscured from sight, everything immaterial. Only Ram and Sita remained in each other's vision.

In time, the fire sizzled out. There was no way a mere pyre could carry against the indomitable strength of the sky. A reprehensible smell of charred wood seeped through. Sita's shoulders shivered but she remained on the blackened pyre, her eyes not leaving Ram's. Wisps of smoke rose, mixing with the rain-washed air.

Embarrassed, Ram lowered his gaze to the ground. It was miraculous, the manner in which not a single flame had touched her. He realized that the heavens were angered at his act. Sita, who only moments ago, was full of excitement at their meeting, now sat aggrieved. Water streamed down her hair that had come undone; the flowers and decorations all gone.

When Ram looked up, there was a deep apology in his eyes, a desire to turn back time. With careful steps he walked to the pyre and extended his calloused hands. But Sita sat motionless. Under the waning light, she saw the long scar on his shoulder. *What was the use of those cuts and bruises, of those fallen bodies, of this wretched destruction?* She saw his lips move but the words failed to reach her. Everything had sucked up too much energy.

Ram didn't give up. He stood in mute silence, hands still outstretched, guilty and desperate. He stood there for hours, unmoving. Finally, Sita's heart welled. But her body had turned cold. She couldn't help her stony gaze. Being offered tenderness after reproach felt hollow.

In time, the silhouette of the trees deepened. The evening turned mournful with the smell of the half-charred wood hanging like heartbreak. She was exhausted. Then, in a moment of sudden impulse, extended her hand. Ram folded her palms in his and gently brought her down.

He told her how wrong he had been. That he had missed her, had searched for her everywhere, fought for her. How he had not slept a wink, crossed that impassable ocean, how all he ever wanted was to get back to her, and that she was his very life. He told her everything she had been pining to hear. Just a little too late. This profuse apology making little difference to her. She simply allowed herself to be led, no longer feeling, or rebelling, or fighting, or accusing. Just quietly hurting.

He held up her chin and expressed his remorse. She wanted to nod back, wanted to smile. This feeling of doubting him was new to her, and it was gnawing, oddly hurting her even more than his words. She didn't like it. She lowered her gaze and buried her sad face in his cold chest, and he wrapped her in his arms.

At long last she was in his embrace, only not the kind she had anticipated. But an embrace, nonetheless. A reconciliation, nonetheless. If only hurt could be erased, such an effort nonetheless. Forgetting everything, Sita brought her own arms across Ram.

Part Seven

28

Lessons on Idealism

The crack of dawn was marked with the usual chill in the air. Sita was fast asleep, her chest softly swelling and sinking, oblivious to everything that was going on outside her cottage. Crunching of leaves could be heard, perhaps even the scampering of rabbits or deer. This was followed by the sound of quick footsteps. A chuckle? An excited dash up her steps before the feeling of being wrapped by cold arms, with joyous cries. 'Ma! Ma!'

'Huh? Luv! Kush! Children! When did you return?' Sita sprang up and gathered them in her arms.

'Just now. Oh, how we missed you Ma!' said Luv.

'Dearly missed you!' chimed in Kush, wriggling his elbow. 'Give me some space,' he said with a pout. 'I am almost hanging off the edge.' A giggle followed as they all snuggled together.

'Look at you both, how frail you have become. All that walking must have been tiring,' Sita said, caressing them both.

'Yes, but equally adventurous!' replied Luv.

'You know Ma, we didn't just go to Ayodhya, but also several small kingdoms on the way, singing and apprising a lot of people about the Ramayana,' said Kush with a sparkle in his eyes.

'Is that so!' smiled Sita.

'Indeed! We stopped at—' Just then his stomach let out a sudden rumble. 'Ma, I am very hungry.'

'Hmm, I can hear that,' Sita nodded, trying to contain her smile.

'Me too. Please, can we have something to eat,' said Luv.

'Okay, okay! Why don't you quickly take a bath and say your morning prayers. And I will arrange for something.'

Both boys jumped to their feet. 'Please will you make us *rasiya*?' Luv asked.

'And some *thekua*. It has been so long since we had your delicious cooking,' pleaded Kush.

Sita smiled at their innocent requests. 'Anything else?'

'Hmm...this will do for now! See you very soon,' Kush said.

Once again, they squeezed their mother into a warm hug, and raced to the Tamsa, waving fresh sets of ochre yellow dhoti in the air, laughing, leaving behind footprints on dewy grass. Sita stood at the threshold, looking on admirably, as brightness steadily crept up the waking sky.

The boys returned to find their mother by the chulha, blowing air through a bamboo pipe to kindle the flames. The sound made them chuckle; they had often made it into a whistling plaything. In this while, Sita too had bathed. Wet hair hung down her back. Smiling, she motioned her sons to the mat of darbha grass. Not only had she prepared an entire meal so quickly, but was now stirring a pot of milk sweetened with jaggery. Luv grinned to find it was his *raisya*. Sita was making sure the rice didn't stick to the bottom. She couldn't quite leave the wooden spoon aside, for otherwise the milk would hiss and threaten to spill out.

The boys took a deep whiff. The rasiya smelled wonderful with the delicate hint of almonds, dry coconut, and raisins. A warm batch of *thekua*, made from flour and jaggery and baked over warm embers, was laid out on a bright green banana leaf, making them hungrier.

They sat across their mother, eyes brimming with delight. Sita too smiled as she served them food. How terribly she had missed them. After a hurried prayer of gratitude for the food, they went straight for the sweetmeat.

'What! Are you not starting with the rice and vegetables?' Sita retorted.

'Please Ma, not today! We are having your sweetmeat after so long. Let us enjoy our fill!' said Luv.

'Yes, there is no one who can prepare sweetmeats quite like you,' said Kush.

'Hmm? Why do I get the feeling it is in fact your praises which are heavily sweetened.'

'Definitely not! Try it for yourself if you don't believe it. Mmm…' Luv said, closing his eyes.

'Mmmmmmm…' Kush echoed, taking a bite of his own. He kept checking for her reactions through squeezed eyes,

It melted Sita's heart. Her sons had definitely turned much leaner after the trip. Probably taller too. The mellow morning light glimmered over their lean arms and their defined shoulder blades. Surely, they couldn't have grown so much in the space of a fortnight. It struck her how closely they resembled Ram—same eyes, same lean fingers, even the curl at the end of their lips was not far off.

'You know Ma, in Ayodhya there are so many different types of food. Well, not that it is anywhere as delicious as yours. But the variety—unimaginable! There are markets just to sell food, and there are people who sell all day. But of course, you have to offer something else in return,' said Luv.

'Is it!' Sita feigned ignorance.

'And Ma, you should have seen their houses, the clothes they wear. So colourful! Nothing like ours,' said Kush.

'Yes, and they don't dress alike, like we do here. Some had very rich garbs, and others...much simpler,' said Luv in a low voice.

'Oh, and wait till you hear about their houses—studded with topazes and rubies!' exclaimed Kush.

'Yeah, apparently gems aren't only to be worn over bodies,' chuckled Luv.

'Oh yes, it was hard to find a spot on the palace wall which was covered in gems or murals. They had the most immaculate carvings,' beamed Kush.

'But did you notice how much simpler the houses on the periphery were?' Luv said.

'Hmm...I guess I was too taken by the buildings in the inner quarters to notice anything else,' replied Kush, munching on his thekua.

Sita noticed an early tinge of concern. Kush, she could tell, was rather taken by the materialistic wealth of the kingdom, and Luv slightly pained to see the disparity. Until now, they had never set foot outside the hermitage, and it must have been a shock to learn the ways of the world.

'If you both have finished eating, let us go and water the plants. Remember the neem, *ashwagandha* and *haritaki* saplings we had planted last month? Well, they have come up quite nicely.'

'But wouldn't you at least eat something, Ma?' asked Luv.

'No dear, I am not so hungry. I will have some later.'

And they all walked towards the medicinal garden, not far

from their cottage. Luv and Kush each carried a pot of water that Sita had filled from the river that morning. Truly, the plants had begun to poke their delicate heads over the ground. It felt good to run their hands through the cool, wet mud, to tend to the little saplings, which over time would grow into valuable trees. But for now, the right care at their tender age was vital. As they tilled, they were careful not to harm any worms or insects, and gently placed back any that were mistakenly taken out. After finishing, they lay down on the grass, enjoying the play of a few squirrels scuttling around for fallen fruits. Sparrows called from the bare branches, seen only as a silhouette against the shimmer of the climbing sun. Here, in the hermitage, their world was simple—mud walls, forest paths, and the company of birds and beasts. But Sita never forgot the royal legacy her sons bore and the throne they would never see. Giving voice to her ever silent musings, she asked, 'So, tell me Kush, if you were to be crowned king one day, what type of kingdom do you hope to rule?

'A king! But why would I be a king?' Kush snorted, shrugging his shoulders and returned to playing with the grass.

'Well, no harm in imagining, is there?'

After a moment's deliberation, Kush replied, 'I was completely taken by the grandiosity of Ayodhya. Its resplendence even outshines Guruji's descriptions. If I were to imagine my kingdom, it would not just have palaces, but streets too glittering in jewels. Houses would be twice as tall as I saw in Ayodhya, and gateways would disappear under the cover of clouds. Chariots would fly. There would be white horses, four tusked elephants, lions, tigers and camels in my stables—animals of every kind, even ones that no one has heard of.'

'And what use would all that be?'

'Why else, but a marker of prosperity!' replied Kush.

Sita smiled, and turned towards Luv, 'And you, son? What kind of kingdom do you envisage?'

'Finally! I thought you had already decided to crown Kush as king.'

'Oh, my dear Luv. If only I had a kingdom to offer. But as for my love, you both are equal successors.' Sita drew them both towards her. 'Okay, now tell me, I'm waiting.'

Luv's face turned sombre. 'Ma, all I know is that there will be no place for inequality in my kingdom. You see how our ashram is. I would like my subjects to have equal wealth, live in similar houses, eat similar food and wear similar clothes. No one's turban will be more elaborate than others, or their jewelleries grander. I want no place for jealousy. Just a truly happy kingdom.'

'But don't you worry that will be a stagnant kingdom then? If everything is equal, how would people find motivation to work hard? They would become disinterested and lazy?'

'Exactly Ma!' chimed in Kush, 'The people who are wealthier are so because of the hard work they put in. Those with weak initiative remain poor,' said Kush.

'Mind you, son, that's not entirely true! Some are genuinely unable to work due to certain challenges, their age or ailments. A king's duty is to provide for every needy.'

'So, do you mean to say the king should divide the wealth equally?' asked Kush.

'My sons, society is not meant to be equal. There will be some physically more evolved, some intellectually so, and yet others, morally. A rightful king must first provide for the vulnerable, and then put others to work based on their potentialities. Besides, prosperity is never to be marked by wealth, or people, or territory—instead by the moral values of the kingdom. And who other than the king is a paragon. Only, he should not be a crude moralist, but flexible enough to adapt his judgment to changing situations—time, place or people. No single truth can ever be good for all.'

'Then what about the laws, Ma?' asked Luv.

'The laws should take into light every pertinent situation,' said Sita, with a serious expression.

'Hmm, and we thought there could be no kingdom more perfect than Maharaja Ram's,' said Kush.

'Children, perfection itself is an ever-changing concept. A ruler should evolve with the times. Do you understand?'

'Err…yes. But I don't think we are becoming kings,' smiled Kush.

'You're so remarkable, Ma. We are indeed very lucky to have you,' smiled Luv, looking into her eyes.

'Didn't Maharaja Ram also say the same!' added Kush.

A cold rush rippled through Sita, but she didn't look up. She continued scraping the ground, then asked in the gentlest voice, 'What did he say?'

'Oh, he was quite taken by our veena playing, and when he learnt that it was you who taught us, he said we were fortunate to be born to such a mother,' Luv beamed.

'And what did he say about the singing?' Sita tried to sound unaffected.

'Kept praising us throughout. He enjoyed the entire description, but most specifically, the parts on Queen Sita. How his eyes glittered each time, didn't they, Luv?'

'Indeed, kept remarking to Prince Laxman on what an astonishing woman she was.'

'Did he say that in front of the whole court?' Sita asked.

'Of course, said it in front of everyone. But we learnt something unfortunate...Queen Sita doesn't live with him anymore. I wonder why she left, especially as Maharaja Ram loved her so much. In fact, he never remarried,' said Kush.

'He never remarried!' repeated Sita, more as a surprised realization than a question.

'No, they say he has taken the *ekpatni vrat* in her honour. A proclamation that he is only faithful to her. Quite remarkable, when it is so common for rulers to take multiple wives. If for nothing else, then at least for the sake of progeny,' said Luv.

'He must love her a lot,' said Kush looking into Sita's eyes.

'People tried every ploy to convince him to get married. When all persuasions failed, they even encouraged him to organize an *Ashwamedh* yajna,' said Kush.

'Is there going to be an *Ashwamedh* yajna?'

'Yes Ma, we saw the *Ashwamedh* horse. It was white as a pearl, with fur as shiny. And there were these beaded anklets on its feet. And how it kept swishing its tail!'

Kush swayed his hands and face sideways to show her. 'It was so beautiful, if only we could keep it for ourselves. I wish you had come with us. The preparations were grand.'

'They are also building a staue! But we didn't get a chance to see it. It was veiled.' said Luv.

'What statue?'

'Of Maharani Sita!' said Kush.

'Her statue! Why so?'

'We were equally baffled,' said Luv. 'You see, the *Ashwamedh* yajna cannot be performed without the participation of a spouse. And since the Maharani no longer lives there—'

'His subjects compelled him to remarry,' interjected Kush, 'Such a ploy!'

'Such a ploy!' echoed Luv. 'But Maharaja Ram, brilliant as he is, asked for Maharani Sita's statue to be built in pure gold and placed next to him.'

Her statue made out of pure gold! Sita's head reeled in disbelief.

'You said you couldn't see her face?' she asked.

'No Ma, we were refused,' replied Luv.

'Despite repeated pleadings!' said Kush. Both brothers looked at each other and swayed their heads in spirited disapproval. Sita let out a sigh of relief.

'But Ma, besides being a ploy to convince him, we don't understand the value behind *Ashwamedh* yajna at all? Are you listening?' Kush shook his mother's arms, dragging her back to reality.

'Hmm, the *Ashwamedh* yajna...well, it is a harmonious way of aligning the kingdoms,' replied Sita. 'Saves unnecessary violence and upheavals and helps share resources.'

'Harmonious maybe, but equally belittling. To either submit or challenge is a choice born out of fear. Sending out a horse like this sends a wrong message towards establishing supremacy,' said Luv.

'Yes, better if the submission were out of love that was fearless instead of fearful!' agreed Kush.

Their thinking struck Sita with wonder. Despite being the descendants of the Ikshvakus, they were not afflicted by the rigid sense of morality that had consumed Maharaja Dasharath and Ram. These visionary boys were not moulded by blood alone.

'But how do we propose this to Maharaja Ram? Remember, how that sculptor ridiculed our concerns. I doubt others would understand either. But Maharaja Ram is different. If only that horse crosses our hermitage...we will capture it.'

'Well, that may not be entirely impossible! Didn't they say the horse would be running eastwards. Let's keep an eye. And let's warn the other boys in the ashram too.' Then looking towards Sita, Kush added, 'Ma, would you be okay if we captured it?'

'Hmm? You do realize it might be seen as an open challenge to the king?'

'So? We are not afraid!' said Kush, puffing his chest.

'Yes, we don't fear anyone, not even Maharaja Ram. Like you said, a ruler should be able to evolve with times. We would never become rulers ourselves, but we can at least suggest changes to the one who rules,' said Kush.

Sita smiled at her sons, not saying anything. A cuckoo called from the branches. The sun was shining brighter by now.

'Oh, I completely lost track of time. The ladies must be waiting at the pavilion. Don't you need to leave for your vedas lessons too?' Saying this, Sita got up. The boys got to their feet too, and scampered off, the talk of capturing the *Ashwamedh* horse getting distant in the air. But Sita wasn't paying so much attention. Her mind was fraught by the other revelation. A statue being built was disconcerting enough—and a golden one—even more so.

29

Garnishing of Gold

Sita reached the pavilion to find the ladies already assembled. It had been a few years that she had been teaching them *Kaoshikii*, which wasn't just any dance form, but one with deep philosophical benefits. Few diligent ones were already practicing in the centre of the large octagonal platform, while the rest lingered along the low parapet gracing the edges. Giggling little girls played some kind of game with pebbles. Set within the dense green tranquillity, the pavilion was a simple but expansive structure of mud with a thatched roof over tall bamboo columns.

'Just look how Vandevi's face is beaming this morning! Happy now that your Luv and Kush are back?' remarked Guruma, and extended her hand to Sita to help her up. Hiding a smile, the old lady added, 'However, I am very angry. Why haven't they come around to visit me?'

'Neither me,' joined in the bright spirited Vasuki.

'Oh! I do apologise for their oversight, and I shall remember to pull their ears for it. They will see you soon after their lessons, Guruma. And you too, Vasuki,' said Sita lovingly pinching the little one's cheeks. Then turning around, she addressed the others 'I also apologise for the delay. I got so caught up talking to the boys. Come, let us take positions whenever you are ready.'

Everyone moved towards Sita, ladies both young and old, and some little girls, eager to start their daily ritualistic practice. Vasuki and her group of friends stood in the first row right behind Sita.

'Are all dancers ready? Let's begin!' Saying this, Sita put her hands above her head and folded them in an upright *Namaskar Mudra*. She tapped her right toe behind her left heel, followed by the left behind her right. She bent right, then left, then forward, then backward, and ended it with firm stampings of each foot.

The ladies followed with synchronised swaying, their eyes closed, submitting in absolute faith to this mystical cycle of sixteen counts. It was a cloudy morning, and a hazy blur of light filtered down the thatched roof. The atmosphere was mesmerising, with everyone's bangles clinking, their feet softly stamping to the chants of *dhin dhin dhin…ta ta*. A mild scent of sandalwood drifted through the air. In that instance, the women themselves looked like trees swaying in submission to the lord. They continued for quite a while, oblivious to the passing of time. The whole atmosphere was so invigorated that when Sita ended the dance with her final call of *ta ta,* it took a while for everyone to slide down their hands and open their eyes.

'Beautiful! Divinely beautiful!' said one of the women, a feeling of calmness evident in her voice. 'Vandevi, I have no words to describe the feeling.'

'It used to make me envious seeing the men perform Taandav, especially the glow on their faces afterwards. I had always pined for a something similar,' said another, wiping sweat with her saree's drape.

'It has improved my confidence by leaps and bounds. My speech is so much freer,' said Vasuki's mother.

Sita smiled, pleased to hear the effort had found its mark. 'This dance can open the *koshas* of the mind—its fine, subtle layers. Ever seen how a lotus unfurls petal after petal? By swaying in such submission, we allow our mind's unfurling. It becomes easier for Shiva's grace to flow through.'

Guruma, who had been listening intently said, 'And we women, equally need to align ourselves with the Lord. Afterall, we are the ones who carry his grace of life forward.'

'Indeed,' Sita continued, 'We nurture his creation both within the womb and beyond. We are one half of his creation that shapes the values of the other half.'

'Surely, we play no lesser a role than men,' said an enthused lady.

'Their contribution is valuable too, which is why the Lord created two opposite forces. Just that we need to work in coordinated cooperation instead of subordinated cooperation,' said Sita, caressing young Vasuki's hair. The little one's eyes sparkled with hope, and she nodded. Smiling, Sita nodded back. Then she turned to address everyone, 'Shall we go and finish weaving before it gets late.'

The group of jovially chattering ladies left for weaving, and from there to churning ghee used for *havan*. The cows offered as alms over time from various kingdoms needed to be tended and fed. Afterwards, they made new pots and left them to dry under the afternoon sun.

It was almost dusk when Sita finally left for her cottage. Judging there was still time for the boys to return from their archery lessons, she took a relaxing route by the Tamsa. The air was filled with the excited chirping, as birds returned to their waiting little ones. Finding a clear spot, Sita sat down. Tamsa was a calm river. The evening sun had cast a column of light over the glazed waters, as if pouring gold from its endless pot. Grey *sarsa* birds took off to the sky, their feet tucked inside, wings spread wide.

Sita rested her head atop her knees and listened to the gentle lapping over round pebbles. She reached out her palms, as if to cup the sun. It made her smile, the big ball of light so small within her reach. The fuzzy light glimmered over her arms, rendering them gold. And that was enough for her thoughts to return to the statue.

Why were they glorifying Ram's devotion? How he had not taken another wife, how he had built her statue. A golden statue! He may be acknowledging her purity through gold, but was he also not refuting the claims by building a statue. Why such a need when she was right here? This immortalising in gold and story was being erased in life.

Golden deer to golden Sita! Life had come a long way in between! One a lure, the other a deception. So what if she had once been lured by that elusive deer, weren't all their minds deceived now, all those people of Ayodhya who were finally revering her only after they were done vilifying her. Building her statue, turning her into some kind of sacred myth from a long-forgotten past, forgetting how they had once burnt her in rapturous flames of indignation with those baseless rumours. The act of burning in fire may well purify the gold, but this begrudging deception of justice only hurt her more.

Sita's hands remained cusped, unnoticed of the sun that had long dipped down. Now all that remained within her reach was darkness. She slid her hands down, and only when they touched the pebbles that she realized how cold it had become.

A restless quietude had filled the place. This darkness, only a matter of time before the moon rose and drove it away. She got up and slowly made her way back—as a full moon, very patiently, started to make its way up.

30

Pointless Moon

Silver light slanted down the window and fell over her sleeping boys. From across the room where she sat on her khatiya, Sita held them in a loving gaze. Hands tucked behind their ears, rosy toes peeping beneath, lips drawn in a resting smile with ends dotted in grooves. Their innocence was waning but not quite gone.

Luv rolled over his side and off slid the blanket. Sita crouched over to cover him. Long hair stuck to his cheeks, and she wiped it away. 'Ma? You…haven't slept? Come…sleep.'

'Mmm? In between…' Kush tried lifting his arm, but it flopped down.

And Sita lay in between, thankful for their love. The shaft of light coming down the window, however, was too strong. Tonight, the moon was full, elucidating everything usually forgotten.

The dazzling milkiness was not far from that night at the exile, when en route Panchavati, Ram, Sita and Laxman had reached Anasuya Devi's hermitage. The night, however, had started differently with the moon swallowed behind furious grey clouds. It poured in thick sheets, obscuring everything from view. There was no cave in sight, and the peepal tree they sheltered under was hardly much help. Lightning blitzed through and stunned over the tree tops, and with all that water gushing downhill, the ground had become slippery. In such a state, the idea of lighting a fire would have seemed absurd, yet Sita could not help herself. She leaned against the tree, clenching her stomach. A small yam each is all they had eaten the entire day. That's when Ram saw a flicker of light downhill. Holding onto each other, and anchoring one slippery foot after another, they climbed down.

Ram knocked on the door, but there was no response. The thumping rain had muffled every sound. He knocked again, and after waiting a while, just as they turned to leave, the door creaked open. There stood an old lady, her back hunched like a tortoise shell. Silvery hair hung in thin frays down her shoulders, and her chin was tattooed in thick black dots. From her ear lobes hung solid hoops of gold, which stretched down the piercings, making them look like gaping screams.

'Welcome! Welcome! We were waiting for you only.' She rattled, and two blackened teeth flashed in her otherwise empty smile.

'Greetings, mother! Do you know us?' Ram asked.

'Know you? Who doesn't? Especially after the blessing you brought to Dandakaranya. Sage Agastya had sent a word. Oh, do come in, the rain is awful. Come, I have boiled the rice, and the stew of *karande* is piping hot.'

Her husband, Sage Atri also came forward. Despite being older than his wife, he looked stronger. Not all his hair had greyed, and neither was his back as curled. He had a kind smile and pretended not to take note of the puddle by their feet as he handed them a fresh change. After a humble yet fulfilling meal, the men retired to Sage Atri's cottage for a scholarly discussions, while Sita offered to clear the dishes. In the time, the rain had turned soft over the roof, yet fine sprays made their way through the window.

Anasuya Devi, breathless with even the slightest of activity, propped herself on the khatiya and gazed at Sita. There was no jangling of bangles over Sita's dainty wrists as she scrubbed the pots, only a garland of simple forest flowers, which too were mostly squashed or missing.

'What do you make of forest life, dear? Tough, isn't it?' Anasuya Devi's voice shook and frayed at the ends.

'Yes, mother. But also contending. After all, hermits like yourselves choose to spend your entire lives here,' Sita replied, her eyes downcast.

Her quick wit pleased Anasuya Devi. Being a strong woman herself, she appreciated those who spoke their mind. 'True. But I had been born a sage's daughter. You, however, were a princess. So unfortunate, that debacle before your husband's coronation… but you could have stayed back. Why did you follow him?'

Sita upturned the washed pots, and considered her words before replying, 'Living without him would have hardly been living at all.'

Anasuya Devi smiled, and it sounded more like a wheeze. Again, flashing her crooked teeth, she said, 'I heard your sister stayed back.'

'It wasn't her wish. She was commanded.'

'And weren't you?'

Sita looked at the wavering light of the lamp in the corner and replied, 'So was I. But what vow could be more sacrosanct than the one made to the wedding fire. I could never abandon Ram, especially not then.' She crouched to remove the burnt logs from the chulha and began clearing away the ash. A shy smile lit her face as she said, 'Besides, he has been exceptionally kind, doesn't make me miss a thing.' Then in a soft voice, added, 'This exile is nothing. If need be, I would follow him to the end of the world.'

'So charming, your praises! Exactly what I was hoping for!' The old lady let out a hearty chuckle which sounded a bit disconcerting, and said, 'You sound just like the *chakor* following the moon. You are the bird…and Ram is your moon.' With that, she let out another chortle which almost choked her.

Colour rose to Sita's cheeks. It was startling to hear the old woman take such keen interest in passion. But there wasn't any lie in what she said.

'I heard your wicked stepmother was challenged to allow you to rule as Ram's regent. That sage Vashishtha had raised quite a furore. A queen in her husband's absence—now that would have been remarkable!'

'Hmm, but there was no point ruling through such travesty of facts. Either Ram should have ruled rightfully, or best we followed the oath together.'

'No greed! I see no greed in you, not an ounce. You are what an ideal wife should be. May Lord Shiva always protect you.' Anasuya Devi raised both hands in a blessing. It took a while for her head to stop bobbing.

She gestured for Sita to come closer, and the younger one took her place by the foot of the khatiya and began massaging her host's cold feet. Her bones looked delicate, and Sita took care running her fingers over them. In this while, the fine sprays too had stopped, and the hostile night turned pleasant. They chatted a long time in the golden light of the lamp, the older imparting advice, and the younger absorbing it in ready obeisance.

'Daughter, I have a gift for you,' said Anasuya Devi. 'There, in that corner, must be a trunk.' Sita could tell she couldn't see very clearly with her rheumy eyes and carefully guided her over. Although the puddle had been wiped off, the floor was still slippery. Shaking with effort, the old lady opened the trunk and took out a bundle wrapped in red cloth. 'Here, this will look nice on you!' she said with a smug smile.

Inside were lustrous ornaments of many different kinds—gold earrings, necklaces, toe rings and carved bangles. There was even a waistband with tinkering bells.

'Oh, kind mother! Touched as I am, I can't accept these. My husband has vowed to live as an ascetic. I am so sorry...' Sita folded her hands.

'Who says these are merely ornaments? These are my blessings.' Anasuya Devi thrust the bunch forward. She lost her balance and had to steady herself by holding on to Sita. 'And don't you worry about your husband. If he says anything, they would only be words of appreciation.' Her toothless grin flashed again.

Anasuya Devi sat Sita down on her *khatiya* and with freckled hands, bedecked her before sending her off. Outside, the ground was cold and gleamed with water-filled puddles. Sita lifted her saree pleats, careful not to muddy them. The wind had settled, and wet fronds of palm glistened in the silence. But it was her fragile heart that pounded wildly.

Ram was at the door, keeping an eye out. It was awkward, that unexpected dressing up, that intoxicating smell of unguents. Ram stood fixated, blocking her way in. Drops of water gleamed at the edges of the thatch roof and plopped down. He then gently extended his arm and drew her in. No words were spoken, at least not for a while, as he ran his fingers over the ornaments, then took them off one by one, his fingers brushing her ears, the nape of her neck. Just then, a hoot was heard, and with a mad fluttering, a bird took to the sky.

'A chakor!' Sita rushed to the window, but all too late.

'What?' Ram enfolded her from behind. Outside, the moon glistened on the dewy grass and the trees behind. On a boulder stood Laxman, ready with a bow and quiver, his frame erect, leg outstretched, as always keeping the night long vigil. But the moonlight elucidated a forlorn look over his face.

'It is not that I am not grateful towards Laxman, yet a part of me is incensed for Urmila,' Sita said, sliding off Ram's arms.

He lowered his gaze. There was no denying the unintentional injustice. That look on Urmila's face, the day they had left for the exile. How she had suppressed the trembling defiance rising up her throat, her eyes sharp with tears. Her longing evident to all except Laxman.

'I did stop him. But he would not listen,' Ram said in a low voice, attempting to ease the tension.

Sita returned her gaze outside. 'If only he also cared for his duties as a husband as much.' The sarcasm was intended more for Ram who kept praising his brother's selflessness. 'And sometimes I wish Urmila wasn't so self-effacing. That she was more ruthless and unapologetic.'

Sighing, Sita came around and lay on the reed mat. However, her back was turned away. Ram too lay in quiet reflection, carrying the guilt of Lakshman's doing. That night, the full moon shone with a pointless light over them both. It shone equally pointlessly over Laksman outside, and over Urmila much farther away. Only the chakor kept flying higher and higher, in a naive attempt to meet its lover.

Part Eight

31

Time for Spring

'What! You're already awake?' Luv groaned, rubbing sleep off his eyes.

Sita had just walked in with a pot of water that she placed by the *chulha*.

'Bathed and ready too?' Kush propped himself on his elbows.

'Not only that but I have also milked the cow. The rotis and a stew of jackfruit are ready in that corner.'

'Did we oversleep?' Luv craned to look out of the window. The embers in the chulha were still warm, but behind it the forest was obscured in a sheet of white blindness.

'Didn't oversleep, but about time you got up. However, I need to leave early.' Sita walked out to spread her washed saree onto the branches of the mango tree.

'Why so?' Luv also walked out. A dense fog hugged the ground.

'Guru Valmiki wants assistance in the *prayogshala*. He is making new medicines that might cure difficult ailments. A few of us agreed to help.'

'Oh yes, he did say something to that regard yesterday,' said Luv.

'Does it mean no lessons then? Are we free this morning?' asked Kush.

'What! No! Other sages will take your lessons. So go, and get ready. And don't forget to eat,' Sita said, pulling Kush's cheeks. 'Oh, and sprinkle some grains for the birds. Look in the red pot…by the sill.' Saying this, she disappeared into the fuzzy whiteness.

By the time she reached the prayogshala, a few disciples had already busied themselves. Sita too started sorting dried leaves of *gular*, *paakar* and *bad*. She ground them over stone mortar and mixed its paste with the strained juice of *bhojvriksh* and peepal. These were then duly separated by Sage Valmiki in pots and sealed before being added with the desired medicinal fruits. Few pots were kept under the sun, and the rest wrapped tightly with muslin cloth and buried under the ground for few months.

Sita had almost finished helping with the tidying and cleaning when she saw Sage Valmiki leave. She rushed out.

'Guruji! We are so grateful for this enlightening experience. Hope our efforts will bring results.'

'And if it doesn't, we will try again. Sooner or later, we will succeed.'

'Your last attempt took years. How you do you stay so motivated?'

'Daughter, why else would I be called a *rishi* if not for the quest for discovery. The great Lord Shiva himself was the founder of *Vaedyak Shastra*. You see, medicines as the best analogy that a cure for every problem exists.'

He started walking, and Sita followed after. 'If the lord wanted,' Sage Valmiki continued, 'he could have simply made his creation perfect. Yet he didn't—he left behind problems. Why? To give our souls a purpose. And when we serve our purpose, serve his creation, is when we actually end up serving him.'

They walked some more before he added, 'Take your example only. You never limited your life to yourself, or even to Luv and Kush. You selflessly served the women in the ashram, teaching them the vedas, new skills…but now it's time to think beyond. What about serving the posterity, serving those yet to be born? You see, this gift of life is very valuable, daughter. And only a mere few are able to realize it.' He raised his hands in blessings even before Sita could join hers. But something caught his attention, and he glided towards the arjuna tree.

'Oh, look, new leaves have started to shoot.' He regarded them admirably, 'Do you know what it means?'

'That it's time for spring?'

'That it is time for change! Just see how tender they are, and then to be fraught with so much resistance from everywhere—wind, cold, animals. Yet they will survive. Why? Because a powerful force protects them. And that powerful force looks after every meaningful change.'

He continued, 'Did you know the arjuna tree is very valuable, its flowers and bark are good for the heart. In time, the whole forest will be abuzz with the ringing of its pods and the return of the tree nymph butterflies.'

'And the chestnut-winged cuckoos!' chimed in Sita.

'And the chestnut-winged cuckoos! The forest is ready to embrace its change. Are you ready to embrace yours?' He looked her in the eye. Then swiftly changed the subject. 'Alright, I am off to the Tamsa to meditate and will only be back tomorrow. Tell the ashramwasis not to worry, and not to come looking.'

And away he went, stopping ever so often by yet more trees, crying each time, 'It's time for change!'

Sita looked confused. *What did Guruji mean? Hadn't she already embraced a fair share of changes? Upheavals thrown at her for no mistake of her own? Was he instead implying not to simply bear, but bring about the change. Become the genesis of change?*

The creamy sunlight had long cleared the fog. Slight warmth in the air was decipherable, yet another inkling that change was coming. Her gaze returned to the tender arjuna leaves, more golden than green, more defiant than delicate. She walked closer. The bark was peeling in places, the trunk was wide and its branches overarching. She sank to her knees and leaned against it, just like she had leaned against the *shimshapa* years ago. A part of the knotted root jutted out, and Sita ran her fingers over it. So much of the root was hidden out of sight—yet it worked silently, holding the tree firm, feeding it with life. Like the root, some lived their lives in shadow, doing their duty without praise. A smile touched her lips, as though the thought was not about the tree alone.

Her gaze turned distant, and the sounds of the outside world fell away. A cuckoo above sat in similar stillness. It stretched its beak to the patch of azure sky, but didn't sing, perhaps reluctant to break that blissful melody of silence.

Oblivious to Sita, a distant whinnying cut through the air. It was followed by the scuffle of feet and rising voices, gathering urgency, until they swelled into the hum of a crowd. Out of the commotion emerged a horse, spotless white, its body restless with energy, its legs skittering in impatience. Regal velvet clung to its back, red as ruby, while golden *ghungroos* clashed and rang with a desperation that refused to be stilled. The horse's head tossed left to right; its tail swished in mad rebellion. Luv had its knotted red rein under his hold, and Kush tussled with the horse to calm it down. But the horse huffed and puffed, and swung its neck, refusing to submit. Not to some little boys who didn't quite reach the height of its back.

'Where have you found this horse?' asked an ashramwasi.

'It is the *Ashwamedh* horse,' hollered Luv. 'It belongs to Maharaja Ram.' He tried calming the horse by stroking its mane, whispering something in its ears. Too angry for any such affection, the horse snorted and sprayed its captor all over.

'Maharaja Ram's *Ashwamedh* horse! Do you even realize what you have done? Set it free right away!' shouted someone from the crowd.

'Why should we? Isn't the whole idea to capture it and pose a challenge?' Kush shouted back, still holding onto the horse's neck. The horse swayed furiously which sent Kush stumbling on the ground. Luv wasted no time and flung across to clamp its mouth.

'A challenge? Whatever would you challenge Maharaja Ram for? Are you out of your minds! Weren't you just singing his praises?' asked the man.

Another person cut in before the children could reply, 'Look children, this is a hermitage, not a kingdom. It doesn't behove us to get involved in these matters.'

'You don't understand! Of course we respect the Maharaja. But letting the *Ashwamedh* horse pass without doing anything sends a message that our submission is out of fear.'

'Fear or otherwise, how does it even matter?'

'It matters. Anything born out of fear never bears good results,' said Kush.

The horse hissed, and once again thick sprays fell on Luv's face. He wiped it out of his eyes. Meanwhile, Kush kept stroking it.

'But this ritual has been carrying through ages. Your ludicrous actions will drag us all into trouble.'

'And who are you to assume our actions are ludicrous? Let the Maharaja be its judge,' said Luv.

'Maharaja? Are you a fool to think you would even get to meet him? He's a king, that too of Ayodhya, a man far too important for petty botherations. Mind you, it will be his army coming.'

'So! Let them!'

'How adamant! Someone, go call their mother. Only she can talk some sense into their thick minds.'

Immediately, two ladies took off to look for Sita while the rest fruitlessly continued to reason with the boys. It took the ladies quite a while before they saw Sita sitting under the arjuna tree.

'Vandevi! Here you are!' said the lady, relief spreading over her face, 'We had been searching for you everywhere. Quick! You must hurry to Luv and Kush—they have captured the *Ashwamedh* horse!'

Sita sat frozen, reacting not even with as much as a flinch. It seemed like she hadn't heard her. The dappled shade made it difficult to tell if she had even noticed their presence.

'Vandevi! Hurry, before it's too late!' the other one said, hand pressed against her heaving chest. But she too was met with the unusual quiet from Sita.

'Is she okay?' the lady asked her companion. In reply, the other one shrugged her shoulders.

They crept closer and began more softly. 'Vandevi? Luv and

Kush have captured the *Ashwamedh* horse. We are very worried about the consequences.'

But Sita was unmoved. A serene smile lit her restful face. Probably some powerful thoughts precluded all noise around.

'Vandevi? Are you even listening? What are you looking at?' the lady asked.

'At this creeper.' At last Sita replied. It was to their most insignificant prodding. 'Look at this *madhumalti*, twirled around in helpless devotion to the tree. Like it has accepted there is no alternative fate for her.'

The women shot confused looks at each other. Indeed, the creeper hugged the tree tightly, and indeed the tree felt like the master of that creeper's vulnerable destiny. But why was that crucial. Why now?

Sita ran her fingers around the creeper's glossy leaves, and it shivered ever so timidly. 'There is no value in love and trust if it is not reciprocated,' Sita whispered, not directly looking at her companions, or she would have seen the stark incredulity in their eyes.

'Err…Vandevi, we understand all this, but now is not the time. Like we said…Luv and Kush, have held the horse captive. They say that they have some questions for Maharaja Ram, and would only release the horse after meeting him. Now please, you need to come,' said the lady.

'Then it is between them and the Maharaja. I have nothing to do with it.' Sita finally addressed the matter, but in an unfazed tone.

'But Vandevi? Wouldn't you at least go and stop them?' asked the baffled lady. 'Please help us. Even Guruji is not in the ashram today.'

'Do their questions come with a wrong intention?' asked Sita.

'What...we...we don't even know what questions they have? But isn't that beside the point.'

'No, that is the whole point. The quest for discovery should never be stopped, especially if the intentions are not wrong. Hope you don't mind, but I want to be left alone.' Replying so, Sita tenderly turned her face away.

Even though she wasn't exactly supporting her sons' actions, neither was she decrying them. Such oddity on Sita's part was beyond the grasp of the simple ashram ladies who until now had only known her as highly conscientious. They shifted on their unsure toes for a while, but receiving nothing beyond a stony silence, returned with their heads hanging low.

32

The Blanket

In time, the horse calmed down. All the stroking and whispering had worked its magic. In fact, by now it had even warmed up to its young captors, and nuzzled its cold, wet mouth against their necks, setting off a ring of giggles. It had even accompanied the boys to their cottage as they fetched their bow and quiver, ready for a battle if there was to be one.

The defeated ashramwasis had also dragged away their impressionable young children, wanting no part in that blasphemous capturing. But hardly a prahar had passed before they had to rush back.

In the receding light of the afternoon, the stir of an approaching army broke upon the hermitage; armour clattering, hooves pounding, spears flashing, the forest itself echoing the din. At its head rode Prince Laxman. The ashramwasis turned to Luv and Kush with anxious eyes, but the boys stood unflinching, their casket of arrows and bow slung in readiness. Now only a miracle could save them. As the prince drew near, the ashramwasis dropped into ready submission.

'You two?' The sight of the offenders surprised Laxman

Both boys bowed with folded hands, mindful of not loosening the hold over the rein. The horse neighed but made no effort to move away.

'My Lord, it was a childish mistake,' implored an old ashramwasi.

'Please pardon their audacity,'

Laxman raised his hand in assurance and looked endearingly at the young boys, who had enchanted Ayodhya only a while back.

'Greetings, My Lord!' said Luv, 'But this is not a mistake. We have genuine concerns.'

'Concerns? What sort?' asked Laxman.

'Pardon us, but they are only for the ears of Maharaja Ram,' Kush replied, holding his chin high.

'Ah! I had my suspicions the first time I met you. Not only are you skilled in music, but equally with words. Alright, so be it! Accompany me to Ayodhya, and I will make sure you are allowed an audience with the Maharaja. But first, set the horse free.'

'We cannot! Our concerns are in fact related to this practice. Unfortunately, we can't set it free, not until Maharaja Ram addresses us,' replied Luv.

'There is no need to be concerned. I can assure you, there will be no effect on the autonomy of your hermitage.'

'Please, all we want is a word with the Maharaja,' Kush replied adamantly.

'Do you not realize the seriousness of the *Ashwamedh* yajna. It cannot be meddled with. Not for any fanciful whims! Leave its rein!'

'We will not! We will not let the horse carry on,' Kush spoke up.

'Enough of this petulance!' Laxman's face reddened, and his eyes took on a frightening expression. 'Or I will not hesitate to raise arms against you.'

'By all means. We too have our bow and arrows ready,' announced Luv.

By now, Laxman, thoroughly incensed, jumped off his horse and pulled a bow from his quiver. But before he could even brace it, a sharp arrow came rending through and grazed his arm. Blood oozed and slithered down. But it wasn't the greatest shock. A dozen more arrows whooshed past and rained down in a cage like formation. Another arrow knocked his bow to the ground.

Everyone was stunned. On the one hand, the impudence of the boys was deplorable; on the other, their skill, commendable.

Not prepared for such agility from mere ten-year-olds, Laxman was deeply embarrassed at his own lack of swiftness. His sweaty hands slipped over the arrows, as he plucked them one after the other, fearing yet another round of outwitting display. Thankfully, the sun plunged into the horizon, announcing an abrupt end to an unsatisfactorily short war.

'As per the warrior rules,' Laxman said, turning back to the dipping light, 'it would be a sin to raise weapons any longer. So, I shall leave.' Laxman jumped onto his horse's back. The bleeding had left a stain over his dhoti. 'I must confess, your valour is remarkable; and only in its honour I shall convey your wishes to the Maharaja. But before you get your hopes too high, just bear in mind that the result could also be disastrous.'

He yanked the reins and trotted off. The clomping of the hooves once again filled the air. With it, the hermits also retreated, uneasy with the uncertainty.

The boys too returned to their cottage. Light was fading fast and by the time they reached their kuitya, an unsettling stillness had taken over the place. They lit a diya by the cow's shed and dropped the animal some fodder. They offered some to the horse too.

'Where is Ma? I haven't seen her all day?' asked Luv.

'She hadn't even turned up at the ashramwasis' request. Do you think she might be upset?' said Kush.

'But we had checked with her, hadn't we—our intent of capturing the horse?' replied Luv, and then peered into the darkness.

'Do you think we could ask the ashram ladies for help?' Kush suggested.

'Ah! They must all be fuming. I doubt they would even open their doors to us. Shall we check by the Tamsa? She often goes there.'

They took the horse and walked over to the banks. But it was desolate with only the mournful gurgling on the pebbles. They went to the *havandkund,* and to the pavilion, but were met with similar stillness. Confused, they returned to their kutiya and sat on the verandah. The horse slumped by their feet, who they stroked in a bid to forget their own anxiety. But Sita still didn't return. It was only when the evening got murkier and the shrill of crickets creepier that their voices took on a weepy touch.

'She has never left us this long, not without telling us. She mentioned the prayogshala in the morning? Shall we go there?' suggested Luv.

'But hadn't the experiment long finished in the morning?'

'Still, no harm in checking?'

They lit a larger diya, wrapped themselves in blankets and

left for one final attempt. In the uncomfortably quiet night, the ringing of the anklet over the horse sounded stark.

The prayogshala was unnervingly still with all the pots and the jars, the pestles and the mortars, the strainers and the mixers, all taking on a strange appearance in the enveloping gloom. They padded through the sheltered darkness. Under the glow of the diya, the crushing pain on their little faces was heart wrenching. An unexpected shadow caught Luv's eyes, halting him mid-step. Something was against the tree outside. Could that be their mother? Or simply more jars? It was hard to tell in the darkness.

'Ma? Is that you?' Luv beseeched. His voice came out dry.

There was no reply. They edged closer. The pat of their feet and the ringing of the horse's anklets, the only sounds.

'Ma? Is that you?' Luv repeated.

Kush shone the diya closer and it made him gasp, 'Why are you—'

'What are you doing here?' interjected Luv.

'Hmm...Luv? Kush! Ah, I am just...I was only—' Sita woke up from a state of deep trance.

'Are you okay, Ma?' Kush asked, taking her hand. It was shockingly cold, colder than the ground beneath.

'I am fine. I am indeed fine. Oh, and is this the horse?'

'Yes Ma, the *Ashwamedh* horse,' said Luv.

'The change is indeed upon us,' whispered Sita.

'Change? What change?' Luv asked.

'Oh, don't bother. I...I guess I just need some time alone. Why don't you go back to the cottage, and I will see you later.'

'No Ma, you are coming with us. It is too late. And too cold,' Luv pulled her by the arms.

'No!' She flicked back, something she had never done before.

'But why not? Don't do this, please get up.' Kush was teary and held out his own arm.

'Please understand!' said Sita, then regretting her previous impulse added, 'Please go, and eat something. I promise I will see you later.'

They stood frozen, far too baffled to see their mother behave this way.

After a while, Luv mustered courage and asked, 'Ma the horse is hungry. We had given it some grass but it is still complaining.'

'Look in the cottage. I am sure you can find some jaggery, or some dried peas. If you are old enough to challenge the ritual, then you should be responsible enough to look after the horse,' she said. 'I am sure you will. Now go. It is quite late.'

The boys knew there was no point coaxing her. Clearly, her mind was made up. She fell strangely silent, and the trill of crickets grew louder.

'Okay, if that is what you want,' said Luv, shifting on his toes. 'But at least take this blanket. Kush, let's place the diya beside Ma.'

Sita peered into their sad eyes, touched by their concern, but said nothing. Together they wrapped her with warmth, tucking her feet and shoulders against the chill. Their cheeks were so round, so close upon her, their eyes averting her gaze. They were acting mature, like they knew she needed the silence and were allowing her so. When had they grown so much? Tears turned sharp in her eyes. An overwhelming desire urged her to gather them into her arms, but she simply watched them leave, dragging away their heavy feet and the whinnying horse.

It was clear the night was going to be tediously silent. But more pinching was the regret that she hadn't embraced her boys when she had the chance, hadn't let them lay their heads on her lap, stroked their sorry cheeks, smoothened their hair. The silhouette of the boys melted into the distance like an already read page from the past, a page that had contained the most vulnerable and the most beautiful writing of her life, and she wondered, as she sat alone in the cold shade of the arjuna tree, if she would ever be able to flip that page and experience the joy afresh. The lingering tear dropped down her eye, clearing her wavering vision. But the boys had already disappeared.

33

Night of Silence

Two more prahars drifted by, while the ground gathered more dew and the air more chill. But nothing deterred Sita. Despite the prickling, she sat frozen under the tree's inky shade, frozen to all emotions. Her soul needed the silence—not of words, but of thoughts. The recent pull of the past had tugged her away from the present, and the present is all she yearned for, for that alone led to the future.

She closed her eyes and listened to the cool air filling her chest. It felt nice; to not speak, to just listen. And she listened to the letting go, to every outgoing breath releasing her from the shame, the achievements, the attachments, the fear of hiding her identity from the world. What was her identity anyway—was it even fully revealed to her? Was she herself not ignorant of her own facets; of her power, of all that she was ever capable of. But right now, she didn't want to think. She wished only to breathe, deeply and slowly, as if each breath were a salve to her hurting soul. In time her trance blurred into sleep.

When she finally opened her eyes, the stars had long blotted back, and a crimson streak crept up the horizon.

The night has passed.

Even though she hadn't said it out loud, she felt it with undoubting clarity. The night had indeed passed. She stood up, brushed off the dust, and corrected the gathers of her saree. Then she folded the blanket and retied her bun. Her eyes were red after the night outside, but her spirit was renewed with contentment.

Tamsa wasn't far. Although the morning was still young, there was no harm in taking a bath now that she was already awake. The forest had also just about started to sing with rising birds.

The river lay blushing in the same hue as its beloved sky, with nascent light lapping the awakening water. Although uncomfortably cold, it didn't bother Sita, who had led most of her life in the forests. Without so much as a sigh of hesitation, she immersed herself, letting the water take over, and wash away any lingering thoughts. She rose and looked at the brightening sun that brought in a new day, a new offering.

The animals gathered by the water momentarily looked up as Sita made her way back to her children, her saree dripping with water, her lips chanting the morning prayers. She pictured them waiting at the cottage, perhaps tending after the horse, perhaps still wrapped in their blankets.

But when she entered her kutiya, there was no sign of Luv and Kush. Their blankets were neatly folded, and the vessels were untouched. Had they not eaten anything? The sight of their crushed faces swarmed in front of her eyes, and she felt a heavy pang. Then her thoughts turned uneasy. Perhaps she had been too harsh the night before. Had they left the cottage and gone looking for her again? What if they had not returned through the night—out there with wild beasts prowling in the dark?

Determined to waste no time, she pulled out a new saree, and had nearly finished changing when she heard a rattle at the door. The same lady from yesterday, stood across her.

'Vandevi! Why didn't you listen to us yesterday?' she said, forehead clenched in deep creases.

'Where are Luv and Kush? What happened to—'

'They are fine.' She cut her sharply, 'But now look, what has happened! Maharaja Ram, he himself is here, and—'

Ram!

Sita's senses stopped responding. The lady was saying something but it failed to reach her.

'What is wrong with you Vandevi? Why are you ignoring us?'

By now, Guruma along with a few more ladies also hurried inside. 'Daughter! Quickly! Or else we will all have to bear the brunt.' Her hand pressed hard on her heaving chest. 'Guruji is also not here! I don't know how else to manage this situation. Hurry!'

Sita staggered back, her knees nearly giving away, before she hit the wall. *Eleven Years!* After eleven long years he was here.

'Go! Why are you still standing here?' yelled Guruma.

How could she go? He wasn't even here for her. How could she simply go and startle him.

'Just apologize to him, and it will all be fine.' The urgency in Guruma's voice disoriented Sita.

Apologise? For what?

Guruma strode up and shook Sita. 'Can you not hear me? What has overcome you? They are your children after all!'

Sita looked about; an uncomprehending look still pasted over. Guruma shook her and roared, 'I'll say this once again.

We have already tried our best. But it is your duty, and yours alone. Do you understand?'

'Yes! Yes. I understand…I…understand!'

She stared at the open doorway—at the brightness beckoning her. Then took a deep breath and walked out.

But as she climbed down the steps, her feet faltered, and she brought up her palms. They were calloused and roughened with forest life. Not the hands fit for a queen. Her ochre yellow saree was rough and plain. And her skin, it didn't hold the same glow as the first time he had seen her in the gardens. Her hair was not as lustruous as when he had weaved it with flowers. She was different from the time he had slept holding her, or from when, with her belly so swollen, he had embraced her. Had embraced her for so long—and—left forever.

Once again, she brought her palms close and considered all the cuts and callouses. Today she would wear them as marks of an honourable independent woman. A woman who shone through all of life's oddities.

The ladies, once again confounded by her behaviour, edged towards her. But before they could do or say anything, Sita strode off.

It was time to meet Ram.

34

The Final Call

To the onlooking ladies, Sita appeared confident, walking with a resolute gait and focused eyes. Only her own heart knew how wildly it pounded.

Her momentum finally faded as she reached the *yajnashala*, where a large gathering had formed beneath the sprawling branches of the banyan tree—familiar ashramwasis alongside men bearing spears and maces, all standing with their backs turned. Her eyes searched for him, but all she saw was a sea of heads. The cries, however, rang clear.

'Glory be to Luv!'

'Glory be to Kush!'

'Glory be to Ram!'

'Oh, you are here!' an ashramwasi, having taken notice, slipped to one side.

'There is nothing to worry. Look, how happy the Maharaja is!' said another, parting way, and she caught his crown's glint.

'Oh Vandevi, you came too late,' they parted further.

'Vandevi is here! Vandevi is here! Give way!'

'Give way, she is here!'

A path cleared—and she saw him. A sudden shock slammed through her, and her chest leapt. Ram stood with the boys, still unaware of her.

But Kush—he raised his eyebrows and cried, 'Ma! Look, the Maharaja himself is here!'

With a gentle swivel, Ram turned, and his serene smile, vanished. All in a moment, gone. His face contorted in deep folds. He blinked. Then blinked again, as if unsure whether his eyes had conjured a vision from the past. Sita felt a deep burning in her stomach.

With slow, sure steps he walked over, crossing the parted gathering of curious onlookers. A racing anticipation burnt Sita's cheeks. And the pounding of her heart—it was loud and embarrassingly clear for all.

'Maharaja!' she spoke softly, hoping he would halt.

And he did! Stung, yet again! This formal greeting, so absurd, but a less formal one, would have been equally inappropriate. Such was the nature of their estranged relationship—a husband and a wife, who had loved each other fiercely, but just not openly.

Ram tilted his face, searching for her eyes that avoided his. Anticipation is such a dreadful thing. Despite the unlikely reality of such a reunion, and despite her own upright heart, Sita had secretly allowed herself its million manifestations. Yet, none of them came in close palpability to the bare display of bafflement, love, remorse and longing she sensed today. The same emotions slipping over Ram's face, like shadows across the lapping waters of a river. His open unrestraint left Sita—one who had been forced to cover herself as Vandevi—very discomfited. Her finger twisted the loose end of her saree. Then she slowly looked up at him, more closely this time.

Their eyes spoke, spilling all their unremitting pain. Only he seemed more crushed, more forlorn. So pallid with the passage of time. Age hadn't affected her so gravely, but for Ram, it had turned the hair under his weighty crown greyer. His forehead carried deep wrinkles, ones she didn't have any memory of. Sunlight gleamed off his pearl necklace, and she saw his shoulder blades glisten, just as they had, when they had sat together on the boulder overlooking the Godavari. His arms that had held her in countless embraces were still strong. The mole beneath his left ear remained unchanged, and beneath it, the battle scar from Lanka had faded with time, but not quite gone. He looked so familiar and unfamiliar at the same time. His throat moved as he softly swallowed, and at once Sita became aware of all the people gathered around.

Sensing a strange discomfort, her sons walked up and held her by the arms.

'Do you...have you met the Maharaja before?' asked Luv in a measured voice.

Kush looked bewilderingly at the king and his mother.

It broke their stupor. What answer could she offer to that, to say under what capacity she knew him? But Ram understood. He finally understood. No wonder the ten-year-old Luv and Kush were his own sons, their likeness, just like him. And no wonder they were her sons, their resilience, just like her. He let out a painful sigh, that rent through the dry air, and despite the swarming in his eyes, he saw with clarity his grown-up boys, and his now-distant wife. He finally saw all that his decree had robbed him of.

'Please return the horse,' Sita said to the boys.

'We already have, Ma,' replied Luv. 'Maharaja has come in peace,' he said in a meek voice.

'Ma, are you okay?' Kush asked, more directly.

'Yes…pay your obeisance to the Maharaja and let us go.'

Ram flinched. She kept calling him Maharaja. How she was punishing him! That aloofness of hers worse than her grievances. And now Sita had gathered her boys, and was ready to leave.

'Please! Stop!'

She bit her lips, and closed her eyes.

'Sita! Look at me!'

Finally! Finally, he had called her by her name!

An unsettling wave of shock crossed over the boys. Their mother, Maharani Sita! A few gasps followed through.

But Sita kept her eyes closed. She wanted no part of it. Her boys, betrayed and let down, slowly stepped away, as Ram moved in closer.

She still wouldn't have opened her eyes if it wasn't for the faint sobbing of her sons. She looked pleadingly at them as they staggered back, shaking their heads in denial. If only such knowledge could have pleased them, but it made them distraught. *The irony of life!* In a mere turn of a moment, their revered idol, Maharaja Ram, had become their father, and their mother, the distant Maharani Sita. What a gain and an equal loss. It felt like they didn't belong to either. Tears streamed down their disbelieving eyes. It broke her heart. Ram also looked at them, knowing all too well that he couldn't even apologize for the heartbreak, which was in effect his doing. He looked remorsefully at these innocent boys who were his sons. Or rather, her sons.

They were not the only ones stunned by this revelation. The gathered ashramwasis, now looked at her with a newfound awe. The same deference was over the faces of the Ayodhyan army. It made the moment tediously unbearable.

'I...I had no idea you were here.' The husband, who could talk to her as if she were his own mirror now spoke with painful restraint.

Once again Sita had no reply. Yet the air thrummed with unspoken words.

Are you startled to see me here?

'Please look at me, Sita.'

And she did. And only saw discomforting distance.

'Life has not been the same ever since you left.'

Left?

'I know I had been harsh...but you must know, you...you complete me like no other.'

Then why didn't you come looking?

'There hasn't been a more devoted wife, more supportive, more understanding.'

A lump went down her throat.

'The way you have been with me through everything...is something...that I haven't offered equally.'

It wasn't her desire to see him beaten, yet she could not deny his words. A tear fell down her eye and blotted her saree. The sight refreshed tears in Ram's own eyes. He walked closer and remained standing. Simply lost, just looking at her.

'Do you...would you be willing to overlook everything? Allow me to...' He began, but not steadily, the words punctuated by so many pauses, arousing so many feelings. 'Please allow me to take you back to Ayodhya along with...our sons.'

The windless silence augmented the intensity of trying emotions. Sita tried not to hear. But she couldn't overlook that the sobbing of her sons had silenced. What now replaced their faces was a hopeful expression. Hope—such a strange thing—springs up at the slightest spark.

She knew the surge of love in Ram's heart was genuine, and as was the look in the downcast eyes of the Ayodhyans wanting to welcome their queen back. And above all, she heard the faint knock of her own heart, prodding her towards a future that could be. She, Ram, Luv and Kush, finally together. She had loved him with absolute honesty. And isn't love bigger than grudge?

Then why did you abandon me in the first place? Sita's questioning thoughts continued.

'I know I have been harsh in my judgment. But it was for the sake of Ayodhya.'

'Ayodhya?' She finally spoke.

Let out in shock, that first word was only an outlet for her reprising shame.

'And what exactly did you end up doing for the sake of Ayodhya?'

'You know the rules. The people were angry. They wanted to know whether you were chaste…I tried explaining, and it made matters worse. They wanted to question you, to appear for a hearing in front of the court. I couldn't let that happen… that ordeal would have been too much. So, I sent you away. I do realize how wrong I was. I should have let you speak. And you could have easily allayed all doubts. At least that suffering wouldn't have been worse than—' his voice drifted off, '—But it's not too late. You can still appear for the ordeal.'

A great queasiness surfaced upon Sita. It felt like she was back in Lanka, standing amidst his horde of army, much like all these people today. Once again, she saw all eyes bore down upon her.

'Wasn't my justification in Lanka enough? I was naïve to think that you had believed me.'

'You are taking it all wrong, my dear—'

Her shoulders flinched at that mark of endearment, something which didn't go unnoticed by Ram. With a dampened voice he continued, 'Of course, I believed you. And yes, the army also saw you walk into the flames…and that miraculous showers. But they were only a handful after all. But Ayodhya murmured…non-stop. It became too much.'

Mortification clung to his voice, dragging the pitch down, cautioning him not to utter any more. Yet he defied all instincts and followed what he was supposed to do.

Ram—always doing what he was supposed to do.

'You must believe I only tried to protect you.'

'How? By first maligning me yourself?'

'Sita! How could you say that?'

'Deny it for all you want, but the truth is—you killed my honour to save yours!'

Her will turned ferociously stubborn. There must have been bewilderment and rebuke for her cold, dispassionate gaze—coming from a woman, a wife who had vowed to support him in good times and bad. She had done so with absolute devotion—until now.

Some moments passed as Ram considered her. 'What could have I done? I had to uphold the fairness of rules.'

Oh, the cruel words! Sometimes they hurt like the sharpest daggers.

He cleared his throat, and began a bit more tenderly, 'Sita, please consider this. Appear for an ordeal and allow us a life together.'

'You say that Ayodhya judged me! On what? Baseless stories? Imaginations? Rumours? Or do you think it was your complete lack of support that stoked their suspicion?'

A look at her blazing face was enough to suppress a thousand rising pleas.

'Raavan taking me by force was bad enough, but you forcing the verdict was worse. The evil I managed to keep at bay with a single blade of grass...yes, that was my weapon in Lanka...my own strength of character...you rammed it down by becoming a silent spectator.'

Ram extended his arm, but she shot hers in defiance, 'No! I refused to give in then, and I refuse to give in now. Accepting your request is a much worse assault on my self-respect...you refused to accept my real truth then, and today—I refuse to accept your forced lie!'

Her voice shook with choked anger. 'You talk about treating the queen in equal regards with others. Well, I was made into a pawn! You ask me what should you have done? When a woman is taken against will...' and she took a pause, '...do you realize what that even does to her. And to return and find the welcome worse than abduction. Raavan was a known evil. But you were my husband. Or should I say an unblemished husband to a tarnished wife!'

'That was not my intention—'

But Sita wasn't listening, 'Well, what you should have done was to make me feel accepted, offer me compassion, not contempt. Not break our trust, our love—' her voice trailed off.

'Don't say that! Our love can never be broken.' His assurance felt weak just like his raspy voice. His quivering eyes made him look old beyond years against her newfound strength. 'I only intended to uphold the fairness of rules.'

'Is that how you dull the pain of injustice? If there is such a rule, mustn't it be challenged? Was a right precedent set for the situation? Forget me...did you do justice by Ayodhya?'

No words. Ram had no words. Sita stopped talking too. And their silence merged with the uncomfortable silence all around. She started to cry openly.

'I am sorry to have hurt you,' said Ram, completely broken. 'What is the meaning of this life if I can't even protect you? For there is none I love more than you,'

The ache in his voice melted her heart. She herself could have wanted nothing more than to be with him, but at the same time knew that she couldn't risk familial bindings cloud her judgement. Her retribution had twisted her fate once, and she wouldn't allow it again. Her eyes glittered, but that was it.

'If it was just for our sake, Ram, I could have come back to you. But now this cause has a collective bearing. My right decision today will avoid recurring harm to others.' She folded her hands. 'With all humbleness I say that the decision for renunciation will be mine this time. I must sacrifice my individual joy for collective benefits. We both must. You only said, I have supported you in your duty. Allow me to carry mine. Allow me, Ram, allow me with a happy heart.'

A heavy ache stirred the air. By now Guru Valmiki had also come and was looking at Sita with compassion in his eyes.

Sita continued, 'In our union we achieved so much. In our separation we are destined for even more.'

There was a kind of stillness where nothing moved, then out of nowhere sunlight streamed through a crack between the clouds and poured directly over her. It illumined her aching face set in firm resolution.

'I have no desire to carry on without you.' Ram said, his voice thick with indescribable pain. It wrenched Sita's heart to see him that way—a rigid exterior, a tender interior, a miserable clash—her beautiful husband. She wanted to embrace him; tell him it would eventually be alright. Although there was a lot of pain now, it would be transient.

'You must carry on,' she said, 'For you have lots to accomplish still. Rule Ayodhya, end the evil in people's heart. Bring up our sons.'

Sita returned her loving gaze to her sons, who were crying with impassioned grief. Tears rolled down their ruddy cheeks and quivering mouths. She opened her arms and they rushed forth to embrace her. She had been their entire world until now, their mother with the tenderest heart. Sita softly wiped the tears out of their hurting faces, kissed their forehead and gently glided them towards their father.

'Ram you are a part of my eternity.' There was a tragic beauty in her expressions. 'You had already become that part when I heard your name the first time, even before we met. I have always loved the sound of our names wrapped together.'

Ram-Sita, Ram-Sita. Memories took her back.

'Sita-Ram.' he said.

'Huh?'

'Sita-Ram. That's how we will be remembered. It is you who's always led me.'

'Sita-Ram! Sita-Ram!'

A chant went up through everyone's welled throats. Her sons were distraught but holding themselves up bravely. Love is a painful feeling. There can't be greater agony to see your loved ones hurt, and to know you have the power to reverse that. It is a weakening feeling. The streaming tears turned the moment blurry.

In that moment all shapes lost their sharpness, everything started dissolving—resentments, love, memories, a future that could have been, principles, regrets. Old grievances slowly rubbed out of memory. There was no more to be said. Nothing mattered anymore. Only the future.

And the thought that had inundated her moments ago, slowly receded back, leaving her clear and composed. Sita looked beautiful as she stood considering everyone, her eyelashes wet, her aura iridescent, her gaze supple.

When her gaze met with Ram's, it separated them from the rest of the world, merging their thoughts and aspirations for one last time.

'Sita!'

'We shall meet again, Ram.'

It was all she said, then she smiled, but she seemed distant. Like she wasn't real, only a figment of imagination. A sound loud enough to split open the ears followed. The ground shook violently and swung, mixing the green of the trees with the blue of the sky, tossing everything, slapping it back again. The ground heaved and cracked open, in rips, in ridges, in deep long fissures. Enormous amounts of dust rose, the earth blasting in wrath, obliterating vision, blurring reality with terror.

Everyone shielded their eyes and staggered back. The earth roared beneath their feet, as if waking from a cursed slumber. Stones split open, trees shuddered to keep their hold, their roots tore from the soil like veins from flesh. With it, screams rang out—not only from mouths, but from the land itself, groaning with warning. Shadows danced in the choking haze, and people stumbled, grasping for as much clarity as for breath. It was as though the very bones of the ground were breaking—and no one could stop it.

And then, she was gone.

When the dust finally settled, everything calmed down and the air became magically clear as before, she was gone. Ram looked helplessly about but the ground had closed back in; all the fissures sealed. The beacon of light who was here only moments ago was gone, turning everything unusually quiet. Ram clutched his wailing sons closer. With an unsettling realization he understood what had actually happened. It was the beckoning of her mother.

The final call.

A throbbing silence filled the place. Sita was here for a purpose, and she had fulfilled it—as a daughter, a wife, a mother and finally a queen. Now it was up to him to honour her vision.

As everyone wept, he stood forlornly still, allowing moments to pass, and a part of his life with it. And whatever was left of it, he would spend remembering her with deepest regards.

She was different in the manner she was born, and different in the manner she went away, lovingly embraced back to the one she had arisen from. Sita, a gift from Mother Earth, had led a very fulfilling life, imparting important life lessons right from her birth. Even in her departure she had made an impact and hoped the world would become a better place. She was more than a wife, a companion, a supporter—more than anything Ram could have wished for.

Sun, the gracious ball of fire was silently setting over the horizon. It looked like someone had smeared sandalwood on the horizon. Ram stood up, gathered Luv and Kush in his arms and walked over to catch the last drop of the golden light before it was too late. From somewhere, a delicate hint of raatrani picked up in the air—its smell most loving, most comforting.

Acknowledgements

Drawing this book to a close feels bittersweet—like both an arrival and a farewell. It's not simply been the making of a book, but the making of memories, the making of dreams—and here I thank a few companions who have been part of the journey.

To the entire team at Rupa Publications—I am deeply indebted. Especially to my editor, Yamini Chowdhury, whose first email of offer was a breath-stealing moment of pure joy and disbelief. Many thanks to my editor Richa Tewari for her guidance throughout the process. Special thanks to Abhipsito Das and Srilagna Majumdar for handling this manuscript with so much care, and for uplifting me with encouraging responses. Thanks also to Padma Pegu for her assurances, to Harshita Sabharwal for her patience, and to Amrita Chakravorty for the beautiful cover.

Many thanks also to my illustrator Onkar Fondekar for handing me the very cover page of my dreams. I fell in love with Sita all over again.

To my mother, Gita Agrawal—no words can honour the magnitude of your contribution. I would have never become a writer if it weren't for you. You gave me the vision to get started, and stood by me through the outlining, rough drafts and final readings. This book may have one author, but if I am the *Yashodha*, then you are the *Devaki*—this story is as much yours as it is mine.

To my father, Pradeep Kumar—thank you for being an exceptional inspiration. For always protecting me in your loving ways and showing me the value in hard work. I am blessed to be your daughter.

To my darling children, Anika and Arnav—you are my magic! If not for the burning desire to stay close to you, this book would have never materialized. The sparkle in your eyes kept me going, as through this long journey, the age of Luv and Kush kept quietly adjusting to match yours. Thanks for your loving patience throughout.

To my brother, Prashant—for your staunch support, for the jolt I needed to start and for the validation that kept me going. This book owes much to your timely nudges, especially the early one on our trip to Sri Lanka.

To my sister-in-law, Saloni—for your genuine enthusiasm, steady encouragement and honest feedback on those early pages.

To my parents-in-law, Manorama Sultania and Ramesh Sultania—for always showering me with your love and blessings. You both are very special.

To my friend, Rita—for being the beacon of positivity through some of my most enduring moments. Thank you not just for seeing me but making me see myself.

Heartfelt thanks to all my friends and family, for your cheers, love and belief. To my teachers, for shaping the way I think. To the book club readers whose encouraging remarks on my reviews fuelled my dreams in ways they may never know. To each and every person offering me help, advice or a special moment of kindness and concern. It kept me going.

Last but not the least, to my dear husband, Achal—for being there for every page, every word, every doubt, every silence and every spark. You have been my constant support, and it would be impossible to gather my gratitude in just a few words, so I won't even try. Let me simply thank you for your love.

And now finally, to you, dear reader—for holding my gentle dream in your hands and offering me your most precious gift—your time.

Printed in Dunstable, United Kingdom

72280490R00180

ZORA FOLLEY

The Distinguished Life and Mysterious Death of a Gentleman Boxer

MARSHALL TERRILL

Pulp Hero Press
The Most Dangerous Books on Earth
www.PulpHeroPress.com

Editor: Bob McLain
Layout: Artisanal Text

ISBN 978-1-68390-095-5
Printed in the United States of America

Pulp Hero Press | www.PulpHeroPress.com
Address queries to bob@pulpheropress.com

Contents

Introduction

Zora Folley was neither a personal hero of mine nor someone who was even on my radar screen just before the start of the new millennium, which was right around the time I commenced my stint as a beat reporter for a Phoenix-based area newspaper called *The East Valley Tribune*, and later, its sister publication, *The Chandler Connection*.

I wrote approximately 5,000 stories over the course of my decade-long career as a newspaperman. I covered everything from City Hall to crime, education to business, entertainment to human interest, and plenty of features. Most of the stories carrying my byline are forgettable; only about a dozen of them remain memorable to me, and at the top of that list is the exhaustive series I wrote about Folley, a boxer from Chandler, Arizona, who perennially ranked among the top heavyweights in the world in the late 1950s and 1960s.

The Folley name is inescapable in Chandler, a city about 20 miles southeast of Phoenix. A park, an aquatic center, and a street near City Hall have been named after the late pugilist. There is a display at the local museum, which I had seen many times, paying tribute to his accomplishments in the ring and the worldwide fame he brought to the city.

Nowadays, Folley has mostly been relegated to footnote status in boxing circles. Old-timers remember that he fought—and valiantly lost—to Muhammad Ali in their heavyweight title match in March 1967. Except for the circumstances surrounding Ali, then facing legal issues regarding his military draft status, it was not a titanic or even especially memorable fight; and unlike his other matches "The Greatest" found it hard to say anything negative about his opponent when trying to drum up publicity for their match, such was Folley's inherent likeability and decency.

Folley's life was a testament to his character. He was a decorated Korean War veteran; a consummate fighter in the ring; a role model for youth; a seemingly happily married father of nine children; a successful businessman; Chandler's first black city council member; and the city's most famous son.

His death at age 41 on July 7, 1972, however, has remained shrouded in mystery for more than four decades, and the few available details concerning what happened hardly square with his distinguished and genteel life.

That's what piqued my interest.

This was a story in my own backyard. The fact that I had access to his family, friends, and associates who knew and grew up with him, and sources in the police department who could help me answer nagging questions about his death, made it an easy decision to pursue the story. It was published as a three-part series in *The Chandler Connection* in the fall of 2003. Most of Folley's family members didn't mind me poking around the decades-long mystery surrounding his demise, and graciously granted me in-depth interviews.

The original 2003 series for the Chandler Connection *on Zora Folley. Photo: Marshall Terrill.*

I was not unfamiliar with professional boxing, having assisted in writing the autobiographies of former heavyweight champion Ken Norton (*Going the Distance*, 2000); heavyweight contender and puncher extraordinaire Earnie Shavers (*Welcome to the Big Time*, 2002; re-released in 2017), and former junior welterweight champion Aaron Pryor (*Flight of the Hawk*, 1996). Through these three men I had seen and experienced the extreme highs and lows and the glamor and dark underbelly of the Sweet Science. I met people from all sides of boxing: businessmen, trainers, fighters, managers, writers, and a long list of famous pugilists and Hall of Fame fighters. They included Muhammad Ali, Joe Frazier, Jake LaMotta, Mike Tyson, Archie Moore, Floyd Patterson, Emile Griffith, Bob Foster, Gene Fullmer, Wilfred Benitez, Sandy Saddler, Willie Pep, James "Bonecrusher" Smith, and the effervescent Ray "Boom-Boom" Mancini.

I must admit that I found it all very exciting in the beginning. My first in-person title fight was Mike Tyson vs. Bruce Seldon on September 7, 1996, in Las Vegas. The fight itself wasn't much. After Tyson barely grazed Seldon's head with a punch in the first round, the challenger fell to the mat. At the 1:49 mark the ref stopped it and declared Tyson the winner-and-still-champion. Chants of "Fix!" came from the audience, but the occasion became much more memorable because it was the night Tupac Shakur was murdered. Shakur was one of several celebrities who had attended the fight and approximately two hours later, 13 rounds were fired into his body from a Glock .40 caliber handgun. Shakur died six days later as a result of his injuries.

Two months later I was back at the same venue—the MGM Grand Hotel—for the first Mike Tyson vs. Evander Holyfield fight on November 9, 1996. I was with Aaron Pryor when he knocked on Don King's trailer door and asked for tickets to the fight. King, resplendent in a fur coat, diamond rings, and electric hair, was dumbfounded, but quickly recovered. "Aaron," he said, "do you show up to the NFL offices and ask for tickets on the day of the Super Bowl?!" But the promoter scrounged up a pair of tickets, and they weren't bad, either.

On that same trip I met Hector "Macho" Camacho, who was surrounded by an entourage and sported his trademark forehead spit curl and a perpetual scowl. He made it clear he was suspicious of the "gabacho" (me!) sitting at his table and pointedly ignored me throughout the meal. My instincts told me his attitude and demeanor would result in a bad ending one day ... and in 2012 he took a fatal shotgun blast to the face, sadly proving me correct.

That was the same year Albuquerque prize-fighter Johnny Tapia met his maker. Through my association with Aaron Pryor, Tapia's wife Teresa contacted me about writing a book on her husband's life. The project was intriguing enough. Tapia's chaotic life included stints in jail, multiple drug overdoses, and bouts of mental illness—all stemming from the kidnapping and murder of Tapia's mother, which he witnessed at the age of 8. While Johnny's volatile life practically wrote itself, I wasn't so sure I wanted to go down that road with Tapia and ultimately took a pass on the project. Frankly, I was weary of dealing with the massive neuroses and warped personalities of so many of the people involved in boxing. As Sonny Liston once said, "Ain't no archbishops ever become heavyweight champion."

So it is a bit of a surprise that I am writing about boxing once more. There are certain lures and triggers for me as a writer. In this case the biggest hook—and what I was haunted by—were the words Folley's son Robert uttered with calm certainty when I interviewed him in 2003:

"We've always had doubts about what happened, but one day the truth will come out."

All well and good, but how was the truth supposed to come out if no one was actively in search of the truth?

Stumbling block No. 1: Zora Folley's autopsy report and the official police report about his death, I was told by several officials, went missing a long time ago.

When I first started working on the story in 2003, I was under deadline pressure. I needed more time to think and ponder about how to find the missing pieces of the puzzle. The greatest piece of wisdom my father ever bestowed on me was, "If you don't know the answer to something, find the person who does." In unraveling this particular case, it took me more than a decade to find my answer.

I have revised and updated the information I gathered for my newspaper series about Zora Folley. Some mysteries have unraveled over time, while others still remain. Folley's distinguished life and mysterious death will continue to fascinate the boxing fans and his fellow Chandlerites who have an interest in him.

With this offering, I hope to finally put his story to rest.

CHAPTER ONE

Fancy Footwork

His career as a longtime contender for the heavyweight champion of the world may now only amount to a mere footnote in boxing history, but his name in Chandler, Arizona, still looms larger-than-life more than four decades after his sudden and mysterious death.

Zora Bell Folley is still the most famous man to ever call the 105-year-old city home. But today Folley has fallen into a weird time warp.

Old-timers will never forget the quiet, gentleman boxer who brought international fame to Chandler when he fought Muhammad Ali in 1967 in New York's Madison Square Garden.

And yet Folley's untimely death at age 41 at a Tucson motel with a group of questionable friends continues to haunt and mystify all who knew him.

To newcomers in the community, the name Zora Folley might, as one New York reporter wrote in the 1950s, belong to a "strip-teaser," or maybe a lower-case socialite.

To those who knew and admired Folley and what he meant to Chandler, that's as big a shame as the runaround Folley got at the peak of his fighting prowess by the people who controlled the richest prize in boxing—the heavyweight championship of the world.

"The history of our people is vital to our city's success," said former mayor Coy Payne, who grew up down the street from Folley's home. "But sadly, I don't think the history of Chandler will reflect too much on Zora Folley."

Folley's history in Chandler began in the early 1940s, when 10-year-old Zora Jr. and his two siblings, Mae Frances and Mary Bell, moved from Dallas, Texas, with their mother, the former Maggie Fowler. She had separated from Zora Sr., a courthouse maintenance man in Dallas. The emigrant Folleys stayed on Dick Old's farm until Maggie got her feet on the ground, working the alfalfa and cotton fields, milking cows and tending cattle.

Chandler, Arizona, was an agricultural town when Zora Bell Folley moved there in the 1940s. Photo: Chandler Museum.

"There was a big need for farm workers at that time because most of the country's young men were off serving World War II," Payne said.

The Folleys eventually moved into the southeast quadrant of Chandler, and young Zora began delivering and picking up milk bottles. Chandler resident Eddie Encinas remembered that when Zora wasn't working, he was a typical kid who liked to swim in the canal near Pecos Road, and that he was a target for bigger kids.

"Zora was a small kid who used to get picked on, believe it or not," Encinas recalled. "But in later years, no one picked on him."

Eddie Encinas. Photo: Eddie Encinas.

Folley attended Ocotillo Elementary School up through the eighth grade. Around that time, he experienced a sudden growth spurt that put his picked-on days behind him for good. At 6-foot-1 and 180 pounds, he was good at most sports. But baseball got most of his attention. "I could hit 'em far when I hit 'em," Folley told *Phoenix Gazette* reporter Bob Allison in 1957.

When he was 16, Folley enlisted in the U.S. Army, where he obtained a GED. He never said why, but admitted to Allison that he added two years to his age to join the military in 1948.

During basic training at Ford Ord, California, Folley got his first taste of boxing. Folley's platoon sergeant happened to be the post heavyweight champion. The sergeant was scheduled to risk his title against a boxer named Lucius Tate, but suffered a last-minute injury and asked for a volunteer to take his place in the fight. Although he had no experience in the ring, Folley raised his hand.

It was Tate's hand that was raised after the three-round bout, in which Folley was knocked down in each round. In spite of that beat-down, he stuck with [boxing] and learned to love the sport," said Willie Arbuckle, Folley's brother-in-law.

Just like one of those old Charles Atlas ads in which puny "Mac" comes back to whip the bully who kicked sand in his face, within a year of his trouncing at the hands of Lucius Tate, Folley beat Tate for the Sixth Army championship. Folley went on to win the All-Army and All-Service heavyweight championships. In 73 service bouts he was beaten only twice.

But that wasn't the only fighting Folley did in the Army. And it wasn't the fiercest.

As an infantryman in the Korean War, Folley saw combat in furious engagements in Pusan, Inchon, and Bloody Ridge. He received five Battle Stars, and said evermore that after experiencing the horrors of war, fighting in the ring held no fear for him.

"I can't get nervous anymore," Folley told Mark Kram of *Sports Illustrated*. "I left that all back there. The Chinee would pour in and come at you screaming, blowing the bugles, and you couldn't stay nervous long. That's all there seemed to be—Chinee, blood and mud. You knew if you could hold on long enough you'd make it."

According to Zora Folley III, his father didn't come back from the famous conflict unscathed. Folley suffered severe frostbite on his feet when his platoon spent weeks in the bitter Korean cold and deep snow without shelter. By the time the Army flew Folley to Tokyo for treatment, he was in danger of developing gangrene.

"My father had feet problems all his life, and that's why he developed such a good defense in the ring," said Zora III. "Fancy footwork wasn't an option."

After his recovery and discharge in 1953, Sgt. Folley returned to a deserved hero's welcome in his hometown. Trouble was, he no longer had a place to live in Chandler. His mother's home had burned to the ground in a cooking accident.

Broke, homeless, and desperate for a way to earn a living, Folley decided to rely on the only marketable skill he had: boxing.

CHAPTER TWO

Turning Pro

Before Zora Folley ever stepped into the professional boxing ring, an Arizona woman knocked him head-over-heels without throwing a punch. Folley and Joella Arbuckle met when Folley was on military leave and visiting his family in Chandler. The Arbuckles had migrated from Oklahoma to Chandler in 1937 when Joella was three. The family's first residence was two tents pitched in a cotton field—one for sleeping and the other for eating.

"My father died at about 40-something, leaving a six-week-old baby, and we moved to a cotton camp in Eloy, Arizona," Joella Folley said in an interview with Chandler historian Lyda Y. Harris. "Picking cotton was seasonal work. When I went to school, it was to Ocotillo and our teachers came all the way from Phoenix. We had to take the bus with no windows. I did not like school and so I quit."

She was 18, and Folley 20, when they married on September 20, 1952. Joella joined Zora in Virginia, where he briefly lived after his return from Korea. "It was the first time I left Arizona, it was an interesting time in my life," Joella said.

Ona Arbuckle was Joella Folley's father. He died in 1940 when he accidentally ate a watermelon laced with cyanide. Photo: Chandler Museum.

According to Zora III, his mother was a deeply religious woman who was loving but firm. Sundays were devoted to church and good food.

"She raised us up on the church whether we liked it or not," he told Chandler historian Melanie Hartman. "Mom, she could really cook. That is one thing we didn't lack; we didn't lack food. Every Sunday after church, it was ready. Pot roast, pork chops. ... My mom used to make pound cakes, great big pound cakes, nice and moist."

When Joella and Zora returned to Chandler at 373 S. Colorado Street, they started a family almost immediately. Zora III was born in 1954, followed over the years by Denise, Mary Bell, Robert, Jeffrey, Francine, Tanya, Dorothy, and Jack.

"He was a fun dad and a real prankster," said Robert of the family patriarch. "But he could be a disciplinarian, too. He had no problem taking the belt to our hides if we got out of line."

Zora III said his father held a take-no-prisoners attitude in the ring as well.

"He had a pretty good jab and a right hand. He would set you up with [the jab] and then, when you least expect it, he would come with the right hand, and hopefully, if he hit you right, it was lights out. He prided himself on good defense. Dad, he believed in hitting and not getting hit."

Folley learned the ropes of pro boxing from Al Fenn, a former promoter, manager, trainer, cut man, and Iwo Jima Marine. After Fenn and Phoenix businessman Bill Swift signed Folley to a management contract in August 1953, the first thing Fenn did was change Zora's free-swinging style.

"He liked to go toe-to-toe and swap a lot of leather, but I told him he couldn't do that anymore," Fenn said. "I showed him how to breathe properly, how to build his stamina, and how to defend himself in the ring."

What Fenn, then the publisher of the *Copper Era* newspaper in Clifton, Arizona, didn't have to show Folley was how to conduct himself outside of it. Their contract included a morals clause, but it was unnecessary. Folley rarely drank and never smoked, and his idea of a grand old time was hanging with his family. Few boxers have been upheld as role models in society, but the Folley had no problem fitting that bill.

Publicity photo of Zora Folley and co-manager Al Fenn, circa late 1950s. Photo courtesy of Al Fenn.

"We used Zora Folley as an example for youth and what they could accomplish if they worked hard and lived their lives right," said Tom Carlson, former teacher and coach at Westwood High School in Mesa, Arizona. "He was a hero not just in Chandler but the entire Phoenix Valley."

In Folley's first pro bout he won a decision against Jimmy Ingram on September 26, 1953, at the Olympic Auditorium in Los Angeles.

After fighting to a draw next time out, Folley blazed through his next 17 opponents and began attracting attention.

Not all of it was innocent. Professional boxing was rife with mobsters, and according to Fenn some of them came sniffing around his impressive young heavyweight and other members of his boxing stable.

"The mob threatened both myself and my partner, Dave McCay," Fenn said in a 2008 interview with boxing historian Christopher James Shelton. "The Nevada mob, an Italian by the name of Ralph Gambino, approached me one day and said that [boxer] Irving Star belonged to them now. Another fighter they wanted was Ray Coleman. The mob called and warned me they would kill Coleman's daughter. I laughed at them: 'Ray Coleman does not even have a daughter.' But those guys knew me and decided to leave us alone."

They left Fenn alone, at any rate. Dave McCay was later murdered in Los Angeles. According to Fenn, he was suffocated with a pillow and his murder was never solved.

"I guess that could have been me," Fenn said.

The Folley Express hit its first bump in the road on June 23, 1955, when Zora faced Johnny Summerlin at the Olympic Auditorium. The tough Detroit veteran (24-4-2) had been a boxing instructor in the army and the year before had dropped two close decisions to the fearsome Sonny Liston. He'd won six in a row since then and made it seven against Folley. Summerlin knocked the Arizonian down in the first round, and the fight was stopped in round six after Folley was down twice more and his corner, fearing his jaw had been broken, threw in the towel.

"That [fight] was a mistake," Fenn recalled to Christopher James Shelton. "Folley was not quite ready for him."

"We brought up Zora too fast," agreed Bill Swift. "He wasn't quite ready for Summerlin, who at that time was a stiff puncher."

Folley rallied back with successive victories over Jack Jerrod, Ted Calaman, and Reuben Wilson, but then lost to Young Jack Johnson in a scheduled 12-rounder at the Olympic Auditorium on December 1, 1955.

Johnson, the California heavyweight champion and a handful both in and out of the ring (he died in 1963 of fatal stab wounds inflicted by his step-daughter), had nearly 20 pounds on Folley plus an even bigger advantage of which he wasn't aware when the bell rang. Folley had injured some ribs sparring with middleweight contender Rory Calhoun in the gym. Zora won the first three rounds with sharp lefts and occasional jolting rights to Johnson's head, but in the fourth Johnson had Folley wobbly after a right to the head and a brutal body attack. Folley was still ahead on points in the fifth, but did not come out for the sixth round on account of several fractured ribs.

"When I started getting hit on the side a sharp pain would go through my body," Folley recalled. "It got to a point where I could hardly breathe. I had to ask my corner to stop it."

Folley didn't lose another fight for two years. On August 15, 1956, he won a unanimous 12-round decision over tough Roger Rischer at Madison Square Garden in Phoenix, and with it the Southwestern heavyweight title. Just over a month later Zora faced his toughest opponent yet in Nino Valdes, the Cuban heavyweight champion and a Top 10 contender who held wins over former champion Ezzard Charles and British champion Don Cockell.

Folley won a unanimous decision over Valdes in their September 9, 1956, bout at Softball Park in Phoenix. The judges gave the Cuban boxer only one of the 10 rounds.

"The fight against Valdes was the big one," Fenn said. "This is what placed Folley on the national map."

On December 3, 1956, Folley made his eastern and national television debut, winning a decision over Wayne Bethea at St. Nicholas Arena in New York City. A month later he beat Bethea again in Syracuse, and then decisioned Howie Baker at St. Nicholas before heading back west.

Folley went 11-0 in 1957, and the next year the fighter called a "man to be reckoned with" by *The Ring* magazine was the top-ranked contender for the heavyweight title owned by Floyd Patterson. But Patterson's manager, Cus D'Amato, had no interest in risking the crown against worthy challengers, and instead had Patterson take on inferior opponents so as to keep the title as long as possible.

"Patterson avoided all the good fighters, especially Folley," said Nigel Collins, former editor of *The Ring*.

Promotional postcard for a March 12, 1957 fight against challenger Johnny Hollis. Courtesy of Arizona State University.

It was an assertion Folley addressed with a touch of bitterness to Mark Kram of *Sports Illustrated* before he finally got a crack at the title from Ali.

"If Floyd had give me a shot, I would have been champion years ago. But he was afraid of me," Folley said. "He kept dodging me, and I was out in the bushes. It seemed like it was always another year or two of just hoping and waiting, and little fights. Always little fights in small towns."

Chasing Patterson wasn't Folley's only problem. He and Bill Swift were forced into bad decisions due to financial considerations. Swift's father was the son of the founder of Swift & Company, the well-known meat packing operation, and his mother's father controlled Morton Salt Company. Bill Swift had acquired additional wealth of his own through real estate and cattle. However, a string of bad investments and a divorce put Swift in the poor house.

"I was broke," Swift told reporter Mark Kram, "and I tried to get a job, but because of my name and my family's reputation for wealth, nobody believed me. There were times when the purses from Zora's fights helped me to support my family. Perhaps if my finances had been better we would not have taken some of those fights and would have saved the losses. As it was, I took fights we didn't need. ... All of this didn't help his career, but Zora never reproached me."

Zora Folley with co-manager Bill Swift, circa 1957.
Photo: Arizona State University.

But also hindering Folley was his textbook boxing style that turned fights into chess matches instead of crowd-pleasing brawls. Wrote Murray Goodman in *Boxing & Wrestling* magazine: "[Folley] is a quiet man by nature and doesn't seem to have the capacity for anger and emotion that makes the fighter with the so-called 'killer instinct.'"

In early 1958, Folley and 24-0 Eddie Machen squared off in at the Cow Palace in San Francisco in what was supposed to be a title elimination match, the winner to get a shot at Patterson. With so much at stake both fighters were overly cautious, and at the end of 12 passionless rounds it was declared a draw.

After Folley knocked out Pete Rademacher, he traveled to London and was outpointed by England's Henry Cooper on October 14, 1958, despite knocking Cooper down in the third round.

Folley and Al Fenn cried robbery, and blamed referee Tommy Little. "He kept telling me to watch my head," Folley said. "He worried me every round."

Promotional poster for Folley-Cooper fight, 1958.

In a rematch three years later, Cooper's head was the concern after Folley almost knocked it into the River Thames with a perfect right in the second round. In 1963, Cooper knocked down then-Cassius Clay before losing on a TKO, and after Clay became heavyweight champion and Muhammad Ali he stopped Cooper in six in a title fight.

The loss to Cooper dropped Folley from the No. 1 spot in the heavyweight ratings to No. 3.

Swift enlisted the help of Jeb Rosebrook, an ad manager for Diamond's Department Store in Phoenix. Rosebrook was a "Mad Man" from New York City and a writer for King Features Syndicate when he moved to Arizona in 1958.

"John Robinson, who owned Diamond's, was a big sports fan, and Zora was the No. 1 ranked heavyweight in the world, but was probably better known outside of Arizona since Phoenix wasn't a big boxing town," Rosebrook said. "He introduced me to Bill Swift and the deal with him was that if we got enough publicity for Zora to get a title fight with Patterson, then we'd work out a percentage."

According to Rosebrook, Bill Swift was "a quirky guy and the black sheep of his family, but he was honest. I remember going to his house on a Sunday afternoon and all of his fighters were mowing his lawn, trimming the bushes, hedges were being clipped.

"On weekends when they weren't doing yard work, he'd gather them up in his station wagon and take them to Mexico to fight in the bull rings. These boxers would fight until the death. You practically had to kill a Mexican fighter to knock him out. They were very macho. They'd get knocked down, the ref would pour water on them to wake them up so they could keep fighting. It was just brutal."

Where Folley was concerned, there was a wall of reserve and politeness that Rosebrook found hard to penetrate.

"To be honest, I didn't know him all that well," Rosebrook admitted. "He was not an outgoing guy or the kind of person to tell jokes or even laugh that much. He was kind of the same person he was as a fighter, and whatever was going on in his mind stayed in there."

It was no act on Folley's part.

"I keep my irritations well hid," the fighter told Mark Kram in 1967. "They're covered up way down deep and I guess that's where they belong."

Folley's impassive demeanor made Rosebrook's job a challenge. He made a pitch to NBC's *The Today Show* to have Folley come on and give the host a boxing lesson.

"It was a good idea and a little out-of-the-box for its time," Rosebrook said. "But then Patterson got knocked out by Ingemar Johansson in June of 1959, and that put a damper on things. We had to wait another year before they fought a second and third match, both of which Patterson won."

Soldiering on, Folley boosted his record to 50-2-3 with a 12-round unanimous decision over Eddie Machen in a January 18, 1960, rematch. But like their first fight it was a dreadful chess match, with Zora's effectiveness undermined by tonsillitis.

"It was probably the dullest fight ever televised," Rosebrook said. "The audience kept wondering who was going to throw the first punch. That fight really hurt Zora's reputation."

Zora Folley takes one on the chin from opponent Eddie Machen. Photo: Historic Images.

Six months later, Folley was destroyed by Sonny Liston in the third round at the Denver Coliseum, a fight later cited by Bill Swift as one of those that wouldn't have been made but for the manager's dire financial need.

After that, wrote Murray Goodman in *Boxing & Wrestling*, "it appeared almost certain that Folley was to be just another heavyweight opponent. He dropped in the ratings and he dropped in ambition. It was fight-to-fight from now on, moving wherever there was a decent pay day."

Folley was still ranked fifth when he squared off against Doug Jones at New York's Madison Square Garden on Dec. 17, 1962. He'd won a 10-round decision over Jones earlier that year, and at the Garden Folley almost stopped Jones in the opening round. But he let him off the hook and Jones took charge of the fight and ended up knocking Zora out in the eighth.

Over the next five years the man *Boxing Illustrated* called "Arizona's *Machine de Boxe*" remained in the rankings with workmanlike but unspectacular victories over contenders Bob Cleroux, George Chuvalo, future light heavyweight champion Bob Foster, and then-undefeated Oscar Bonavena.

Doug Jones' 1963 victory over Zora Folley was a major setback to his status as a heavyweight contender.

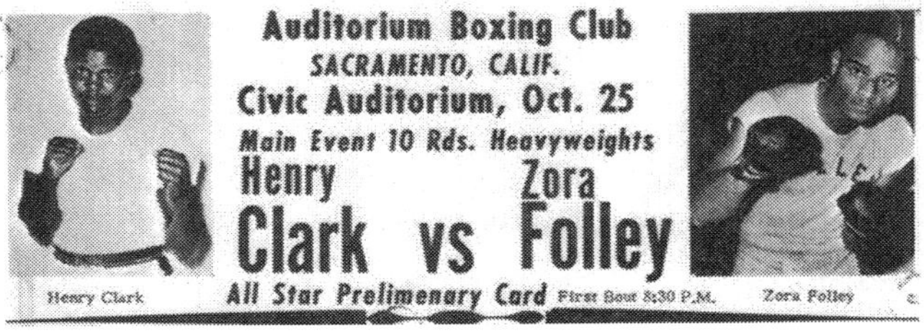

Promotional material for Henry Clark vs. Zora Folley, October 25, 1966.

Meanwhile, Cassius Clay became heavyweight champion in 1964 and became Muhammad Ali after that. He successfully defended the title eight times, but made as much news outside the ring. Ali's membership in the Nation of Islam and his "I ain't got nothin' against no Vietcong" antipathy to the war in southeast Asia were causing no end of legal problems for the young champion.

CHAPTER THREE

Facing Ali

After dispatching Ernie Terrell in a lopsided and humiliating 15-round fight at the Houston Astrodome on February 6, 1967, 25-year-old Muhammad Ali told the Associated Press that he was leaning toward Folley for his next title defense.

"It will either be Zora Folley or George Chuvalo next, but I'm sure it's Folley," Ali said. "I think Folley can put up a better fight than Terrill. He's a better boxer."

Folley certainly thought so. "I can beat [Ali]," he told a reporter after the Terrell fight. "I saw plenty of openings."

The fight was slated either for Detroit's Olympia Stadium or New York's Madison Square Garden in late March. There was still much uncertainty given Ali's 1-A draft status with the Army. Ali claimed he was a minister with the Muslim sect, and told the Associated Press, "I just don't understand it. We are fighting in Vietnam for people's freedom and I am being criticized for my religious beliefs. That seems hypocritical to me."

Ernie Terrell had criticized Ali's stance and further drew his ire by refusing to call him by his adopted Muslim name. Not only did Ali label Terrell an "Uncle Tom," but he repeatedly humiliated Terrell in the ring by asking, "What's my name?" and punctuating the question with a volley of stinging punches to his face. It was the 39-5 Terrell's first loss in five years.

Folley got one of the best valentines of his life when Ali announced on February 14 that they would square off in Madison Square Garden on March 22. It would be the Garden's first heavyweight title bout since Ezzard Charles whipped Lee Oma there on January 12, 1951.

Ali and Folley at a February 1967 press conference announcing their fight. Photo: Historic Images.

"Folley is a civilized, intelligent man who knows me by name," Ali said. "It will be a good clean fight."

It was also a good pay day for both men—Ali was to receive $150,000 plus 50 percent of the live gate and all other ancillary rights, including a home TV network broadcast. The fight would also be broadcast live in Canada, Japan, Mexico, and parts of Europe.

Folley's purse was $25,000 and 15 percent of the live gate and ancillary rights, and ultimately would total about $70,000, almost doubling his previous personal high of $40,000.

Folley, whose record stood at 74-7-4, was both thankful to Ali and confident of victory.

"Everybody knows I have been a top contender for the last 10 years," he said. "The top man always ducked me. I am glad we have a man of the caliber of Muhammad Ali who will fight all of the contenders. I am very confident that, come March 22, you will have a new champion."

The former war hero went so far as to defend Ali's name change and his refusal to be drafted into the military.

Muhammad Ali was stripped of his title after the Folley fight for his objection to the Vietnam War. He didn't box again until October 1970.

Muhammad Ali's button to protest the Vietnam War.

"I don't think he's a slacker. That's his religion," Folley said. "I've met several more people that way, some Jehovah's Witnesses. I can tell you about my religion—I'm a Baptist—but I don't judge the next guy. ... If he wants to be called Muhammad Ali and says that's his name, I'll call him that."

Ali was a heavy favorite, but Folley's innate decency and refusal to be drawn into rasslin'-style pre-fight ballyhoo perplexed the preening champion.

At a press conference one of Ali's entourage tried to goad Folley.

"What's his name?" inquired the needler, sitting between the champion and Folley.

"Muhammad Ali," replied Folley without hesitation.

"Thank you, brother," Ali said. "That Folley's such a nice, sweet old man, eight little kids, calls me Muhammad Ali, thanks me all the time for giving him a chance. How am I ever gonna get mad at him and build up this fight?"

Folley commenced his training by walking the seven miles from his Chandler home down Highway 93 to a gym in Mesa. The jaunt usually took him about three hours, depending on his pace. It gave him a lot of time to think about, analyze, and come up with a strategy for the upcoming fight.

"I think my experience will overtake a lot of his speed," he told reporter Murray Olderman. "I know a lot more about the ring than he does.

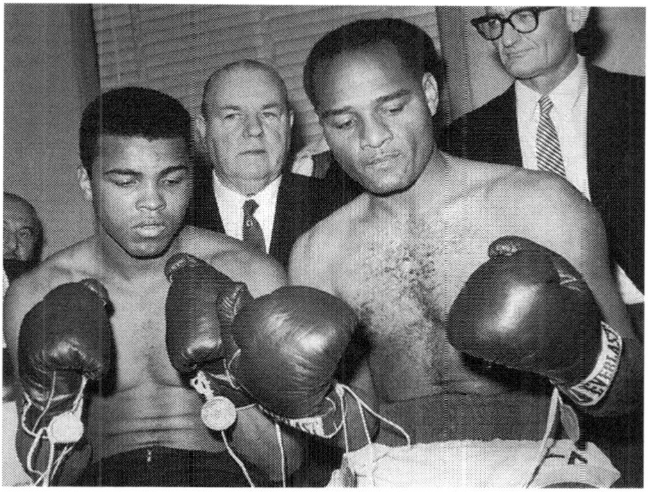

Ali and Folley in upstate New York, preparing for the big fight, March 1967. Photo: Historic Images.

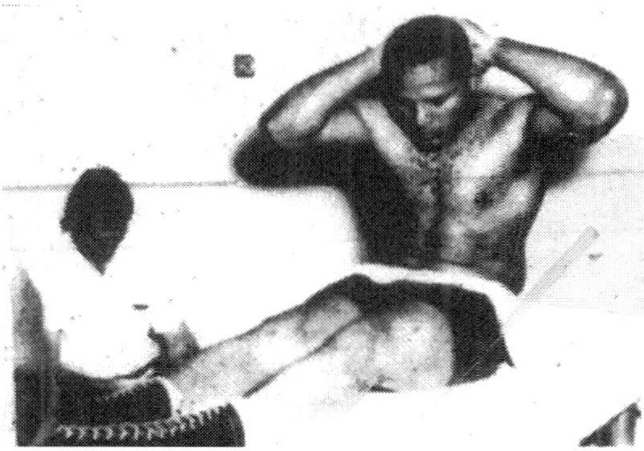

Folley preparing for Ali. Photo: Chandler Arizonan.

"I know it by the inches and by the foot. I can cut the ring off so short he'll forget about that speed and stuff. ... I think I can discourage [Ali]. He's never been tested. I'm not sure he'll stand up under punches."

The Chandler community rallied around Folley, and before his departure for New York City more than 300 residents showed up for a gala dinner and program in his honor at the San Marcos Hotel. The March 1 event was billed as the "Zora Folley Appreciation Dinner" under the sponsorship of the newly organized Chandler Jaycees. Jaycee President Russell Jennings served as master of ceremonies, and Chandler mayor George Nader was the main speaker. Proceeds from the dinner benefited a local youth program. Wearing a suit and tie and proudly sporting wife Joella on his arm, Folley was presented with a brand-new wristwatch.

Joella and Zora Folley the night they were honored by the Chandler Jaycees, March 1967. Photo: Chandler Arizonan.

Folley headed east on March 6 and checked into Grossinger's, a legendary 1,200-acre resort hotel in New York's Catskill Mountains. Ali was encamped 10 miles away in Monticello at Kutsher's Hotel and Country Club. Both resorts were two hours northeast of New York City and the perfect place to train—great facilities, good mountain air, with easy access to the media capital of the world.

Their camps, naturally, were in direct contrast with each other. Folley's was quiet and focused, while Ali's camp took on the usual circus-like atmosphere, with an even more heightened sense of drama this time on account of his looming Army induction date of April 11. Ali was coy about what would happen then.

"My main concern is Folley," he told reporters. "My decision is made. I won't tell you what it is. I have to report to the government, not reporters. But I know what I have to do."

When a reporter noted that there were Muslims in the Army, Ali replied, "The jails are full of Muslims."

Helping to prepare Folley for the fight was Ken Norton, a young pro fighter just out of the Marines who would become heavyweight champion himself a decade later.

"He helped me quite a bit when I was starting out," Norton said. "Zora was a very good man and was more helpful to me than any other fighter I worked with."

Zora III was 13 at the time, and for him the highlight the night his father fought for the heavyweight championship was sitting at ringside and getting his picture taken with former champion Joe Louis. The ringside was dotted with former ring greats, including Sugar Ray Robinson, Rocky Graziano, Emile Griffith, Sandy Saddler, Willie Pep, James "Cinderella Man" Braddock, Joe Frazier, and Ernie Terrell (wearing sunglasses to hide the puffy eyes Ali had damaged a few weeks earlier). Entertainer Sammy Davis Jr. was there along with numerous other celebrities.

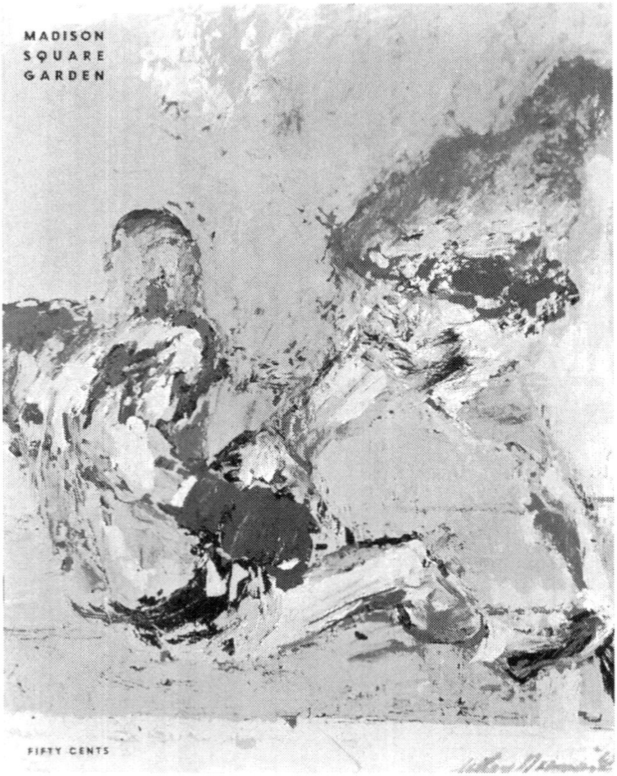

Famed artist Leroy Neiman designed this fight program cover for the Madison Square Garden match.

Ring announcer Johnny Addie introduced Ali, at 6-feet-3 and 211½ pounds and sporting white trunks, and the 6-foot-1 Folley, who tipped the scales at 202½ pounds. Folley was also giving away age and reach, which is why oddsmakers made him a 7-1 long shot to beat Ali.

The 34-year-old challenger outpointed Ali in the first two rounds, though many observers pointed out that the champ seemed to be "playing around," content to mostly dance around the ring.

"I was not carrying him," Ali adamantly stated afterwards. "He was a better fighter than Sonny Liston, Floyd Patterson, or Ernie Terrell. He was slick, tricky, and a good boxer."

The third round saw Ali get busy, using his fast left jab to keep Folley from getting set to punch. In the fourth round Folley dropped flat on his face from a left-right combination to the jaw. He sat up with a startled look on his face at the count of five and was back on his feet at nine.

Ali moved right in on Folley, who seemed dazed but instinctively fired back with a double-fisted barrage. A right connected and sent Ali to the ropes, bringing a roar from the Garden crowd of 13,780.

Almost a continent away, about half of the residents of Chandler listened to the live radio broadcast of the fight at the local high school football field. Future mayor Jay Tibshraeny, who was a young boy at the time, was one of the thousands rooting for the hometown hero.

"It was definitely the biggest event that ever took place in Chandler at that time," Tibshraeny said. “This fight brought us national attention and it unified the city in a way that only a sporting event can.”

The Chandlerites’ hopes waned as Ali’s jabs drew blood from Folley’s nose and raised a lump under his left eye, but then soared again in the seventh when Zora scored with a big right to the champ’s head. But at 1:48 of the round an Ali right dropped Folley for the second time. He was almost on his feet at referee Johnny LoBianco’s count of eight, but then tumbled back down and it was over.

“When you see your father get knocked down, it’s more than just a boxing match,” Zora III said. “It was devastating.”

Muhammad Ali raises his hands in victory after knocking out Zora Folley in the seventh round of their March 21, 1967 bout. Photo: Historic Images.

The teenager cried and Ali came over to comfort him, putting his arms around the young man and telling him, "What are you crying about? Your father is a great fighter. A man doesn't have to win a fight to be a champion."

"I fought well," Folley said. "I gave it all I had. He was just a better fighter. ... I'll keep fighting. I still think I can beat any heavyweight but Ali. I'm not ashamed of my showing."

It turned out to be Ali's last fight until 1970. He refused military induction the next month and was stripped of his title.

Over the following three years Folley went 5-3-2. On September 29, 1970, he was knocked down five times and stopped in the first round by rising contender Mac Foster. "Matches of this sort are not good for the game of boxing and should not be countenanced," said *The Ring*. "That kind of requiem for a heavyweight is bad business all around."

It was a sad end, after 17 years and 96 fights (79-11-6), to one of that era's most distinguished careers in heavyweight boxing.

But as endings went, the worst was yet to come.

CHAPTER FOUR

Death of a Boxer

If Zora Folley had been the stereotypical down-and-out ex-prize fighter, the circumstances of his death probably wouldn't raise many eyebrows.

In fact, however, he actually gilded his status as one of Chandler's most solid citizens after closing out his career as a heavyweight contender in 1970. The dapper, congenial Folley found employment as a salesman in the truck division at Rudolph Chevrolet, though his new bosses were at first unsure about taking him on.

"I told him he wasn't qualified, that he was too nice a guy. But I saw a little bit of a spark," said Frank See, then truck sales manager at Rudolph. "I saw that he was determined. I laid it on him and told him what he'd be up against and we let him try."

The owners hoped Folley's celebrity status would bring customers to the lot, though it didn't work out that way at first because Folley was reluctant to trade on his celebrity and it showed in his initial sales stats.

"We've tried to motivate him to use his reputation to his advantage, but he hasn't used it," said Frank See at that time. "If he did, I think he'd be doing three times as much business."

The Gentleman Boxer was now fighting a different kind of battle—to break out of his shell. To help him, the dealership offered to split the costs of enrollment in a Dale Carnegie personality course. Folley agreed to take the course, but insisted on paying the whole cost himself.

But he made clear that he wasn't going to pretend to be someone he wasn't just to get a commission.

"I don't growl, if that's what they mean," Folley told an Associated Press reporter. "If you take someone away from their own personality, I think that's phony. I do things my way."

Folley's way worked. He ended up making close to $24,000 a year, averaging 30 sales a month. And his customer base was not exclusively black. In fact, "Ninety-nine percent of my business is not with blacks," Folley said. "It would be stupid to expect all blacks who come in to buy from me, but it's not stupid to expect blacks to come here because there's a black salesman here."

A Rudolph Chevrolet sticker on an early Chevy Nova. Photo: Chevelles.com.

The respect accorded to Folley across the board came not only from his boxing but also his position as counselor with the Chandler Career Center and his participation in the Migrant Opportunity Program. So it was not unusual for Folley and others in Chandler to consider him for an expanded role in the community. At the behest of supporters, in December 1971, he announced his candidacy for Chandler city councilman in the January 1972 primary election.

"I have lived here since I was 10 years old and am proud to live in Chandler," Folley told the *Chandler Arizonan*, a weekly paper. "I have represented Chandler all over the world for the last 20 years in the sport of boxing. I don't box anymore, but would like to represent Chandler as a city councilman."

Three open council seats were up for grabs, and on January 18, 1972, voters elected Everret Jones, Marcia Metcalf, and Thomas Wood to fill them.

Folley didn't have much time to lick his wounds. On April 13, Councilman Jones notified Mayor Raul Navarrete that due to a family crisis he would have to resign and leave Chandler. Longtime activist and teacher Coy Payne, later the city's first black mayor, proposed that Folley be appointed to replace Jones on the council. Payne pointed out that while African Americans had served on several boards and commissions, the local black community needed representation on the all-white council.

The city fathers agreed and appointed Folley to fill the unexpired two-year term. Zora was sworn in by City Magistrate Coy Beasley on April 27, 1972. A photo of Folley raising his right hand to take the oath of office appeared in the next issue the *Chandler Arizonan*. It was the last public photo of Folley.

Zora Folley being sworn in as a member of the Chandler City Council by City Magistrate Ed Beasley, April 1972. Photo: Chandler Arizonan.

No one was more respected in the community than the war hero turned heavyweight contender whose innate dignity had stood out in the slimy world of boxing like lipstick on a frog.

"He's the only heavyweight champion they'd put on a Wheaties box," said then-mayor George Nader before Folley's fight with Ali in 1967.

Which makes what happened on July 7, 1972, so perplexing to his family and friends to this day.

For one thing, nobody knows what Folley, a seemingly happily married man with nine children, was doing at a motel in Tucson with a man named Artis Hudson Broom, Broom's wife Dorothy, and a Mesa woman named Ann Young.

Chandler residents recall Broom as a typical celebrity "hanger-on." His close friendship with Folley appeared completely out of character for the former fighter, though they'd known each other since Broom was 16.

"[Broom] was a guy who liked hanging around my dad because it was exciting," said Robert Folley. "I remember bumping into him when he was in his fifties and he could not look me in the eye. I didn't care much for the man."

Broom was once stationed at nearby Williams Air Force Base. Robert Folley speculated that Broom's and his father's military backgrounds formed the basis of their friendship. Unlike Folley's, Broom's military record was hardly distinguished. He enlisted in the Army on January 21, 1957, and was discharged that same year on November 4.

According to Maricopa County Recorder documents, in 1971 Broom and wife Eura lived in Chandler at 551 S. California, Apt. A-3. By 1972, Broom was residing with his other wife, Dorothy Broom, at 1030 S. 10th Street in Tucson.

Folley was with Artis and Dorothy Broom and Ann Young at the Sands Motor Hotel, 222 S. Freeway, at the intersection of Interstate 10 and Congress Street. According to a police report they were engaging in horseplay near the motel pool when an accident occurred.

Vintage postcard of the Sands Hotel in Tucson, Arizona.

"He and Broom were goofing off at a late hour to see who was going to throw who in the water with his clothes on," Tucson police sergeant Lyle Murphy was quoted in an Associated Press article on July 9, 1972.

The article went on to say that a motel clerk told police that one of the women ran into the office and told him Folley was badly hurt. "An ambulance was called and Folley was taken to the Pima County Hospital, where he underwent emergency surgery. But at 1 a.m., July 8, Zora Folley, 41, died from his injuries.

According to a Sands clerk who insisted on anonymity, those injuries included a large bump on his head and another gaping wound in the back of Folley's head.

Robert Folley recalled the horror he felt when he put his hand on his father's head at the wake and felt the latter wound. "I remember it so vividly to this day," Robert said. "I've always thought something was inconsistent about his death, and it's always upset me."

Willie Arbuckle, Folley's brother-in-law, said he heard a different version of the accident.

"From what I understand, the pool had a dividing wall between the kiddie and the adult sections, and when Broom pushed him Zora tried to make a dive out of it and hit his head on the dividing wall," Arbuckle said.

Joella Folley never spoke on the record about her husband's death and politely refused my request for an interview in 2003. She died on October 1, 2011.

Joella Folley, circa 2011.

Former Chandler vice mayor Lowell Huggins, a friend of the late boxer, spoke for many when he said, "I've never felt comfortable with the facts surrounding Zora's death and I still feel uncomfortable."

Huggins was a member of the Chandler Police Department at the time of Folley's death. After hearing about it on his police radio, Huggins made the 100-mile trek to Tucson to personally check out the scene of the accident. But he wasn't allowed on the motel premises, which wasn't uncommon since Huggins was not with Tucson law enforcement.

The autopsy and police reports concerning what was officially ruled an accidental death were not available when I originally requested them in September 2003.

Dr. Bruce Parks, former chief medical examiner for the Pima County Office of Medical Examiners, said then that he looked for but could not find Folley's autopsy report or any other records at the facility, and that there was not any way to find out if the documents still even existed.

"We think they were in our archives and on a list to be destroyed," Park said. "It was standard policy," he added, to delete such documents after a certain amount of time had passed.

Tucson police said in 2003 they did not know if the police report had been destroyed or was stored somewhere on microfiche. The records division said that if the latter were the case a report number would be needed to pull up the document. But the report number could only be obtained from the autopsy report, which had apparently gone up in smoke.

The missing documents fueled speculation and various dark theories over the years about Folley's death. Multiple versions, some wildly conspiratorial, of what happened that night have circulated in the Chandler community and boxing circles and forums. A popular one hinted that Folley had been rubbed out by the mob, which wasn't wholly unreasonable on its face since in the early 1970s Tucson was a haven for such Mafia overlords, capos, and underbosses as Joseph Bonanno Sr., Peter Licavoli Sr., Mo Dalitz, Peter Notaro, and Charles J. "Bats" Battaglia. In the late 1960s, 10 bombings in 12 months that damaged homes and local businesses had suspected ties to the Mafia. Things got so heavy that U.S. Rep. Morris Udall asked FBI Director J. Edgar Hoover to assign more agents in Tucson to fight organized crime.

A national magazine reported in 1972 that when Folley died two "suspicious" men had been seen lurking around the motel.

Peter Licavoli was a well-known mobster who ran his empire from a 72-acre ranch outside of Tucson. Photo: Detroit Police Department

Nigel Collins, then editor of *The Ring* magazine, said in 2003 that public information about Folley's death didn't quite add up.

"It could be that maybe to the white establishment, the death of a black man wasn't a big deal," Collins said. "I think racism could have played a role in that there wasn't a full investigation."

Some boxing writers lumped Folley's death in with the similarly sudden and murky demises of former heavyweight champion Sonny Liston and heavyweight contender Eddie Machen. Liston died of an alleged drug overdose in Las Vegas on December 30, 1970, and a month after Folley's death Machen went out an upper-story window in San Francisco. It was ruled a suicide.

Whether their deaths were in fact connected, or the deceased boxers were merely recipients of, as Collins wrote in his book *Boxing Babylon*, "a concrete pie in the face from the cosmic clown," is a question that will be debated as long as people never tire of a good mystery.

Certain facts about Zora Folley are not debatable.

More than four decades after his death, he remains Chandler's most famous resident. A year after he died, the city dedicated the park in Folley's name. In 1983, childhood friend and former Chandler mayor Coy Payne successfully lobbied to have a community swimming pool named after the late fighter.

The City of Chandler Folley Pool, 600 E. Fairview Street. Photo: Marshall Terrill.

"Zora Folley was a very honorable and soft-spoken man," said grocer Eddie Basha, who served as a pallbearer at Folley's funeral. "He was a very prominent citizen and did more to put Chandler on the map than anyone else I know. He brought only fame and repute to his community."

Well and good. But how a man dies is also a reflection of how he lived, and as the years passed, the burgeoning rumors, innuendo, and conspiracy theories kept Zora Folley from resting in peace, and they harassed me long after my newspaper series about the boxer I'd never met.

"Closure" is an overused word, but it became my Great White Whale.

CHAPTER FIVE

Starting Over

Even though I had left my Chandler newspaper beat five years prior, I maintained my former sources and relationships in person and through social media. There is a bonding experience between a reporter and a source that is hard to describe. A deep trust must be established and maintained because the reality is that his reputation is all a reporter has. And despite Chandler now being a thriving metropolis of about 250,000 people, it still remains small where the flow of information is concerned. If trust is established, the information—as long as you protect your source—is unimpeded.

I was really put to the test when a source invited me to the Hells Angels clubhouse in Mesa. It was a fundraiser for one of the famous biker group's high-ranking members who was out on bail for several RICO violations and raising money for his trial. Sonny Barger, the Hells Angels founder and legendary leader, was going to make an appearance. It was Barger who kicked the hell out of writer Hunter S. Thompson, which the gonzo journalist chronicled in his 1965 book *Hells Angels: The Strange and Terrible Saga of the Outlaw*

Motorcycle Gangs. I certainly wasn't about to disclose to Barger (or anyone else for that matter) that I was a reporter. I aimed to strictly abide by Barger's "be nice to me and I'll be nice to you" philosophy, and even brought him a signed copy of one of the books I wrote on actor Steve McQueen (they rode motorcycles together back in the 1970s) and didn't make any waves. I also brought one for the guest of honor. The books were a big hit with these gents. I don't know if they ever read them or not, but it made them happy at the time. I recently asked my wife, to whom I had been married for at least five years when I attended the party, if I'd ever told her about that night. She shook her head no. I was pretty solid when it came to keeping a confidence.

Beyond trust, there was mutual respect with my sources. I wasn't a hard-ass reporter and didn't judge anyone hastily or hold grudges. I simply wanted the crucial information so I could build whatever story I was working on around what was irrefutable. As long as I stuck to the facts and quoted people correctly, I could remain fair and balanced. That approach allowed me to go back and question all my original sources for the 2003 newspaper series I had written on Folley.

The first person I approached was Lowell Huggins, who had known Folley since he was a teenager.

"Zora Folley was the finest person I ever knew," Huggins reaffirmed in 2013. "He was my friend and I miss him terribly."

Lowell Huggins. Photo: City of Chandler.

Huggins, a 20-year member of the Chandler Police Department, had tempered his remarks to me in 2003 regarding Folley's death because at the time he was a member of the Chandler City Council and knew it could be potentially explosive. Then he would go only so far as to call Folley's death very suspicious; but now, long retired from local government, Huggins let loose.

"Zora Folley did not slip and fall and hit his head on the side of the pool," he stated. "He was the most coordinated man I ever met. I boxed with him, worked out with him, and that story is just plain false.

"Artis Broom, for whatever reasons, killed Zora Folley. The only answer I don't know is why he killed Zora."

Huggins recounted to me again how, after hearing a police dispatcher announce Folley's death over the radio, he drove to Tucson. Huggins reiterated that he was barred from the premises of the Sands Hotel by Tucson police, leading him to believe something suspicious was at play. That night has haunted Huggins for more than four decades and the memory of it brought him to tears more than once during our two-hour meeting.

The second person I approached was former Chandler police chief Bobby Joe Harris. He was a U.S. Marine sergeant and drill instructor who was wounded in Vietnam. He was a natural born ass-kicker, but with a brain and street smarts. He was also a reporter's dream in terms of providing a quote. Harris shot straight from the hip and spiced up any municipal story that needed a little fairy dust. He was smart, funny, and instinctual, and lived through Chandler's transition from a blue-collar town to its current tony incarnation as Arizona's Silicon Valley.

Harris was hired from Clovis, New Mexico, by the Chandler Police Department in 1971, a year before Folley's death. Harris was a sergeant on the Clovis Police Department and made $602 a month, with no retirement. He gave up his rank and seniority to join the Chandler force, which paid $622 a month and offered a retirement package after 20 years.

"Me and my wife Judy thought we'd gone to heaven and died," Harris says today.

At the time of Harris' hire date, Chandler was an agricultural city of roughly 15,000 residents whose economy relied heavily on nearby Williams Air Force Base.

City of Chandler billboard welcoming Williams Air Force Base personnel. Photo: Chandler Museum.

"Chandler was a rough-and-tumble bar town, and if Williams hadn't existed the city would have dried up and blown away," Harris said. "Chandler had 13 bars in a one-mile stretch and most of them were filled with cowboys, rednecks, agricultural and migrant workers. And they liked their liquor and they liked to get rowdy. One of the things we did on the force for fun was count all the bullet holes in the bars to see if there were any new ones since the last time we were there."

Harris understood these men and cut them a lot of slack. But the law was the law, and if they broke it, he stepped in—but not alone. The stories of Harris and his German shepherd, Warlock, the department's first certified K-9, are legendary in Chandler. Warlock literally took a bite out of local crime and many a backside when he and his partner patrolled the streets in Harris' 1974 Ford Torino, the granddaddy of all muscle cars.

When Warlock bared his fangs the toughest bar fighters and miscreants froze in their tracks and meekly surrendered. In some cases a Warlock growl induced its target to have a childish accident on the spot, and brought a confession before Harris even slapped on the cuffs.

"Miranda rights meant nothing to Warlock," Harris quipped.

Chandler Police Officer Bobby Joe Harris and his legendary K-9 assistant Warlock, circa 1974. Photo: Bobby Joe Harris.

Harris' other equalizer was a black polycarbonate baton, commonly referred to as a "nightstick," which he freely employed on those uncowed by his K-9 assistant. It dented the thick skulls of many career criminals, degenerates, and lowlifes who had it coming. Sometimes when the liquor wore off the troublemaker would sheepishly apologize, and Harris would shake his hand and let it go. That kind of lawman no longer exists except on TV.

Harris moved up the ranks quickly. Eight months after he was hired he made detective; six months after that he was promoted to sergeant. In 1994, Harris became Chandler's chief of police and helped the department transition during the city's largest growth spurt. He remained the department's head man until 2003, the same year I wrote the Folley series, which he read.

When I interviewed Harris in 2013, he spoke of the only time he was ever in the same room as Folley—at the boxer's funeral.

"There was talk that Muhammad Ali might show up, and the top brass were concerned there could be some trouble," Harris said. "Ali was a very controversial figure at the time and so the police chief, Bill Louthan, set up a detail. I just happened to be one of the workers."

Folley's funeral took place at the United Methodist Church on Williams Field Road in Chandler on Wednesday, July 12. Mayor Raul Navarrette and members of the Chandler City Council joined wife Joella; sons Zora III, Robert, Jeffrey, Jack; daughters Denise, Maybelle, Francine, Tanya; Folley's sister Mary Frances Sullivan of Dallas; co-managers Bill Swift and Al Fenn; and hundreds of Chandlerites in paying final respects.

Ali was a no show.

Military rites were conducted by a bugler, firing squad, and honor guard from Fort Huachuca at Folley's gravesice in the Mesa Cemetery. His headstone, paid for by the U.S. government for Folley's military service, was a small white marble slab.

Mesa Cemetery entrance. Photo: Marshall Terrill.

Concerning the many unanswered questions about Folley's death, Harris' advice was pointed.

"You've got to find that police and coroner's report," he said. "Otherwise it's mere speculation."

That was easier said than done.

Rumors had abounded for years that the two reports were purposely destroyed by the Tucson police and pathology departments. Officials told me in no uncertain terms in 2003 that the reports were not accessible. When I persisted, it was made clear that I was wasting their time and my own.

So I headed to the library and spent hours upon hours scrolling through old newspapers on microfilm. I don't recommend it for the weak-eyed.

Folley's death was reported in *The New York Times*, *Los Angeles Times*, *Pittsburgh Post-Gazette*, *The Arizona Republic*, and *The Arizona Daily Star* in Tucson. Most accounts called what happened a "freak accident," the result of a "friendly scuffle" or "midnight prank."

Folley Dies In Accident

What Folley was doing at midnight at a hotel almost a hundred miles from his home and family, in the company of Artis Broom and two women, was not explained.

It's important to note that this was 1972 and the world was decades away from the era of the 24-hour news cycle and instant access to public records we take for granted today. Accordingly, rumors and speculation ran rampant in boxing circles and in Folley's hometown of Chandler.

As a former reporter, I knew exactly what information the press back then was fed—what police call the "initial report"—a handwritten document by the field officer or first responder on the scene. What baffled me was why the reporters didn't follow up by accessing and printing the supplemental and more detailed report filed by the investigating detective. Was it a cover up by police? Was it to protect Joella Folley and her nine children from potentially embarrassing information? Or did the Fourth Estate, known at that time for winking at the indiscretions of presidents, diplomats, movie stars, and sports celebrities, simply back off the story to allow Folley to rest in peace?

Bobby Joe Harris offered a possible explanation.

"Access to public information was hit-and-miss in those days. I'm not sure what the public information policy of the Tucson PD was in 1972. I don't think Arizona even had public information laws at that time," Harris said. "I know that

Chandler's information was handled by the police chief back then. The chief did not allow troops to talk to the media and officer names were seldom if ever released. The Folley incident was sort of a scandal and the media did not hit on those sorts of stories as they do now. Plus, the 'powers that be' were more protective of it. It's also possible that another story might have popped up and became a bigger priority."

Phoenix, Tucson, and Chandler-based news publications reported that the pathologist's report on Folley would be released on Monday, July 10, 1972. But an AP story carried in *The Arizona Daily Star* on Tuesday, July 11, said: "The Pima County pathologist's official report on Zora Folley's death has been delayed and will not released until Wednesday [July 12]." That was the day of Folley's funeral, and the autopsy report wasn't made public then, either, possibly out of consideration for the grieving family.

But the autopsy report wasn't released to the press after that, or ever. It was never mentioned in print again.

What happened to it?

In 2003, Dr. Bruce Parks of the medical examiner's office in Tucson told me he looked for but couldn't locate the document. I believed him at the time and still do.

On September 25, 2013, I left a message with the office of the medical examiner. About an hour later I received a call back from Michelle Gough, a pathology transcriptionist. I explained what I was looking for, and mentioned what I'd been told a decade earlier. She took down the information and said she'd see what she could find out. A day later, Ms. Gough called back with the stunning news that she had located the eight-page pathologist's report from July 8, 1972, and would email me a PDF of it for $125.

More than four decades after Zora Folley's mysterious death, the long-vanished pathology report had suddenly reappeared.

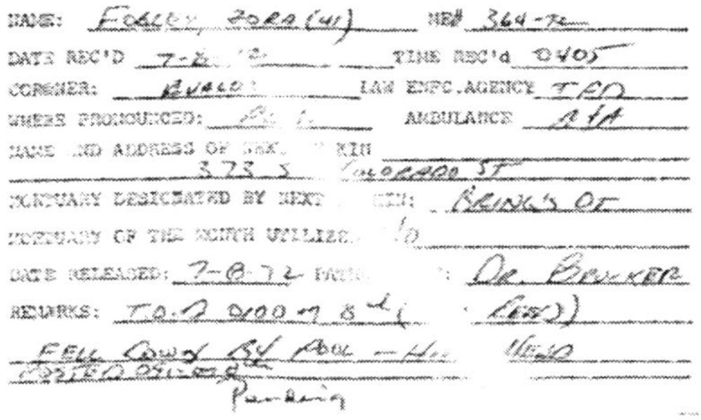
NAME: Folley, Zora (41) ME# 364-72
DATE REC'D 7-8-72 TIME REC'd 0405
CORONER: Brucker LAW ENFC. AGENCY TPD
WHERE PRONOUNCED: [illegible] AMBULANCE A+A
NAME AND ADDRESS OF NEXT OF KIN
373 S. Colorado St
MORTUARY DESIGNATED BY NEXT OF KIN: Bring's OE
MORTUARY OF THE MONTH UTILIZED: [illegible]
DATE RELEASED: 7-8-72 [illegible]: Dr. Brucker
REMARKS: [illegible]
Fell down by pool — hit head
[illegible]

Cover page of Zora Folley's pathology report.

According to the report by coroner Edward Brucker, Zora Folley was pronounced dead by Dr. G. Reed at 1 a.m. on July 8, 1972. Then Folley's corpse was transported at 3:45 a.m. by A & A Coach Service from the Pima County Hospital to the office of the coroner's pathologist on Pennington Street. Under the "Apparent Type of Death" category, the coroner checked "Natural," and not "Accidental." But then he wrote, "Fell down by pool—hit head."

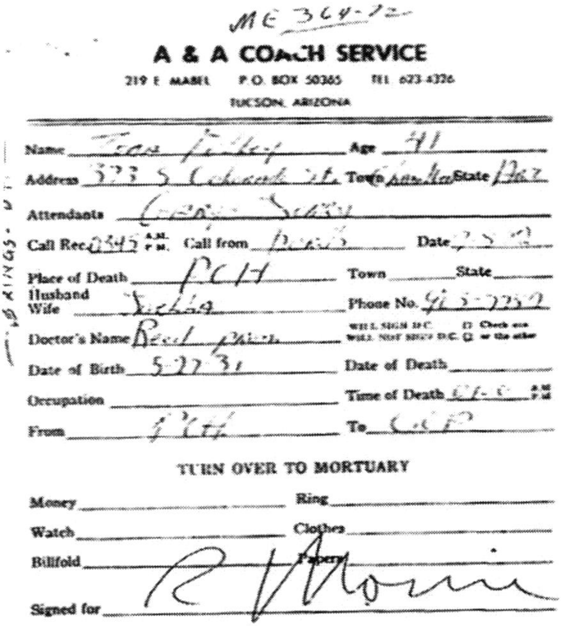

ME 364-72

A & A COACH SERVICE

219 E. MABEL P.O. BOX 50365 TEL 623-4326

TUCSON, ARIZONA

Name Zora Folley Age 41

Address Town State

Attendants

Call Rec. A.M. P.M. Call from Date

Place of Death PCH Town State

Husband Wife Phone No.

Doctor's Name WILL SIGN D.C. WILL NOT SIGN D.C. Check one or the other

Date of Birth Date of Death

Occupation Time of Death A.M. P.M.

From To

TURN OVER TO MORTUARY

Money Ring

Watch Clothes

Billfold Papers

Signed for

Invoice from the ambulance service.

Brucker had Folley's blood, urine, and bile tested for traces of drugs and alcohol. The results came back on July 11, and indicated that Folley was clearly inebriated at the time of his death. His blood alcohol level was 0.17—slightly over the limit of 0.15 at that time and almost twice the limit in Arizona today.

So alcohol clearly played a part in Folley's death. I can't say that this came as a huge surprise to me.

6. LABORATORY EXAMS:

Blood:	ethyl alcohol level = 0.17g/100ml. (G.L.C.)
	acid and neutral drugs = none detected (T.L.C.)
Urine:	alkaloids including morphine = none detected (T.L.C.)
	amphetamines = none detected (T.L.C.)
Bile:	alkaloids including morphine - none detected (T.L.C.)

Folley's post-mortem lab report

In one of the many articles I read about Folley, the United Press International reported that on December 26, 1959, Folley was arrested and jailed by Phoenix police after his car was involved in a minor accident. A passenger in the other car was slightly injured but did not require hospitalization. Folley was booked in the city jail on a drunk and reckless driving charge, where he spent six hours sobering up. He was eventually released on a $300 bond.

Zora Folley quenches his thirst with a jug of lager in London, England, January 1961. Photo: Keys Press Agency Ltd.

The last photo of Folley published before his 1972 death, when he was sworn in as a member of the City Council, showed a man who was obviously no longer in fighting trim. Folley had aged considerably since he hung up the gloves two years earlier, and his face had the tell-tale bloated quality you frequently see in ex-athletes who have let themselves go.

Under "Cause of Death" Brucker listed "Cerebral Concussion," and on four diagrams of Folley's head—front, left side, right side, and back—it was indicated that the fatal trauma occurred at the lower back of his skull. Therefore it seemed probable that Folley had slipped and hit the back of his head. But there was still one missing piece of the puzzle, without which the mystery of Zora Folley's death was unsolvable. That was the police report filed by the investigating officer at the Sands Hotel, containing information about what Folley was doing there based on interviews with his companions and evidence gathered at the scene.

Ten years ago I'd been told that it, too, was gone for good. But was it possible that it, like the newly materialized pathologist's report, was awaiting exhumation from its own musty bureaucratic rabbit hole?

The last photo taken of Zora Folley, January 1972. Photo: Chandler Arizonan.

CHAPTER SIX

Inching Closer

I knew from my decade-long tenure as a journalist that most police departments in Arizona purged their reports from their filing system after seven years. This didn't include murder cases, but Folley's death had not been deemed one despite the questionable circumstances surrounding his death.

The supplemental police report, I felt, would hold the long-lost information I needed to crack the decades-old mystery. If indeed it still existed. Not only would the report spell out what happened that fateful night in July 1972, but it would also list the names of eyewitnesses who'd asked newspapers to keep their identities a secret. If I could locate this document I could potentially interview the people who were there that evening and either corroborate or disprove the official version of Folley's death. If they were still alive.

Too many *ifs*.

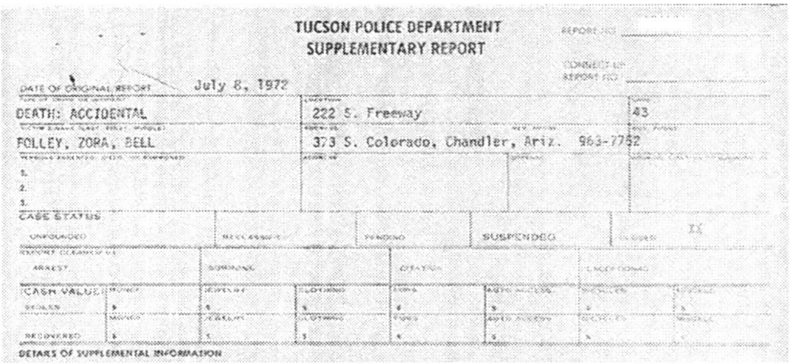

TUCSON POLICE DEPARTMENT
SUPPLEMENTARY REPORT

DATE OF ORIGINAL REPORT July 8, 1972

DEATH: ACCIDENTAL | 222 S. Freeway | 43

FOLLEY, ZORA, BELL | 373 S. Colorado, Chandler, Ariz. 963-7752

1.
2.
3.

CASE STATUS
UNFOUNDED | | | SUSPENDED | XX

ARREST

CASH VALUE

STOLEN $ | $ | $ | $ | $ | $ | $

RECOVERED $ | $ | $ | $ | $ | $ | $

DETAILS OF SUPPLEMENTAL INFORMATION

Tucson PD's supplemental report on Zora Folley.

I asked the Folley family in 2003 if they had a copy of the police report in their possession, and they did not. (In fact, the family had little in the way of photos and boxing memorabilia. The largest collection of materials on Zora Folley was located at the Chandler Museum at the City Hall complex, which was culled together by museum staff and paid for by generous donors.)

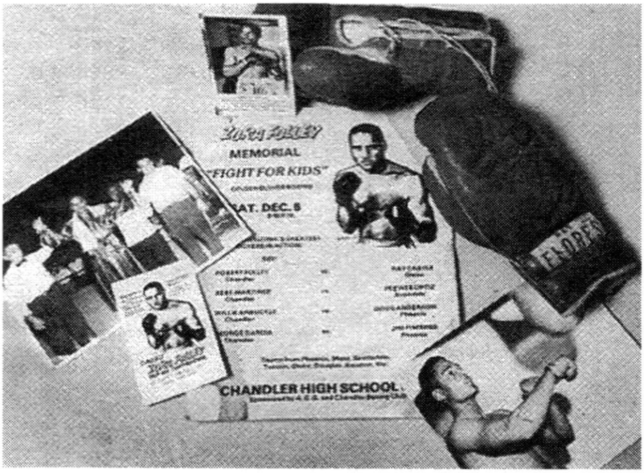

Folley memorabilia. Photo: Chandler Connection.

Joella Folley was still living in the house at 373 S. Colorado Street when I interviewed Zora III and Robert Folley a decade ago for my newspaper series, but did not wish to speak to me on the subject. She remained in her bedroom the entire time I was there. I remember feeling her presence and thinking how odd and ironic it was that the person closest to Zora Folley was just several feet away behind a locked door.

It was probably just as well. I spent a couple of hours with Zora III and Robert, discussing their father's life, his military service, the Ali fight, and their special memories of him. By far the most memorable exchange wasn't about their father or his exploits in the ring but the mystery woman who was with him on the last day of his life. When I asked them if they had ever heard of Ann Young, they said no. But they suspected why she was there.

"My father probably had a little thing going on the side with her, like a lot of professional athletes do," Robert said matter-of-factly. "No big thing."

I didn't print his response in the *Chandler Connection* out of respect for his mother. Something didn't seem right about it at the time, and so I chose not to run the quote.

Former manager Al Fenn also suspected that Ann Young was a mistress or girlfriend, and in a 2008 interview with Christopher James Shelton said:

"I guess Folley was stepping out on his wife. The guy he was with was a professional celebrity hanger-on. They were meeting with these two women. I believe that the men began with horseplay, trying to impress the women.

"Oh, I hear the talk that Folley was murdered. They say it was the husband or boyfriend of one of the women that found them, became jealous, and whacked him."

In 2013, former Folley publicist Jeb Rosebrook laid the most interesting tidbit of information on me, which he had kept to himself for almost four decades.

"In July 1972 I got a phone call from my former boss, John Robinson, informing me that Zora was dead," Rosebrook said. "He told me Zora was down in Tucson to meet an old friend and they started wrestling around when Zora slipped and fell and hit his head near the pool.

"John also told me Zora was getting a divorce. Knowing Zora had nine kids with his wife Joella, the information came as a bit of a shock. The Sunday *Republic* had just written an article about Zora, how he had taken a Dale Carnegie sales course and started selling cars and was doing well for himself. It was a lot of information to process."

I spent months on ancestry web sites in an effort to track Ann Young down. It led me down some interesting paths, including a lady whom I strongly suspected might be a black widow, but nothing I could hang my hat on. Clearly the Ann Young I was looking for didn't want to be found. Her tracks were covered up so well I didn't even know her age or race. Maybe she had kids or grandchildren that didn't know anything about Zora Folley or what happened to him in her company, and opening up that decades-old mystery would create all kinds of complications for her and her family. I could imagine that the prospect of suddenly having that long-closed chapter of her life opened for public inspection might keep her up most nights.

Artis Broom died on July 5, 1997, but his former wife Dorothy might still be alive. A search of ancestry websites showed that they had been married in a civil ceremony in Las Vegas on March 15, 1972, and then resided at 2102 N. 3rd Avenue in Tucson. A Vegas wedding was likely Artis' idea. Had they applied for a marriage license in Arizona, Broom might have been busted for bigamy.

On a 1966 mortgage document on file at the Maricopa County Recorder's Office, Artis claimed he was married to Annie L. Broom and they lived at 51 E. Boston Street in Chandler. But the recorder's office shows no marriage or divorce certificate for the couple. In 1969, Eura L. Broom was listed as Artis' wife, and they lived at 184 E. Saragosa Street in Chandler.

A document dated May 5, 1972, indicates that Artis and Eura, then living at 551 S. California Street, owed $37.77 in back taxes for 1969. That was about two months after Dorothy Ann Carey became the third Mrs. Broom in Las Vegas.

A quick internet search for Eura revealed that she was still living in Chandler. Hoping she would be able to fill in some big blanks, I sent her a letter in May 2014 asking for an interview over the phone or in person. There was no response.

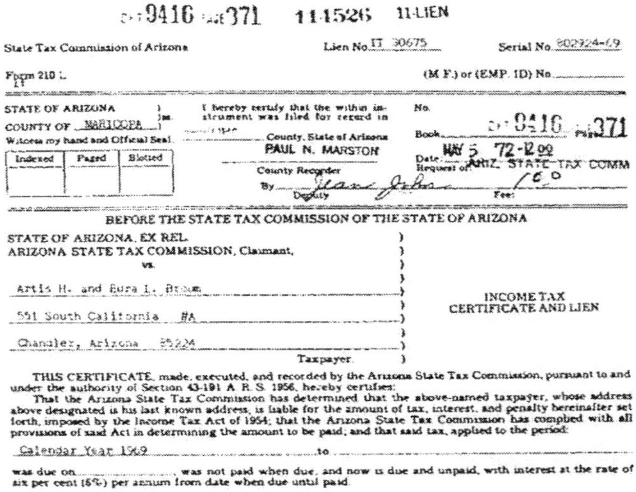

9416 371 11-1526 11-LIEN

State Tax Commission of Arizona Lien No. IT 30675 Serial No. 802924-69

Form 210 L IT (M.F.) or (EMP. ID) No.

STATE OF ARIZONA) ss.
COUNTY OF MARICOPA)
Witness my hand and Official Seal.

Indexed	Paged	Blotted

I hereby certify that the within instrument was filed for record in County, State of Arizona
PAUL N. MARSTON
County Recorder
By Jean John Deputy

No. Book 9416 Page 371
Date MAY 5 72-12 00
Request of ARIZ. STATE TAX COMM
Fee: 1.00

BEFORE THE STATE TAX COMMISSION OF THE STATE OF ARIZONA

STATE OF ARIZONA, EX REL.
ARIZONA STATE TAX COMMISSION, Claimant,
vs.
Artis H. and Eura L. Broom
551 South California #A
Chandler, Arizona 85224
Taxpayer.

INCOME TAX
CERTIFICATE AND LIEN

THIS CERTIFICATE, made, executed, and recorded by the Arizona State Tax Commission, pursuant to and under the authority of Section 43-191 A. R. S. 1956, hereby certifies:

That the Arizona State Tax Commission has determined that the above-named taxpayer, whose address above designated is his last known address, is liable for the amount of tax, interest, and penalty hereinafter set forth, imposed by the Income Tax Act of 1954; that the Arizona State Tax Commission has complied with all provisions of said Act in determining the amount to be paid; and that said tax, applied to the period:

Calendar Year 1969 to

was due on ________, was not paid when due, and now is due and unpaid, with interest at the rate of six per cent (6%) per annum from date when due until paid.

A 1972 tax lien on Artis and Eura Broom

But with the help of a private investigator, I learned that Dorothy Broom was alive and living in the Pacific Northwest with the 42-year-old daughter sired by Artis. With fingers crossed, I sent a letter to her similar to the one I'd written Eura.

On May 30, 2014, I emailed the Tucson Police Department's records division in hopes of finding the long lost police report on Folley's death. In September 2003 I'd been told they didn't know if the report had been destroyed or had been put on microfilm and filed away somewhere. If the latter was the case, a report number would be needed to pull up the document, and it would be listed on the autopsy report.

Now I finally had the pathologist's report, but there was no police report number on the document. Now what?

At 12:10 p.m. on the same day, I heard back from the Tucson Police Department.

"I'm not sure that they can assist you without a report number," the emailer wrote back "but you can check out the Arizona State Library and Archives website. Otherwise, you may want to check with *The Arizona Daily Star* newspaper."

I immediately called Dennis Preisler, director of Archives and Records Management at the Arizona State Library. I explained to him what I was looking for, and he said while he would not be able to locate the police report without having a specific case number, he would pull all of the Tucson police reports from 1972 if I wanted to scroll through all of the microfilm. He warned that it would be a lot to sift through. I gulped and said okay.

When I met Preisler at the library on June 2, he had a cart containing two white storage file boxes filled with more than 100 reels of microfilm. The files were not arranged in any sort of chronological order but were numbered on the Dewey Decimal System. *Eeny-meeny-miny-mo,* I sighed as I plucked out a reel in the middle to begin my search. It was from April 1972, and by the time I was done looking through that one reel alone four hours had passed. I did the math in my head—100 reels times four hours = 400 hours—and groaned.

Hours later when I staggered out of the library I turned on my cell phone to check for messages. There was only one, and when I saw who it was from the headache I had from squinting at all that microfilm was zapped by a rush of adrenaline.

The message was from Dorothy Broom.

CHAPTER 7

Can I Get a Witness?

I didn't have much time to prepare for the telephone interview Dorothy Broom agreed to give me in her voice mail. It was only a five-minute drive from the Arizona State Library to my office in downtown Phoenix. But I didn't need much preparation. I'd known the questions that I needed answered.

At my office I dialed Broom's number and recorded the following conversation at 5:30 p.m. on June 2, 2014:

MT: Hi, Dorothy. Thanks for taking my call.

DB: Yes, I received your letter in the mail.

MT: I wanted to make sure this is the correct Dorothy Broom who was married to Artis Broom from Chandler, Arizona.

DB: Well, yes, I was married to Artis Broom who was from Chandler; but I lived in Tucson, Arizona.

MT: I'm writing a book and many people, including the Folley family, have always wanted to know what happened the night Zora Folley died. They've always felt Zora died under mysterious circumstances. You and Ann Young are the only two who can tell us for sure since you're the only living eyewitnesses.

DB: I can give you the best that I can remember, you know?

MT: I certainly appreciate it.

DB: Okay.

MT: So before I get into the incident, let me ask you how your ex-husband, Artis H. Broom, and Zora Folley met?

DB: I really don't know, because when I met them they already knew each other. I met them through a mutual friend of mine from work when I lived in Tucson. I think her name was Ella Bea Musgrove. That's how I met Artis. And then I met Zora through Art. At the time I met them, I didn't know Zora was married or that Art was.

MT: That's interesting because I did a background check on Artis and noticed he had another child the same age as your daughter. They were born in the same year.

DB: Yes...

MT: What did Artis do for a living?

DB: He was a construction worker.

MT: And he was working in Tucson in 1972?

DB: Yes.

MT: I know you're going to find this funny, but I have to ask because there are so many rumors circulating about Artis. One of the Chandler police officers I interviewed said he remembered Artis because he had diamonds embedded in this teeth.

DB: (Laughs) No. He didn't have any diamonds in his teeth. If he did, I would have knocked them out and sold them after what he put me through.

MT: (Laughs) So can you recall what happened that night at the Sands Motor Hotel on July 7, 1972? I have newspaper accounts that say Zora was trying to throw Artis into the pool and they got into a "friendly scuffle" and then Zora slipped on the cement and cracked his head open. Is that a true account?

DB: I remember we had met them [Zora and Ann Young] over at the Sands and had dinner there. At the time I was pregnant and we were sitting at the veranda or lounge at the swimming pool. Zora and Artis were in the swimming pool and horsing around. Zora went to dive and there was some sort of divider in the pool—a cement divider—when he jumped in and dove. He hit his head on that piece of cement divider, whatever that was, in the pool.

MT: Was it a cement divider that separated the shallow end and the other part of the pool?

DB: Yes, I think so.

MT: So Zora dove in by himself? He wasn't pushed by Artis?

DB: He dove in by himself. No, he didn't get pushed in. He dove in by himself. They had been playing around; they were in the water already.

MT: The newspaper account stated that Artis was in his clothes and that Zora was already in his swimming trunks, trying to throw Artis in the pool and get him wet.

DB: No, they were both in the pool swimming.

MT: So Zora got out of the pool and dove in, not seeing the cement dividing wall?

DB: Yes.

MT: Well, it was at night and past the posted hours of swimming, so I'm sure no pool lights were on.

DB: Right.

MT: Wow. So it was an accident?

DB: Yes, it was. A complete accident. A terrible accident. I'll never forget it as long as I live.

MT: The newspaper stated that Zora had three holes in his head: The front, the top and the back...

DB: See, I don't know anything about that. All I know is that when he hit his head and [was] laying there, I remember Art grabbing him and trying to pull him up out of the water. At that point, we were all just freaking out. Somebody called out for someone to call an ambulance.

MT: It still seems a bit odd to me that he crushed his head if he was in the water. He'd have to have some sort of force or steam built up to have such an impact. Did he dive off the pool deck into the wall?

DB: I don't remember that. I don't remember when he pushed off. It seemed like I remember him diving but I can't remember if he dove from the pool deck or the...

MT: Diving board?

DB: No, the patio or pool deck, and hit his head. It wasn't a diving board, I know that.

MT: And you and the other lady were at a table having drinks?

DB: Well, I don't drink and I never have, but I was sitting there because we just had dinner. I had a Coke because I was pregnant at the time.

MT: Do you know if Zora was alive when he was pulled out of the pool, or was he dead on the spot?

DB: I don't know. I don't remember. When they called the ambulance and the driver got there, I don't know if he was dead or not. They kept people back from the scene. At that point, I was just scared.

MT: How big was Artis? How tall of a man was he?

DB: I think he might have been 5'8" or 5'9".

MT: I would assume he was in pretty good shape because he was a construction worker?

DB: Yes, he was in pretty good shape. As far I know.

MT: And the lady who was with Zora that night, Ann Young, what can you tell me about her?

DB: I don't remember her name, but I do recall I thought that was his [Zora's] wife at the time. There were a lot of things I found out afterwards that I didn't know ahead of time.

MT: Was she a white woman or a black lady?

DB: A black lady.

MT: All of this time I've been trying to locate a white woman by the name of Ann Young.

DB: No, no, no. I can't remember what her last name was, if it was Young or what.

MT: The newspaper had her listed as Ann Young from Mesa. One newspaper account had her listed as 18 years old.

DB: Ah, no, no. That's not the one. They got somebody else mixed up because this woman was older than 18. This was not an 18-year-old woman. She was older than me, I think, because I was in my thirties at that time. So no, she was older than that.

MT: Are you sure this wasn't his wife, Joella?

DB: No, no. See, this is all the stuff that I found out later. I had actually spoken to Joella and talked with her...

MT: Did you know Joella has passed on?

DB: No, I didn't.

MT: She died in 2011.

DB: No, I didn't. I can't remember this woman's [Ann Young] last name, but she wasn't an 18-year-old woman.

MT: Do you know if she was from the Phoenix area or Tucson?

DB: She must have been from the Phoenix area. She wasn't from Tucson.

MT: Somebody I interviewed suggested Zora was in town for a council meeting or a regional meeting. Was he in town for that or was he there to specifically visit with Art?

DB: He was just in town to visit and see Art, and visit with us.

MT: You might recall lots of rumors were swirling around that Artis killed Zora or that Zora was killed by the Mafia?

DB: No, I never heard of that. No, no.

MT: How did Zora's death affect Artis?

DB: Well, it affected him to the point where he started drinking a lot. He was kind of despondent and that's when we started having problems. As a matter of fact, that's when we separated. After that, things didn't gel and I left and went away. I moved to Las Vegas first, stayed a while, then came back to Tucson. Then I left Tucson and moved here.

MT: I noticed that Artis passed away in 1997. How did he die?

DB: I don't really know because I've been up here since 1977. Someone told me that he had a stroke. I have my youngest daughter by him, the one I was pregnant with.

MT: What year did you and Artis get divorced?

DB: In 1979.

MT: He has a widow named Eura and had two kids by her.

DB: Okay...

MT: I saw his headstone and it read, "Loving Husband and Father." Sounds to me as if he could have possibly turned his life around?

DB: I don't know because we separated in 1973.

MT: So Zora's death in 1972 really did have a big effect on your relationship?

DB: Yes. My daughter was born in November of 1972. Now that I think back, we separated in the first part of 1973 because it was after she was born. She was born November 15, 1972.

MT: And if memory serves me right, Artis had another kid at the same time...

DB: I don't know. I found out a lot of lies after we separated. A lot of things about him I didn't know, that I should have looked into before we got involved.

MT: What was Zora like as a person?

DB: Very, very nice person. Very nice and respectable man, from what I knew about him. They came down to visit a couple of times and had dinner, just sit around and talk and laugh. Basically, that was it.

MT: Do you know why you chose to have dinner at the Sands Hotel that night?

DB: I don't know who picked it. I guess Zora picked it because they were registered there at the hotel. We just met them over there. I had my own place at the time.

MT: That's interesting because the newspaper report said Zora was not checked into the hotel, but I guess he was...

DB: I guess he was, too, because they didn't stay with me. And we met them over there that evening.

MT: He probably checked in under another name.

DB: It could be, because that's where we had dinner.

MT: I think that's all I have to ask you and I can't thank you enough for helping put this issue to rest once and for all. I think this will bring the Folley family major, major closure. Their son once told me he thought Artis had something to do with Zora's death.

DB: No, no. No, I can truly say that's not the case. When I read your letter it kind of threw me for a loop, but I can certainly understand the family wanting closure. I would want the same.

MT: Thank you so much, it's certainly appreciated.

DB: Okay, I hope so. Call me back if there's anything else I can tell you.

What a classy, above-board lady. I hoped that my stirring up the past hadn't been too hard for her. After our conversation I couldn't help reflecting on the damage caused to so many lives—Dorothy Broom's, her daughter's, Zora Folley's and his family's—by a cockroach like Artis. Frankly, that he was Zora's sidekick didn't say a whole lot for Folley's judgment.

The few loose ends that needed to be tied up concerning Folley's death now depended on finding that supplemental police report on one of those 100 or so reels of microfilm. Which depended on my eyes not falling out of my head, first.

CHAPTER EIGHT

Zora's Folly

Day three at the Arizona State Library. My eyes looked like cherry tomatoes, my back, shoulders, and head ached, and God only knew if I was any closer to finding the police report than when I'd sat down at the microfilm reader seven hours earlier.

But after my galvanizing interview with Dorothy Broom the previous day, Phoenix sheriff Joe Arpaio and a platoon of taser-happy deputies couldn't have stopped my search for the needle in a haystack that would pop once and for all the Hindenburg-sized balloon of mystery, doubt, and plain hot air hanging over the death of Zora Folley.

At about 4 o'clock on June 4, 2014, an hour before closing time, my discomfort disappeared like a puff of smoke. There it was on the screen in front of me.

I made two copies of the initial and supplemental report. One would go into a safety deposit box and the other to the Folley family.

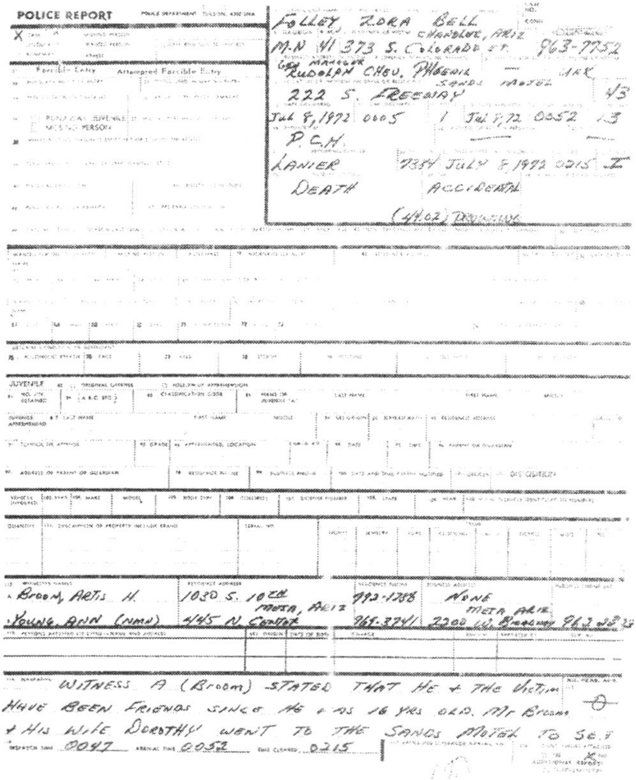
POLICE REPORT

FOLLEY, ZORA BELL
CHANDLER, ARIZ
M-N 41 373 S. COLORADO ST. 963-7752
GEN. MANAGER
RUDOLPH CHEV. PHOENIX — UNK
SANDS MOTEL
222 S. FREEWAY 43
JUL 8, 1972 0005 1 JUL 8, 72 0052 43
P.C.H.
LANIER 7354 JULY 8, 1972 0215 I
DEATH ACCIDENTAL
(44.02) DROWNING

BROOM, ARTIS H. 1030 S. 10TH MESA, ARIZ 992-1288 NONE
YOUNG, ANN (NMN) 445 N. CENTER 969-3741 2200 W. BROADWAY MESA ARIZ

WITNESS A (BROOM) STATED THAT HE + THE VICTIM HAVE BEEN FRIENDS SINCE HE WAS 16 YRS OLD. MR BROOM + HIS WIFE DOROTHY WENT TO THE SANDS MOTEL TO SEE

0047 0052 0215

The long sought-after Zora Folley police report, which details the night of July 7, 1972.

The first box filled out by Officer Lanier listed the witnesses to Folley's death. There were the names and addresses of Artis H. Broom and Ann Young. Broom gave his address as 1030 S. 10th Street in Mesa, Arizona, which was different than his and Dorothy's home at 2102 N. 3rd Avenue in Tucson.

Ann Young provided two addresses in Mesa: 445 N. Center St., (residential) and 2200 W. Broadway Road. I recognized the latter address as that of the Motorola semiconductor plant, at one time Arizona's largest employer. The plant opened in 1969 and Young must have been one of 2,600 people employed there.

While not listed as a witness, Dorothy Broom was mentioned several times in the body of the report.

Writing at 2:15 a.m on July 8, 1972, a little more than an hour after Zora Folley had been officially pronounced dead at the Pima County Hospital, Officer Lanier said:

> "Witness A [Artis Broom] stated that he and the victim have been friends since he was 16 years old. Mr. Broom and his wife Dorothy went to the Sands Hotel to see victim. Stated victim was swimming in the pool. Victim and witness had a few drinks and victim tried to throw Broom in pool with his clothes on. Victim and Broom were pushing each other and victim, who was wet, fell back into pool striking his head on the side of it. Broom jumped into pool and pulled victim out. Victim was taken to Pima County Hospital where he was pronounced dead at 0100 a.m. July 8, 1972 by Dr. G. Reed. Notified Dr. Edward Brucker, Duty Pathologist at 0128 a.m., July 8. Sergeant McDaniels was supervisor to arrive at hospital and notified Lt. Johnson of details. Talks with Mrs. Broom and witness B [Ann Young] confirmed Mr. Broom's story. Mr. Broom notified victim's wife and sister in my presence. N.F.I. [No further information]"

Say what you will about his character deficiencies, but Artis Broom had brass balls. That early morning phone call informing Joella Folley that her husband was dead must have been a bitch to make.

The supplemental report, filed on July 11, 1972, three days after the initial one, contained the real meat of what occurred.

TUCSON POLICE DEPARTMENT
SUPPLEMENTARY REPORT

DATE OF ORIGINAL REPORT July 8, 1972
DEATH: ACCIDENTAL 222 S. Freeway 43
FOLLEY, ZORA, BELL 373 S. Colorado, Chandler, Ariz. 963-7752

The top portion of the supplemental report.

A registration card indicated that clerk Claira Nuttall checked Folley into the hotel around 9 p.m. on July 7. But not under his real name. Folley registered as "William Fountain." He listed 1210 E. Camelback Road as his address—not his home but the address of his employer, Rudolph Chevrolet. He indicated on the slip that he would be checking out the next day. Folley handed over $9.63 (including tax) in cash and received a key to room 219.

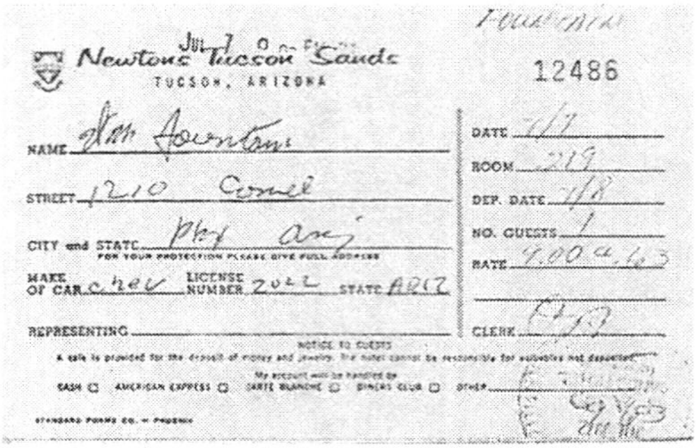

Newton's Tucson Sands
TUCSON, ARIZONA
12486

NAME Wm Fountain
STREET 1210 Camel
CITY and STATE Phx Ariz
MAKE OF CAR chev LICENSE NUMBER 2022 STATE ARIZ
REPRESENTING
DATE 7/7
ROOM 219
DEP. DATE 7/8
NO. GUESTS 1
RATE 9.00 9.63
CLERK

CASH ☐ AMERICAN EXPRESS ☐ CARTE BLANCHE ☐ DINERS CLUB ☐ OTHER

Zora Folley's Sands registration slip shows he checked into the hotel under the alias of William Fountain.

Sgt. Wolff was the first detective from the Tucson Police dispatched to the Sands, and noted his arrival at 11 p.m. July 8—almost a full 24 hours after Folley's death. He first spoke to the owner of the hotel, Keith Hanlin, who advised Wolff that clerk Manuel Franco was on duty at the time of Folley's death.

Franco told Wolff that he had started his eight-hour shift at 11 p.m. on July 7. At 11:45 p.m., he said, he received a phone call from room 219.

Room 219 of the Sands Motel. Photo: Marshall Terrill.

He identified the caller as Artis Broom. Broom asked Franco if he could buy a pair of bathing trunks for a late-night swim. Franco replied that the hotel did not sell or supply trunks, and politely told Broom that the pool was closed. Shortly after that call, Franco went out to check the pool area and saw Folley and Broom standing on the deck. He later noted that Folley was wearing swimming trunks. Contrary to the initial report that indicated Broom was fully clothed, Franco said he had on a pair of cut-off blue jeans.

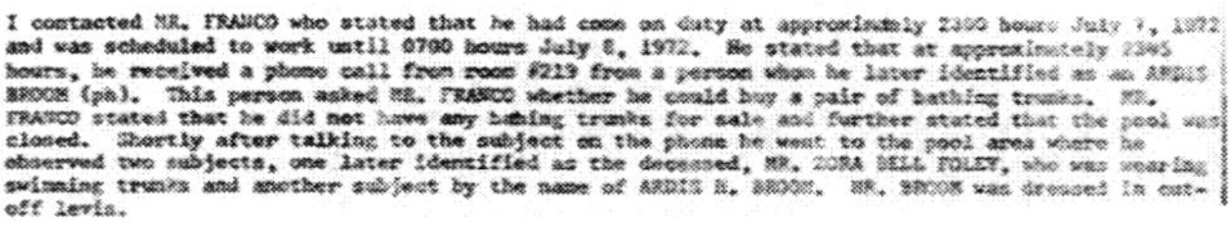

I contacted MR. FRANCO who stated that he had come on duty at approximately 2300 hours July 7, 1972 and was scheduled to work until 0700 hours July 8, 1972. He stated that at approximately 2345 hours, he received a phone call from room #219 from a person whom he later identified as an ARDIS BROOM (ph). This person asked MR. FRANCO whether he could buy a pair of bathing trunks. MR. FRANCO stated that he did not have any bathing trunks for sale and further stated that the pool was closed. Shortly after talking to the subject on the phone he went to the pool area where he observed two subjects, one later identified as the deceased, MR. ZORA BELL FOLEY, who was wearing swimming trunks and another subject by the name of ARDIS B. BROOM. MR. BROOM was dressed in cut-off levis.

Manuel Franco's statement to Tucson PD.

Franco told Wolfe that he firmly informed Folley and Broom that the pool was closed and asked them to leave the area immediately. Then he returned to the front desk to register another hotel guest who'd just arrived.

Moments later, just around midnight, Dorothy Broom and Ann Young rushed to the front desk and told Franco that "an accident had occurred."

Franco picked up the phone and called first for an ambulance and then called the Tucson police.

"This was all of the contact that he had with the incident or with the parties involved," Sgt. Wolff wrote in his report.

This clerk, MR. FRANCO, advised both MR. FOLEY and MR. BROOM that the pool was closed and that that they would have to leave the pool area. He, however, was then called to the desk by a party who wished to check in and while he was in the process of checking that party in to the hotel, he stated that he was advised by the two females who were in the company of MR. BROOM and MR. FOLEY that the accident had occurred. He stated that he called the ambulance and the police department and that this was all of the contact that he had with the incident or with the parties involved. MR. FRANCO lives at 926 W. Columbia and does not have a telephone. MR. FRANCO works the desk between 2300 hours and 0700 hours and can be reached at the Sands Motel if needed.

Franco's contradictory statement to Tucson Police.

But it was Manuel Franco, speaking on condition of anonymity to a newspaper reporter on August 8, who said he had found Folley with "a large bump on the forehead, a hole on the top of his head and another wound on the back of his head."

Why Franco would tell police that he didn't personally investigate what happened at the pool, but then tell an entirely different story to a reporter the night of the incident, can't be explained. He died in 2004. Why the Tucson police didn't re-interview him after his contradictory statement to the media is puzzling as well. Did they not see the story in the paper, which was first published on July 9 in the *Arizona Daily Star*, the *Arizona Republic*, and an AP story that was printed around the country?

After Wolff's investigation, he turned the case over to Detective M. Reyna of the Tucson Police. On July 12, Reyna contacted Sgt. Gomez of the Mesa Police Department and asked him to interview Ann Young to "ascertain what type of relationship existed between her and Mr. Folley and whether or not they had been registered under the name of Fountain in the room."

Ann Young told Sgt. Gomez, when he finally made contact with her at 1:07 p.m. on July 14, that Zora Folley had picked her up at 5 p.m. on July 7 at her Mesa residence, and then they drove to Tucson and he checked into the Sands under the name of

William Fountain. She said she had known Folley for approximately five years, and that they frequently went to Tucson on weekend trips.

That was a punch to the gut. Ann Young and Zora Folley had been carrying on an adulterous relationship since around the time of his championship fight with Muhammad Ali, when the face he presented to the world was that of a loving husband and proud father.

In the course of my journalism career I've interviewed and followed enough celebrities to realize that often their carefully crafted public images are doffed like an overcoat when the cameras are off. In fact, this sort of behavior has become the norm in today's world and I have come to expect it. I'd hoped that wasn't the case with Zora Folley, but there it was in black and white.

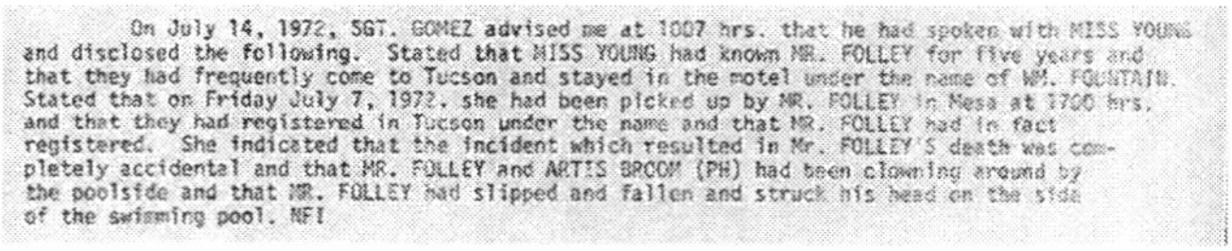

On July 14, 1972, SGT. GOMEZ advised me at 1007 hrs. that he had spoken with MISS YOUNG and disclosed the following. Stated that MISS YOUNG had known MR. FOLLEY for five years and that they had frequently come to Tucson and stayed in the motel under the name of WM. FOUNTAIN. Stated that on Friday July 7, 1972, she had been picked up by MR. FOLLEY in Mesa at 1700 hrs. and that they had registered in Tucson under the name and that MR. FOLLEY had in fact registered. She indicated that the incident which resulted in Mr. FOLLEY'S death was completely accidental and that MR. FOLLEY and ARTIS BROOM (PH) had been clowning around by the poolside and that MR. FOLLEY had slipped and fallen and struck his head on the side of the swimming pool. NFI

Ann Young's statement to Sgt. Gomez of the Mesa Police Department.

In the final paragraph of his supplemental report Detective Reyna wrote that Ann Young "indicated that the incident which resulted in Folley's death was completely accidental and that Mr. Folley and Artis Broom had been clowning around by the poolside and that Mr. Folley had slipped and fallen and struck his head on the side of the swimming pool. N.F.I."

No further information.

My decade-long search for answers was over, but I was far from ecstatic. The family and admirers of Zora Folley would not be ecstatic, either. There had been no mob rubout or murder by Artis Broom or strangers unknown.

The cause of Zora Folley's death, it turned out, was plain old human folly.

A view of the former Sands swimming pool, 2014.
Photo: Marshall Terrill.

CHAPTER NINE

Ringside Wrap

Like untold boxers before and after him, Zora Folley did not leave this world a wealthy man.

On November 5, 1973, his widow Joella filed a petition with the Arizona Superior Court in Maricopa County for her late husband's estate. The four-page document listed two main assets: a $3,000 trust for her nine children and their home at 373 S. Colorado Street, which was worth $18,000 at the time.

b. That all of the following described real and personal property of the estate of ZORA B. FOLLEY, deceased, remaining in the hands of the Executrix be, and the same is hereby distributed to JOELLA FOLLEY, surviving wife, to-wit:

Interest of Decedent in the Davis-Folley-Wilson Trust created in the Stipulation for Settlement in cause no. 12,131 in the Navajo County Superior Court	$3,000.00
Real property described as follows:	
Lot 75, of DOBSON ADDITION, as per map recorded in Book 36, Page 18 of Maps, in the office of the County Recorder of said County.	$18,000.00

Zora Folley's two listed assets at the time of his 1972 death.

While never a superstar of the ring, Folley had nevertheless occupied a place near the top rung of his profession for more than a decade. Unlike many of his contemporaries, his habits and lifestyle, like his personality, were low-key and even staid. "A stoic gentleman," writer Murray Goodman called him back in the early 1960s. That was mostly how Folley had stood out from many of the top heavyweights of his generation.

"If he wasn't the kind of guy he is, I wouldn't fool with him," Bill Swift once said, speaking for himself and co-manager Al Fenn. "We don't need the fight game to make a living and if we had a troublemaker it wouldn't be worth it."

Zora III says his family remains proud of his father's accomplishments.

"We should be proud that our father was not only a great boxer, but a great man, and had good character, good quality and [was a] very loving father. I miss him, and lost him too early."

While his fame was earned with his fists, those who knew Folley best say his character and integrity were his greatest gift to his hometown. Chandler has honored him often over the years.

While still alive, Folley had a city street named after him. A year after he died, the city dedicated Zora Folley Memorial Park at 601 E. Frye Road. A decade later, Folley's childhood friend and former Chandler mayor Coy Payne successfully campaigned to have a municipal swimming pool at 600 E. Fairview Street named after the fighter. Folley was also among the charter inductees in the Chandler Sports Hall of Fame in 2004.

Zora Folley in the mid-1960s standing next to the street sign in Chandler, which was named after him. Photo: Chandler Arizonan.

My hope in finding and printing the truth about Folley's death after all these years is that it will not in any way diminish the regard for him of his fellow Chandlerites and others who admired him. Folley was a hero on the military battlefield and a man who conducted himself with class and integrity in a profession in which both qualities are as rare as hen's teeth.

But Folley was a human being whose personal, hidden frailties—everybody has them—contributed to his ignominious downfall. His questionable friendship with Artis Broom still makes no sense and remains one of the great mysteries of Folley's life and death. Folley was a man of impressive dignity and gentleness. Nobody ever used those words to describe Artis Broom.

Maybe he had a groupie mentality that fed the ex-fighter's ego or maybe they were legitimately friends. Whatever the case, the pair remains close in death, as I discovered when I paid my respects at the grave of Chandler's favorite son at the City of Mesa Cemetery and found Artis Broom's grave just a few hundred yards away.

Tombstone of Artis Broom.

I was even more stunned to learn that same day that the house in which Ann Young, Folley's *femme fatale*, lived at the time of his death was a proverbial stone's throw from the cemetery. I wonder what she thought every time she passed by the eternal resting place of the man whose fate might have been so different but for their liaison.

Ann Young's residence in 1972. Photo: Marshall Terrill

Kneeling at Folley's headstone on that sunny day in June 2014, I wished him eternal peace. Then a quote from former heavyweight champion Joe Frazier came unbidden to mind. It's not exactly a fitting epitaph to a near-champion admired by so many, but it seemed like an appropriate summation of the tragedy of Zora Folley:

"Boxing is the only sport you can get your brain shook, your money took, and your name in the undertaker book."

Final resting place of Zora Folley.

APPENDIX A

Police Report

POLICE REPORT POLICE DEPARTMENT TUCSON, ARIZONA

X

Forcible Entry — Attempted Forcible Entry

RUNAWAY JUVENILE
MISSING PERSON

FOLLEY, ZORA BELL
CHANDLER, ARIZ
M-N 41 373 S. COLORADO ST. 963-7752
GEN MANAGER RUDOLPH CHEU, PHOENIZ — UNK
SANDS MOTEL
222 S. FREEWAY 43
JUL 8, 1972 0005 1 JUL 8, 72 0052 13
P.C.H. — —
LANIER 7384 JULY 8, 1972 0215 I
DEATH ACCIDENTAL
(44.02) DROWNING

JUVENILE — ORIGINAL OFFENSE — FOLLOW UP APPREHENSION

DISPOSITION

WITNESSES NAMES	RESIDENCE ADDRESS	RESIDENCE PHONE	BUSINESS ADDRESS	BUSINESS PHONE
A. BROOM, ARTIS H.	1030 S. 10TH MESA, ARIZ	993-1788	NONE	
B. YOUNG, ANN (NMN)	445 N. CENTER	964-3741	MESA ARIZ 2200 W. BROADWAY	962-2875

NARRATIVE: WITNESS A (BROOM) STATED THAT HE + THE VICTIM HAVE BEEN FRIENDS SINCE HE WAS 16 YRS OLD. MR BROOM + HIS WIFE DOROTHY WENT TO THE SANDS MOTEL TO SE.3

DISPATCH TIME 0047 ARRIVAL TIME 0052 TIME CLEARED 0215

ADDITIONAL REPORTS: X NO

CONTINUATION OF NARRATIVE

VICTIM. MR BROOM STATED VICTIM WAS SWIMMING IN THE POOL. VICTIM + WITNESS HAD A FEW DRINKS + VICTIM TRIED TO THROW BROOM IN POOL WITH HIS CLOTHES ON. VICTIM + BROOM WERE PUSHING EACH OTHER + VICTIM, WHO WAS WET, FELL BACK INTO POOL STRIKING HIS HEAD ON THE SIDE OF IT. BROOM JUMPED INTO POOL + PULLED VICTIM OUT. VICTIM WAS TAKEN TO PIMA COUNTY HOSPITAL WHERE HE WAS PRONOUNCED DEAD AT 0100 AM JULY 8, 1972 BY DR. G. REED. NOTIFIED DR. BRUCKER, DUTY PATHOLOGIST AT 0128 AM. JULY 8, 1972. SGT McDANIALS WAS SUPERVISOR TO ARRIVE AT HOSPITAL + NOTIFIED LT. JOHNSON OF DETAILS. TALKS WITH MRS BROOM + WITNESS B CONFIRMED MR BROOMS STORY. MR BROOM NOTIFIED VICTIMS WIFE + SISTER IN MY PRESENCE. N.F.I.

IF ADDITIONAL SPACE IS NEEDED, USE CONTINUATION REPORT

ADDITIONAL ARREST INFORMATION:

ADDITIONAL PROPERTY INFORMATION:

OFFICE OF THE CORONERS' PATHOLOGIST
1990 West Pennington Street
Tucson, PIMA COUNTY, Arizona 85701

CASE NUMBER: ______
AUTOPSY
DATE & TIME: 2-8-72 9 1/2 am

PATHOLOGIST: [illegible]

DECEDENT: Foley Zora ______ AGE: 41 SEX: M RACE: N
Last First Middle

ADDRESS: 323 S. Colorado M W S D LAW AGENCY: TPD

1. APPARENT TYPE OF DEATH: JUSTICE OF PEACE: Avalos

1a. ☒ Natural	1b. ☐ Suicide	1c. ☐ Accident	1d. ☐ Homicide	1e. ☐ Other
	☐ Gunshot (cal., weap)	☐ Traffic Passenger	☐ Gunshot (cal., weap)	
	☐ Poison (substance)	☐ Traffic Driver	☐ Knife	
	☐ CO (auto, resid)	☐ Traffic Ped.	☐ Beating	
	☐ Hanging	☐ Gunshot	☐ Strangulation	
	☐ Other	☐ CO	☐ Other	
		☐ Drowning		
		☐ Other		

2. CIRCUMSTANCES: Fell Down By Pool - Hit Head

2a. ☒ No physician in attendance.
☐ Phys. in att. but refuses to sign.
☐ Phys. in att. but physically unable to sign.

2b. ☐ Unobserved death.
☐ Observed death.

2c. ☒ At residence
☐ At public place

3. LAST SEEN ALIVE: ______
Time & date Place By whom

4. FOUND DEAD: ______
Time & date Place By whom

5. PRONOUNCED DEAD: 0100 - 8th ~~Home~~ Res. Dr. Reed
Time & date Place By whom

6. LABORATORY EXAMS:

Blood: ethyl alcohol level = 0.17g/100ml. (G.L.C.)
acid and neutral drugs = none detected (T.L.C.)
Urine: alkaloids including morphine = none detected (T.L.C.)
amphetamines = none detected (T.L.C.)
Bile: alkaloids including morphine - none detected (T.L.C.)

CODABLE CONDITIONS OTHER THAN THAT PRODUCING DEATH:

CAUSE OF DEATH: [illegible]
Cerebral Concussion

* Appended diagrams

[signature]
Coroners' Pathologist

Copies to:

[illegible]

ROOM LAST NAME FIRST INITIAL IN OUT

1210 [illegible]

STREET NO. OCC. RATE

Phx., Az.

CITY STATE

12486

Newton's Tucson Sands
222 SOUTH FREEWAY
TUCSON, ARIZONA 85705
(602) 624-1751

TRANS. FROM TO

DATE	SYMBOLS	CHARGES	CREDITS	BALANCE	PICK-UP
[illegible]-70 PAID			* 9.[illegible]	* 9.03G	* 9.[illegible]
[illegible]-70 ROOM		9.[illegible]			
[illegible]-70 TAX		.[illegible]3		* .00G*	

JUL 7 [illegible]

Newtons Tucson Sands

TUCSON, ARIZONA

12486

NAME Wm Fountain

STREET 1210 Cornell

CITY and STATE Phx Ariz

FOR YOUR PROTECTION PLEASE GIVE FULL ADDRESS

MAKE OF CAR Chev LICENSE NUMBER 2062 STATE ARIZ

REPRESENTING

DATE 7/7

ROOM [illegible]

DEP. DATE 7/8

NO. GUESTS 1

RATE [illegible]

CLERK [illegible]

NOTICE TO GUESTS

A safe is provided for the deposit of money and jewelry. The hotel cannot be responsible for valuables not deposited.

My account will be handled by

CASH ☐ AMERICAN EXPRESS ☐ CARTE BLANCHE ☐ DINERS CLUB ☐ OTHER

STANDARD FORMS CO. — PHOENIX

TUCSON POLICE DEPARTMENT
SUPPLEMENTARY REPORT

REPORT NO.

CONNECT-UP REPORT NO.

DATE OF ORIGINAL REPORT: JULY 8, 1972		
TYPE OF CRIME OR INCIDENT: DEATH/ACCIDENTAL	LOCATION: 222 S. FREEWAY	43
VICTIM'S NAME (LAST, FIRST, MIDDLE): FOLEY, ZORA BELL	ADDRESS: 373 S. COLORADO CHANDLER, AZ. 963-7752	NONE
PERSONS ARRESTED, CITED, OR SUMMONED: 1. 2. 3.	ADDRESS	OFFENSE

CASE STATUS:				
UNFOUNDED	RECLASSIFIED	PENDING XXX	SUSPENDED	CLOSED

REPORT CLEARED BY:			
ARREST	SUMMONS	CITATION	EXCEPTIONAL

(CASH VALUE)	MONEY	JEWELRY	CLOTHING	FURS	AUTO ACCESS.	BICYCLES	
STOLEN	$	$	$	$	$	$	$
RECOVERED	$	$	$	$	$	$	$

DETAILS OF SUPPLEMENTAL INFORMATION

I was instructed by Lt. Wright to contact Personnel at the Sands Motel reference the accidental death of ZORA BELL FOLEY. I proceeded to the motel at approximately 2300 hours this date and contacted the manager a KEITH HANLIN who is presently residing at the Sands Motel. MR. HANLIN advised me that the person who worked the desk at the time of MR. FOLEY's death was a MANUEL FRANCO.

I contacted MR. FRANCO who stated that he had come on duty at approximately 2300 hours July 7, 1972 and was scheduled to work until 0700 hours July 8, 1972. He stated that at approximately 2345 hours, he received a phone call from room #219 from a person whom he later identified as an ARDIS BROOM (ph). This person asked MR. FRANCO whether he could buy a pair of bathing trunks. MR. FRANCO stated that he did not have any bathing trunks for sale and further stated that the pool was closed. Shortly after talking to the subject on the phone he went to the pool area where he observed two subjects, one later identified as the deceased, MR. ZORA BELL FOLEY, who was wearing swimming trunks and another subject by the name of ARDIS H. BROOM. MR. BROOM was dressed in cut-off levis.

This clerk, MR. FRANCO, advised both MR. FOLEY and MR. BROOM that the pool was closed and that ~~that~~ they would have to leave the pool area. He, however, was then called to the desk by a party who wished to check in and while he was in the process of checking that party in to the hotel, he stated that he was advised by the two females who were in the company of MR. BROOM and MR. FOLEY that the accident had occurred. He stated that he called the ambulance and the police department and that this was all of the contact that he had with the incident or with the parties involved. MR. FRANCO lives at 926 W. Columbia and does not have a telephone. MR. FRANCO works the desk between 2300 hours and 0700 hours and can be reached at the Sands Motel/if needed.

I then interviewed the bell boy, a RAY TOHIDIZADEH. This subject was working as a bell man from 1500 hours to 2300 hours on 7 July 1972. He resides at 510 W. Prince and has no telephone. He stated that he did not see MR. FOLEY; that he does remember a Negro subject who checked in but he believed that he checked into room #208. He could offer no further information. I then talked to the bartender, a MRS. LAURA COCKRAN. MRS. COCKRAN resides at 1030 E. Adelaide, and her phone number is 624-0807. She stated that she had come on duty at 1700 hours 7 July 1972 and closed the bar at 2400 hours, that date. She stated that she did not see any blacks in the bar during her time of tending bar. She could offer no further information.

I was informed by the manager, MR. HANLIN, that a Negro male checked into the motel at approxi-

Officer Reporting Sgt. Wolff Con't Ser. No. Date Time

FORM P.D. 81 Force Division

CONTINUATION SHEET
TUCSON POLICE DEPARTMENT SUPPLEMENTARY REPORT

REPORT NO.

CONNECT-UP REPORT NO.

DATE OF ORIGINAL REPORT: JULY 8, 1972 OFFENSE CLASS: DEATH/ACCIDENTAL PAGE 2 OF 2

CONTINUATION OF NARRATIVE:

mately 2100 hours 7 July 1972. This subject gave his name as WILLIAM FOUNTAIN. He checked into room #219 and checked in as a single occupancy. The subject FOUNTAIN stated that he lived at 1210 Camel, Phoenix Arizona. Make of car was a Chevrolet, license #2022 dealer Arizona plate for '72. I talked to a CLAIRA NUTTALL who stated that she worked the desk from 1500 hours to 2300 hours on 7 July. She stated that she checked in MR. FOUNTAIN and that if she could see a picture of the deceased, MR. FOLEY, she couldn't be able to tell whether this was the subject who represented himself as WILLIAM FOUNTAIN. MISS NUTTALL is in the process of moving and can only be reached at the Sands Motel; however, she will be off work on Wednesday July 12, 1972 but can be reached on the following day, this being the 13th of July 1972.

I feel that the subject who checked in as WILLIAM FOUNTAIN ~~is~~ was actually the deceased subject ZORA BELL FOLEY. A copy of the registration was obtained from the manager, MR. HANLIN, and will be attached to the case report. NFI....

TUCSON POLICE DEPARTMENT
SUPPLEMENTARY REPORT

DATE OF ORIGINAL REPORT July 8, 1972

DEATH: ACCIDENTAL — 222 S. Freeway — 43

FOLLEY, ZORA, BELL — 323 S. Colorado, Chandler, Ariz. 963-7792

1.
2.
3.

CASE STATUS: UNFOUNDED / RECLASSIFIED / PENDING / SUSPENDED / CLOSED

CASH VALUE — STOLEN $ — RECOVERED $

DETAILS OF SUPPLEMENTAL INFORMATION

I contacted MR. HANLON, the manager for the SANDS MOTEL, and he informed me that the clerk who is working the night desk, registered was CLAIRE NUTTALL at 933 N. Alvernon, 881-1100.

On July 11, 1972, I was able to contact MISS NUTTALL and show her a photo of ZORA FOLLEY and stated she remembers the individual coming up and registering and remembers a NM registering that night and stated that she did not feel that she could positively say whether or not the individual was the same individual who registered by the name of WM. FONTAINE. She was sure the subject that registered under that name was a NM as she asked him how to spell his name. A copy of the SANDS MOTEL registration slip #12486 was obtained and is kept as part of the case file in Records.

I spoke with the other clerk ANN BAILEY who had been on duty earlier that day and she stated she was not able to supply any information and she had not seen the subject.

I then contacted SGT. GOMEZ of the MESA, ARIZ. P.D. 969-7211. I requested on July 12, 1972 at 1540 hrs. that he please contact MISS ANN YOUNG, who resides at 445 N. Center in MESA, ARIZ., 969-3741. I asked him to please interview MISS YOUNG and ascertain what type of relationship existed between her and MR. FOLLEY and whether or not they had been registered under the name of FONTAINE in the room.

On July 14, 1972, SGT. GOMEZ advised me at 1007 hrs. that he had spoken with MISS YOUNG and disclosed the following. Stated that MISS YOUNG had known MR. FOLLEY for five years and that they had frequently come to Tucson and stayed in the motel under the name of WM. FOUNTAIN. Stated that on Friday July 7, 1972, she had been picked up by MR. FOLLEY in Mesa at 1700 hrs. and that they had registered in Tucson under the name and that MR. FOLLEY had in fact registered. She indicated that the incident which resulted in Mr. FOLLEY'S death was completely accidental and that MR. FOLLEY and ARTIS BROOM (PH) had been clowning around by the poolside and that MR. FOLLEY had slipped and fallen and struck his head on the side of the swimming pool. MFI

Officer Reporting K. REYNA — 3595 — July 23, 72 — 0900
da
INV. SUP. DETAIL — DETECTIVE

OFFICE OF THE CORONERS' PATHOLOGIST COUNTY 65 4XXX
190 West Pennington Strea
Tucson, PIMA COUNTY, Arizona 85701

CASE NUMBER:
AUTOPSY
DATE & TIME: 7-7-72 - 7/17 pm

PATHOLOGIST: E-B

DECEDENT: Foley Zola (Last) (First) (Middle) AGE: 41 SEX: M RACE: N

ADDRESS: 373 S Colorado N W C D LAW AGENCY: TPD

1. APPARENT TYPE OF DEATH: JUSTICE OF PEACE: Avalos

1a.	1b.	1c.	1d.	1e.
☒ Natural	☐ Suicide	☐ Accident	☐ Homicide	☐ Other
	☐ Gunshot (cal.,weap)	☐ Traffic Passenger	☐ Gunshot (cal.,weap)	
	☐ Poison (substance)	☐ Traffic Driver	☐ Knife	
	☐ CO (auto, resid)	☐ Traffic Ped.	☐ Beating	
	☐ Hanging	☐ Gunshot	☐ Strangulation	
	☐ Other	☐ CO	☐ Other	
		☐ Drowning		
		☐ Other		

2. CIRCUMSTANCES: Fell Down By Pool - Hit Head

2a. ☒ No physician in attendance.
☐ Phys. in att. but refuses to sign.
☐ Phys. in att. but physically unable to sign.

2b. ☐ Unobserved death.
☐ Observed death.

2c. ☒ At residence
☐ At public place

3. LAST SEEN ALIVE: ______ (Time & date) (Place) (By whom)

4. FOUND DEAD: ______ (Time & date) (Place) (By whom)

5. PRONOUNCED DEAD: 0100 on 8th (Time & date) PCH (Place) Dr. Reed (By whom)

6. LABORATORY EXAMS:

Blood: ethyl alcohol level = 0.17g/100ml. (G.L.C.)
acid and neutral drugs = none detected (T.L.C.)
Urine: alkaloids including morphine = none detected (T.L.C.)
amphetamines = none detected (T.L.C.)
Bile: alkaloids including morphine - none detected (T.L.C.)

CODABLE CONDITIONS OTHER THAN THAT PRODUCING DEATH:

CAUSE OF DEATH: Cerebral Contusion

* Appended diagrams

E. Burns
Coroners' Pathologist

Copies to:
Signed 7-10-72

SOUTHERN ARIZONA PATHOLOGISTS, P.C.

TRANSFER OF PROPERTY

CA NO:

PATHOLOGIST: EB

NAME: Folley, Zev AGE 41 (M) DATE: 7-8-72

ITEM: BLOOD FROM: [illegible] TO: [illegible] DATE: 7-11-72

URINE FROM: [illegible] TO: [illegible] DATE: 7-11-72

BILE FROM: TO: DATE:

~~GASTRIC CONTS.~~ FROM: TO: DATE:

MODE OF DEATH: TIME OF DEATH: TIME OF AUTOPSY:

DRUGS TAKEN OR FOUND ON DECEASED:

OTHER DRUGS SUSPECTED: EMERGENCY THERAPY:

MATERIALS TAKEN FOR ANALYSIS & ANALYSIS DESIRED:

Blood: CO

ETOH ✓

General Screen ✓

Other:

Urine: ✓ Gen scr.

Stomach content: ✓ NO STOMACH CONTS AT [illegible]

Other: Bile ✓

RESULTS

Blood ethanol 0.173 Gm/100 ml (GLC)
[illegible] 0.144 Gm/100 ml
[illegible] ([illegible]) - 0.152 Gm/100 ml

Blood {[illegible]} {[illegible]} none detected (TLC)

Urine alkaloids including morphine none detected (TLC)
" [illegible] none detected (TLC)

Bile - alkaloids including morphine none detected (TLC)

DATE REPORTED: 7-[illegible]-[illegible]

Toxicologist

Pathologist

APPENDIX B

Boxing Record

Zora's Folley's complete boxing record, presented in reverse chronology.

LEGEND:

W (Win), L (Loss), D (Draw)

KO (Knockout), TKO (Technical Knockout), UD (Unanimous Decision), MD (Majority Decision), PTS (Points Win)

1970-09-29 Mac Foster L KO

1969-11-05 Billy Joiner W UD

1969-06-16 Tommy Sims W KO

1969-01-29 Sonny Moore W TKO

1968-07-06 Oscar Bonavena L MD

1968-05-14 Al Jones D PTS

1968-03-11 Roger Russell D PTS

1967-11-13 Brian London L PTS

1967-10-03 Nick Sosa W KO

1967-09-18 Wayne Kindred W TKO

1967-03-22 Muhammad Ali L KO

1967-01-17 Floyd Joyner W KO

1966-12-13 Jefferson Davis W UD

1966-10-25 Henry Clark W UD

1966-06-28 Jefferson Davis W KO

1965-12-06 Bob Foster W UD

1965-02-26 Oscar Bonavena W UD

1964-11-14 Gerhard Zech W KO

1964-04-17 Karl Mildenberger D PTS

1964-03-17 Tod Herring W TKO

1964-01-17 George Chuvalo W UD

1963-10-17 Billy Daniels W UD
1963-09-19 John Collins W KO
1963-07-27 Ernie Terrell L UD
1963-05-23 Bob Cleroux W UD
1963-04-02 Dean Bogany D TD
1962-12-15 Doug Jones L KO
1962-11-19 Dave Furch W UD
1962-08-29 Al Gonzalez W KO
1962-08-01 Doug Jones W UD
1962-06-12 Paul Andrews W TKO
1962-04-18 Bob Cleroux W UD
1962-02-15 Mike DeJohn W KO
1961-12-05 Henry Cooper W KO
1961-09-28 Sonny Moore W UD
1961-08-30 Ben Marshall W KO
1961-05-11 Alejandro Lavorante L KO
1961-02-10 Norman Letcher W TKO
1960-09-16 Willi Besmanoff W UD
1960-07-18 Sonny Liston L KO
1960-04-05 Clarence Williams W UD
1960-01-18 Eddie Machen W UD
1959-11-18 Alonzo Johnson W UD
1959-10-02 Monroe Ratliff W TKO
1959-08-04 Howard King W MD
1959-07-07 Alvin Williams W KO
1959-04-07 Willi Besmanoff W UD
1959-03-10 Hank Thurman W UD
1959-01-29 Alex Miteff W UD

1958-11-24 Joe Bygraves W TKO
1958-10-14 Henry Cooper L PTS
1958-07-25 Pete Rademacher W KO
1958-05-19 Art Swiden W UD
1958-04-09 Eddie Machen D PTS
1958-01-01 Garvin Sawyer W UD
1957-12-04 Edgardo Romero W TKO
1957-11-21 Duke Sabedong W KO
1957-09-10 Monroe Ratliff W UD
1957-08-05 Edgardo Romero W TKO
1957-07-09 Jeff Dyer W UD
1957-06-18 Julius Griffin W TKO
1957-05-20 Jimmy Wood Tucson W KO
1957-04-18 JD Harvey Yuma W KO
1957-03-12 Johnny Hollins W KO
1957-02-11 Howie Turner W UD
1957-01-09 Wayne Bethea W SD
1956-12-03 Wayne Bethea W SD
1956-09-25 Nino Valdes W UD
1956-08-15 Roger Rischer W UD
1956-05-28 Rocky Robinson W KO
1956-05-08 Ponce de Leon W KO
1956-02-28 Watson Jones W KO
1955-12-01 Young Jack Johnson L RTD
1955-09-24 Reuben Wilson W KO
1955-09-08 Ted Calaman W TKO
1955-07-28 Jake Williams W TKO
1955-06-23 Johnny Summerlin L RTD

1955-05-16 Howard King W TKO
1955-04-07 Calvin Brad W TKO
1955-02-24 Kirby Seals W TKO
1955-01-20 J.D. Reed W TKO
1954-12-18 Kid Zanzibar W KO
1954-11-26 Jimmy Ingram W UD
1954-10-23 Georgie Woods W SD
1954-10-01 Sandy McPherson W UD
1954-08-28 Kid Percy W KO
1954-08-13 Kirby Seals W UD
1954-07-12 Frank Buford W UD
1954-06-10 Johnny Rebel W KO
1954-04-13 Jackie Condon W TKO
1954-03-26 Battling Blackjack W KO
1954-01-26 Howard King W TKO
1953-12-07 Lonnie Malone W TKO
1953-11-17 Cornelius Brown W RTD
1953-09-29 Calvin Chambers D PTS
1953-09-22 Jimmy Ingram W PTS

Bibliography

Books

Collins, Nigel. *Boxing Babylon*. Citadel Press, 1990.

Hartmann, Melanie. *Southside Neighborhood: 100 Years of Recipes and Stories*. City of Chandler and Arizona Humanities Council, 2012.

Rosebrook, Jeb. *Saturday: A Novel*. Dutton, 1965.

Articles

"Zora Folley: A Man to Be Reckoned With." *The Ring*, December 1957.

"Velvet Paws in the Cow Palace." *Sports Illustrated*, April 21, 1958.

"A Tiger on the Trail." *Sports Illustrated*, July 21, 1958.

"Heavyweight in Weighting." *Sports Illustrated*, August 1, 1960.

"Folley-Machen." *Boxing Illustrated*, April 1960.

"Zora Folley vs. Henry Cooper." *Boxing Illustrated*, February 1962.

"What Is Folley's Fate?" *Boxing Illustrated*, 1962.

"The Enigma of Zora Folley." *Boxing and Wrestling*, June 1963.

"Zora Folley Bounces Back." *Boxing Illustrated*, August 1963.

"Folley-Chuvalo!" *Boxing Illustrated*, April 1964.

"A Book Fighter Who May Change Ali's Style." *Sports Illustrated*, March 20, 1967.

"After Muhammad, A Graveyard." *Sports Illustrated*, April 3, 1967.

"Folley Decked 5 Times in One Round by Foster." *The Ring*, 1971.

"Zora Folley on Council Ballot Next Tuesday." *Chandler Arizonan*, January 12, 1972.

"Three Councilmen Elected." *Chandler Arizonan*, January 19, 1972.

"Zora Folley Still Mild." Associated Press, April 11, 1972.

People. *Sports Illustrated*, April 24, 1972.

"Zora Folley Installed as City Council Member." *Chandler Arizonan*, April 27, 1972.

"Zora Folley Dies in Accident." *Arizona Daily Star*, July 9, 1972.

"Folley Rites Set." *Arizona Daily Star*, July 10, 1972.

"Folley's Death Blamed on Fall in Swim Pool." *Sheboygan Press*, July 10, 1972.

"Zora Folley Funeral Set." *Arizona Daily Star*, July 11, 1972.

"Community Joins In Last Tribute to Zora B. Folley." *Chandler Arizonan*, July 12, 1972.

"Zora B. Folley... A Man to Remember." *Chandler Arizonan*, July 12, 1972.

"Pool Accident Causes Death of Boxer Zora Folley." *Jet*, July 27, 1972.

Obituaries. *The Mesa Tribune*, A-12, July 10, 1997.

Obituaries. *Arizona Republic*, A-12, July 11, 1997.

"Folley's Mystique Bobs and Weaves into City Lore." *Chandler Connection*, September 20, 2003.

"Folley Pays His Dues, Battles 'The Greatest.'" *Chandler Connection*, October 2, 2003.

"Circumstances in Folley's Poolside Accident Still Murky." *Chandler Connection*, October 10, 2003

"The Final Interview of Boxing Legend Al Fenn, Manager of Zora Folley." *Ringside Boxing Zone*, October 2008.

Acknowledgments

I would like to respectfully acknowledge the following people who made this work not only possible, but made it flourish:

Pete Ehrmann, who served as editor, cheerleader, and patron saint of this project. Pete's encyclopedic knowledge of old-school boxing was crucial as well as his knowledge of the Folley case. I could not think of a better partner.

To that end, former Chandler police chief Bobby Joe Harris also provided great insight into the case and was a gentle motivator.

Former Chandler vice mayor Lowell Huggins, a friend who could always be counted on.

Dorothy Broom, who bravely recounted for me of the night Zora Folley passed.

Michelle Gough, who found the long-lost pathology report, which blew the Folley case wide open.

Dennis Preisler at the Arizona State Library, who was helpful and encouraging in helping me locate Zora Folley's police report.

The talented Sara Bielski, who designed the cover.

Boxing historian Christopher James Shelton who kindly permitted me use of his 2008 interview with the late Al Fenn.

Mike Fitzgerald for his friendship and eagle eye.

Other contributors include Willie Arbuckle, the late Eddie Basha, Dave Bigos, Tom Carlson, Nigel Collins, the late Eddie Encinas, the late Al Fenn, Robert Folley, Zora Folley III, Nate Meyers, the late Ken Norton, Dr. Bruce Parks, Jim Patterson, Coy Payne, Jean Reynolds, Jeb Rosebrook, Stuart Rosebrook, and Robert Spindler.

About the Author

MARSHALL TERRILL is the author of more than 20 books, including best-selling biographies of Steve McQueen, Elvis Presley, and Pete Maravich. For more information on his books, visit:

www.MarshallTerrill.com

32294680R00074

Printed in Poland
by Amazon Fulfillment
Poland Sp. z o.o., Wrocław